TWO WORLDS APART

To Freddy & Lian
with love

Gail Thompson

Gail Rose Thompson

outskirts
press

Outskirts Press, Inc.
http://www.outskirtspress.com

ISBN: 978-1-9772-1872-8

Library of Congress Control Number: 2020903479

Cover Photos © 2020 Wikimedia Commons and 123RF, LLC. All rights reserved - used with permission.

Outskirts Press and the "OP" logo are trademarks belonging to Outskirts Press, Inc.

PRINTED IN THE UNITED STATES OF AMERICA

DEDICATION

To my dear Mel

With gratitude to friends and family members who have taken their time and expertise to read drafts and make comments and corrections.

TABLE OF CONTENTS

1

Though longing for you scatters in the wind
All my lifes work
Still, by the dust on your dear feet, I have
Kept faith with you.
Hafez

Ali 1979

The sky was that true cerulean blue one finds only in Persia. As Ali left the dark stable, he squinted and held his hand to shade his eyes; the Qashqa'i hat he wore had no brim. It was a dark brown felt and rather like a skull cap, except it had ear protectors for cold weather, that were almost always turned up as it seldom got very cold in this part of Khuzestan. The sun was approaching noon and he had to get Zahra Khonume across the river to Dezful and on to Ahwaz in time to catch her flight. He didn't want her to go. He knew it might mean a whole new way of life for her, but for him it would be a terrible change. America seemed so far way; it was another world. He knew she'd been there before and had returned home, but something told him it would be different this time.

He trudged across the sandy yard towards the stable block on the other side, above which Zahra had her apartment. It was an old building of mud with an onion-shaped dome which kept it very cool in the hot months. He slowly mounted the steps to the second story and opened the door to the main living room.

Zahra was standing in front of the mantelpiece examining one of the many photographs the mantle. To look at those pictures was to read the history of her life. And what an interesting life she had lived. Recently he had often found her staring at one or the other of these photos. He knew it would be hard to get her attention —he knew she must have some misgivings about leaving. She was probably in some sort of dreamland contemplating her decision. He was reluctant to startle her in case she turned around and snapped at him, or worse he might find her eyes full of tears. It had happened that way before.

Zahra

Zahra put her bags by the door for Ali to take down to the car and turned to look over the room she loved so much. The high-domed ceiling had been whitewashed and along with the many windows, it gave the room a light spacious feeling. A huge fireplace was the central focus of the room, but there was no need for a fire in the hearth on such an unseasonably warm day in mid-February. Along the huge mantle, made from a thick Cypress beam, there were many photographs, all framed in Persian silver. The images cataloged her life!

She looked at the picture of her mother, her father and herself taken more than thirty years before, on the day she left Persia to go to boarding school in America, and suddenly she was thirteen again.

"Ba Khodah Behrid, Zahrajun!" It was her father's voice giving the blessing as she walked under the Koran holding the traditional handful of Iranian soil in a white handkerchief.

Her mother and grandfather were holding the gold-edged Koran up high above her head as she passed below, like a strange game of London Bridges. She half expected them to lower their arms to *"chop off her head!"*

There had been so much family dissention about her mother's decision to send her away to school. World War II was finally over and things in Europe were settling down. Louisa had decided it was time for her only child, to go to school in her homeland and learn about her American heritage. Until then Zahra had been a Persian teenager with no idea what life on the other side of the world was about. She was totally protected and pampered in her affluent life, but her mother wanted her to venture abroad for the sake of a better education than she would attain in Iran.

"When we were married, Hassan, you made a promise that our children would be educated in my country. After all these years, are you now going to rescind that promise?"

Zahra had been about to walk into the living room when she heard her mother's voice. She stopped to listen. "Louisa, Louisa, my love. I will keep my promise. But it is too soon. You bore me only one child, my beautiful Zahra. I would have been happy with ten children and then it would have been easy to keep my promise. You know how I love my girl. We must keep her here a year or two more. Then it will be time. I promise I'll send her, but not now."

"Hassan! She will be going to America this year. She's ready to start High School and I want her to study at the same school for all four years. I have already made the arrangement for her to go to Mary Willet, a private girls' school in

Richmond, Virginia where I went. She will be close to my mother in Charlottesville. It's time for her to learn about my culture. Now she is only Persian! Please Hassan, you must sign the papers for our passports and the permission sheet to let us out of Iran. I have never begged you for anything before. I've tried to be an exemplary Persian wife; I've loved you and still love you despite your many infidelities. I've learned your language, loved and been accepted by your overbearing family, given you a beautiful Persian daughter and totally lost my own identity. I beg of you to do as I ask!"

As far as she knew, Zahra's mother had never asked her father for a thing. Why was it so important that she go to the United States to school? She had a wonderful life. She adored both her parents. She was doing well academically at the Razi School, the top of her class. She had many friends. She agreed with her father that it was too soon for her to go away. She knew that she had to go at some time, but not now!

She heard her father Hassan say, "Very well, Louisa. Get me a pen. I will sign now in front of you and then Abraheem can take care of things in the morning." There was a sad submission in her father's voice that Zahra had never heard before. Why was he letting her go? Tears welled up in her eyes and she ran up the wide oak stairs to her room.

That was two months ago and now she was actually at the airport about to get on a big silver bird. She had never flown on an airplane before. Despite her sorrow at leaving her family, friends and country she was excited to get on this plane that would swish her off to Europe first and then on to her mother's homeland. How her existence would change.

Zahra's mother, Louisa Kadjar, had been raised in Virginia; her father had been an industrialist and had made a vast fortune. When his daughter was in her late teens, he was asked by the President to serve as ambassador to France. Louisa had loved Paris and the many Embassy parties. It was at a masked ball given by the Italian Ambassador that she met Hassan Kadjar. She had danced with him most of the evening trying to guess his nationality. He'd known who she was from the beginning, as he had been trying to get an introduction to the beautiful daughter of the American Ambassador for months. At midnight, when the masks were removed, she saw a handsome, swarthy face with velvety brown eyes. She still didn't know who he was, but he told her he was a minor diplomat at the Persian Embassy.

There was a long exciting courtship during which she was given fabulous pieces of jewelry by Hassan and entertained by Royalty. It took her some time to realize that this man who claimed to be a minor diplomat was in actuality the nephew of the Shah of Persia. He was a Prince! When his tenure in Paris was up, he asked her to marry him, which she did without hesitation, and he took her back to his country where she had been ever since. Over the years, she had become almost more Persian than he was.

Hassan's Uncle Ahmad, who was the shah, had succeeded his father, Mohamad Ali Shah, at the age of eleven, who himself had succeeded his own weak and incompetent ruling father, Mozaffar od-Din Shah in 1907 after he had been forced to pass a constitution that curtailed the monarchial power. When Mozaffar tried to rescind this new constitution, he aroused much opposition and thus Ahmad Shah, though very young, was put on Persia's Peacock Throne. He inherited a kingdom in turmoil and one that was frustrated by the influence of British and Russian Imperialism. When he came of age, he took the reins of power from his regent, who had lived and governed in a lavish lifestyle, and tried to fix the damage done by his autocratic father. Even though he appointed the best ministers he could find, he was still proved an ineffective ruler, faced with internal unrest and foreign intrusions.

During World War I, when British and Russian troops fought against the Ottoman forces in their county, the people of Persia were not used to being used as a battleground. The local movement tried to challenge the power of the young Ahmad Shah. The newly born Soviet Union annexed portions of northern Persia and then marched on Tehran. By 1920, Ahmad Shah and his government had virtually lost all power. At the beginning of 1921 he was pushed aside by the military coup of Colonel Reza Khan who first made himself Prime Minister, and then in 1925 had himself crowned as the king, taking the title of Reza Shah Pahlavi.

There had been turmoil those first two years that Louisa had been living in Hassan's country though it really didn't affect their lifestyle a great deal until Ahmad Shah went into exile in Europe. The new shah declared that the Kadjar dynasty was terminated after a hundred and fifty years. Louisa's husband, being a true Persian, immediately pledged himself and his assets to the new government, headed by Reza Shah. Those of the Kadjar family who cast their lot with this new Pahlavi dynasty fared well. Few of their lands were taken and their personal wealth was left untouched. For Louisa and Hassan their life hardly changed, save the family was no longer on the throne and Hassan was not able to call himself Prince.

In the first few years of her married life, Louisa had miscarriage after miscarriage. Eventually her French-trained doctor told her that the reason was that she was not abstaining from sexual intercourse during her pregnancies. The next time she must abstain from the day she missed her first period. She felt this was a ridiculous medieval fallacy, but Hassan was by that time being unfaithful in the Persian way, so it was an easy procedure to follow. She told him what the doctor said, and he left her alone. The resulting next pregnancy produced Zahra. She had a difficult pregnancy and birth and was then told by her doctor that she would never have another child.

Zahra was a good baby. She rarely cried, ate well, and was not prone to colic as were many of the babies of Louisa's Persian friends. She grew strong and beautiful. Louisa would listen to her friends telling about the problems they were having with their children and yet, she never had the opportunity to experience these things. Her daughter was a very sweet, intelligent little girl. As she began to grow up, they developed an honest, simple and rewarding relationship.

Now it was the summer of 1947 and Louisa was about to get on a plane to take her only child to America where Zahra would commence her Western education. She had not been back to

America since her marriage. She was very nervous about going there. She was afraid it was not as it had been when she left. Her parents had been to visit her in Persia on several occasions, but she had not seen her mother since her father had died two years before.

The trip to American seemed to take forever. Zahra and Louisa stopped in Rome for a few days, staying at the Grand Hotel. There was shopping at Via Vittorio Veneto for fashionable frocks, shoes and handbags, for in this vibrant city, they saw how out of date their Persian attire looked. Louisa had never travelled to Europe as many of her Iranian girlfriends had. The horrible flea-infested Orient Express on which she arrived in Tehran when she was first married made her sick. Just the thought of it prevented her from even dreaming of trips to Europe. It was only when she realized she'd be able to fly to her destination that she became convinced she needed some time out of her adopted homeland and should accompany her daughter to the commencement of a new chapter in her life.

In Paris they stayed on the Champs d'Elysee, their room overlooking the wide, tree-lined street. There were visits to Dior, where the majority of Zahra's wardrobe was purchased. She didn't realize that she would most likely be the only girl in her class that had her clothes made for her at the top fashion house in the world. In Persia all one's clothes were hand-made, copied from pictures in European magazines.

London was beautiful that August; the weather was warm but not too hot, and the gardens were a sea of colors. The roses seemed to almost equal the glorious pink and red roses of the Kadjar's own garden. Roses had been cultivated since antiquity in the East and had been taken by the Crusaders back to Europe from Persia.

This was the first time Zahra had been in an English-speaking country. She did have a good command of the language due to the fact that she and her mother spoke English exclusively when they were conversing. However, she had a difficult time understanding the accent of the Londoners. It worried her that perhaps she would have a language problem when she got to school. French was more her second language than English, for her parents most often spoke together in French, a language with which they were both comfortable and which was the tongue of the cultured in Tehran. Farsi was, of course, Zahra's mother tongue.

Buckingham Palace seemed very grand in comparison to the Golestan Palace where the new Shah Mohamed Reza Pahlavi was residing. She knew that the Golestan was where her father had been born, but now the Pahlavis lived in the palace that had belonged to her father's family. The vastness of this great British palace, along with the magnificence of Windsor Castle, put seeds of doubt in her mind about the importance of the country where she had been raised. Her mother was constantly reminding Zahra that she must not compare the countries; Persia – or Iran as it was now called – was great in its own right and with the oil industry developing, it would become one of the greatest nations of the world.

2

When friends meet heart to heart, this is the key
To happiness's treasury;
May no one hesitate at such a time
Or hold back then, reluctantly.
Hafez

Ali 1979

Ali knocked on the door jamb before entering Zahra's apartment. She didn't hear him.
He coughed but still she didn't acknowledge
that she knew of his presence. He picked up her
readied bags.

He remembered the first days he came to
work at Andimeshk when he was a young boy
of eighteen, the fifth son of an Arab sheik who
bred beautiful Asil (pure) Arab horses known
for their speed and stamina. His elder brother,
Reza, would be the head of the tribe upon his
father's death, so for a young Arab boy it was

best to cross the desert to find work, either in the small towns or on farms established in the area. He'd heard his father talk of the beautiful woman, Zahra *Khonume*, who had taken over the breeding of the Bakhtiar Aghili Stud, which was owned by the powerful chief of the Bakhtiar tribe Mehdi Khan, so he was not surprised when his father suggested this would be a good place for him to find work and a new life.

His father had given him a beautiful young bay stallion of the Saglawi line. He knew this stallion would help his son as an introduction to Zahra, who all the tribes' people knew would do just about anything to improve the quality of her herd.

There are five primary strains of the Asil horses that go back many centuries. The legend says that the religious leader Mohammad was camped on the side of a beautiful river of crystalline waters with a hundred mares. He cruelly decided not to give water to these mares for three days, and then on the fourth day, he released the mares. They all rushed towards the river to quench their thirst. At that moment, he blew his horn to command the mares to return to him, but of the hundred, only five came back to their master. He blessed those five mares and at that moment decided that they would be the only mares he would dedicate to breeding. From that day forward those mares were known as "The five of the prophet Allah" and were baptized individually with the names Abbayab, Saglawiyab, Koheilan, Hamdaniyab and Habdan which were now the five main strains of the Asil horses of Iran.

And so, the sheikh sent his son to Zahra, knowing she would take him in, especially if he sent the boy with a young Saglawi stallion. Ali had arrived at the Aghili Stud farm one evening, dusty after his two-day ride, from his father's winter home. His horse was as tired as he. The beautiful bay stallion Shahid, as he was called, was of fine pedigree. He was tall for a Saglawi, measuring more than 15 hands. He had a re-fined, wedge-shaped head with a straight nose and wide flaring nostrils. His eyes were big, kind, and intelligent. His lineage would work well with the Bakhtiari herd in producing su-perior horses. This parting gift from his father would give him an insured position with Zahra at Aghili.

He asked the little man crouching at the gate if he could speak to Zahra *Khonume*; the man shrugged and nodded. When he went through the arched opening in the high mud wall, he saw her standing by the stall door of a tall black stallion. She saw him and beckoned him. "From where have you come all covered with dust and alone?"

He told her that he had come from his father's lands about two day's ride from Aghili. She remembered Sheikh Karim Salih. She told the boy that he could stay the night and that they would talk in the morning. She sent him to the grooms' quarters and made sure that he was fed and had a mat to sleep on.

Once back in today's world Ali trudged down the stairs with the suitcases and put them in the back of the old Land Rover.

Zahra

Zahra was looking at the class picture from her freshman year. There were twelve young girls in uniform all smiling, standing in the school library with the head mistress Grace Pearce. The height of the houses in Richmond had startled Zahra. Granted she had seen New York on her way, where the height of the buildings had amazed her, but she had expected that Richmond would be a city with flat-roofed houses like Tehran. She could not imagine her mother having lived in anything other than their own house in Persia, which was by standards there, very beautiful, but by American standards primitive. It would certainly not be possible to sleep on the peeked roofs of Richmond in the hot summer months as she did in her own flat rooved home. Her mother had told her that the climate was about the same temperature as Tehran, for the two cities were almost on the same latitude. But Richmond was low and very humid, whereas Tehran, at an altitude of about five thousand feet, was dry.

That first day, walking into the large, high-ceilinged hall of Mary Willett School, Zahra felt like a little baby. She clung to her mother's hand. The principal of the school greeted them joyfully for she had been a student at the school when Louisa was there. Miss Pearce had been one of the prefects whom Louisa had looked upon as a perfect model to follow when she herself entered the school. She wondered why the woman had remained single, for she'd certainly been very popular as a girl.

"Well, Louisa, it's wonderful to see you, and this must be Zahra. My, you look like your mother did at your age, even though you're as dark as she was fair. Welcome to Mary Willett. I hope you'll have four wonderful years with us."

Louisa smiled and said, "Grace, it is so good to see you. You've hardly changed at all. I'll always remember that first day here when you were assigned to be my senior friend to make sure that I learned my way. You were so kind to me. I hope you've got a similar system now. Zahra's really nervous about being here, aren't you dear?"

"Well, I'm more nervous about having to stay away from home for four years than anything, I guess." It was the first words she had spoken, and Grace Pearce was enthralled by the slight accent and the deep lilting voice of the fourteen-year-old.

Grace

Many people had wondered why she, the Queen of the May festival at college, the most popular girl of her own graduating class, had never married. It was simple. She loved girls! And so she had gone into teaching at her old alma mater. Over the past twenty years she had advanced to the position she had wanted. It was not that she was at all lecherous about it – she wasn't; she just loved being with girls, particularly beautiful young ones like this new student who was obviously so totally naïve and innocent.

How she was attracted to this child.

She, Grace Pearce, daughter of the founder of the R. J. Pearce Tobacco Company and sole heiress to the fortune, was still, at the age of forty, sought after by many a young bachelor, as well as many old divorcees or widowers. After her amazing first experience with the opposite sex, she was exposed to the worst tragedy that could befall anyone. She decided that she'd never get serious about a man again. But the memory of that first time always remained with her and she had never again been able to enjoy the sex act with men. Although she didn't totally abstain, for she had learned that word spreads fast, especially in a small town like Richmond. Engaging in the odd affair, never mind how distasteful to her, kept her reputation clean.

She had been in sophomore year at college, Sweetbriar naturally, as it was her mother's alma mater and had been named after the plantation of distant relatives. Indiana Fletcher Williams had inherited the land through the Fletchers and when she died, she bequeathed it to become a school for young women in memory of her daughter who had died at the age of sixteen.

One Friday afternoon, it had been arranged that Grace's cousin would pick her up to spend the weekend with her maternal uncle and his family. Harry was just two years older than she and was due to graduate that spring. He was a typical clean-cut University of Virginia type who played on the football team and who all the girls panted after. When her friends heard that Harry Brown was picking her up at the dorm for the long weekend, they all hung around just to get a glimpse of him and hopefully an introduction from Grace. She hadn't realized how many close friends she had until that time!

"Well, girls, I'm off," she said as she saw him drive up in his bright red Morgan sports car. They all rushed to her at once, saying, "Just introduce me to him!" "I'd do anything to meet him." "I think I might swoon!"

So, ten or twelve girls followed behind as she walked to the car. As Harry jumped over the side of the car door, they giggled that fashionable college girl laugh. He ran up to Grace and lifted her off the ground, giving her a great big hug. "Gracey baby! You look fantastic. Mom and Dad have a great weekend planned!"

It took her a minute to catch her breath, once he had let her down, but when she finally did, she kept her word to her friends, introducing them to him one by one. "Harry my friends want to meet the hero of the UVA Cavaliers Team. This is Sally, Pam, Judith, Ann, Gail, Jean, Jane, Olga, Harriet and Julie." They all tried to look their most seductive, for Harry's reputation with the girls was well known. Maybe one of them would catch his eye and he'd invite her to a fraternity party or something.

"It's nice to have met yawl," he said, with his prominent southern accent. "I should have known that my cousin would have a bunch of beautiful-looking friends. I hope we'll see yawl at the next post-game party. Make sure you come and introduce yourselves to me again. Just say you're friends of mine if you have trouble getting into the Frat house."

He took Grace's bag, which had been lying on the sidewalk where she dropped it, and put it behind the seat. Then, taking her arm, he ushered her into the passenger seat of the fancy little car, walked around to the driver's side, and hopped in.

"Well, bye yawl!" he called starting up the car and driving off.

The two cousins were silent for some time. They had a two-hour drive ahead of them, and there was no rush to converse. He was thinking how absolutely fresh and innocent she looked this warm fall day; if she wasn't his cousin, she'd be just the type of girl he would marry. Not that he was seriously thinking of marriage, but he was about to graduate and so many of his friends were going to marry in the spring.

For her part, Grace was thinking about how

all her friends had been so excited at meeting this cousin of hers with whom she had practically grown up. Because she was an only child, her parents had made a point of letting her spend as much time as possible with her cousins, so she'd never thought of Harry as anything special. She hadn't seen much of him since he'd gone to Virginia, but on the big holidays the families spent time together. Grace always thought of Harry as just Harry. Now she was looking at him in a new perspective. He was unusually handsome, tall and well built. He had a winning smile that would probably melt any girl's heart, and eyes that twinkled and crinkled at the corners when he laughed. Yes, he really was attractive. Maybe if he weren't her cousin, she would like to date him, even get pinned to him. She felt a strange tightening in her throat and her crotch at the thought of it.

"Gracie baby, why are you so silent?"

"Oh, I was just thinking about how all the girls in my dorm were dying to meet you. I couldn't figure it out because I've always thought of you as just Harry. But I guess you're something special to everyone else."

"Why aren't I something special to you?" He turned to look at her with a look she'd never seen him give before. The feeling went from her crotch to her stomach.

"You're just my cousin for heaven's sake. I haven't ever thought of you as anything else. I guess I love you like other kids would love their brother."

The two cousins talked about what they had each been doing over the past few months as they drove home to the family farm in Culpeper County. By the time they reached Locust Ridge they were laughing and joking as if they were young kids again.

The weekend was blissful; they were up early Saturday morning in order to get the horses ready to go out cubbing with the Warrenton Fox Hounds at 6:30. They played tennis, swam in the pool and partied late. The whole family had the usual sumptuous Sunday luncheon around the pool before they drove off to college again.

Dusk was setting in as they drove through the gates of Sweetbriar on Sunday evening. Grace was sad that it was over, for she couldn't remember ever having such a good time with Harry. He'd definitely changed in her eyes, from a cousin to an attractive young man.

"It was fun this weekend, Harry. Thanks so much," she said leaning over to kiss him on the cheek as they had pulled up in front of the dorm.

Suddenly Harry grabbed her shoulder, burying his face in the nape of her neck. Then cautiously, tenderly, he started kissing her neck, her chin and her soft innocent mouth. He parted her lips with his inquiring tongue until she too began to respond to the moment of passion. He took her face in his hands, staring deeply into those beautiful blue eyes. "We have to see each other more often. I love you more than a cousin, Grace. Will you come to my frat party next weekend?"

"I think we feel the same way. Of course!" she said, not daring to think of what the complications might be.

He picked her up the following Friday at the dorm again, but this time she didn't mention to her friends that she was going away with her cousin. He'd arranged for her to stay at the girls' dorm with the date of one of his friends. When she saw him drive up, she ran out of the building and jumped over the door into the Morgan. He laughed as she pecked him on the cheek, ruffling her blond hair as they drove off.

When he introduced her to his friends, he didn't mention to anyone that she was his cousin. The parties were deliciously fun, full of innocent cajoling and minor necking on the dance floor. The game had been won by Virginia and he had, of course, been a star on the field, which made him in demand at the post game party. But Grace found that she blended in well with his friends.

They had decided that they would picnic on their way back to Sweetbriar on Sunday if the day was fine. It dawned a soft golden fall day, so they set off mid-morning with a picnic of wine, cheese and French bread. Harry had a spot picked out just a half hour outside of Charlottesville, where it was obvious, he had been before. Along the bank of a small stream, under the limbs of a huge grandfather oak, they laid out a plaid motor rug. There was some hiking to do and paddling in the stream to keep them occupied before they decided it was time to go ahead with their lunch, for they each knew that this would be a very special picnic.

Lolling back on the soft wool blanket, they sipped wine, and discussed their aspirations, dreams, and hopes, to pass the time. Then Harry began to shower her with soft tender pecks around the nape of the neck and face. His hands began roaming over the small hills of breasts that seemed to welcome him. He was well-experienced in the art of sex, but he couldn't tell about her. He was almost sure that she would be a virgin and yet she didn't protest his activity as he slipped his hand under the waistband of her panties. She was already moist, he discovered, as he slid past the patch of soft hair. She even welcomed his exploring finger as it carefully pushed into her.

He heard a soft sigh escape her lips as he fumbled with his belt and slid off his trousers. He felt he might explode. Kneeling beside her, he unbuttoned her blouse, slipping it and her bra off. She lay with eyes, closed not uttering a word. When he had taken off her skirt and panties, he gazed at her perfect naked body with its white middle and golden tanned extremities. It was so unblemished, so perfect to his eyes that just looking at it made him harder.

"I'm a virgin, you know," she muttered as he deftly straddled her.

"I'll take care of you. It'll hurt a little, maybe a lot, but I'll make you come first, so you'll enjoy part of it. Just relax and let me take care of you."

He wanted to come so badly he couldn't stand it, but he had good practice and knew that he must let her have a small climax first. Otherwise it would ruin it for her this first time. He suddenly felt her body reaching for him and he pressed on the front of her vagina as she began to shudder and moan. Then he knew it was his turn. He plunged quickly into her never entered tight, tight vagina, and in an instant, she was no longer a virgin. The ringing in his ears coincided with her scream of pain, so that he could hardly discern which was more forceful. She was weeping as he lay spent upon her; he slowly rolled off and lay staring up into the branches of the old oak.

"I'm sorry it hurt you. It always does the first time, you know. It won't again. Next time it will be much more fun."

"What've we done? Do you know what we've done?"

"We've only expressed our feelings for each other."

"But it's supposed to be saved for marriage."

"Don't be so silly, Grace. I'm going to marry you this spring after I graduate. It's not like you're being a loose woman."

"But, how can we? We're first cousins. It's not allowed. Our parents will die. Oh my God. Mother will have a stroke."

"Stop it. It doesn't matter. We can marry. Who's to stop us? Will you marry me, my love?"

"Oh, I want to so much, yes."

They kept it a secret until just before Christmas at which time they had decided they would become officially engaged. It was during one of the family weekends that they both sat down collectively with their parents to break the news.

The hue and cry started immediately. "It's impossible for first cousins to marry!" "You don't know what you're doing." "You're both two young and inexperienced to think of marrying." Their comments were hard to take but they stood their ground, together. It seemed that the families were more afraid of what people would think than of the consequences, so they agreed to go along with the marriage only if the two promised not to make an official announcement until after Harry had graduated.

Harry and Grace spent every weekend together, discovering each other totally, mentally and physically, and they became more certain of the rightness of their union. Grace herself felt totally fulfilled, both sexually and mentally, to the point that she sometimes wondered what more there could be to her life.

She was totally surprised one Friday when Harry didn't arrive to pick her up at the time they had arranged. Maybe he was held up at class or had decided to finish that term paper that was due, so she wasn't worried. When there was a call for her in the dormitory office, she knew it was him explaining the problem.

"Hello!" she said breathlessly into the phone.

"It's all right, darling, just hang on. I'm coming to get you. Just sit tight and I'll tell you all about it." It was her father. She didn't understand and began to panic.

"What's the matter? Where is Harry? He was supposed to pick me up. Something's happened! Tell me!"

"He had a car accident, Grace. He's in the hospital. I'm coming to take you to him. Don't worry. Just sit tight and wait."

Don't worry! She died a thousand deaths before her father arrived.

By the time she and her father reached the hospital in Charlottesville, Harry had been pronounced dead! His death nearly killed her, too. She lost the year in college and in many ways never recovered. She did complete her B.A degree and then went on to study for a Master's in education, but she would never date any of the young men who asked her out. She had had her one perfect romance and she never wanted another. Now she had only school and all those lovely girls who reminded her so much of herself in those happy days.

Zahra 1947

Yes, Louisa was pleased to discover that they still had the same system as when she went to school at Mary Willet. Zahra's senior friend would be in shortly to take her to her room to meet her roommate. The following half hour was spent filling out forms for Zahra's admittance to the school. There would be some problems, for the educational system in the U. S was different from what she had been studying in Iran. Zahra would probably excel in languages, but her mathematics and sciences would be below the American standard, for young girls were not expected to be proficient in the sciences in her country.

After knocking lightly, Jeanie Bowman walked into the principal's office. She was a tall, slender, dark-haired girl with slightly protruding teeth. She could not be called pretty, but she was quite attractive in that late teen way; quite wholesome looking. She would be Zahra's senior friend.

Zahra felt terribly frightened when she left the soft pink of the principal's office with Jeanie; it was as though she were being sent into the desert without water. And yet, when she came to the oasis of what was to be her room, she saw a welcome sign and her own suitcases which helped. Anne Williams was to be her roommate for the next year. It turned out that they got on so well, they continued to be roommates for the four years until they graduated from the school. They both had a mad passion for horses and loved to ride. That was enough of a bond to start with.

That first evening, Anne told her that they needed to dress for dinner in the dining hall.

Zahra had no idea what she would wear and asked Anne which of her many beautiful outfits from Paris she should put on. Anne was flabbergasted at the number and formality of Zahra's outfits. They were too much for dinner in the dining hall, so she went through Zahra's suitcases and trunk and found a plain tweed skirt and a coral colored cashmere sweater set.

Since she and Anne had taken too much time with their introductions, they dressed hurriedly. They were going to be late, which was not tolerated by the headmistress. They rushed down the oak spiral staircase and walked into the hall at one minute after six. Anne found a place for Zahra at the table where she usually sat with her close friends; quick introductions were made for it was time for the Head Girl to lead the school in the grace. This habit seemed strange to Zahra for her family did not pray before their meal.

Zahra sat at the table amongst the other girls who were chatting frivolously about the happenings at school that day. She felt left out and very shy. She was out of her element and uncomfortable. She knew she would have to be strong like her mother if she was going to survive the next four years at this strange school in this country so distant from her beloved Persia, as her father still called it. She knew she'd always remember those first few days. She was a timid Persian girl, who felt completely lost to begin with. She was homesick for her protected life in Tehran with its beautiful mountains. In fact, she could see the loveliest of all, Mount Damavand, from the balcony of her bedroom. Here at school she saw only the bricks of the next building and heard the traffic from the streets of Richmond.

Her roommate, Anne Williams, was a kind girl. and when she found Zahra crying quietly in the room, she would put her arm around her to comfort her. As time went by, her English became proficient and she mastered the math and science. In no time, she became one of the top students in her class.

Vacations were the part she dreaded the most, but as she became friends with the other girls in the school, she found she was never in need of a place to spend those days. Her grandmother lived in a huge house in Charlottesville filled with antique furniture, very dark and depressing. Her first visit there had been her last; her grandmother had no idea who she was. Grandma was becoming senile and was looked after by an old couple who didn't like their territory to be disturbed by a young girl who had nothing to do there but snoop around and read books.

Zahra's roommate, Anne, lived on a horse farm not far from Middleburg, Virginia and Zahra was looking forward to visiting with her during the Thanksgiving holiday. In her mind's eye she pictured North Cliff, as the Williams' farm was called, to be like the one that her family had in Nowruzabad just outside of Tehran. At her family's farm, there was a large mud building with high domed ceilings which kept it cool in the summer months. Inside the front door was a huge room with tiled floors which was used for entertaining the many guests they had every Friday, the holy day of the Muslim religion. It was tradition to have family and friends visit at noontime, after those who did go, had left the mosque and taken the half hour drive to the farm. There was always a huge meal set out by the servants: *gorme sabsi, khoresh-e-badenjune*, plenty of rice served different ways, and of course a large leg of lamb from the sheep that had been killed the day before. Fruit in abundance and sweets were served first, to prepare the palate for the heavy meal. After lunch everyone would go to the stables to see the horses and watch the children ride the ponies. Usually Zahra and her cousins would show off their expertise, galloping around the open desert fields at the back of the house, jumping over piles of sticks that had been pruned from the pomegranate trees and rocks that had been picked up and formed into small walls to divide the sections of the fields. She missed those old days.

3

What memories! I once lived on
The street that you lived on,
And to my eyes how bright the dust
Before your doorway shone!
Hafez

Ali 1979

He climbed back up the steep stairs to see if
Zahra was ready to come down to the yard
and leave but when he entered the apartment,
he saw that she was still looking at the photographs on the mantel.

"Khonume!" he spoke, and she turned to
look at him a bit surprised. "We need to leave
soon if you are to be on time for your plane."

"Just give me a minute, to make sure I
haven't forgotten anything. I'll be right down."

He remembered the meeting that first full
day of his long-lasting stay at the Stud. He had

awakened early, as he heard the other grooms getting up. When he went outside, they had a small fire to make tea and warm the *nun* from the previous evening; they were very cordial to him, offering him tea and bread. He took a big lump of sugar between his teeth through which he sipped his tea and accepted a large piece of *nun* that had been warmed in the fire; he also took a large bit of goat cheese; it was a delicious fare after his long ride and the few pieces of dried bread and water he had carried with him.

Shortly, he was called by the little man who had been at the gate the previous night, and told that Khonume would see him in her office. He was escorted into what he thought was a stall but behind the curtain that covered the opening was a lovely room with a wooden desk behind which she sat.

"Good morning Ali. Did you sleep well?"

"Yes, very well, thanks to you and Allah."

"I see you have brought a young stallion with you."

"Yes Khonume, he is a gift from my father to you. He is of the best Saglawi lines and his pedigree goes back six generations." The Saglawi line was known for its refinement and almost feminine elegance, a type of horse more likely to be fast rather than have great endurance.

"I am so glad to hear you had a good night. Your father is a good friend of mine, as he is also to my dear husband Mehdi, and I thank him for such a beautiful and important gift. Thanks to him, we were able to develop our herd to be one of the finest in this part of the world. When we had only a few mares that we were breeding and needed to infuse new blood into our herd, Mehdi and I rode the route you took these past few days with four of our best mares so that we could breed them to your father's fabulous Koheilan stallion, Arruz. As I am sure you know, he won an across-the-desert race from Iranshahr to Kasch. He travelled those one hundred fifty kilometers in ten hours," she recalled.

They discussed the fact that Ali had come to Aghili looking for work and Zahra said, "I will let you stay here for one month so that you can learn the way I run this breeding farm. If you show me that you are a hard worker and a good horseman, you may stay on, if that is what you want."

And thus, Ali commenced his tenure which had lasted many years through good and bad times. To him she became like a goddess whom he loved dearly, though from afar.

Now she was going to leave this beautiful place that he called home and he would be the one to oversee it for her, until her return. The great responsibility of it all made him anxious.

Zahra

Zahra had been looking at the picture of herself and Anne Williams sitting on two beautiful Arab horses that were owned by Anne's family. It was the Thanksgiving holiday and the school had a celebration planned for those girls who came from too far way to go home, but Anne had invited Zahra to come to her family's farm in Middleburg, Virginia. Zahra was thrilled because she knew the Williams had horses and she truly missed the horses she had left at her family's farm, Nowruzabad.

A chauffeur-driven black Lincoln picked them up at the front door of the school the Friday before Thanksgiving. Since she had arrived at Mary Willett that day in September, Zahra had only left the environs of the school area a few times. She'd been devastated when her mother left her there alone, but she had been brave and was settling in well with her schoolwork and the other girls.

Now, on her way to Anne's house, she watched as they drove out the school gates and through Richmond until they came to Route 1, a winding road that took them through the hilly countryside. She was amazed at the trees, which had turned to the beautiful crimson and gold colors of autumn foliage. She kept picturing the William's farm like that of Nowruzabad with its desert and irrigated paddocks for the horses to graze, and the low mud brick stables surrounding the yard, like a horseshoe.

After a two-and-a-half-hour drive, they drove through big brick gateposts onto a driveway that was lined with tall, golden-leaved trees. There were huge fields as big as twenty of the paddocks at Nowruzabad, and the house they approached at the end of the long circular drive was big, built of gray stone. It had a pillared front porch and many small-paned windows. The house was at least three stories tall and very imposing in comparison to her parents' humble farm outside of Tehran, which by Persian standards was very impressive.

The door was opened by a uniformed maid who hugged Anne. "It is wonderful to see you, sweetie," she said. Then turning to Zahra, she added, "And this must be your friend from school. You too, are welcome, young lady. Now off you go to the den; your mother has just come in from the hunt and is eagerly awaiting the two of you."

They went through a closed door in the large hall and walked into a wood-paneled room with bookcases on three of the walls and a huge fire burning in the hearth. "Anne, my darling girl!" cried a beautiful blond woman, opening her arms to her daughter. She was dressed in buff britches, tall black riding boots with patent leather tops, a white shirt, and silk stock tied around her neck.

"And you must be Zahra! Come girl and let me give you a hug too! We are all so happy to have you here with us over the holiday. You must call me Joan," she told Zahra.

"Your dad is on his way home from Washington and I expect your brother soon, too. Why don't you girls go up to your room to freshen up and change for dinner? We'll have a cocktail here before dinner. Come down about seven."

They went up to Anne's room, which was large with two four-poster beds. Anne showed Zahra the closet and dresser for her clothes, and they sat down to plan what they would do the next day. Of course, they would go to the stable to see the horses, and for sure go for a ride. Zahra couldn't wait to see the horses and ride. She missed that activity almost as much as she missed her mother.

Anne picked out one of the Paris dresses from Dior for Zahra to wear, since dinner was usually quite formal at the Williams' home. Anne herself would wear a blue velvet dress with a lace collar that had been made for her by the local dressmaker in Middleburg.

Zahra looked out the window at the rolling hills of North Cliff. She saw a large pond surrounded by weeping willow trees. She couldn't believe it! There were weeping willows in her garden in Tehran. Oh, she missed Tehran, the capital city of her homeland, Iran. The country's name had been changed by the Shahanshah and the Majlis, the governing body of the country, in 1935. The word Iran meant "Land of the Aryans" in Persian and had been used from the times of the Elamite Kingdom in 2800 B.C. and through the Sassanian era. But the rest of the world had called the country Persia, since Persian was the official language. Really Persia and Iran could still be used interchangeably.

"Oh! I so badly want to go and run over the fields. Can we do that, Anne?"

"Not till morning. It will be dark soon, and we need time to unpack and get ready for dinner."

At just before seven, the girls tripped down the oak staircase and ran into the den. Mrs. Williams wore a long flowing green taffeta dress

with three strands of pearls at her neck; she
looked beautiful. Zahra remembered how lovely
her mother had looked when there were formal
dinners at the big house in Tehran and again
had a flash of homesickness.

"Where's Tom?" asked Anne and then added, "I guess late, as usual!"

Her mother said, "Your brother will be down
soon, I'm sure. He just came in from deer hunting a little while ago. He needs time to change
his clothes."

"He always gets to do the fun things that I'm
never allowed to do! It's not fair!"

"He's four years older than you and a boy.
Hunting deer is not for the ladies."

"It will be for this lady when I grow up, and I
know Zahra, too, will be a deer hunter with me.
Won't you Zahra?"

Zahra didn't know anything about deer
hunting in America. Her father would go hunting with his friends in the Alborz mountains on
horseback several times every year, but they
would bring back ibex, mouflon and sometimes
gazelle, which the houseboy hung in a cold
room after dressing them; she thought maybe
they were a kind of deer, but she didn't know.
Women in Persia seldom went hunting with
the men, but her father had given her a rifle
which he taught her to shoot. He'd even taken

her hunting with him a few times. She loved riding across the desert and up into the arid mountains around Nowruzabad with her father and his friends. Of course, they took at least two servants who would lead the pack mules with their horses. The servants would prepare the picnic lunch from the mule packs and help scout for the game, which was extremely hard to spot with their desert colors against the barren mountains.

Soon Mr. Williams appeared in a maroon velvet dinner jacket with a black bow tie. He made Zahra feel very welcome. He was tall man with fair hair that was starting to thin. It took a while for Tom to appear, and when he did, Anne was a little perturbed with him.

"You're always late! Here I have a friend visiting from school and we are just starving, and you take your own time to come for dinner."

"Now Anne!" said her mother. "We'll all move into the dining room now, shall we?"

Zahra couldn't keep her eyes off Tom. He was so handsome. He had thick blond hair, a straight yet not narrow nose, and a mouth that was always smiling as he teased his sister. He made good conversation with his parents and was very courteous to the girls. He seemed so much nicer than her own seventeen-year-old cousins who never gave her the time of day and acted with a superior attitude; she didn't miss them!

The holiday was a whirlwind for Zahra. She and Anne rode the horses every day, going on long trail rides over the hills, and through pristine fields graced by low stone walls on the Williams five-hundred-acre farm. Zahra was thrilled that they had four Arabs, Arabian horses as they called them, the same breed of horse she had at home. The bloodlines she didn't know but they looked like her family's horses. They were comfortable, brave and very well trained; never a spook or a shy which she was used to from her own horse, Leilah.

"Do you know that Arab horses are called Asil in Persia?" Zahra mentioned while the family was having diner one evening. "The word Asil means pure. They're thought to be descendants of the horses bred for thousands of years. If you come to visit me in Persia, you will visit Persepolis which was the Capital during ancient times. There you will see the carvings of ancient horses on the walls of the ruins. There were many tribes back then – still are – and they all knew that in times of war as well as peace, success was only possible if they had good horses. Even today, horses are very special, and their breeding is done very carefully to keep the strains pure," she explained.

During Zahra's visit, they went to the quaint little town of Middleburg which was established in 1787 by a Revolutionary War Colonel and Virginia statesman named Leven Powell. He purchased the land from a cousin of George Washington when it was called "Chinn's Crossroads." The Colonel changed the name, as it was midway between Alexandria and Winchester on the Ashby Gap trading route, and thus it was called Middleburg. One day the girls had lunch at the Red Fox Inn, the oldest building in town, which had been built by John Quinn in 1728 and became a popular stopping point for weary travelers going to the frontier town of Winchester. During the Civil War, "The Beverage House," as it was called, was used by Confederates. Most notably, it was where General Jeb Stuart met with Colonel John Mosby and his famous Mounted Rangers, at the beginning of the Gettysburg campaign. As fierce battles raged around Middleburg, the inn served as both headquarters and as a hospital for the Confederates. In 1937, the building had been saved from the wrecking ball by a local citizen who hired architect William Drew to remodel it. By the time Anne and Zahra came along, it was the place to go for luncheon or an evening of dining out, if you lived near Middleburg.

For Zahra, the holiday was over too quickly.

Soon they were back in the black car. driving to Richmond and school.

Overall the next four years of high school zipped on by. Zahra spent weekends with some of her other schoolmates but most of her vacation time was spent with the Williams.

In the summers, she and Anne would help with barn chores and go riding as much as possible. Anne was a Pony Club member which was one of the leading equestrian organizations in the world that provided instruction and competition in horse sports as well as stable management for children. As an advanced rider she volunteered to teach the young children twice a week, so Zahra went along to help. When August came, they went out three mornings a week to walk the hounds of the Warrenton Hunt. The year-old hound puppies were walked out with a group of older hounds as a beginning of their training for hunting with the pack. At home the Persian people were not overly fond of dogs, and so she hadn't had much experience being around them. She loved the cool misty mornings when they would get up at dawn and ride their bikes the mile to the hunt kennels. She loved these happy hounds wagging their tails and sniffing the ground, trying to catch the scent of something to chase. Sometimes Tom would come out as well as Anne's mother, but most often it was just the two girls, along with the hunt staff and other hardy members of the club.

For Zahra, walking the hounds was fun to do, but most of all she enjoyed cubbing because she would often view the sleek rust color foxes with their thick bushy white tipped tails as they streaked through the fields having escaped the covert. When the puppies had learned to stay together with the older hounds, they would be taken out cubbing in the early mornings three days a week. Those days before the hunting season had commenced, the pack was introduced to finding fox cubs in small hidden woods and chasing them inside this covert while the mounted riders surrounded the area trying to prevent the fox from exiting. Once the cubbing season was over the puppies would be integrated into the pack and would hunt the fox if they proved their worth.

The first time she went cubbing, with Anne and her mother she was nervous. To her, this was a strange sport. In Iran riders on horseback would hunt the gazelle. The method used in Khuzestan needed a great deal of patience and good judgement about pace and distance. The chances of the gazelle escaping were about seventy-five percent. Once a gazelle was spotted, the hunters would start riding at a walk in a large circle around them, usually not more than two hunters together, slowly decreasing the circle. The gazelle would soon become agitated, jog off a distance, stop, change direction, start off again, and eventually go into a canter. All the while the stalker must keep calm, keeping his pace no more than a fast walk. The horse knew – not yet! Not until the gazelle made up its mind what direction it would escape, at which point it would go into a smooth run, which was flat out. Now nothing would make him change direction. This was when the rider or hunter unleashed his horse at a at a converging course diagonal to the gazelle's direction. In this first burst of speed, the gazelle could do up to 90 kilometers per hour. Thus, the need for proper calculation was crucial. The horse was galloping full out and had its head for the rider gathered the reins loosely in the left hand, which at the same time supported the barrel of the gun. In ancient times this sport was done with a bow and arrow; thus, both hands were completely occupied! The terrain was mostly flat, but there were rocks, fox and rat holes, dry flood beds and other things of nature on the ground. The horse must make the decisions while going at full speed. The distance he ran depended on the angle and speed of both horse and gazelle. Choosing the angle and maneuvers when nearing the gazelle was where an expert hunter was separated from an amateur. The gazelle should pass within a convenient shooting distance in front of the horse and hunter. Too slow, the gazelle was gone. Too fast, they would pass behind. The hunter needed to be a good shot as well as an acrobat!

Fox hunting was so different! The huntsman gathered the hounds into a pack and cast them into a covert or small group of trees where a fox might be hiding or have its den. It usually took the hounds quite some time to find the scent, but once one hound found it and started baying the others usually joined in. As they followed the scent, they broke out into the open and proceeded to follow the scent as a pack. The hunters on horseback followed the path of the hounds and had to have good control of their mounts. Never should the huntsman nor the Master be passed. During the hunt, the hounds would lose the line and cast again to pick it up, usually with the guidance of the huntsman. This process continued until the scent was lost completely or the fox was caught and killed, which happens seldom, by the hounds or went to ground in a hole and was safe.

Zahra loved the speed when hounds were on the chase, but there was a lot of standing around waiting while the dogs found the scent. She and Anne rode together, but there were usually about twenty or so other people in the field. That seemed strange to her, for at home, hunting was mostly a solitary sport and in America it was like a spectator sport. There were post and rail fences to be jumped as well as coops and stone walls to go over. That was the fun of it for her! It was invigorating, and after a day's fox hunting, she would be very tired but satisfied. About ninety-five percent of the time the fox got away, so Zahra never did see a kill in the many times she went hunting with the Williams family.

As time went on, Zahra settled into the American way of life. At school she worked hard and did well at her studies. She also took part in the seasonal sports; field hockey in the spring, soccer in the fall, and basketball during the winter months. The weather seemed much like that of Tehran although the summers were not as hot but were much more humid and debilitating. At home, though the temperature would get up into the hundreds by eleven o'clock in the morning, the air was very dry, so it didn't feel as hot as it did in Virginia. A person needed to drink a lot more fluids in Iran, because due to the dryness of the air, one didn't feel the perspiration, as it would evaporate quickly. In the kitchens both in Tehran and at the Noruzabad farm, there was always *Sharbateh Sekanjebin*, a delicious mint drink and *Aab hendevaneh*, a thirst-quenching watermelon drink which was excellent for hydration. The house boy would carry a tray with a pitcher of one or other of the drinks to the family and guests every half hour or so, no matter what was happening.

Though Zahra recalled her home in Persia constantly during her school years, it seemed that in no time, high school was over, and it was time for graduation. Zahra's parents were going to make the trip to Richmond for the big day. She was very nervous to see them because she had come to love her life in the States and didn't want to go home. Most of her classmates were going on to college and she had decided that she wanted to do the same thing.

Now she would have to persuade her parents to let her stay a few more years so that she could graduate from college. She and Anne had already put their applications in for Cornell University in Ithaca, New York and were anxiously awaiting their acceptance letters. They had it all planned. They would live in the women's dorm, as all freshmen were obliged to live in the dorms that first year. After that, they would get an apartment for the final three years of college. She was so excited; she could hardly contain herself.

It would be with trepidation that she would approach her parents. She'd have to time it just right, once they had arrived and spent a day or so relaxing after their long trip. They were going to stay at the John Marshal Hotel which was said to be "The Finest Hotel in the South." It first opened its doors in October 29, 1929, the day after the infamous Wall Street Crash. The hotel was a sixteen-story building of the neoclassical style, with art deco and Moorish touches. It had cost the huge amount of two million dollars to build. There were over four hundred rooms, each of which had its own telephone and bathroom. There were two restaurants and two ballrooms, one of which was the Garden Ballroom on the sixteenth-floor rooftop. She knew that they would both love the luxury during the week they stayed there.

Her parents planned to take her to New York City and then on to Iran, with a week's stay in Paris on the way. Somehow, she would have to take them to Ithaca from New York so that they would see the beautiful Cornell Campus. Cornell had been established in 1865 by Senator Andrew Dickson White of Syracuse and Ezra Cornell of Ithaca. As Senators they had met, become friends and learned of their separate plans and dreams, which drew them toward their collaboration in founding Cornell University.

Senator Cornell oversaw the construction of the first university buildings, starting with Morrill Hall. He then spent time investing the federal land script in western lands for the university, that would eventually net millions of dollars. He had been poor most of his life, was self-educated and a hard worker. He'd amassed a great fortune as a self-made businessman and austere, pragmatic telegraph mogul who made his fortune on the Western Union Telegraph. Now he wanted to spend this income to do the greatest good for the poor. He had concluded that the greatest end for his philanthropy was the need for colleges that taught practical pursuits such as agriculture, the applied sciences, veterinary medicine and engineering and in finding opportunities for the poor to attain an education.

Senator White was well-educated and entered college at sixteen. He had dreamed of going to one of the elite eastern colleges, but his father sent him to a Christian school, Geneva Academy, in Oregon. He did ultimately attend Yale, but he longed for the great colleges he'd read about at Oxford and Cambridge. He had a dream of "a university worthy of the commonwealth (New York) and the nation." He served as a professor of history at the University of Michigan but continued to develop his thoughts on a Great American University. White worked on the development and administration of the Cornell University and became its first president.

Thus Andrew D. White and Era Cornell became the developers of the first American university and therefore agents of a revolutionary curricular reform.

Visiting the beautiful campus, with its late seventeenth century buildings, with Anne and her family had given Zahra the inspiration for her own higher education.

4

Enjoy this moment's happiness
Savor it well;
The pearl will not remain
Forever in its shell.
Hafez

Ali 1979

Ali trudged back up the steps to try to hasten Zahra, but when he opened the door a crack, he saw that she still seemed to be mesmerized with the photographs on the rugged mantel. "It's getting late Khonume," he spoke softly through the narrow opening. She turned to look at him but did not respond. She acknowledged that she had heard him and motioned that she would be down shortly.

He had been happy here at the Bakhtiari Stud farm over these many years. Golam Reza, the old man who had been at the stud since his b... h, had befriended Ali from his first days, taking him under his wing like a father as he had no sons of his own, only daughters who worked in the homes of several of the Bakhtiari families who lived in grand homes in the cities of Shiraz, Esfahan and Tehran. He knew all that had happened at the stud for many years, even before Zahra became the one who was to run it. Though he was old and crippled now, Zahra kept him on to do what jobs he was able; he'd been with the family so long she didn't have the heart to let him go. He had a home forever.

Ali had envisioned himself in the same role as Golam Reza in the years to come, but now it seemed there would be a change, for Zahra Khonume was leaving, maybe forever. Ali was set to take on the role of his mentor and heroine, though he was full of self-doubt as to whether he could handle the job to her liking and his own satisfaction. It was a daunting responsibility.

Zahra

Zahra looked at the picture of Anne and herself with their parents. The Williams were all so blond and the Kadjar family so dark. It was graduation day from Mary Willet School. The two girls were dressed in their white graduation dresses and looked so fresh and young. Oh, how she wished she were feeling so young and unencumbered today. She had such foreboding feelings about what she was about to do with her life.

Those days after her graduation were wonderful. She went to stay with her parents at the John Marshal Hotel in their luxurious suite with two bedrooms and a sitting room. It was good to catch up on the news from Tehran. Her cousin, Bahman, had gone to England where he was studying engineering at Manchester University. He had met a nurse there and was now married to an English girl. Zahra's mother thought they were going to have a baby soon which would be very exciting for the family to have a new generation coming along. Her best friend from home, Mimi Zanganeh, was engaged to marry her cousin Reza; the wedding would be just before Now Ruz the following March, so it was expected that Zahra would be in the wedding. Zahra said nothing about that, as she had not yet broached the subject about going to university in September.

There were graduation parties given by the parents of her classmates at the Country Club of

Virginia, a beautiful old clubhouse on the edge
of a smooth, green-grassed, hilly golf course.
The ball room opened out onto a large patio
where the dancing took place under the stars.
At one of the parties, she was seated at a table
with her parents and the Williams family when
a handsome young boy she had met at one of
the mixers with St. Mark's, the brother school
to Mary Willet, came up to ask her to dance. She
loved dancing and was very light on her feet as
she glided under the Virginia stars.

When the young man brought her back to
the table after the music stopped, she saw that
Tom was staring at her. As the music started up
again, he came over to ask her to dance. She was
quite surprised because she had always thought
he considered her the pesky friend of his little
sister, who just wouldn't go away. He'd been
away at Cornell for the past couple of years, so
she hadn't seen as much of him as when she first
started spending time at North Cliff Farm. He
spent most of his summers working as a coun-
selor at a boy's camp in North Carolina, so he
was seldom home except for Christmas.

"You look so lovely tonight, Zahra!" he said
as he put his arm around her. He too, was a good
dancer. They seemed to float across the floor
to the music of the Glen Miller Band, which
had been brought in by the Roman family for

their daughter, Suzie's, party. "You know I've missed you a lot since I went away to college and haven't spent much time at home," Tom added. "My mother kept me posted about what you and Anne have been up to while I've been living my college life."

Zahra said nothing, as she couldn't think of a thing to say to this handsome brother of her best friend. Since she had first met him, she'd had a crush on him but let no one know, not even Anne. She'd mentioned to her friend Mimi in a letter that she thought he was handsome and so nice, but that was all. Now here she was in his arms, drifting around the dance floor. It took her breath away. She was in a dream but couldn't utter a word.

"What's up? The cat got your tongue tonight?"

"No, it's just that I don't know what to say. You're always teasing me as you do your sister. So, I was surprised that you asked me to dance, especially since there are so many beautiful girls here at the party. There are lots of college girls here, too. I thought you'd be more interested in dancing with them, instead of your little sister's Persian roommate."

"I've had lots of opportunity to dance with those college girls, but none are as beautiful to me as you. I've been waiting since that first day I met you at North Cliff, during the Thanksgiving holiday, you remember? Anyway, I was waiting for you to grow up so that I could become more of a special friend to you."

Again, she couldn't speak and just followed him along to the song, "That Ole Black Magic," her favorite Glenn Miller piece.

When they got back to the table Mrs. Williams said, "You two were the most beautiful couple on the dance floor. You looked like you had danced together before."

"Thanks, Mrs. W. It was the most fun." Zahra answered, her eyes meeting Tom's. He smiled back with his engaging soft smile.

Now her heart was beating like a horse after a two-mile gallop. She felt her face get hot and knew that her parents were observing her with concern. She knew that she would be promised to a suitable Iranian in the not too distant future. She must persuade her parents to let her go to Cornell; now there was more reason than ever for her to go there to college.

The following day, Zahra's parents were giving a luncheon in her honor at the John Marshal hotel. Her classmates and their families were all invited. It was to be a true Iranian lunch that her mother would supervise in the hotel kitchen; the chef had been amenable to this plan as he was interested in learning about Persian food. The Kadjars had brought *arroz* (rice) with them, as well as many kilos of the finest beluga caviar. The guests arrived at noon and were greeted by Zahra, Louisa and Hassan. Zahra was embarrassed that her father's English was so accented and limited. As the people were going through the receiving line, she kept hearing him use the wrong words in his sentences. But she loved him and was proud of his good looks. He was of average height with a head of thick, wavy, salt and pepper hair, his features were chiseled, with high cheek bones and a distinguished, prominent nose. He wore a perfectly tailored, light tan silk suit which accentuated his good looks.

The luncheon was to be served in the Iranian fashion of a buffet. As was the custom, there was a beautifully decorated table with fruit and sweets to start. The sweet would freshen the palate before the actual meal. People helped themselves to the sweets and fruit which they ate while standing around conversing. Meanwhile, the large buffet table in the center of the room, adorned with several porcelain horses and roses (the Persian flower), was being filled by the servers with traditional Persian dishes. Of course, there was the huge dish of caviar served with blinis (a small round pancake); there was also *dolmeh, kuku sabsi, kabab, gormeh sabsi, khoresh* (stews) of many flavors including *fesanjan* and *badanjan* and *polo* (rice) including *lubia polo, albaloo polo*, and *baghali polo*. It was a typical Persian buffet with many of the most well-known national foods.

Louisa had spent many hours with the chef preparing the dishes which needed attention throughout the preparation. The outcome was a well-balanced mixture of herbs, meats, beans, vegetables and cheeses. She herself had made the *Nuna lavash* (unleavened flat bread) to go along with the meal as no such bread was available in Richmond. It made her heart feel good as she watched all these Americans enjoying the food of her adopted country. The luncheon was quite a success that had everyone talking about the delicious food. Many of the girls' mothers wanted to know if Louisa would give a class in Persian cooking.

Zahra and Anne spent most of their time talking with classmates, discussing their summer and fall plans. The girls were all excited about going to college in September. Louisa stood nearby talking to Anne's mother when she overheard Zahra say that she had been accepted by Cornell University. She was taken aback because the plan was for Zahra to be home in Iran in the fall to be presented to Society. Already Hassan had had several prospective suiters speak to him about his beautiful daughter. Now Louisa would again have to persuade him to do something for her that she knew he wouldn't want to do – let her child finish her education.

That evening Louisa went to Zahra's room at bedtime so that she could find out what was actually on Zahra's mind. "Honey, I heard you telling your friends that you've been accepted to Cornell. Is that true?"

"Well, yes! I was going to talk to you and Papa once all the parties are finished and we were on our way to New York."

"Why would you wait so long? Do you really want to go to college? Your father and I have such plans for you in Tehran. I am in shock!"

"Mom, I really love it here in the States. I have so many good friends. Anne and I are both going to Cornell. I want to study more; there is just so much more I must learn. I want to get a degree so that when I do come home to Iran, I'll have some respect, unlike my friends who all stayed home except for shopping sprees to Europe with their mothers. There is just so much more to the world. I love literature and I also want to study agriculture, so I'll be able to make improvements to the farming methods at Nowruzabad."

"Do you know how much this will hurt your father? He's missed you so much these past four years. He wants to be able to ride out with you at Nowruzabd and introduce you to Tehran's society; he has so many plans for you."

"I don't want to go back to a place where I'll be smothered! I know how it is at home. The next thing I know, I'll be forced to marry some man that I don't even like because he's rich or a prince or a politician. I'm too young to do that!"

Her mother looked sympathetic. "I understand how you feel," Louisa said. "I was once young and adventurous, that's how I ended up marrying your father and living my life in Iran, which I love and would never change. It's just that it's going to be so difficult to persuade your father to let you stay here."

"Well, let's wait till we get to New York to talk to him. We still have two more days here and I don't want him to be all angry and miserable when we're around my friends. You know how he can be!"

"Good idea. We're having lunch out at the Williams' farm tomorrow; I am so looking forward to seeing it, having read your letters and seen the pictures you sent us. Then we have one more day before we take the train to New York."

The next day, the William's chauffer picked Zahra and her parents up at the hotel in the late morning so that they would arrive in time for lunch at one o'clock. On the way to Northern Virginia, Hassan and Louise commented on the lovely scenery. It reminded Louisa of the countryside near Charlottesville where she had grown up, and to Hassan who had never been to America before, he thought it was much like the lushness and greenery of Europe. Iran had such a different topography, though it too, was beautiful with its ever-changing shades of brown sand on the desert and tall mountains.

The day was beautiful, sunny, not too hot for May, so they sat on the patio before lunch. Naturally, the discussion, ended up on horses as that was a common interest to all. Tom Williams, Sr., told the story of how he had become involved with Thoroughbred horses when he bought the farm, even though Arabian horses were his interest at the time.

Being in the Middleburg area, one just had to have Thoroughbreds, so he had let his neighbor sell him three brood mares that were in foal to a horse named Sickle. Sickle was bred and raced in England by Edward Stanley, the 17th Earl of Derby; he was by Phalaris the twice-leading sire in England and Ireland. He retired to stud at Lord Derby's stud in 1929 but was then leased to an American, Joseph Widener, who took out the option to buy the horse for $100,000 during a three-year period. As it turned out, on the advice of his neighbor, these three foals of good pedigree went to the Saratoga Fasig Tipton Auction as yearlings. As Sickle had produced three stakes winners from his first crop in America, they all sold for a great deal of money. Thus, Tom was hooked into the breeding business.

After lunch there was, of course, a tour of the stables which now housed a band of ten Thoroughbred brood mares as well as a few Arabs, and Joan Williams fox hunters. Zahra wanted to give a pat to the lovely gray Arab mare she had ridden so much during her time staying at the Williams' home, so she quietly moved off to the small barn where the Arab horses were stabled. As she was in the stall patting the mare, Rosy, her intuition told her that someone was watching her. She turned to see Tom open the stall door. He came over next to her and also patted the mare. The next thing Zahra knew, he had his arms around her and was kissing her cheek and then mouth, his tongue parting her lips. She felt a chill run through her, but it was good.

"Zahra," he said. "I've been wanting to do this forever. I hope you feel the same way about me as I feel about you. I know you'll be leaving for New York in the next couple of days, and I won't be able to see you until school starts in September, but I want to spend a lot of time with you once you get settled there."

"Tom, I like you so much, but I didn't think you felt the same about me. I am so happy! But you must know that my father probably won't let me go to Cornell. He wants me to go back to Persia to be an Iranian socialite. My mother and I are going to try to persuade him to let me stay here and go to college, but I don't know if he will."

Again, Tom took Zahra in his arms holding her close and kissing her again.

Suddenly a voice from the doorway startled them. "What are you two doing?" It was Anne at the stall door. "I thought this would happen between the two of you. I think it's great!"

"You mustn't tell a soul! I am going to have a hard-enough time persuading my father to let me go on to college anyway; if he thinks Tom is part of the reason, he surely won't let me stay here in the States."

Traveling to New York on the train was fun. It was an overnight train, and her parents had a state room next to hers. They had a wonderful dinner in the dining car with champagne and caviar, the latter of which had been refrigerated since the Kadjars arrived in the States.

Her father leaned over after dinner and said, "Zahra June, I'm so excited for you to come back home. I've done a lot of new construction to Nowruzabad. More stables, an addition to the house for guests, and a small apartment for you to have, as I know after your time here you will want to have some independence at times."

"Papa, I am not ready to come home yet. My mind has been opened here. I want to complete my education. I want to go to Cornell University to study agriculture. Think of it – that will be a big help with the modernization of the farming at Nowruzabad. If I do that, and come home to Tehran an educated woman, I'll have many suitors which, I know will make you happy, for there are many wealthy and politically important men that would want me as a wife."

Hassan shook his head and sighed. "What *ashgol* (garbage) you speak my lovely daughter! These past few days with you, I've seen that you are becoming more like your mother and less like the Iranian daughter I hoped you would grow up to be. I gave in to your mother four years ago. and I guess I'll have to give into you now. I don't want to, but I know how you will torment me if I don't."

End of discussion! Zahra was ecstatic that her father was willing to allow her to follow her dream. They went as a family to see Cornell with its gothic stone buildings, stone arches, beautiful paths lined by roses leading to magnificent waterfalls and the lake! Magnificent Lake Cayuga, the largest of New York's Finger Lakes, was such a sparkling blue with huge trees on its shoreline.

Hassan was enchanted with the scenery. He loved his own country and had been amazed by the greenery when he went to Europe. But this New York State, with its soft mountains, majestic trees and sparkling lakes was like being in a dream. How could he tell the light of his life no when she wanted to live there? And so it was decided that Zahra would go with her parents to France and Switzerland, where her father had banking interests, for the summer, then go back to America to attend University.

5

An ambush waits on every side
Wherever we might tread,
And so life's rider rides slack-reined,
Giving his horse his head.
Hafez

Ali 1979

A li turned to leave Zahra's apartment. He walked down the steps, worrying about the ferry across the river to Desful. If the ferry happened to be on the other side of the Dez River when they got to the dock, they would have to wait for it, and that would take many minutes and would delay their arrival at the airport in Ahwaz. The ferry was a rickety affair that would just barely hold the Land Rover and a few people. It was towed from one side of the river to the other with a series of ropes and pulleys that were handled by strong tribesmen of the region.

For centuries, people used to cross the river in small punts, but as agriculture improved and goods and animals needed to be taken to the markets in Desful, and then transported to the cities, it became necessary to have a ferry. Mehdi and Zahra had designed it and borne the cost of building it, for they were instrumental in improving farming in the tribal areas.

It was at least a two-hour drive from Desful to Ahvaz where Zahra would take a plane to Tehran from where she would fly away to America. They must get there in time. He had a huge lump in his throat; he didn't want her to leave. Maybe she would never come back. He loved her so! How could he run this stud farm, as she had told him he must, without her? At one moment he wanted her to hurry up so she would get to the plane on time, but the next he hoped she would not make her flight and would stay in Iran forever.

Zahra

Zahra saw herself and her parents in the picture taken one of the nights they had dinner at

Maxim's in Paris. The dinner was superb; they had ordered the golden caviar that her mother loved so much along with a delicate coq au vin. It had been a lovely evening during which they had talked about her dreams of getting a degree from the University of Cornell.

The trip to Paris had a picture image of the time Zahra and Louisa had been there on their way to the States four years previously, with the exception that Zahra had more control of her wardrobe, which again came from Dior, Chanel and Louis Vuitton. She chose outfits that were casual and comfortable and would suit the collegiate life of Cornell. But of course, her mother insisted that she have a few cocktail dresses and ball gowns. The cold winters in Cornell required warm clothes, so naturally there were a couple of fur jackets with matching hats and a full length mink coat; she knew that she would not wear the mink at school but perhaps if she and Anne went to the farm in Middleburg it would come in handy when they went out in the cold winter evenings.

After a pleasant few days in Paris, they were off to Switzerland. Geneva, the second largest city in Switzerland, was the most international. Here her father had banking business, so they stayed for the week. Hassan spent his days doing business, so Zahra and Louise had time to tour the city and many museums as well as to take day trips. The trip on the historic paddle steamer around Lake Geneva was a fun-filled afternoon and the day visiting Montreux with its Chateau de Chillan was delightful.

When Hassan was finished with his business, he decided that they should go back to France to visit his cousin Roqnehdin, who had a villa on the Mediterranean just outside Nice. They could spend the month in the sun of the French Riviera, swimming, boating, touring and of course gambling in nearby Monte Carlo; how Persians love to gamble!

Zahra was thrilled by the beauty of the Nice area with its warm, clear, summer air; the temperature was rarely over 25 degrees Celsius (80F) nor lower than 20 degrees (68F). Nice was probably founded around 350 B.C. by the Greeks of Massilia (Marseille) and was given the name of "Nikaia" (Name of the Greek goddess of victory) in honor of a victory over the neighboring Ligurians. The city soon became one of the busiest trading ports on the Liguria coast. The Terra Amatta archaeological site displays evidence of an early use of fire, right in the center of the city.

Through the ages, the town changed hands many times. Its strategic location and port significantly contributed to its maritime strength.

For centuries, it was a dominion of Savoy, then became part of France between 1792 and 1815, when it was returned to Piedmont-Sardinia until its re-annexation by France in 1860. The fresh air and soft light of the area attracted many of Western culture's most outstanding painters, such as Marc Chagall, Henri Matisse, Niki de Saint Phalli and Arman; their work could be seen at the many museums. There was plenty of sightseeing for Zahra and her mother, while Hassan relaxed at the villa or on the beach after his nights at the tables.

For Hassan, the evenings were his time of enjoyment. Monte Carlo is situated on a prominent escarpment at the base of the Maritime Alps along the French Riviera. Near the western end of the quarter is the famous Place du Casino which has made Monte Carlo a place of extravagant display and reckless dispersal of wealth. Hassan would take his girls to dinner, at restaurants serving the best of French cuisine, then they would cross to the casino where they'd watch him play – craps, Blackjack, or Chenin de Fer, also called Baccarat. His favorite was Chemins de Fer because there was a possibility of using strategy, whereas the other two games were games of chance. In Baccarat, both players could make choices, which allowed skill to play a part. This was a comparing card game played between two hands, the "player" and the "banker." Each Baccarat coup has three possible outcomes: "player" (player has the higher score), "banker" and "tie." Winning odds are in favor of the bank. The girls would watch for a time, hoping that Hassan would come up with the needed number 9 but that usually didn't happen. One night though, when he was on a roll, they stayed into the early morning hours to watch Hassan break the bank. There was great celebration with champagne before they were driven back to the villa.

And so, the summer continued, until it was time for Zahra to return to New York, to the college that she was so excited to attend. The whole family went back to Paris for a few days to collect Zahra and Louise's clothes and to have one last time together before they would go their separate ways. Louise and Hassan would leave the day after Zahra had taken the plane to New York, so they both went to see her off.

Hassan was quiet on the taxi ride to the airport, but as she checked in, he came up to her, put his arms around her and whispered in her ear, "Are you sure this is what you want to do? I so wanted you to come home with us. I can't believe I'm again letting you go back to America. Oh, I know you'll come home with a good education and I do respect you for wanting that and as times are changing, it's becoming more important for young people to be better educated in order to keep up with modern times. But I will hardly know you when you come home; you have already become a grown woman without my realizing it or having anything to do with it."

Zahra loved her father and understood how he felt, but she wanted to continue her life in America before she would have to become the wife of some uninteresting Iranian.

6

Oh white giant with feet of chains
Oh dome of the world. Oh Mount Damavand
By: Mohammad Taqi Bahar

Ali 1979

Ali checked the oil in the Land Rover. He re-called when he learned to drive under the tutelage of Golam Reza, who himself was at best a sporadic chauffer of the old vehicle. Golam Reza had learned to drive the old car by chance. Mehdi's father, Arab Shehbani Khan, had bought the vehicle when cars and trucks were first being imported to Persia from Europe, where many people had them. He had been vis-iting in Paris and had decided to buy a car for Tehran and a Land Rover for Andimeshk. He would be the only khan in Khuzestan that had a motor vehicle.

The Khan had the vehicle sent to Bandar

Bushehr which was a port of entry for items being shipped from Europe. Golam Reza had been sent to pick it up at the port. He and two other workers from the farm rode on their sturdy Persian horses several hours to reach the port on the Persian Gulf. It took some time and much arguing with the port officials for Golem Reza to take possession of this "metal beast." His papers were all in order but the Arab in charge didn't want this fancy *"Cameron,"* as he called it, to leave the docks.

When Golam Reza was finally given the keys, he didn't know what to do with them or how to drive it! He'd seen pictures of people driving cars, but he wasn't sure what to do. The dock hands all watched with glee in their eyes, laughing. Finally, a truck drove into the port with some exports, so Golam Reza went to the driver to seek his help. The driver showed him how to start the engine and demonstrated how to use the clutch to change the gears, use the accelerator to move it forward, and to step on the brake to stop or slow it down.

After some brief practice, he finally went jerking out the gates of the port to drive his charge to Andimeshk. It took much longer to get back home, as he was afraid to go fast for fear, he wouldn't be able to stop. He found the feeling of speed in the car much more frightening than racing full tilt on his horse. Golam Reza was never comfortable driving the vehicle. But he was the one to teach Ali how to drive. By the time Ali started his driving career, the Land Rover was many years old, as one could tell by the dents and dings on its body. He, too, went jerking off that first day he drove.

"Not so fast!" Golam Rea was more terrified with someone else at the wheel, but he was happy to be able to pass one of his responsibilities on to someone else. It didn't take long for Ali to become comfortable with driving, and soon it became his duty to do all the driving and take care of old "Rostam" as they called the vehicle. The oil level was good and the benzine was full so all he needed was his passenger who was taking her time.

Zahra

Zahra was looking at the picture of herself with Tom and Anne in front of Clark Hall at Cornell. That first year had gone by so quickly she could hardly believe it. She and Anne had shared a room in the women's dorm, though they never spent much time there. They were taking different majors so they didn't see much of each other during the day, but after class most days they would meet at the Trillium dining hall for a cup of tea and a snack, to plan their social calendars. In the warm months, there was tennis, which they both played well, and of course wonderful skiing on the snowy winter days.

But most of all, the girls loved going up to Netherfield Acres to ride. Bob Smith, the son of a friend of Joan Williams, who was studying agriculture at Cornell, had become friends with the girls, and Tom and he had asked them out to ride with him. His family had owned their land for generations and had been instrumental in founding the Millbrook and Rombout Hunt, so the girls were invited often to hunt during the season. And of course, there was the social life! Frat parties every Friday and Saturday night were the place to be. Tom had joined the Sigma Chi Fraternity in his sophomore year so that was where the two girls had their first introduction to fraternity life. However, there were many other frats on the row, so they would often start out at Sigma Chi and then travel on down the street, going to the frat house that seemed to be having the best party.

During the first year, Tom kept his distance from Zahra. He introduced her and Anne to his

friends and to frat life, but he felt that she needed to experience college life without the encum-
brance of a "boyfriend." Every now and then
when they met, he would hold her hand and kiss
her on the cheek, but that was all. Each time
he did, she hoped the situation would become
more intimate, but it didn't. She and Anne were
both very beautiful; Anne had long wavy blond
hair, blue eyes, soft features with full lips and a
willowy stature. Zahra, with her olive skin, huge
dark almond eyes, long jet-black hair and full
breasted figure was a stunner. Both girls were
sought after by the boys and never remained on
the sidelines when there was dancing. And there
was much dancing, to the records of the Glen
Miller Band, Bing Crosby, Vaughn Munroe and
others. Anne's favorite piece was Dinah Shore's
"Buttons and Bows" while Zahra loved Glenn
Miller's "Moonlight Serenade."

Tom was busy with his classes in business
and agriculture but found time to play sports as
well. He was on the Cornell Polo Team. During
spring and fall there was a lot of practice, especially before the games with University of
Virginia, which was the archrival of The Big Red
polo team. Those games were always rough and
tough. The Virginia boys were noted for their
horsemanship, and the fact that their playing fields were able to be used most of the year

meant they had more hours of training. But in the final game of the season of Zahra's first year, the Big Red trounced UVA five to two, with Tom scoring two goals.

The party after the game was held in the Big Red Barn on campus. As school was out the following week, the barn dance became a celebration of the victory as well as the final party of the college year. There was lots of beer, donated by the Genoese Brewing Company, which helped with the costs of the polo team, and lots of dancing.

The last dance of the evening was to Bing Crosby's, "I'll Be Seeing You." When the tune began, Tom took Zahra's hand and led her to the dance floor. She had hardly seen him all night. As the star player of the game, he was in much demand with his teammates, replaying every second of the game they'd won and accommodating the many girls who wanted to dance with him.

Zahra was going home to Persia for her summer vacation; her parents had insisted that she needed to spend some time with them. It had been almost five years since she'd been to her country. They wanted her to reconnect with them and their way of life for the two months she would be there. They'd spend time at their home on the Caspian Sea because there was a summer social season where they planned to introduce her to society. Of course, she knew her father was hoping to keep her in Iran, persuading her to forgo her education and get married, but she was determined to return to Cornell in September. Tom held her close as they danced, singing a few phrases of the tune.

"You know I've been wanting to dance with you like this since the beginning of the school year, but I wanted you to have some independence and get into the college way of life without relying on me to take care of you, which I know you would have done if I'd given you the chance. Now you're off to Persia next week." Then he sang along with the song in the background, "See you in September." He held her tighter, dancing cheek to cheek and flowing with the rhythm of the music.

After a moment, he continued, "It will be different in the fall when you come back. I'll let everyone know that you're mine. If you will be. Will you?"

"I've been waiting all year for you to pay me some attention; of course, I'll be yours!'

"Then come outside with me for a minute." He led her by the hand, out the big barn door to a pile of straw bales. They sat down and he took both her hands in his and lightly kissed her on the lips. Not a passionate kiss but a loving one.

"I want to give you my frat pin to wear so that everyone will know we're pinned. It will be a part of me that you'll be able to take home with you." He fastened the pin onto her cashmere sweater.

She took the pin in her fingers and looked down at it and then threw her arm around Tom and kissed him passionately. They kissed and fondled one another for some time before they were interrupted by someone coming around the corner near them.

"What's going on here? I wondered where the two of you had gone," Anne said as she approached.

"Zahra and I just got pinned," said Tom.

"I don't believe it, Tom. You've hardly had any time for Zahra and me all year and now all of a sudden, you're getting pinned? When I caught the two of you in the stable last spring, I thought something was going on between you two. But then nothing happened, so I figured I was wrong." She grinned happily. "Now I was right! I'm so happy! I just can't believe it! I can't wait to tell Mummy; she will be so happy. She loves Zahra like a daughter and now maybe she *will* be a daughter."

The following Friday, Tom drove Zahra to the New York airport. They had a tearful hug and kiss before she went through the boarding gate and she waved from the top of the stairs, as she went into the plane. He stood and watched as the plane taxied out.

It was a long flight to Tehran. There was a stop in Paris where she had a two-hour layover, then another stop in Istanbul, and finally on to Tehran. The trip took twenty-four hours in total. She'd lost a whole day!

Hassan and Louisa were at Mehrahabad to meet her at the steps of the plane. They hugged and kissed her in greeting. Zahra couldn't believe the wave of heat that she felt. She'd forgotten how hot it was in Tehran in the summer. As they waited for her luggage to be taken off the plane, Hassan signaled to Abraheem, their driver, to pick up the luggage and put it in the trunk of the car. As he did so, Abraheem said, "Miss Zahra, welcome home. It is so good to see you; I wouldn't have recognized you. You have turned into a beautiful woman. When you left you were just a young girl."

Louisa had brought a chador for Zahra to put on as they left the airport. Though the women of Tehran's society did not wear the chador often, when they were in such a public place it was respectful. As Louisa placed the chador over Zahra's head, she noticed the fraternity pin on Zahra's blouse. "What is that, Zahra? It looks like a fraternity pin."

"It is, Mamma. I just got pinned to Tom Williams last weekend!"

"Don't you dare mention this to your father! He'll forbid you to go back to college! I am shocked! You must realize that your father wants to select the man for you to marry."

"I don't want to, and I refuse to marry some man he chooses. It would probably be someone much older than me, some important politician or businessman that he thinks would be suitable. No, I will marry someone I love."

"Well, just don't bring up this pinned business to him. We don't want any drama while you're here. Tom did seem such a nice young man when I met him during your graduation. Have you been seeing him all year? Now tell me all about it. But only in English. We don't want your father to understand what we are talking about."

"No, we've been friendly all year, but he's in his third year and very busy with polo, hockey and sculling so I didn't spend a lot of time with him. He did get Anne and me introduced to some of his friends and also to his frat brothers, but we weren't together much. I knew he liked me a lot, and I've had a crush on him since the first time I met him. Last spring when we went to the Williams's farm, he kissed me when

I went to the stables and I kissed him back. But then, when I got to Cornell, he kept his distance, so I thought he hadn't really meant it. And there were so many girls hanging around him, I figured I was just an insignificant friend of his sister. Then at a party to celebrate our team winning a polo match, and the end of the school year, he gave me his fraternity pin which means we are almost engaged."

Hassan had finished supervising Abraheem's loading of the luggage, so they all got into the Kadjar's big black Chrysler limousine and drove through the streets of Tehran to their house in Shemran. Zahra remembered the house as being big but when they pulled through the gates into the walled park-like setting, she was surprised at the massive size of the flat-roofed two-story edifice. And it was beautiful, with huge double-carved oak doors set in a stone façade. The large windows on the main floor all had carved stone window boxes filled with multicolored flowers, while each of the upstairs windows had a small wrought-iron balcony with a flowerpot in one corner, again filled with colorful plants. The tall wall around the garden was draped with bougainvillea in full mauve bloom. Seeing her home, Zahra realized, that yes, she had missed it these past five years, though she had been so busy with school and the American life that she hadn't thought of the house she'd been brought up in. She knew she missed her parents, family and friends, but she had forgotten about this comforting old house.

She was exhausted from the trip, but she raced up to her room. Vases of roses had been placed as a welcome. It had been decided that she would take a nap before the welcome home party that had been planned for her. As she lay on her big bed, stretched out with arms akimbo, she could see the beautiful pointed peak of Mount Damavand through the French doors that opened out onto her balcony. Damavand was the highest mountain in Iran at 5,610 Meters. It had a special place in Persian mythology and folklore. It was said that the three-headed dragon, Azi Zahhak, was chained within the mountain, there to remain until the end of the world. The mountain was also said to hold magical powers in "Shahnameh" (the Persian Book of Kings by the poet Ferdowsi).

Zahra fell asleep gazing at Damavand and dreamed of her life in America. Her mother woke her in time to dress for the party. She had put out one of the beautiful cocktail dresses from Sassoon for her to wear, which surprised her.

"I thought this was to be only our family and close friends. So why do I have to be so dressed up?"

"Well, you know your father! He's also asked a few of his business friends and their families. He wants to show off his beautiful daughter."

"Oh no! So now it's going to start! He's going to try to find me a suitable husband while I'm here. I'm going to talk to him tomorrow morning. I am pinned and know to whom I'll be married, so, he just needs to stop this foolishness!"

"Zahra June, I advise you not to mention your relationship with Tom to him. But you may tell him that you don't want him trying to arrange anything because you'll be leaving to go back to university at the end of the summer. Now, shall we go downstairs to have a good time?"

It was good to see her aunts, uncles and cousins as well as her girlfriends, Mimi Zanganeh and Avid Motamed, who came with their parents. They had lots of catching up to do, for she had been away for such a long time and had no idea what her friends had been up to.

"I'm to be married next month, Zahra" said Avid. "You're my oldest friend so I hope you'll be in the wedding. I'm so glad you will still be here."

"Of course, I'd be happy to, but who are you marrying? Mamma didn't tell me anything about this, and you never mentioned it in your letters. Are you in love?"

"Well actually, it's a business acquaintance

of my father, but he isn't as old. He's quite hand-some and very pleasant and of course he has a lot of money. You know how important that is. There he is now, just coming in the door. Let's go over so you can meet him."

He was a good-looking man of about for-ty, Zahra thought. Average height, a full head of salt and pepper hair, a typical large Aryan nose. His perfectly tailored silk suit made him look very distinguished. Of course, it was an ar-ranged marriage of convenience, which made Zahra feel sorry for her best friend. She herself was so lucky to have been able to go away and meet someone she was attracted to and who had similar interests, that she could truly love. Poor Avid!

People mingled for a long time, having drinks before the wonderful food was brought out for all to enjoy. At the parties in Persia, there was always a room set up with a bar for those who imbibed in alcohol, and a room where you could smoke opium if that was your pleasure. And of course, there was always tea served in small glass cups.

Towards the end of the evening, a tall, dark, and very handsome man of about thirty came into the bar and went up to Hassan. "I'm so sor-ry to be late, Hassan, but I just got back from Andimeshk this afternoon and was given your invitation by my houseman. I knew the party would go on till the wee hours, so I decided to come on. Now, where is this daughter of yours in whose honor this fete has been given?"

Hassan led him over to a group where Zahra seemed to be having a good time. "Zahra." Hassan interrupted. "I want you to meet my good friend Mehdi Bakhtiar. He has just arrived and wants to meet the guest of honor."

"How do you do?" said Zahra putting out her hand and making a little curtsy, as was the custom. *Oh, my God*, she thought, *he has already started*! She and Mehdi Bakhtiar had a delightful conversation about her experiences riding horses in the States. He'd obviously been given the information that she loved horses. He told her about his stud farm in Khuzestan where he spent much of his time. She was impressed with his knowledge of horses and felt that he too had a love of the equine.

He left her side to mingle and Avid came up to her. "Do you know who that is?" She pointed his way.

"His name is Mehdi Bakhtiar."

"I know that! He is the most eligible bachelor in Tehran! And he is the Khan of the most important clan of the Bakhtiar tribe."

Zahra was not impressed. "So? What does that mean?"

"You don't know about the Bakhtiari, the largest and oldest of all the Persian tribes? They're supposed to be decedents of Cyrus the Great. They weren't just nomadic peoples with great military prowess, but they also had villages and large land holdings. They were very powerful when Reza Shah came to power, but he was able to establish authority over them and persuade them to settle more in the towns and villages. There are still many who practice the nomadic life but those who were detribalized have become well educated, assimilated into Persian life and are an important part of national politics. Mehdi was educated at Oxford and is now the most important Khan in Khusestan, perhaps all of Iran. Do you think your dad is cooking something up?"

"I'm sure he's trying but it won't work because I'm in love with someone back in the States."

The following morning after a breakfast of freshly squeezed orange juice, and *nun-e-barbari* with butter and tea, Zahra went to seek out her father. He hadn't gone into his office as it was her first day home and he wanted to spend time with her. Hassan had planned a trip to Noruzabad for a ride in the country for he'd bought her a new horse that he wanted her to ride.

"Papa, *ruz beher*. It is so good to be here with you." She hugged him. "That was a lovely party and I had a lot of fun. Thanks so much."

"Nothing but the best for my Zahra."

"I need to talk to you about something so that we can have a great summer together. I know you're always thinking about finding me a suitable marriage, but I don't want you to do that during this vacation. I'm going back to Cornell in two months and I will not be persuaded to forget my goal of getting a degree from university. So, forget about introducing me to prospective husbands."

"Of course, I won't do that. What makes you think I would do something like that?"

"Why did you invite that man Mehdi Bakhtiar to the party? I know why! But please forget it, so we can have a great time together while I'm home"

"I understand what you're saying, and I will comply with your wishes. I do think, though, that Mehdi, who you met last night, is interested in you."

"That's too bad. He can't have me."

The summer went on well and too quickly. They rode almost every day they were in Tehran, during the early morning hours when it was cool. When the weather became hotter during the middle of *Shahrivar* (July) they went to the summer house in the north by the sea.

The route to the Caspian Sea, the largest inland body of saltwater in the world, where they spent several weeks, was treacherous. They drove to Qazvin, then headed east up the Alborz Mountains on a dirt road that circled the mountains. It was quite a terrifying drive, but the destination was worth it.

The house at Ramsar was right on the water. They swam in the ocean almost every day, even though they had a pool. They ate fresh fish and of course caviar, as the Caspian is the home of the beluga Sturgeon, the largest freshwater fish in the world. Life in the Ramsar area (the Riviera of Iran) was very social in summer, so there were parties almost every night. On several occasions, Zahra saw Mehdi Bakhtiar, who always asked her to dance with him. She found him very pleasant, a good conversationalist, and a great dancer!

Avid's wedding was the week before Zahra left to go back to the States. It was a spectacular event. Persian wedding ceremonies stemmed from the ancient Zoroastrian religion rituals. There were two stages: the legal and contractual ceremony, or *Aghd*, and the reception. During the *Aghd,* the bride, groom and their families signed the official marriage contract. The ceremony took place in a room with a *Sofreh-ye*

Aghd, a special cloth that was set on the floor facing east. The bride's friends and women of the family held a silk scarf over the couple, who sat on the floor, with the man to the woman's right (Zoroastrians considered the right side to be the side of respect).

There were two candelabra and a mirror, which represented light and fire, on the *Sofreh*, along with many items such as gold coins, eggs, nuts honey, incense. Each of these things had a meaning that would help the couple to have a good marriage. The groom entered and sat first so that when his bride, whose face was veiled, sat down and lifted her veil, his first look at her was through the mirror. Zahra, holding the scarf for her friend, could only think that when she and Tom were married, she wouldn't want to go through all this formality. He would not understand it and she didn't want it. But then again, her parents would expect it. Leave out the ceremony? How could she ever do that to them?

Her farewell to her parents was tearful and very different from her first departure from her homeland. She climbed the steps to the airplane, and as she had when she left America, she turned at the top and waved. She couldn't wait to get back to the States and see Tom.

7

I long to kiss his lovely lips,
And if he said he thought I should,
How would that be?
Obayd-e Zakini

Ali 1979

Ali walked back up the stairs slowly, wondering how to get Zahra to leave her reverie and get going. He was becoming more nervous about missing the plane. Maybe she didn't really want to go to America. She had told him about going to school and university there and he was in awe that she was so well educated; few women in all the country had been educated and especially in this tribal area of Khuzestan. He really didn't understand the things she told him about her life there. It was something he couldn't comprehend as it was so foreign to him, but he had looked at her pictures many times and tried to imagine how her life there had been.

In America they raced the horses on an oval track that had lush grass, trees and beautiful gardens. She'd shown him pictures of a place she called Saratoga where she went to the races with people who were like her family, there. The people were fair skinned with blond hair and wore tailored western clothes; the women wore big flowery hats to the races.

Here, in Khuzestan, the horses raced from one point to another, for many kilometers across desert lands. Horses had to be very strong, fit, and sound to win. He thought that those American horses must be frail and weak since they only ran one or two kilometers and on such a manicured surface. To him it would not be very exciting.

He remembered the time that Mehdi Bakhtiar had ridden Arrus II in the Khuzestan cross desert race from Desful to Shushtar, a distance of sixty kilometers. It had been a beautiful day on *Sizdah Bedar*, the thirteenth day after *Now Ruz*, which was a day of partying and picnics in the countryside. A group of forty horses had congregated in the main square of the small town. The mud buildings around the square had been decorated with colorful banners of red, white, and green, the colors of the Iranian flag. The tri-colored flag itself hung on a tall flagpole in the center of the square, waving slowly in the light breeze, with its golden lion in the center.

The square was crowded with people, all of whom had come to see the start of the race. Some wore pantaloons and head dresses while others wore western-like pants and jackets, their best clothes for the special day of celebration. The women wore colorful skirts and beautiful head scarves as, well as long necklaces and earrings of silver and semiprecious stones. It was a day to celebrate the New Year which comes in Persia at the time of the Vernal Equinox. Forty excited horses milled around, waiting for the flag of the starter to fall, to commence the race. Arrus II had been prancing under Mehdi who was the ever-dapper Khan of the Bakhtiar tribe. He was dressed in britches and brown calfskin French-made boots. Other horses reared, kicking and whinnying as they all circled in the square. The official Land Rover that would drive to Shushta to await the finish of the race was driven by the mayor of Dezful, with Shushta's head man in the passenger seat; and in the back were four other officials all calling out orders to the riders. Finally, the officials signaled to the starter who let the flag fall. As it fell, the horses and their riders took off in a southeastern direction from Dezful, heading at an all-out gallop for Shushta. The expert horsemen knew when to race head to head and when to conserve their horses' energy by letting them rest at the walk or trot. Mehdi was a brilliant horseman and was expected to win.

Those spectators who had vehicles ran to them so that they could follow the horses across the desert. Others rode their horses, mules or donkeys slowly into the desert, only to await the results which would be announced by those returning from Shushta a few of hours later. The celebration for the winner and the prize money, which was considerable, would be presented by the Mayor of Shushta.

Ali, who at the time was still a young boy, rode in the back of the old pickup truck driven by his father. He would never forget the excitement he felt as they drove through the desert on the bumpy dirt track as the horses raced alongside. The riders had to know the terrain, for there were ditches and gullies that needed to be skirted to avoid disaster. Mehdi knew his desert and rode with a great feel for the animal and terrain. It was really no contest, as Arrus II ran into the town square of Shushta minutes before any of the other horses. Mehdi walked him around the square as he waited for his competitors who straggled in slowly. The presentation was made amongst loud cheers from all the watchers who seemed in awe of the beautiful black stallion glistening in his own sweat, puffing but not overly tired. How fit he had to be! Ali would never forget it!

Zahra

Zahra was looking at herself with Tom and his parents in the "Win" picture at Saratoga. The North Cliff horse "Lucky North" had won the Saratoga Special a couple of days after she'd arrived back from her summer trip with her family in Iran.

She had arrived at La Guardia airport early in the evening after the long trip from Tehran. She hadn't stopped in Europe this time as she was too excited to get back to the States. She wanted to arrive early enough to have week or so to relax before she started back to Cornell. It had been arranged that she would spend time in Saratoga where the Williams had rented a house for the racing season.

Of course, Tom and Anne had both decided to meet her so they could all get caught up on the drive to Saratoga. The big Lincoln was waiting at the curb when they exited the airport with her many bags. She'd brought gifts for all the Williams family, and naturally her mother had insisted that she needed more clothes, most of which she knew she would never wear. But they filled the suitcases.

She told Tom and Anne what she could about her trip home, leaving out the fact that she knew her father was seriously looking for an eligible man to whom she would be betrothed. She had tales of her wonderful rides in the desert near Nowruzabad, the fabulous time on the Caspian where there had been swimming and fishing, and of course she described in detail the wedding of her friend, Avid. The siblings were aghast at the fact that the marriage had been arranged and the poor girl didn't have a choice in the matter, but she explained that that was still the custom in Iran.

"What will they say when you tell them you're in love with an American and won't be marrying anyone who is chosen by your father?" asked Tom.

"My mother noticed your pin, Tom, but she wouldn't let me tell my father. She said it would break his heart to think he wouldn't be able to select my husband from the many suitable bachelors in Tehran society. But who said anything about marriage?"

"Once you're pinned, the next step is an engagement ring and then marriage. That's the

American custom," Tom replied, giving her a kiss on the cheek.

"Come on you two, enough of that lovey-dovey stuff," Anne chided. We're going to have a great day tomorrow at the races; you can talk about all that stuff when you're alone."

Tom smiled and said, "I guess I didn't tell you when I last wrote to you, my love, that Dad has the favorite in the Saratoga Special. It's a really important race of the season so we're all excited about it. We've had such a good time here. The yearlings we sold brought much better prices than we expected and the few racehorses we have are all doing well. Why, we've had three winners already!" Tom had been in charge of the sales of the yearlings all summer and was thrilled that they had all sold so well. He'd turned down a couple of good job offers in Albany in order to work on the farm; as a result of the sales, he'd be getting a good commission which would probably be far more than he'd have made at a desk job in the city.

The following morning, they were all up early to go watch the morning workouts at the track. It was the custom during the Saratoga season to go to the track to watch horses work while sitting out on the deck having a sumptuous breakfast served by waiters in white shirts and black ties. There were Mimosas, eggs Benedict and omelets of all varieties to enjoy while discussing the day's race card and the chances for one's own horses, if indeed you had a runner for the afternoon.

"There he is!" Tom yelled. "He's coming along the backside now. Do you see the big chestnut with the white blaze and four white feet, Zahra?"

She strained her eyes and then Mr. Williams gave her his binoculars and pointed in the direction she should look. She saw the tall beautiful chestnut stallion that looked to have a long rhythmic stride galloping around the hedge rimmed track.

"He's just going to gallop a half mile to loosen him up for this afternoon," Tom explained as the horse passed them at their trackside table.

The crowd that afternoon was huge. Trying to get through the congestion up to the Williams's box, right on the finish line, was complicated. Zahra had never before been to the races in America, so it was a bit confusing to understand the Racing Form, and things like odds on the horses, but she had a good time watching the races and all the activity around her.

"The next race is ours, so we will all go down to the paddock to see Lucky and talk to the trainer and the jockey," Joan Williams told Zahra.

There was great excitement under the beautiful oak and maple trees that were scattered in the paddock with a number by each. The numbers designated where the horses would be handled and held in waiting for the call, "Riders up!" The Saratoga Special Stakes was a race for two-year-olds run annually since 1901. Not only was it a winner-take-all race but it was six furlongs, which was a long distance for a two-year-old at that time of year. Lucky North had won his Maiden race by five lengths at Belmont four weeks previously and was expected to take the lead and keep it.

The jockey Johnny Longden, who had been the leading money-winning jockey in 1943 as well as the man who captured the Triple Crown of Thoroughbred Racing by winning the Kentucky Derby, the Preakness Stakes and the Belmont Stakes on the horse Count Fleet that same year, had agreed to ride the Williams' horse. As he walked up to trainer "Sunny Jim" Fitsimmons to get his final instructions, he was introduced to the family and Zahra, who was quite taken with his winning smile and small stature. When the call for "Riders Up" came, he was given a leg-up by Sunny Jim on the beautiful chestnut with its coruscant coat shimmering in the sunlight.

They all watched as the colt took the lead out of the gate and crossed the finish line ten lengths in front of the other horses with his huge, long, flowing stride. Then they all rushed down to the winners' enclosure where a picture was taken, and the beautiful silver trophy was presented to the family.

Zahra's college classes were due to begin the second week in September. The Saratoga season, which Zahra was able to partake in for almost ten days, was finished. She would be a sophomore, and as planned she and Anne would be living together in a small student apartment just off campus. It was exciting to have their own home and to be able to decorate it themselves. Zahra had brought a trunk full of Iranian Esfahani fabrics and a few small Persian carpets to add a bit of a Middle Eastern flavor to their abode. Anne had decided to help Zahra give the new living quarters a real Persian atmosphere, with wall hangings of fabric, and carpets, brass and glass work they found in local thrift shops. They spent days decorating the apartment so that when they had a small get-together with their close friends it would be just as they wanted it. "No one else will have such an exciting-looking place," Anne said when they were finally finished their decorating.

"You don't think it will seem too affected, do you?" Zahra never wanted to advertise the fact that she was Iranian, though she was proud to be one.

"No, Zahra. It's beautiful and has such a cozy atmosphere, I know our friends will love it. Let's invite a few friends over for beer and munchies this weekend."

During those first few weeks Tom too, was very busy as he was a senior and had a lot of commitments, both academically and for sports. There was the polo team, which he would captain, and the sculling which had a busy training schedule in the fall. He hadn't seen Zahra nor Anne at all for two weeks when they called to invite him and a couple of his polo playing team members to come over to their "Kasbah Opening," as they called it.

With Tom and his teammates, there were eight attractive young men and women at the party. He was so excited to finally get to see his Persian love that as he entered, he took her lovely small chin in his right hand and kissed her tenderly on the lips in front of all to see. "I've missed being with you since we got back to school, Zahra. We had such a good time being together almost every day in Saratoga and now with classes, rowing and polo, I haven't had the time I want to spend with you. Please forgive my negligence." He kissed her again, this time with both arms around her, to keep her close.

"I've been busy, too, so don't worry. Anne and I have spent a lot of time getting the apartment decorated and my classes are quite challenging so far. So even though I missed you, my time was pretty full."

The get-together went on till quite late, but as everyone was leaving, Tom took Zahra aside to see if she would go out to dinner with him the following evening.

He picked her up at seven and they went to the Lakefront Inn, which had a quaint little bistro with good fare. He told her about the rowing team, which competed mostly in the spring but practiced during the fall until the weather got too chilly. The polo team would be going to Charlottesville, Virginia in a couple of weeks and he was hoping she would make it a weekend trip with him because he was planning to spend the night at his parents after the game.

After dinner they drove in his convertible to the park that overlooked Lake Cayuga. It was a warm fall evening with a full moon shining, its reflection shimmering across the lake. "You know I want to marry you, Zahra," Tom began. "Even though I gave you my pin on the night before you left, I was so afraid you'd come back from your trip home to tell me that you weren't sure about us. Our time in Saratoga was like a dream for me. Even though I spent a lot of time with the horses, when you told me you loved me and missed me, I was the happiest man there."

Zahra was touched by his passionate speech. "I love you Tom, and I want to be married to you, but we have to wait until we're both finished with our degrees, because I know my family won't consider letting me get married here in the States. It will have to be in Iran, and I know that's going to make it very complicated for us. I have three more years before I graduate but you'll be finished this spring. Do you know what you're going to do after you graduate? You've never mentioned much about the future to me."

Tom took a deep breath and sighed. "I've thought about a lot of things. Dad's horse business has become pretty viable in the last couple of years, so I could probably manage that, but I really think that I need to do something else in the business world. I could maybe take a couple of years more of school and get a Masters, and then we would both be out of school at the same time.

"And then there's the problem of the draft. With the Korean thing, the government is getting pretty strict about drafting people like me and it's better to volunteer if you want to have a decent time in the service. With my degree, I'd qualify for the officers' training program. They also have great post service programs to further your education, so if I volunteer, when I get out in two years, I could get my Master's then.

I don't know. I'm going to have to do a lot of thinking in the next few months."

"Oh no! I don't want you to go into the army. You could get killed and then what would I do?"

"Let's not worry about things like that now. We've just started the fall semester, so I have months to make my decision. Let's get out of the car and go down by the lake to look at the moon."

They got out of the car and Tom picked up the plaid motor robe he had conveniently tucked behind his seat. They walked down the grassy slope towards the lake and found a smooth spot, under a gnarly old oak tree, to spread out the blanket.

They sat there cross legged, silently holding hands, watching the moonlight flicker between the puffy cumulus clouds lazily crossing the sky. Finally, Tom kissed her cheek and then tenderly took her in his arms, kissing her passionately. She moaned softly when he began to caress her small firm breasts. She could hardly stand the tingling she felt between her legs. She began to shudder and pulled her whole body close to him. She felt him hard against her and wondered if they would do it. But she was afraid. Her married friends in Iran had told her about their experiences with the sex act and she didn't think it sounded pleasurable at all, so why was she feeling this way? She wanted him and just knew it would be a blissful experience. Once again, he kissed her neck and pressed his mouth hungrily on hers, and then he sat up. He kissed her fingers and said, "We must stop here now. Our time to make love will come, but I want it to be in the right place and at the right time, my love."

She felt disappointed but she knew he was right. They would be lovers before long. And she wanted to be prepared for the event that she knew would be so special. The girls in the dorm last year had told her about the need for protection, so she knew she must go see a doctor before she could ever consent to their joint desire.

Two weeks later, she was in his car beside him driving down to UVA, to a polo match on Saturday afternoon. On Friday night, she would stay in the girls' dorm there, with the girlfriend of one of his Virginia buddies, and then they would drive to Middleburg Saturday evening to stay at the Williams' farm for the night. They would drive back to Cornell the following day.

Saturday dawned crisp and clear. The leaves on the Virginia trees were just beginning to change color, whereas the leaves in New York State were already brilliant red, orange and yellow. The game was at ten, so the bleary-eyed girls rushed around, getting ready to go off to the polo field by nine thirty. This was quite an accomplishment considering the late night most of them had had staying up talking till the wee small hours of the morning. Zahra was not much of a drinker, so she was feeling better than the girls who had been drinking wine and beer all evening. but she wasn't much of a late-night girl, either, so she too had a hard time rousing herself.

When they got to the field, the players were on their ponies warming up. They hit some balls and worked the horses to make sure they were ready for the game. Polo requires that the horses are fine tuned to every command, no matter how slight it might be. Just leaning a little one way or the other in the saddle is a signal for the horse to change direction, speed up or slow down. A good polo pony will follow the ball itself when pointed in its direction. They must also stop on a dime, be able to gallop from a standstill, and turn sharply to position the rider so he can get a good hit. The maneuverability of the animal is extremely important, especially as about sixty to seventy-five percent of the of the player's skill depends on his mount.

Zahra knew a lot about the history of polo. The game originated in Persia sometime around the sixth century B.C. to the first century A.D., depending on which history one deemed to be correct. It was said that Emperor Alexander

(912-913) died from exhaustion while playing and John I of Trebizond (1206-1210) died of a fatal injury during a game. The mediaeval royal polo field built by Shah Abbas I in the seventeenth century was in Esfahan at the Naqsh-e Jahan Square. As time went on, polo passed from Persia to other parts of Asia. It was said that the game first came to the United States in 1876 and was played at a stable on the corner of 39th Street and Fifth Avenue in New York City.

Zahra knew the game well as she had gone many times with her father to the Ghargoushdare polo field, which was just a few kilometers from their farm at Nowruzabad. There were four players per team and usually eight seven-minute chukkas (periods) between which the players must change their mounts, since the game was so fast and tiring for the horses. There was a four-minute interval between chukkas and a ten-minute half time. The play was continuous and was only stopped for penalties, broken tack, or injury to horse or rider. It was much like ice hockey, with the object being to hit the small white wooden ball between the goal posts.

Tom was a superb player and rider. Zahra was proud to stand cheering for him on the sidelines. As she watched him, she hoped he would go to Iran with her one day to show his prowess at the sport that was so important there. Surely that would persuade her father that he would make a worthy son-in-law.

At the end of the 7th chukka, the score was Virginia 7 to Cornell 6. It would be hard to get two goals in the last chukka, but Cornell, the underdogs, were going to give it all they had. The 8th was fast and furious with the ball screaming from end to end without stopping. In the last minute of play, Tom, who was the Number Three player, the best player on the team, hit a long powerful shot from their goal line to the Number One player; amazingly the teammate hit it right between the goal posts. Now it was a tie game, which meant there would be a five-minute break for the players to switch horses and get their breath.

When the "Sudden Death" chukka commenced, Virginia took the ball right down to the Cornell line and their Number One hit a fast ball towards the goal, which luckily missed by just inches. Next the Cornell Number Two had the ball, which he took up the field to Tom, who hit it through the Virginia goal posts. The crowd went wild! The win for Cornell put them in the playoffs.

Following the game, there was a luncheon in the tent that had been erected on the side of the field, where the two teams, their families and friends relived the game chukka by chukka. Tom came up behind Zahra who was talking with the

Number One player from the Virginia team and caressed her back lightly. "I think it's time we got on the road, love. We have to drive to North Cliff and it'll take an hour or so. Are you ready to go?" She said her goodbyes to her companion and the girls she had stayed with the night before and walked with him to the convertible.

"What time are your parents expecting us?" she asked as he opened her door.

"Well, actually they aren't home. Mom called to tell me they were going to New York for the weekend to some racing party, so we have the whole place to ourselves tonight."

"Uh, do you think that will be OK with them?" she asked tentatively.

"No problem, Zahra It'll be fine with them and it's going to be great for us." He winked at her and she knew this was going to be their time.

There were welcoming lights in the house when they drove up the driveway of North Cliff, so Zahra thought maybe the Williams had changed their minds and had not gone to New York after all, but as she hopped out of the car she saw that Aida, the maid, was there at the door to welcome them. "Tom, your mother told me you two would be coming to spend the night, so I have planned supper for the two of you. I hope you don't mind eating a little early, say six-ish, because I had planned to go to evening church with my family. You know, I thought no one would be here tonight with your parents in New York for the week-end."

"That'll be perfect Aida, because we need to get up at the crack of dawn tomorrow, to drive back up to school."

They had their early supper in the cheery breakfast room, accompanied by a bottle of Beaujolais Superior. They decided to walk down to the stables to have a look at the horses before darkness set in, and then Tom suggested that they go to the library to sit by the fire. The evening was becoming cool. The fire had been laid and set by Aida before she left for church. Tom went over to the bar and poured two glasses of port for them to sip as they warmed themselves by the crackling fire.

"So, is this going to be our special time, Tom?" Zahra asked bravely as they sat chatting about the horses.

"You guessed it, my love. It's the perfect time and place. Let's go up to my room to see how we get along."

"I want you to know that I'm prepared. I went to the doctor last week when I knew we were going to Charlottesville. If we're going to make love, I don't want to become pregnant. It would ruin both our lives if that happened," she said shyly.

"You're amazing! Are all the Persian girls as smart as you?"

"Persian girls don't have premarital sex. The men all want to marry virgins. I've never talked to my Iranian friends about it; the subject is *taboo*. My birth control information comes from American girls only. My two friends in Iran who are married have talked to me about the sex act, but it doesn't sound very exciting the way they describe it. To tell you the truth, I'm a bit nervous and scared."

"I promise you I'll try not to hurt you. But they say it does hurt a little bit the first time, although I've also heard that girls who ride horses a lot have an easier time. Being a rider like you are, you should be fine," he tried to calm her nerves.

When they got to his room, he opened the door for her, then quietly closed it behind them. He kissed her softly on the lips and began to undo the buttons on her cashmere cardigan. Slowly he undressed her until she stood completely naked in front of him.

"Now you get to undress me," he huskily whispered.

She started with his shirt, unbuttoning it and letting it slip to the floor, and then she began with his belt. She noted a bulge in his pants as she undid the top button and began to pull down the zipper. The next thing she knew, they were in each other's arms skin to skin, kissing each other on his big bed. Things progressed well from then on.

"Oh my God! I had no idea it would feel like that," she commented, still panting slightly as they lay in each other's arms much later. "It was so erotic and wonderful. I don't think I'll ever be able to get enough of you."

"You may be sorry you said that, because I'm getting ready to have you again. You're an amazing lover. You know how to make me so happy. I love you more than anything."

The following morning, they drove back to Ithaca with Zahra snuggled next to Tom, listening to Glen Miller on the radio.

As the college year passed, they spent as much time with each other as their busy lives would allow them. They were so in love and happy, they believed life would continue happily until they were finally able to marry and be together forever.

8

How long will you be like
A cypress tree,
And lean your lovely head away from me?
Jahan Makek Khatun

Ali 1979

Ali waited outside on the small porch by the two chairs and round table where Zahra would often sit in the inclement weather to read or to work on the pedigrees of her horses. So much of her time of late had been spent on compiling and editing the stud book for the Persian Asil horses, and now he'd be responsible for keeping it up to date; it was a never-ending job that he prayed he would be capable of doing. He hoped she had heard his footfalls on the steps so she would come to the door ready to leave, but there was no sound from inside.

As a young boy, his father had told him about

how the Bedouin tribes, of which they were a part, had for centuries tracked the ancestry of each horse through an oral tradition. Their horses were of the purest blood and crossbreeding with non-Asil horses was forbidden. Mares were the most valued, both for riding and breeding, so pedigree families were traced through the female line. Mares didn't nicker at approaching enemy tribes and they carried their masters into battle with courage and pride, standing loyally by the fallen. The only requirement of the sire line was that he be pure Asil.

He remembered when Zahra had first told him about her project to try to get the Asil horses in Iran recognized by the Word Arab Horse Organization. Ali could not figure out why she would want the horses in their country to be recognized by other countries. They were Persian horses that were raised and lived in Iran. Who cared about the rest of the word? The chiefs of the tribes were very fastidious about their horse breeding programs and would share the services of their pure-blooded proven stallions with each other's mares. He believed that the Persian was the bravest, strongest, and fastest of all the Arab horses in the world and he knew from his father that the blood of the horses of his country was kept pure by all the tribespeople. Had Zahra Khonume become a bit *divoneh* (crazy)?

No one in Iran would want to breed their horses to the *ashgal* (garbage) from any other country, so what was she thinking, with this crazy idea of hers?

Zahra

With tears in her eyes, Zahra looked at the picture of Tom in his army uniform. Days before he was to graduate with his Bachelor of Arts in Business, he'd received a letter from the United States Draft board telling him to report to their office. He had contacted his father who had tried to pull strings that would make him ineligible for the draft, but the best he'd been able to do was to persuade the head of the Defense Department to let him enlist rather than be drafted.

The Korean War had begun in June 1950 when the Korean People's Army of the North, backed by the Soviets, crossed the 38th parallel into the pro-Western Republic of Korea. By July, American troops had entered the war on behalf of South Korea. Now it was two years into the war and Tom would be going overseas as soon as his basic training was complete.

When Zahra heard the news, she was devastated. She'd been so sure that their life would continue as it had during the college year, and that Tom would take his masters and in two years they would be able to marry. "You must be strong, Zahra," Tom had whispered in her ear as he held her tightly the night, he told her the terrible news.

"I'm a strong person, Tom, but I'll be so worried about you. I won't be able to think. War is just plain dangerous and so many men have been killed over there in that dreadful place already. Oh, I just can't believe this is happening to us."

"I'll be in Alabama for my boot camp and training for several months before they deploy me, and that won't be dangerous. I'm sure I'll get a short leave after that, so we'll be able to be together then," he assured her.

She knew things would be very different. but she was so proud of him at his graduation that she could forget the future for that one day. She knew she'd worry about things once he had gone off to Alabama; she didn't want to spoil the occasion. He was awarded the "Best Athlete" of his graduating class. It gave her shivers to see her handsome man in his robe and mortarboard on the podium receiving his awards and sheepskin.

There was a round of luncheon parties after the ceremony, and the Williams held a congratulatory dinner at the Ithaca Hotel for Tom, in its famous

Moosehead restaurant. The dinner was for about twenty family members and close friends who had come to Tom's graduation. Champagne was served before the desert and many stood up to congratulate and "roast" the guest of honor.

"I want to thank everyone here for coming to this special dinner to celebrate my graduation and especially my parents for their total support of me during my life. I'll be starting a new chapter in the next few weeks when I leave for my military training. I'm of two minds, for I really don't want to leave my privileged life, however I'm proud to be an America and I will do my utmost to fight for our country. I will miss everyone here," he commented as he glanced at Zahra with a wink, "but I look forward to boot camp, and then my officer's training before I go off to Korea."

Everyone clapped for him and champagne glasses clinked as all toasted, "To the United States of America!"

Tom had planned a three-day holiday for Zahra and himself at a cottage that his family owned on Lake Champlain, at the northernmost part of the Great Appalachian Valley, between the green Mountains of Vermont and the Adirondack Mountains of New York. The lake was drained northward by the long Richelieu River into the mighty St. Lawrence which flowed out to the Atlantic Ocean. The lake was named after Samuel de Champlain who discovered it in 1609, at which time it was known as the northern gateway to the Iroquois lands. At the beginning of the Revolutionary War, the British occupied the Champlain Valley. However, it didn't take long for the rebel leaders to realize the importance of controlling the lake. The British forts of Ticonderoga and Crown Point had big supplies of artillery and were weakly guarded. When the colonial militia attempted to expel the British from Boston, they were unable to do it without heavy artillery, so they successfully attacked the two forts and brought the guns to Boston where they succeeded in routing the British.

The cottage was within driving distance of Saratoga, so they drove up there one morning in time to have lunch at their favorite restaurant, Siro's. During the racing season, they had often grabbed a bite there before going to the races, and many an evening after the races, everyone went together for a late dinner. They would all stay, chatting with the racing crowd which often included trainers and jockeys, as well as owners.

It was a cool day in early June when Tom and Zahra arrived in Saratoga Springs, but even so, they were able to sit outside on the patio where they had a delicious light lunch of shrimp salad and fresh French bread. It was fun to talk to the restaurant owner, Siro himself, at a time when he wasn't as busy as he was in August, the last time they were there.

"So, you two are staying at the lake house for the week-end?" he said with a chuckle and a wink. He was always a jolly fellow. "I guess you're serious about each other. Just remember to invite me to the wedding when you have it."

"Oh, we will," Zahra said. "It won't be for a couple of years because I have to graduate, and Tom will be out of the Army by then. But you'll have to travel to Iran, because the wedding will be in my country."

"If I'm invited, Zahra, I'll be there. I think Iran sounds like an interesting place and I'd love to visit there."

They spent the weekend like an old married couple, taking long walks on the beach and in the woods, playing Scrabble in the evenings, until they happily fell into each other's arms in bed. They went frequently into town to shop or eat at one of their favorite restaurants. Too soon, though, it was time to get back to reality.

Zahra was going to stay in Ithaca that summer to take a couple of extra summer courses in agriculture, and Tom had to get ready to go to boot camp. They drove back to Zahra's apartment where they would have to say good bye for a few months, but they had the hope of being together once again before Tom was deployed.

9

If Sorrow sends her soldiers here
And wants a bloody fight,
My serving boy and I will put
Them one and all to flight.
Hafez

Ali 1979

Ali shuffled his feet and walked around the balcony hoping to make enough noise to jar Zahra into coming to the door. "*Sabre con, Ali. Umadam hala.*" She was coming, she said. How many times had he heard her say that, when she was trying to put something off until another time?

He remembered times she had gone to Tehran to beg someone, anyone, for money to give or loan her, in order to be able to buy feed for her horses and her people as she had run out of her own savings. He knew how proud she was and that she hated to have to beg, but she had no other choice. She had to do it. She would go to see old friends of her family who wanted to help her in the situation she found herself, now that both her parents had left this world.

It had taken her hours to come out of her rooms on those days, but it hadn't really mattered because they were driving the old Land Rover all the way to Tehran, if it would make it. This time there was a problem with time, for the plane would not wait for her.

Zahra

Zahra stood seemingly hypnotized by the picture of herself and her parents standing in the garden of the old Tehran house. Her father was smiling broadly at her, though he looked a bit thin, and her mother seemed pensive. Zahra remembered the sadness she felt when she went home that summer and how her life would be changed once she was back in her homeland.

Her mother had written to her telling her the exciting news that they had finally installed a telephone in the house in Tehran and now she'd be able to call and talk to her every now and again. It was very expensive to call the U.S. but it would be fun if they could speak to each other sometimes. The first time her mother called, and Zahra answered the phone, the static and whooshing sounds made it difficult to hear, and she found herself yelling into the phone, to make sure her mother heard her. It was a rather unsuccessful experience, so she told her mother not to bother calling again unless it was really important. Letters had worked during the past few years so why bother changing their routine?

Then one afternoon, just after she arrived at the apartment having spent most of the day studying in the library, Anne told her that her mother had called. Anne said Zahra should not go out because her mother would call again in an hour.

"When did she call?" Zahra asked anxiously, for she knew it must be important. What could it be? She couldn't imagine. She'd had a letter a few days earlier telling her that her parents had gone up to the house on the Caspian Sea for couple of weeks when the weather in Tehran got too hot, and they had had a wonderful time partying with their friends and enjoying the cooler sea air. They must be back home in Tehran now, because she knew there was no phone in the Ramsar house. But maybe her mother had gone to the village to make the call from one of the phones there.

Anne said, "I think it was about four or so. She should be calling any minute now, I would think."

When the phone rang Zahra jumped to answer it. "*Mama, che shot*?" she spoke into the receiver.

"This isn't your Mother, my darling. It's me," said Tom, who was on the other end of the line.

"Oh Tom, I can't talk for long now. Anne just told me that my mother is going to call any minute now. I'm worried because we agreed that she wouldn't call unless it was something important, because the reception from Iran is so poor that I could hardly hear her the last time she called. Will you be able to call me again later, or can I call you back after I've talked to Mama?"

"I'll call you in an hour or so and remember that I love and miss you."

"Oh! I love you too, so much. It's not the same here without you. I'll wait for your call. And hopefully my mother's call won't be something terrible. Maybe she just wants to talk."

"Bye, love. I'll talk to you in a bit," he finished.

"Bye," she answered as she put the phone in its cradle.

When her mother finally called an hour later, Zahra was in a state; she just knew that something dreadful had happened at home. She picked up the receiver on the third ring and taking a deep breath answered, "Hello."

"Zahra is that you?" she heard her mother's voice crackling through the echo on the line.

"Yes, Mama. Is something wrong? I thought you were only going to call if it was important."

"It is something very important! You must come home as soon as you can make the arrangements. Your father has been diagnosed with cancer and it seems he doesn't have a long time to live. He wants you to come home so that he can spend time with you before he dies."

"Oh no! Are you sure it's cancer?"

"Yes, and he needs you."

"I'll be finished my summer classes in two weeks, so I'll make arrangements to come home right after that. I'll have a few weeks before the fall semester starts up so that should work. I am so sorry he's sick, but maybe he'll get better. People don't always die of cancer."

"My darling, you don't understand. You may not be able to go back to school this fall. Your father wants you to be here with him for his final days."

"We can talk about that when I get home, Mama. Can I talk to Baba?"

"Well, actually he's not home just now. He went to do some business in the bazar."

"So, he's not sick in bed?"

"No, no. He's able to live his normal life at present but the doctor said that he won't be able to do that for too long."

"Well, I'll be home in about three weeks then. Give him my love and a big kiss. I'll telegraph you my arrival date and time. I love you Mama and I'll see you soon." She softly hung up the phone.

When Tom called, she tearfully told him about her father. She was upset about his condition, but she really thought he would get better. Her mother had always been a bit of an alarmist. Persians were all pessimistic about illnesses. She was sure everything would be fine in the end. Her only worry was that maybe she wouldn't be allowed to come back for her third year of university. Once she got home who knew what would happen. She was afraid that maybe she wouldn't see Tom before he was deployed to Korea.

"My darling it will all work out in the end. Don't get yourself all upset."

"I have just two weeks left in summer school, so I'll have to make arrangements to go home the following week. You said you wouldn't be able to get away from your training until the end of your three months and that's more than a month away," she whined into the telephone.

"Let me see if I can get an early pass, somehow. I really need to see you before you go back home to Tehran."

As it turned out, Tom had somehow finagled himself a pass, and the next time they spoke they made plans to meet in New York the weekend before her flight to Iran. His family usually stayed at The Plaza on Fifth Avenue, so they would meet in the tearoom late Friday afternoon. She would take the morning train to New York, get a cab and go directly to the hotel, where she could check her bags. Then she'd have some time to shop for a few presents she wanted to take home to her family and close friends.

It was a hot New York summer day, so she was happy to enter the cool of the hotel about three-thirty, after her shopping was finished. Tom expected to be there by four-thirty, so she decided to go to the Palm Court, where they were to meet, to rest while she waited for him. It had been New York's iconic destination for afternoon tea since The Plaza had first opened in 1907. The nineteen-story building, which was considered a skyscraper in those days, had been called the greatest hotel in the world. It had been built on the site of a smaller hotel of the same name, facing the Grand Army Plaza, commemorating the Union Army in the Civil War. She sat in the large airy tearoom with its mirrored walls, marble columns and dramatic leaded glass ceiling overhead, which allowed in the natural light.

From her seat, she could clearly see the lobby and her heart missed a beat when she saw the handsome soldier walking towards her. She quickly stood up and was in his arms as he kissed her tenderly on her soft parted lips. He held her at arm's length, thirstily drinking in her beautiful smooth almond complexioned face.

"It's so good to see you. You look more beautiful than I remember, my love. Shall we have some tea and sandwiches before we go up to the room? We probably won't make it for dinner." He smiled sheepishly at her.

Their suite was large and airy, overlooking the beautiful foliage of Central Park, with a sitting room and a huge double bed in the bedroom that also overlooked the park. Once the bell boy brought their bags and left, it didn't take any time for them to undress each other lovingly and fall into the comfortable bed. Their lovemaking was both tender and desperate, for they both had their fears of what the future would bring for them.

While she was having a luxurious bath in the large marble tub, Tom walked in, dressed in grey flannel pants and a navy sports jacket. He sat on the stool facing her, taking in her beauty, and thinking how lucky he was.

"So, what do you say that we go down to the Oak Bar and have a glass of champagne to celibate our luck in love?"

"That sounds like a great idea. Maybe we could have a snack. I'm famished after all the exercise you put me through," she joked.

The Oak Bar which was attached to the Oak Room, was cozy with its long wooden bar and a few booths and tables. Its style was Tudor revival with a plaster ceiling and a floral foliage motif carved into the wood. There were three Everett Shinn murals which were painted by the artist, whose modern realism of urban life was one with the Ashcan school of the 1920s. Tom and Zahra sat in a booth in the back corner of the bar, sipping their Moet Chandon and eating rare steak and a salad.

"I have something for you, Zahra, though I know I shouldn't give it to you until I've spoken to your father, but with the circumstances, that would be impossible." He pulled a small velvet box from his pocket and put it on the table. "Will you marry me?" he said.

She looked at it and then lightly touched it, hesitating.

"Open it," Tom said. "It won't bite you."

She tentatively opened the box that had the writing *Tiffany & Co.* in blue letters on the inside of the white silk lid. She took in a sharp breath when she saw the large square-cut center diamond flanked on either side by graduating baguettes.

"You know I'll marry you, Tom. But this ring? It's so beautiful! I'm so surprised. How am I going to tell my father and mother? I'm certain I'll be able to persuade Baba, but we'll have to wait until I'm finished with my degree and you're out of the army. Oh, my God, I forgot! You might have to go to Korea. When will you find out? I won't be able to stand it."

"Just calm down and say yes, so I can put this on your third finger," he laughed.

"Yes, yes. I love you so much."

On Saturday night, they went to see a Broadway play and had a late dinner at Sardi's, which was the in place to go after the theatre for patrons and actors alike. On Sunday morning they did some window shopping along Fifth Avenue, but they spent a lot of time making love and just being together. Monday morning came too soon! Tom had a military flight out to Alabama early and Zahra would be leaving, for Tehran via London, on a late afternoon flight from Idlewild Airport. The airport had been dedicated as New York International Airport by Mayor Fiorella LaGuardia in 1948 and named for the Idlewild Golf Course after the land on which it was built. They had a tearful goodbye, but both believed they would be able to be together again for forever the next time they met.

10

My heart how long will this last?
Calm down, and rest;
You'll certainly upset the world if you
Don't stop this quest!
Jahan Malek Khatun

Ali 1979

Ali walked back down the steps. He had already checked the oil, and there was enough gasoline in the old vehicle, so he decided to clean the windscreen. He was getting really impatient but told himself that maybe it would be just as well if Zahra missed the plane. Then she would have to wait a few days to get new reservations and during that time she might even decide not to leave at all.

About five years before, Ali had driven her to Tehran because she'd arranged a meeting with the chairman of the Royal Horse Society to persuade him to give her money to keep her breeding program going. That time, she'd kept him waiting two hours so they ended up having to drive in the heat of the day. He thought that was not a good idea because old Rostam would sometimes heat up when they drove long distances. They'd planned to leave at sun-up, when it was cooler, so the drive across the desert to the ferry would be more comfortable. But when she came down at eight the sun was already beating down ferociously. "It's going to be a long hot drive today, Zahra Khonume," he said as he helped her into the Land Rover.

"That doesn't matter, Ali. It's many hours' drive and I'm not in a hurry. I'll need to do a lot of thinking on the way so that I have a good speech when I go before the head of the *Anjoman Sultaniteh Asb*, the organization that encourages and helps to keep our Persian horses pure. I need their *rials* (money) if we're going to be able to keep the herd"

"*Bali* Khonume, I understand but we will be lucky to arrive in Tehran before late tonight I fear, even if the roads are good and we have no trouble with Rostam."

"Don't be a pessimist, Ali. We'll be in Tehran in good time and I'll have my meeting with *Agha* Mansarpour tomorrow morning. I believe all will go well." Zahra was a true optimist when it came to raising money for her beloved horses. The *Anjoman* was sponsored by the Imperial Court of Shah Mohamed Reza Pahlavi who was a real enthusiast and lover of horses. She was confident that he would want to continue to support the Iranian Asil horses and especially the herd of his old friend, Mehdi Bakhtiar.

Zahra

Zahra was holding the picture of her mother all in black with a veil covering her face; the chador she had been wearing was draped over the chair beside her. It had been a bad couple of years for her before that terrible day of black. The memories brought tears to Zahra's eyes as she recalled those days. The only blessing was that she knew her Baba was in a better place.

When she had arrived in Tehran after the twenty-four-hour flight it seemed as if nothing had changed. There was the same black limousine with Abraheem waiting at the curb as she and her parents came out of the front door of the Mehrabad airport. They had hugged and kissed each other and there was no mention of her father's health on the way driving up to Shemran. She'd turned her new glittering engagement ring around so the shimmering stones were facing her palm, so it would be unnoticed. Her father told her he was planning a welcome home party for the following week and then they'd go up to the Caspian house to enjoy a couple of weeks of the late summer weather. Everything seemed normal and there was not an inkling of her father's supposed cancer. Could this have been a trick to get her back home?

When she awoke the following morning, after a much-needed sleep, her eyes took in the view of her beautiful snowcapped Damavand through the window. The sun was shining brightly, and she could tell it would be a typical hot, dry, sunny August day in Tehran. She felt lucky that her father had installed the water cooler for the house while she was away, for the temperature in her room was quite bearable. There was a light tap on her door and her mother peeked in.

"I thought you might still be asleep after your long flight yesterday," Louisa said as she walked into the room.

"No, I'm slowly waking up and so happy to see my favorite view hasn't changed since I've been away. I've always loved looking at the mountain when I wake up; it's one of the things

I miss when I'm in the States."

"I want to tell you about your Baba. He's been having some back pain the past couple of months and then I noticed he was losing weight and that he was starting to get a yellowish tinge to his skin, so I took him to see Dr. Riahi. He told us that the jaundice condition could be caused by several things, but he wanted to do some tests. When the results came back, we were told that your father has pancreatic cancer. The prognosis is not good and at present there seems to be no safe operation that can be done here in Iran. A Dr. Whipple has performed some operations at the Presbyterian Hospital in New York, but it's very dangerous, and most of the patients died within two years or sooner. We'll have to let the cancer take its course and hope for the best, Zahra *Junam*."

"But Mamma, he doesn't look sick. Is this type of cancer a bad one?"

"It is said that few people survive more than five years. We'll have to wait and see. The Doctor doesn't know how long your baba has had it."

"So can Baba just go on as usual until he starts feeling really bad?"

"That's what I understand, *Junam*. So, we will just have to live life day to day," her mother explained.

"Well, what about my going back to school?"

Zahra was worried that she might have to stay at home and not be able to finish her degree.

"I don't think you should plan on going back this next semester. You can wait until we know more how things are going to be, before you make any decisions about that. Your father really needs you here. I think it will kill him if you leave now when he knows he doesn't have a lot of time left."

Zahra said nothing. She loved her father and didn't want him to die but he could be around for another five years. She was twenty now and if it took that long for him to die, she would miss out on her education. And what about Tom? Would he wait for her to come back in five years? He might even have to go to war if the Korean problem was not solved soon. And she wanted to see him before he was deployed. What a mess this was. She wasn't sure she'd be able to adapt to life at home after having lived in that wonder world of America for so many years. She felt confused and depressed.

Her mother broke the silence. "I see you have a pretty substantial diamond ring on your left hand. Does that mean that you and Tom are engaged?"

"Yes, he gave me the ring the night we got to New York last week. Isn't it beautiful?"

"I'm sure he is a charming young man, but I would suggest that you lock that ring away in a

safe place for the time being. I don't want to upset your father. You know he'll never approve of
your marrying a non-Muslim and an American
to boot."

So, she wouldn't be able to flaunt her beautiful ring if it was hidden away someplace. And
she surely couldn't tell any of her friends because no matter how close they were to her, they
were surely closer to their mothers and would
tell her secret to them, and then of course their
fathers would find out and finally her own baba
would hear the news. No, she'd have to find a
hiding place to keep it safe until she left to go
back to America. Oh! Please, *Allah* let it be in
time to start the fall semester!

Slowly she climbed out of her bed and looked
around the room. Under the window was the
small Kuwaiti chest where she kept all her me-
mentos. It had a secret drawer under the shelf on
the right side, which would make a perfect hiding place. Slowly she slid the ring off her finger
and put it back in its blue velvet box, opened the
brass decorated top of the chest, and slid it into
the compartment. It would be safe there, but she
would have to find a lock, for she'd never felt the
need to lock the chest before. She would have to
go to the Tajrish bazaar to find a small antique
padlock. She decided she would get Abraheem
to drive her there as soon as she finished her

breakfast of *nun-e barbari* with goat's cheese, orange juice and of course delicious tea.

Persians drink *chai* (tea)in the morning, after each meal, as well as all through the day. Every morning a gas burner flickered under a kettle that would continue to boil all day and late into the evening. This kettle contained tea, one of the most important cornerstones of Iranian culture. Tea production was a major industry in the Caspian Sea provinces of Gilan and Mazandaran and was a large part of the economy in that area. Before 1900 there was no tea produced in Iran, but a Persian diplomat by the name of Kashef al Saltaneh, who was posted to India as Iran's ambassador, decided that he would introduce the growing of the product to his own country. At that time, the English had a strict monopoly on tea production in India, with rigid rules against non-Europeans engaging in its trade. Kashef, who was actually Qadjar Prince Mohammad Mirza, had studied in Paris and spoke fluent French. Thus, he was able to pose as a French businessman and learned the trade. He eventually smuggled thousands of saplings into Iran, and after six years of experimentation introduced his product into the market. This distant cousin of Zahra's was known as the father of Iranian Tea.

Her first few days home went by in a flash.

She went out to Nowruzabad to see the horses and ride across the desert with her father. He seemed his normal self except for the fact that he seemed more tired in the evenings and retired to his room earlier than she remembered. Most nights, she and her mother would sit on the patio drinking their tea after supper, and then when the mosquitos came out, which they always seemed to do as darkness set in, just in time for the British TV comedies, they would move into the cozy den to spend an hour or so watching Hyacinth boss her poor husband around in the show, "Are you Being Served?"

"I just love this show!" Louisa would say every time they sat down to watch. "It is just so British. Can you imagine any Iranian wife getting away with what she does to Richard? Why, your father would have divorced me years ago if I had dared to behave in that manner. Not that I wouldn't have loved to at times. I guess American wives are pretty bossy too. I've seen that "I Love Lucy" show a few times and that Lucy seems to do lot of yelling and bossing around herself."

Zahra watched the shows patiently with her mother until she excused herself, supposedly to go upstairs to her own room which was adjacent to Hassan's wood paneled domain. However, after an affectionate mother-daughter embrace, Zahra could then slip off to her father's study where she could write to Tom about the events in her life at home in Iran where she felt like a stranger.

Her father seemed to be carrying on his life as if there was nothing the matter with him. He went off to the bazaar most mornings to do his usual business. He would return in time for the sumptuous lunch of *khoreshts, baghali polo*, and other types of rice, as well as salads, that would be put on the table. Often Zahra's friends Mimi and Avid, who were both married now, came to have lunch with the Kadjars. After lunch, Hassan would usually go up to his room to have a nap and the girls could spend time gossiping about their lives.

Mimi and Avid had stories to tell Zahra about their married lives and how hard it was to be submissive to their husbands, who were several years older than they. When the topic of sex came up, Zahra was quite shocked that neither of the girls seemed to enjoy their experiences with their husbands. It sounded as though their husbands did nothing to arouse them and it was a "wham, bang, thank you, ma'am" experience for both of them. They had read books with descriptions of the pleasurable sex lives of the characters, but it didn't seem that either of them had had an enjoyable time or had come to a climax during their married lives. At first Zahra was afraid to enter into the discussion because young Persian girls were supposed to be virgins until they were married. She didn't want them to think ill of her, as she thought they might if they knew she had already given up her own virginity. But as the weeks went on, she finally decided to tell them.

One afternoon, she finally broached the subject. "When I hear the two of you complaining about having to give yourselves to your husbands, I feel badly for you. You seem to be searching for any excuse to avoid having sex, which I'm sure doesn't make your husbands very happy."

"Just wait until you're married, and you'll be saying the same things, Zahra," said Avid.

"I will tell you a secret, but you mustn't say anything to anyone, especially your mothers."

"We promise," her friends said in unison.

"I'm not a virgin. I have a fiancé with whom I've had sex and I enjoyed every minute of it."

"Are you telling the truth?" questioned Mimi.

"Of course, I'm telling the truth. Having sex is one thing, but making love is another. You see, Tom, that's his name, he and I love each other with a passion and so when we join together, we want to please each other in order for us both to have great pleasure and fulfillment. To me, making love is exciting, pleasurable and ecstatic all at once."

"Maybe you can tell us about it and help us learn to enjoy it with our husbands," suggested Avid.

"I can't say that I have a passion for my Ali Reza, but I like him all right. Maybe I need to learn some ticks of the trade," Mimi commented.

"Well, if you want, I'll help you both by telling you about my experiences and I also have a couple of books that you can borrow. I keep them hidden at the bottom of my suitcase, so let's go up to my room and I can get them for you. You read them, and then we'll talk about it the next time we're together. But you must keep them hidden or we'll all be in trouble; don't let anyone see you reading them and if they're discovered, don't you dare say where you got them."

So, the American educated and liberated Zahra would help her Persian friends learn how to enjoy a part of their marriages. Persian wives traditionally had the role of being the caring central figure of the family. They were expected to be good hostesses, for most husbands entertained frequently and expected to have their friends admire their choice of a wife. The husband was like a bantam rooster who strutted around puffing out his chest with pride, so he expected his wife to provide an outward display of obedience and willingness to serve him at all times.

Once a boy child has been born the husband feels he has been fulfilled, as there would be an heir to his domain. Daughters were accepted and loved as well, but it was a disappointment if a girl was born first. It was expected that the wife should try again soon to have a boy child. Most Iranian men didn't marry at an early age because they wanted to be established in their lives before they settled down to support a wife and children. And children were the most important reason to marry, although the men would have little to do with their upbringing. That was the duty of the wife, whether she did it herself or managed her household of servants to do it. As a result, sex was considered an act designed to produce children first and pleasure second. Many men had sown their wild oats way before their marriages, so the consummation of the marriage was often perfunctory and the feelings of the bride, who was a virgin and inexperienced, were hardly considered.

Hassan had invited all his business associates, family members and friends to the "Welcome Home" party he held for Zahra a couple of weeks after she had arrived. She insisted that he include the few girlfriends she had, and of course, her mother had a group of her own lady friends who were included so the number of guests reached almost a hundred. The party was

held in the beautiful garden around the pictur-
esque kidney-shaped pool with its underwater
lights. The roses were in full bloom and the cen-
terpieces with yellow and white roses on each of
the ten round tables that were scattered about
the pool added to the atmosphere of the party,
similar to the Arabian Story, *A Thousand and
One Nights*. The buffet tables were laden with
Persian cuisine that was both colorful to look at
and delicious to eat.

By the time the guests started to arrive, at
about ten o'clock, the evening had become pleasantly cool. Zahra's friends, Avid and Mimi, were
among the first to arrive, along with several other young couples who gathered together, talking and sipping dry rose wine. There was a band
playing lilting Persian music, so the girls went
out to the area cleared for dancing and began to
dance the traditional *Baba Karam* folk dances.
As the music continued, some of the men joined
in and the dance floor became crowded.

Zahra, dreaming of Tom, was throwing herself into the music, when suddenly her shoulder was tapped and a tall, attractive gentleman
asked, "May I join you, *Khonum*?"

"*Bali,Agha*," she answered surprised. And
then she recognized him – Mehdi Bakhtiar the
divinely handsome man her father had introduced her to the last time she was home. Her

heart skipped a beat as he looked deeply into her eyes and she had to suppress a shudder as he lightly touched her waist when they began to dance. What was happening to her? She had just left the love of her life a few weeks ago and had been exchanging love letters with him; she was engaged! How could she be attracted to this older man? No, she wasn't attracted to him. It was just that he was as handsome as a movie star and she was flattered that he had sought her out to dance with him. That was all!

The trip to the Caspian house was wonderful. The weather was perfect, with the sun sparkling on the azure blue sea every morning as she got up to go down to the beach for an early morning swim. She had always loved the feel of the salty warm water of that beautiful Caspian Sea in the cool early mornings. She and her father loved to sail in the small dingy almost every afternoon as the wind came up. She played tennis with friends who came to visit, she learned to waterski one afternoon when Prince Golam Reza came to visit with his new boat and water skis, and of course there were parties in the evenings. The Casino at Ramsar was a short drive, so many nights her father would take her and her mother with him when he went to gamble. And there was a lot of interaction with Mehdi Bakhtiar. He seemed to be at every party. He came over to play tennis, which he did very well. He came with Prince Golam Reza and helped her up on the water skis. He was at the Casino when she went there. He was ever present.

When they went back to Tehran, it was evident that her father's health was not good. He'd lost more weight; his skin was getting a yellowish tinge and he seemed unusually tired. Some mornings, he didn't go to the Bazaar, so Zahra was not surprised when her mother told her that she didn't think she should go back to Cornell that fall. She had intuitively known that this was coming, but still, it came as a blow to her. She had hinted in her letters to Tom that she thought she would have to stay in Iran. He wrote that he was enjoying his military training, though he complained about the summer humidity and heat he was experiencing. He missed her terribly but knew she was in a safe place and felt it was good thing that she had gone home to be with her parents. He wished her father well, but knew how serious pancreatic cancer could be, so if she couldn't go back to school for the fall semester, it wouldn't be the end of the world; she could miss time and go back at a later date.

Life continued along during the autumn months. The weather cooled down, and her father seemed to rally. Zahra spent days out at Nowruzabad, riding and taking care of her horses. She actually moved into the little apartment that had been built for her and spent several nights a week there. She loved being out in the desert, where the sky was so big at night and she could hear the hyenas and wild dogs howling. She spent a lot of time working with and training the two beautiful horses her father had bought for her. One was a five-year-old blood bay Turkoman/Darashouri stallion that was a bit difficult to handle. She spent hours brushing and handling him with gentleness so that he would learn to trust her. She could tell that he must have had some rough treatment before he came to Nowruzabad as a three-year-old colt. She named him Shahram, which in Farsi meant Archangel; the Archangel *Mika'eel* is mentioned in both the Quran and the Bible, so she felt it was a fitting name for this beautiful animal that she planned to train to be an angel. Her other horse was a seven-year-old purebred Darashori, bay with four white feet and a white blaze, that her father had bought from a Sheik friend who lived south of Esfahan in the city of Yazd. This horse she had named Yazdegerd, after the twelfth Sasanian king who was said to have had a peaceful disposition and been a benevolent and astute ruler. This horse had the same disposition as his namesake and was beautifully trained for riding across the desert and hunting.

Summer became autumn, and then the snow began to appear, so she would go with friends to ski at Ab Ali a couple of times a week. Skiing had been introduced to Iran by the Germans when they were building the railway across the country for Reza Shah. The resort was just a few miles northeast of Tehran, so it was easy to drive there for a few hours of skiing in the beautiful powder snow of the Alborz Mountains.

Before she knew it, the cold snowy winter months had passed by and it was time to prepare for Nowruz, which is the Persian New Year. The *Khaneh Tekani* or spring cleaning began in the Kadjar house at the beginning of March. Louisa supervised as the help scrubbed and polished every nook and cranny of the house. Zahra was expected to totally clean her room and go through her closets and take any clothes that she thought she would not wear again and give them to the poor. It took over a week for her mother to be satisfied that all in the house was spic and span.

The origin of Nowruz dated back about 3,000 years to Zoroastrianism the ancient Persian religion that predates Christianity and Islam. It was the day of the vernal equinox that marks the beginning of spring and the first day of the month of *Farvardin* in the Persian calendar.

The curtain raiser to the holidays was

Chaharshanbeh Soori, a fire festival held on the last Wednesday of the calendar year. The festival was full of special customs and rituals, especially jumping over fire. As the sun set, people lit fires and gathered around to jump over them in a ritual during which they asked the fire to take their paleness and problems and in return give them energy and warmth. The New Year is all about celebrating special moments and sharing joy and gratitude with family and friends who sit around a specially prepared *Haft Seen* Table as the clock ticks toward the approaching year.

"Zahrajun, this is the first Nowruz you have spent at home since you went away to school six years ago. I want you to help me set up the table," Louisa told her daughter. "Do you remember all the seven *S* items we put on it?"

Zahra smiled. "Of course I do. First we need the *Sabzeh* I saw growing in the kitchen which denotes rebirth and renewal. Azizeh planted the barley seeds a couple of weeks ago and I see that the dish has a lush grass growing in it now. I'll bring it out to the dining room where you have the table set up. And I'll collect the rest of the S's and bring them out."

Together they decorated the table with the *Senjed* (dried lotus fruit for love), *Sib* (apples for beauty and health), *Seer* (garlic for medicine and taking care of health), *Samanu* (sweet pudding for wealth and fertility), *Serkeh* (vinegar for patience and wisdom that comes with aging) and *Sumac* (a spice for a sunrise of a new day). In addition, they brought out the Holy Quran, a mirror symbolizing reflection, colored eggs for fertility, coins for prosperity, and a goldfish in a small glass bowl for new life. The table with its white cloth looked beautiful and ready for the thirteen-day celebration of dinners, family visits, and reflections on the year ahead.

On the thirteenth day, *Sizdah Bedar,* it was customary for the family to go out to the country and spend time with nature, so the extended family of aunts, uncles, cousins and many friends all gathered at Nowruzabad for a joyous day of picnicking. After a delicious repast while sitting on deep red Turkoman carpets along the bank of the small stream that flowed through the garden, the *Sabsi* was ceremoniously thrown into a stream of running water to release the evil of the old year and usher in the good of the New Year.

That evening, Zahra drove into the Tehran house with her parents. She had plans to have lunch with Avid and Mimi the next day. She was in her room reflecting on the wonderful Persian celebrations of Nowruz when her mother called her from downstairs, where the only phone in the house was located. "*Zahrajunam,* come quickly! You have a call from America! Hurry before the line gets fuzzy!" Louisa shouted up the stairs. "I think it might be Tom," she whispered as she gave the receiver to her.

"Hello!" she said breathlessly.

"Zahra, it's so good to hear your voice. Your letters have been wonderful, but I've been dying to talk to you; with the time difference it's hard to do. I just wish I had my arms around you now and could kiss your perfect soft mouth."

"Oh, Tom, I can't believe it's you. I've missed you so much. I love you and want to be with you, but we're so far apart now it's frightening." She was still out of breath, but from excitement now.

"I just had to call you because the war with Korea has escalated and my unit is being deployed to go there. I think we'll be leaving in a few days, but it's not definite. I probably won't be able to call you again, but I'll still write to you and you can continue sending your letters to the same address; they'll be forwarded to me" he explained.

"Oh no! I don't want you to be in a war. It's too dangerous!" She bombarded him with questions. "Do you have to go? How long will you be there? What if something happens to you?"

"Yes, I have to go. I have no idea how long I'll be there. I'll do my best to stay safe and I'll carry your picture beside my heart. I have faith that all will be well, and we'll be together again, before too long. You know I love you more than anything, my darling."

"I love you too, and I'm missing you terribly. I will pray to *Allah* to keep you safe. Please don't let anything happen to you. I can't believe this," she sobbed.

"I'll be okay my love, I promise," he said as the connection failed.

"What's the matter?" her mother asked. Zahra had slumped in the little chair near the telephone and was sobbing.

"Tom's going to war! I can't believe it! I'm afraid he'll be shot dead by some crazy Korean. All the news I've heard about that war is horrible. The weather conditions are terrible, and the soldiers suffer malnutrition and disease. And what are they fighting for? The United Nations and the American forces are trying to stop Russia from spreading its Communism, but it seems stupid to me that the States are even in the war. Why is it their problem when they're so far away from that country? Oh God, I don't understand."

"There, there darling, don't get yourself into a state. It's not for us to understand the politics of the world. I'm sure all will be well, and Tom will stay safe. Just pray to Allah and have faith. That's all you can do."

Hassan walked into the hallway from his

office where he had been relaxing. "What's all this crying on *Sizdah Bedar*? This is supposed to be the happiest day of the year."

"Oh Baba, you remember Tom Williams? He's my friend Anne's brother. You met him when you were at my graduation in Virginia. Do you remember him?" she blurted out through sobs.

"Of course, I do. He was very polite to me and made sure that I understood what his father was saying to me. He kept telling Mr. Williams to speak more slowly. And he was a handsome fellow in a Nordic way."

"Well, he went into the Marines this year and now, he's being sent to that horrible war in Korea," she told him in a shaking voice.

"Oh, I'm sorry to hear that. War is a terrible thing. We here in Iran tried to stay neutral in World War II but then the British and Russians invaded us because they thought our country was pro-Nazi. So many Iranians were killed in useless battles. The next thing we knew Reza Shah abdicated and was sent into exile in South Africa and his inexperienced playboy son Mohamad Reza took over the throne.

"Our oil was the real reason the Allies were here, but we did eventually declare war on Germany. The Tehran Conference in 1943 really put us on the map, so to speak. The big three leaders Winston Churchill, Joseph Stalin, and Franklin Roosevelt planned their war strategy and also had the first meetings about the formation of the United Nations here in Tehran. Our young Shah sat in on those meetings, and it was then that he began to realize the importance of developing Iran into a great power, which he is continuing to do today, praise be to *Allah*," he pontificated.

When Zahra continued to snuffle, Hassan put his arm around her and said, "The way you are carrying on makes me feel that you are sweet on this young man. I noticed when we were in Virginia that you two paid a lot of attention to each other, but I thought it was just "puppy love." Did things develop into something more when you were at university?"

Zahra looked at her mother, who gave her a warning glance. Should she come out and tell her *baba* the truth about her feelings for Tom, or would it be a mistake? Maybe he would forbid her to ever go back to school at Cornell; or maybe he'd be happy for her and make the path to marriage with Tom smoother than she expected. She couldn't decide what to say.

Finally, she blurted out, "Baba, yes I'm in love with Tom and he loves me too. When he gets out of the Marines and I graduate from Cornell we want to get married."

Ba Khoda, che kar mikonam? What would he do, he wondered to himself? He had pictured her married to a successful Iranian business-man and now, she wanted to marry an American and probably spend her life in the United States. It would kill him. But he was going to die any-way so why would he forbid her to do this? He didn't have a lot of time left. The doctor had told him another year or two. He wanted her to love him and be with him to the end. So perhaps he should tell her it was all right. When he was gone, it wouldn't matter. Maybe Louisa would be happy to move back to her homeland after he was gone. He didn't know. He'd wanted a big social wedding for Zahra with all the prominent people he knew; why even some of the Pahlavis would attend. But now he knew she wouldn't want that. If he pressed her it would make her unhappy and she would most likely hate him for forcing it on her.

"*Zahrajunam,* if you are truly in love, I'm happy for you. It will be a long wait by the time you finish college, but if that ends up being what you really want, how can I stop you? I would prefer it if you'd marry a nice Iranian boy and spend the rest of your life here. but I won't be here forever, and you must live your life the way you want. Look at your mother! She fell in love with me and has spent her whole life here in Iran, which is not her birthplace. She's been mostly happy, I hope," he looked at Louisa, who nodded with tears welling up in her eyes.

"You aren't angry with me, Baba?"

"How can I be angry with someone who is in love? No, I'm just a bit disappointed, that's all, but I'll get over it, *Junam*. I'm just lucky and so happy that you're here with me, now."

So, the next day, when she went out to Xanadu Restaurant with Avid and Mimi she was finally sporting her beautiful diamond engagement ring. She was still worried and unhappy that Tom was off to Korea but at least she could now talk about him freely with her friends and parents. The girls were glad there was now a name and pictures of the lover who had taught her and them, vicariously, the art of making love. They both had admitted that their own relationships with their husbands had improved since their tutoring in the American way. Their only sadness was that they were going to have to wait so long for their friend's wedding. Would she really wait until after she graduated, or would they get married sooner if the war ended and Tom came back safe and sound? Who knew, but the speculation was fun talk about.

Nowruz melted into summer and the season at Ramsar was upon her once again. The water activities in both the Caspian Sea and the pool at the house kept her occupied during the days. The parties in the evenings at the beautiful villas owned by friends and family were always entertaining. It seemed everywhere she went, she would see the handsome Mehdi Bakhtiar; he was ever present and she had a feeling that it was not by coincidence.

"Zahra *Khonume*, you are looking ever so ravishing tonight," he addressed her one evening at a dinner party that was held at the palace of Prince Golam Reza, the Shah's brother.

"*Kheli muchekeram*," she thanked him politely, looking straight into his dark brown, alluring eyes. Yes, she felt an attraction to him, but it was not right; she was now an engaged woman.

"I hope you will allow me a dance when the music starts later on, *Khonume*."

And after the sumptuous buffet of delectable Persian dishes, rice and of course the golden caviar that only the royal family was able to obtain, there he was at her elbow, leading her to the dance floor. He held her lightly as they floated around the floor amongst other couples, both young and old, to the music of Frank Sinatra, who had come to Iran at the request of the royal family, all of whom were great fans of his.

"I love this song," Mehdi said as Frank started to croon, *All the Things You Are* and his grip on her tightened slightly. She felt herself touching his body. When the song was over, he led her out the tall French doors to the balcony that overlooked the garden and pool.

"I see you have a beautiful diamond on your left hand. I'd heard rumors around town that you are engaged to marry an American. I must congratulate him, whoever he is, for his luck at winning your heart. I must tell you, I was disappointed when I heard this. I had hoped that I might be the one to sweep you away. I'm sure your father didn't tell you, but I'd asked him if I might court you, myself. He told me you were strong willed. and would most probably make your own choice, which it looks like you have."

"Mehdi, I thank you for the great compliment. I would have been honored to be courted by you if I had not fallen in love with Tom Williams. He is my roommate's brother and I've known him since I first went to the States to school. Unfortunately, he's now in the Marines and fighting in Korea. I'm so worried that something might happen to him because war is such a horrible dangerous place."

"You must have faith that *Allah* will take care of him. Be sure to pray for him every day and hopefully he will be safe. I will pray for him too and maybe that will help."

"You are so kind, Mehdi. I hope we can

become good friends."

"I can't think anything I would like better, with the exception of being more than your friend. But I respect your situation and promise to be a good friend upon whom you may rely no matter what." He gave her a hug and took her hand as he led her back to the party.

Her father seemed to be in his element. When they went to the casino, he was unable to be a loser during their stay in the north. The house was full of family and friends for the whole of the month of *Mordad,* so there was fun and laughter all the time. However, the thought of the danger that Tom was in was never far from the front of her thoughts. When she was with her friends, she could talk of nothing else, and became a bore to them all. They were mostly contented in their marriages, and her few unmarried friends were consumed with thoughts of what man they would be arranged to marry, or if they might make a love match as she had done.

Zahra lived for the ever-dwindling number of letters she received from Tom as he came closer to the combat zones and had less time or opportunity to write to her. She tried to understand but began to hate this dreadful war and the government of the United States that had sent her lover on this horrible mission.

When they returned to Tehran, she broached

the subject of going back to Cornell, but her mother insisted that it was an impossibility despite the fact that Hassan seemed to be doing well with his cancer. Only *Allah* knew when her father's time would be up, and she needed to be with him when the time came. She couldn't argue, for she knew that what her mother said did make good sense. But by now she would be two years behind in her studies. She spent as much time as she could at Nowruzabad and also began going to the newly opened Pahlavi Children's hospital to volunteer. She would spend hours there two or three times a week, playing with the handicapped children being treated there, and reading Old Persian Fairy Tales to them. She dreamed of the day she and Tom were married and had children of their own.

When she walked into the Tehran house one *Shanbeh* morning, after she had spent the past couple of days in her little abode at Nowruzabad, her mother greeted her holding a small brown paper envelope. "This came for you early this morning Zahra June. It's a telegram. Hopefully it is good news."

Why would she be getting a telegram? She had no idea. She had never received one before and didn't know who it could be from. She took the small silver letter opener on the hall desk and carefully slit it open. As she unfolded the flimsy paper, she saw it was from Anne Williams.

"TOM IS MIA STOP WILL CALL YOU TUESDAY 6PM TEHRAN TIME STOP ANNE"

"What does this mean, Mama?" she asked as she showed it to Louisa.

"It means he is missing in action, darling. I am so sorry, but it doesn't mean he is dead; he's just missing."

"Oh *Allah*! How could you do this to me?" she screamed and broke into tears.

Tuesday would not come. She spent the three days crying in her room. Her mother brought her food, most of which she wouldn't touch. At five in the afternoon on *Do Shanbeh,* she went down to the front hall and waited for the phone to ring. She jumped when it finally shrilled loudly at exactly six o'clock. She shouted into the phone, "Hello, is that you, Anne?"

"Zahra, we're so upset, but you mustn't despair. We got the news on Friday that Tom was in a bunker that was under Korean fire and was hit by a bullet. When his unit realized they were being pushed back, they all moved back from the enemy lines but as they did the Koreans came over the bunker and dragged some of our wounded over to their side. Tom was one of the soldiers they took. They'll probably take him to a prison camp." Anne's voice was shaky and choked up.

"What will happen to him? I've read in some of the few news reports we get here, that the conditions in the prison camps are terrible. The men are starving and dying of all sorts of diseases."

"I know. We have so much bad news about the camps. There's nothing we can do but pray. We've had reports that there are armistice negotiations going on but there hasn't been much progress. Dad has some good friends who are close to President Truman, and they've promised to find out what they can. They say they'll keep us informed, so I'll call you whenever I get news."

"And how is your mother doing?"

"She's depressed about Tom, but you know her – she's keeping herself busy with her charity work. And of course, her horses and fox hunting keep her mind off things. She's amazingly resilient. She says she believes he'll come home safe and sound, and she won't think of the negative side of it. I wish I could be so positive."

"My heart is aching, but she's right. Life goes on, and we must live it. I'll try to be like her, and you should, too."

The connection was beginning to get staticky as it always seemed to do on overseas calls. "I'll call you as soon as I hear something, Zahra. Remember we love and miss you."

"Bye, miss you too," she said. As she hung up the receiver, she began to sob.

Her mother had been in the next room when Zahra was on the phone. She came running in, and asked, "What is it, darling?"

"Tom's been captured, and they think he'll be taken to a prison camp! I can't believe it. What will I do if he never comes back?"

"*Zahrajunam*, you are a strong young lady. You'll be fine. You will think positive thoughts, you will continue your work at the hospital, you will see your friends, you will be the kind, wonderful daughter you are to your father and me, and your young man will come back to you."

So her life went on without much change, though her thoughts were mostly about Tom. Another year went by, with no word about him. She and Anne talked on the telephone several times and finally the war was over, and prisoners of war were released, but not Tom. He was officially presumed dead. There was nothing she could do, for there wasn't even a funeral she could go over to the States to attend. It was the end of her relationship with Tom. She cried a lot, but that didn't do much except make her eyes red and make her feel sick.

One morning, a couple of months after Anne had told her the devastating news, she got up and looked out the bedroom window at her beautiful mystical Mount Damavand with its white cone and pale chartreuse green look of spring. "It's time to start over," she told herself. Nowruz was only a week away, so it was a fitting time for her to pull herself together. She looked at her beautiful engagement ring and slid it off her finger slowly. Then she unlocked the small Kuwaiti chest and put it back in the secret compartment where it had been two years before when she had first come home because of her father's illness.

She helped her mother with the *haft sin* as usual, so all was ready for family and friends when the day arrived. The days of celebration were busy. The house was full of people almost daily, from noon until late in the evening, And of course, there was time spent visiting the homes of relatives and close friends.

Her father, Hassan, was beginning to feel poorly. He had lost a lot of weight and his energy level was low. When Abraheem was not there to drive, Zahra wielded the big Chrysler along the narrow streets in Shemran where most of their friends lived.

"It's good to have an alternate chauffer on staff," Louisa said jokingly, as they were on their way to Prince Golam Reza's for lunch one day during the holidays.

"Well, at least my daughter learned how to

drive a car while she was living in America, so all that expense was worth it," Hassan interjected, laughing.

"If I ever get back there, I'll have a Bachelor of Arts, too. Then you'll really have your money's worth," she replied with a laugh.

When they drove up the steep driveway to Golam Reza's palace, which was high up on the side of the mountain in Niavaran, a large group of people were there. The area was beginning to be developed now that so much new wealth seemed to exist, presumably due to the growing oil industry. The prince had just finished building the modern, though not ostentatious, residence the previous year. It was the day before *Sizdah Behdar,* so everyone was talking about where they would be going to have their picnics and the day in the country. Of course the Kadjars would be hosting a picnic for their close friends and family out at Nowruzabad to the west of Tehran.

"*Mubarak Khonume,*" Mehdi Bakhtiar took Zahra's hand and kissed it as she walked into the large reception room that overlooked the pool garden and the mountains. "I haven't seen you out and about for the past month or so."

"*Nowruz-e-Mubarak,* Mehdi. No, I've been keeping close to the home front. As you may know, my father has not been doing so well during the past few weeks. The cancer is taking its toll, so we have kept a low profile."

"Yes, he told me just now that it's getting to be a strain on him to be as active as he has always been. He did tell me to be sure to come to Nowruzabad tomorrow for the *Sizdah Bedar* picnic. He suggested I come early enough to take a ride out in the desert with you. I don't like to presume but I'm sure you have a horse in your stables that would suit me."

"That would actually be quite lovely. With all that has been happening, I haven't ridden out for some weeks. Yes, please, do come around eleven and I'll tell the boys to have two horses ready for us. I'm sure Mama won't mind. She has plenty of help for tomorrow and certainly won't miss me. I'm not really that domestic, though she's been trying to coach me in the ways of the Persian kitchen."

After their conversation, she thought to herself, *so my dear, sweet, sick baba is at it again.* She chuckled to herself. Even though he'd been extremely kind and sympathetic when he heard the devastating news about Tom Williams, he obviously thought it was now time to find an appropriate husband for his only daughter. She didn't want to marry anyone except Tom, which was now truly impossible. Well, she would be polite to Mehdi and pretend to be interested if it would make her father's last days happier.

The doctor had said that he was getting close to the end. He'd lost a lot of weight and his skin was getting more yellowish every day. She and her mother had both noticed that he wasn't eating much. He was having trouble walking and was keeping more to himself, either at his desk or lying on the sofa in his walnut paneled office.

Two mornings after *Sizdah Bedar,* Louisa was sitting at the dining room table alone, having her tea and *nun-e-barbari,* when Zahra came down from her room to have breakfast before going to the Children's Hospital. "I'm worried, *Zahra June*. Your father didn't want to get up to come down for his breakfast. He looks terrible and seemed so weak and depressed. I didn't want to make a big deal about it, so I told him I would bring his tea up when I finished mine."

"You need to call Dr. Riahi. He'll come over, and I'm sure he can give him some medicine for the pain. I know he keeps saying there's not much pain, but I don't believe him. To me, he looks like he's hurting a lot, and he's just hiding it, so we won't worry."

"I'll go call him now and then take your *baba* up some tea and rice with *mast* for digestion."

Zahra got up from the table, but she hesitated at the door as she was leaving the room, "Do you want me to stay home Mama? I can call the hospital to say I won't be in today."

"No, no. The good doctor will come soon, I am sure. You go about your business and I'll take care of things here. This afternoon we really need to sit down to plan what we will do if he dies."

"You mean *when* he dies, Mama."

When an Iranian Muslim dies, the body must be buried within twenty-four hours. It is taken to a designated place, such as a mosque or the cemetery, where the *Mordeh Shoor* is performed by a professional Muslim body washer of the same sex as the deceased. The whole body is lightly washed three times, and then all the body openings, such as ears, nostrils and genitals are blocked with cotton balls. Prayers to *Allah* are recited during this ritual to attain forgiveness for the individual's sins during his lifetime.

Next the body is covered with a shroud and carried to the coffin by four men, where it is put on the ground and raised up three times to symbolize the deceased's refusal to leave his earthly life behind. Finally, it is put inside the coffin.

Usually a Quran is placed on the dead person to protect and bless him. The coffin is then carried to the gravesite where the gravedigger has dug the hole. At the gravesite the body is placed on the ground and once again lifted three times. On the fourth, it is lowered into the grave where the grave digger and a family member will position it on its right-side facing Mecca. It is regarded as blissful to touch the grave soil and spread a handful on the grave. Rosewater is always sprinkled on the grave as the Mullah recites verses from the Quran and gives condolences to the survivors.

As Zahra had not attended a funeral since she had returned home, her mother needed to explain the rituals of death to her. The family was Muslim but they seldom went to the mosque, and she had not been taught much about her faith over the years. When people asked if she was Muslim, she always said that she was, but in reality, she didn't know. She believed in *Allah* being the Supreme Being of her faith, but then the God that was worshiped in America and the Christian world was also the Supreme Being. She hadn't analyzed it seriously, but to her they were one and the same.

"We will need to have a memorial service at the house on the third day. This *Khatm,* as it's called, will be attended by all our family and friends as well as your *baba's* business associates. We need a large picture of him to put in the mosaic frame that I bought at the bazaar a couple of weeks ago, because I knew we were getting closer to this moment. We will put the picture on an easel at the far end of the reception room and surround it with large flower arrangements," Louisa explained.

"Will there be a Mullah?" Zahra asked.

"Oh yes. We'll have one of the Mullahs from the Sepahsalar Mosque, a friend of your *baba*, who will come to read verses from the Quran and direct the service. I want to have Reza, your cousin, play traditional Persian music on the sitar after the service, and we will serve the traditional sweet desert, *Halva*, dates, and of course, tea and sugar."

"But Mama, don't we need to serve a meal as well?"

"Oh, yes of course. Azizeh and her helpers will put the food out on the dining room table after the service and when everyone has finished their remembrances of Hassan," Louisa explained, haltingly. Then she began to get choked up and touched her eyes with a handkerchief.

"Mama, this is so morbid. I don't want to talk about it anymore. Let's go up and sit with *Baba*. Maybe he'll be awake, and we can talk about some of the fun times we've all had together."

So, they climbed the wide oak staircase and went into Hassan's room where he was lying propped up on pillows with his eyes open. They sat on either side of him, each holding his hand. When he spoke, his voice was soft. "You know my loves; it is not going to be long before I'm not with you. I don't want you to be like so many screaming, howling women I've seen at funerals. Louisa, you were not raised in my faith and Zahra, I have been neglectful in not teaching you the Muslim ways, but I believe there is only one omnipotent being. He will take me in my way and you in yours – it's all the same." He took a deep breath, and then smiled at his two beautiful girls. "Now let's talk about the day we drove to the Lahr Valley last summer and had such a good time fishing for brown trout."

A week later, when she woke in the morning, Louisa walked into Hassan's room, and he was no longer there. His face was peaceful in death, so she felt he had not been suffering his last few days. Dr. Riahi had been at the house every afternoon and had given him an injection to keep the pain away; she thought it was morphine but she didn't ask. She had told the doctor she wanted him to be sure to keep Hassan comfortable and that he had done.

She went to Zahra's room and lightly tapped on the door. "*Biah injah*, Mama," Zahra told her to come in. "*Baba's* gone, isn't he?"

"Yes, my love, his time is up." Louisa whispered. They held each other and cried and talked about how much they loved him and would miss him. Louisa would now be without her one true love, and Zahra would no longer have a doting father to indulge her every wish.

They had carefully planned for this moment. They each went about the things they had discussed and within no time the house was humming with activity. The service itself would be at the *Zahir-od-dole* cemetery which was just up the hill in Darband not far from the Tashrish Bazaar. Once Dr. Riahi had come to write the death certificate, Hassan's body would be taken there for the preparation for burial. Zahra and Louisa would notify family members and a few close friends by phone and then they would go to the gravesite where the service would be held in the early afternoon when all was ready.

In the Muslim religion it is believed that the departed soul is dependent on the living family for the first three days after death and that the spirit is lonely and susceptible to evil. During those days, the family should pray and fast in order that their loved one will enter heaven, which is said to be a sunlit paradise where anything is possible.

The day of the *Khatm,* (third day after death) attended by over a hundred people mourning Hassan's death, came and went without any major incident. Before she knew it, close relatives and friends were visiting the grave for the *Hafteh* (seventh day) when more prayers and verses from the Quran were said. And then the fortieth day arrived, when the simple flat black Persian marble gravestone was set over the grave with more rituals, and Zahra was finally able to cast off the black she had been wearing and don her preferred colorful clothes. She was sad that her father had died but she was also mourning the loss of Tom. She had talked with and written to Anne several times but there was never any change in the fact that Tom was presumed dead.

11

Lovers don't finally meet somewhere.
They're in each other all along.
Rumi

Ali 1979

Ali walked across the stable yard. He might as well do something useful while he waited for his mistress to come down from her apartment. He checked the water in the trough beside the stable door to see that it had enough for the horses when they came into the yard, from grazing on the desert, in the evening just before sunset. The other grooms would be keeping an eye on things because he most probably wouldn't be back before dark, so he wanted to be sure the trough was full. The drive would be long and he would wait at the airport until he saw the plane carrying Zahra Khonume leave the tarmac and fly up into the sky.

He remembered his first days at Andimeshk, when he was trying to learn how the Khonume took care of her horses. It was different from the nomadic care his father gave to his extensive herd. Sheik Karim's horses roamed the desert by day and night when they were on their travels from south to north and vice versa. They would all be fed at the camp in the mornings, where they came to get their forage which was placed in several large piles. The herd divided itself up into small groups, with five or six horses eating at each pile. There were, of course, some skirmishes amongst them, but very seldom did any of them get hurt. When they were in the South in the winter months, they would be tethered at night near the few small buildings and tents so the dogs could warn if any predators lurked in the area.

At the Bakhtiari Stud, which was surrounded by a high mud wall and had long narrow barns with box stalls, the horses were put in the stalls at night when they came in from their daytime desert grazing. There was either straw or dried grass in each manger, along with a scoop of barley waiting for each horse where they would spend the night.

"When the horses come in, Ali" Zahra had told him, "you must watch that each one stops at the water trough and drinks its fill. They have their pecking order, but you must be sure each horse gets enough water, for that is the most important substance for a horse's sustenance. I don't leave my horses free in the desert as your father does. I'm afraid the wolves and panthers that live in the mountains over there will come down and attack my young horses at night," she had explained to him when he first started working for her. "The horses must drink well in the mornings before they're let free all day and then again when they come back to the stables in the evening. It will be a part of your job to make sure the horses drink enough water." As time went on, he learned how the Khonume wanted her horses cared for and always made certain that her system was followed.

Zahra

She was holding her wedding portrait. She saw herself wearing a long white dress with a delicate lace veil covering her shiny dark hair that was pulled back into a bun at the nape of her neck. The dress had been made of a light woven cotton made in Azerbaijan that was covered with very fine lace that had tiny crocuses, for-get-me-nots and roses, which were her favorite flowers, woven into it. The long sleeves and neck were made solely of the lace. She loved that picture. She always knew she was beautiful, but on her wedding day, she had really felt it.

It seemed that the anniversary of her father's death arrived before she could blink an eye. She had been obliged to stay in Iran with her mother to help her settle the estate and to be with her through the period of mourning. Zahra was still sad because of the loss of her father but she knew he was in a better place now and she hoped that her life could get back to some semblance of normal. She knew she was not going to go back to Cornell. What would be the point? Tom was dead and Anne had become engaged and was getting married soon. There would really be no reason for her to complete her degree. It would be of no use in Iran where she knew she'd be living the rest of her life, except for the advanced agriculture practices she would study, but she had learned enough to help her with Nowruzabad she felt. If she went to America, she'd just be sad and mournful without Tom at her side. She had told Anne that she couldn't go over to the States to be a bridesmaid because she was still in mourning, though that was a little white lie. She just didn't want to go away again.

During the past year, she'd spent a lot of time with her friends, Avid and Mimi, and had also met many other young women her age through them and at the hospital. She had her horses and now she was the one who was there to manage Noruzabad. The farming was developing well, and they had a good crop of pomegranates and persimmons, as well as the only fields of French asparagus in the area. The crops they harvested, along with barley and alfalfa, had made the farm a paying proposition. She wanted to continue with that work, as it gave her a real feeling of fulfillment. Her father would be proud of her.

During the past months, Mehdi Bakhtiar had begun dropping in to have tea with Zahra and her mother once a week or so. He was as charming and handsome as she had remembered him before her *baba* died, but she'd never shown him a reason to think she was interested in him in any way, other than friendship. The last *Sizdah Bedar,* when her father had been alive, she'd ridden out with him into the country, and they had a great time riding across the desert and into the mountains to the north of Nowruzabad. They had raced back across the desert towards home, and she'd won by about twenty meters, but he had chided that she'd given him the slowest horse and thus she had an unfair advantage. They had laughed and joked and enjoyed each other's company. But then her sweet *baba* died, and she had no thoughts of Mehdi or any other man in her life with the exception of the memories of Tom.

"Mehdi came by again today," Louisa told her when she came back from her hospital work one afternoon.

"And?"

"I just thought you would want to know," was her mother's reply.

"I'm sure he came to see you, not me. He was a friend and admirer of *Baba*."

"I think he is interested in you, Zahra. He's not married and getting to the age when he should be. He never said anything to your father after he found out you were engaged to Tom, but before that he had made some overtures about you, to him."

"Mama, stop! I'm finally settling into the fact that I've lost my father, and the love of my life is dead. I'm beginning to feel that I can have a good life here without complications, so please don't start match making."

"All right, all right. I'll keep my nose out of your business. But you're a very beautiful young lady and I'm sure suitors will come along now that the period of mourning is officially over; you must be aware of that."

Zahra sighed, "I'll handle all those suitors

when they come flocking to the door, Mama, don't worry."

Zahra kept herself busy to keep her mind off her recent losses. She attended parties given by friends of the family and her many young married acquaintances. She did love music and was always happy to dance with the group when the music began, as it always did at these Persian house parties. Mimi's husband had become an investor in the new "in" place to go, *Shehkoof-e-Now,* which was a chic European-type night club in which Prince Golam Reza, along with his sister, Princess Ashraf, were investors. So it was, that Zahra would often go there after dinner with friends. There was a celebrity singer or group appearing there most weekends and it became her haunt. She would usually go with some of her friends but often she would have Abraheem drive her and he'd wait to take her back to the house when she was ready.

She had never been much of a drinker, but as she started to party frequently, she began to partake in alcoholic beverages more often. She was usually able to realize when she was reaching the level of having too much to drink and would then stop and switch to tea or water. She loved to party and dance, for it gave her a release that she hadn't been able to find the past couple of years that she had been back living in

Iran. She loved her life at Nowruzabad when she was planning and managing the agricultural business of the place, and she always had time for a ride in the desert. She felt fulfilled with her work at the hospital helping the children. And now she was enjoying a good party life, where she could let her hair down. Yes, she was getting used to and enjoying life in her birth country.

One *Chahar Shanbeh,* while she was at the night club enjoying herself with Mimi and Avid, dancing with a group to the music of Googoosh, the young female vocalist who was all the rage now, she felt a tap on her shoulder. She turned and saw Mehdi Bakhtiar, looking ever so handsome in a white silk shirt, open at the neck under his navy-blue blazer. Her breath caught in surprise, as she looked into his deep brown eyes. "May I have the honor of dancing with you, Khonume Kadjar?" he asked.

"Hello, Mehdi. You surprised me! I didn't expect anyone to cut in while I was dancing with my girlfriends. -- Yes, of course I'd be very pleased to dance with you." She used her Persian manners, though she really didn't want to dance with Mehdi. When she was near him, he made her tingle in a way she didn't want to feel, and she was afraid to be so close to him in his arms. But what could she do now?

As Mehdi took her in his arms, Googoosh

began to sing the beautiful ballad, *Bad Az Tou,* which was a love song about a cheeky girl who wouldn't commit to her admirer. The rhythm of the music was slow, and as they glided around the dance floor, Mehdi began to softly sing the words along with Googoosh. He held her loosely but close and she could feel his whole body against her own. She tensed. "Relax Zahra, I'm not going to make an indecent pass at you; I have too much respect for your dear father. I just want to enjoy the music and dance with the beautiful woman you are."

When the song ended, he led her back to the table where her friends were sitting, "*Muchekeram, Khonume,*" he thanked her. "I hope to see you again soon. You are as beautiful a dancer as you are to look at." She was flabbergasted and couldn't answer as he walked way.

"Zahra, I knew Mehdi would come around to court you. He's had eyes for you since the first time he met you at your coming-home party a few years ago. I've watched him looking at you whenever he is around," Avid said to her as she sat down.

"Oh, don't be ridiculous. I'm not in the mood to be courted. The two most important men in my life are now gone, and I don't have room for another just yet."

"You have to admit, he's gorgeous to look at

and he's one of the nicest men I know. He is good friends with my husband, Ahmad, so he comes to our house often, and I promise he is so sweet and kind. He loves playing with the kids and is always ready to give a helping hand if needed. You would be very lucky to have him. You can't bring people back from the dead, so you might as well look to the future. You aren't getting any younger, you know. The Bakhtiar tribe is one of the most important in the country. Mehdi is the eldest son, so he became the head of the tribe when his father, the Khan, was killed. Just think, you could be married to one of the most important men in the county."

Zahra held up her hand, "Just stop! I have no intention of marrying anyone at the moment. Maybe someday in the future I'll fall in love again, but not just yet."

Spring turned into summer and it was *Mordad* (July) again. Their seaside house in Ramsar beckoned Zahra and Louisa. They hadn't gone there during the year of mourning as they were both missing Hassan too much and felt that the summer house would feel empty without his happy personality roaming about it. He'd always been at his best when they were staying those few weeks in the North to get out of the oppressive heat of Tehran at that time of year. He had loved swimming and fishing in the

blue waters of the Caspian Sea and going night-
ly to the Casino to try his luck at the tables. He
could relax and forget the worries of everyday
life in the real world that one time every year.
Now it was their time to forget life in Tehran
and leave the house and Nowruzabad farm in
the hands of their loyal workers. They decided
they would spend the month in Ramsar.

"I think we should have a big party at the
house as soon as we get settled in. What do you
think of that?" Louisa asked Zahra as they were
driving up the mountains on the Chaluz Road.

"I'm sure it would be fun, if that's what you
want, Mama. Most of our friends are at their
summer homes too, so we will really have a big
crowd. You haven't done much socializing lately
and it will be good for you to see the people you
and *Baba* used to spend time with again. Yes, I
think it's a great idea. We'll start planning and
making the guest list tomorrow first thing."

And so, the planning began. They decided
to hold the party on the first day of *Shahrivar,*
the beginning of the sixth month of the year and
the last month of summer. As they went through
their list, they realized that they would most
likely have at least sixty of their friends and acquaintances if they counted on one third of the
invited guests not coming. It was a good number
and there would be plenty of room, as the house

was large, and the garden and veranda could also be used for mingling. They would decorate the porch with candles and flowers and have a caviar bar there with *blinis* and iced vodka before the main meal was served on the long teak dining room table. In addition, there would be a table with fruits and sweets and a samovar of tea for those who didn't imbibe in alcohol. There would be traditional Persian sitar music before and during dinner, and then after the meal the veranda would be cleared for dancing to the music of Ramesh, the young man whose music was almost as popular as Googoosh. After the year long period of mourning they had kept, they both had fun arranging things for their first party.

One afternoon, shortly after the invitations had been delivered. Mehdi Bakhtiar dropped by to have tea with them; his own summer house was just a few kilometers up the coast. "I was honored to receive the invitation to your party. I will definitely accept, but I also want to contribute something to show my respect for Hassan. I will supply the best French Champagne we can get. Prince Golam Reza has a special import license and often brings things into the country for me; I'll ask him to bring in a few cases of Dom Perignon. Also, Princess Fatimeh is involved with the caviar business and will be able to get some of the rare golden caviar that is so hard to find; I will supply that as well. This will be the best party of the Ramsar season, I am sure."

"No, no Mehdi you can't do that. It's too much," Louisa told him.

"It's not too much when I want to do it, Khonume," he replied.

"But you are being too kind. It is impossible," she said using the Persian *taarof*.

"You must accept this small contribution I want to make," he answered.

And so it went on in the Persian way of *ta-arof,* which is an Arabic word indicating the process of getting acquainted. But in Iran for centuries, the etiquette has been a form of polite negotiation in discussions, with both sides understanding the socially implied rules. It also derives from the fact that Iranians care so much about the image they present to others. Naturally Louisa was obliged to eventually accept Mehdi's offer, and they then turned their attention to other matters.

As he was leaving, Zahra showed him to the door, "It was good to see you, Mehdi, and again, thank you for your contribution to our party."

"My pleasure. It was good to see you too, Zahra. I was hoping that you would join me for dinner at the Casino tomorrow evening. I have reserved a table; Avid and Ahmad will be joining us."

"Oh, I don't know. I'd hate to leave my mother alone." She was not ready for this.

Mehdi smiled. "Well, perhaps she'd like to come along. You mention it to her, and I'll give her a call when I get home, just to confirm."

"Well, let me think about it." After all, she did like him, and he was dashing; perhaps it would be fun.

"It would please me very much. Please say yes."

"All right, thank you. I'm sure it will be fun." She wondered if she could keep her head a whole evening with this charming sexy man who made her almost quiver.

"I'll pick you and your mother up about nine thirty tomorrow evening then," he took her hand and kissed it, then turned and walked down the steps towards his car with a springy step.

Her mother looked at her, surprised, "I have no intention of going to dinner at the casino with you and Mehdi. I told him no, when he called a few minutes ago. I planned to play cards with some of my own friends tomorrow. You go and have a good time."

That she did. They dined and danced and went to the tables where Mehdi and Ahmad played blackjack for a time. Once Mehdi came away a winner, they danced some more. It was after two in the morning when they got into the car at valet parking. Mehdi put the red Ferrari in gear and drove out the white pillared gates of Ramsar's Casino. Once they were on the twisty coastal road, he took Zahra's hand, "I had a marvelous time tonight being with you, Zahra. I hope you enjoyed yourself, too."

"Thank you so much, Mehdi. I really had a good time," she answered as he drove up to her house. He got out to open her door, and they walked up the path to the front door. He kissed her hand and turned to leave.

She was feeling giddy. She'd had a wonderful time and loved the feeling of being with him. He was considerate, entertaining and irresistible. She had felt almost breathless sitting in the fast car with her hand in his. It was a feeling she had never expected to feel again. It wasn't a feeling of love, like she had for Tom when they became interested in each other. That time her heart had been racing like a horse after a long run. No, this was a sensual feeling like she had felt just before she and Tom would make love. It frightened her that she could have this feeling of lust for someone she had never even kissed and who she only knew as an acquaintance of her father. Was she becoming a loose woman?

Of course, there was no possibility of having intercourse with this man. She didn't love him, and she was in Iran. It was taboo to have premarital sex. He would want to marry a virgin, which she was not. Now that she thought about it, her marriage prospects were not good, because she had been deflowered. Some people believed that girls who rode horses a lot broke their hymen while participating in that activity, but she knew that idea would not hold water as far as she was concerned. After all, she had spent a lot of time in America, where it was known that it was common for couples to have sex even while they were just dating. She would just have to keep her cool and get used to the fact that she had her memories with Tom, and that was probably all she would ever have as far as a sex life was concerned here in this society.

When the night finally arrived, Zahra and her mother's party ended up being a great success. The caviar was served in a beautiful ice sculpture of a jumping sturgeon with its mouth open, and the fresh blinis that had been made by Azizeh in the Kadjar's kitchen were mouthwatering. Dinner was served at ten-thirty and devoured in no time by the crowd, who surrounded the table like a flock of vultures. Then came baklava and other sweets, along with the dry bubbly Dom Perignon which flowed like water as the music of Ramesh commenced and couples began to fill the dance floor on the veranda.

It was after two in the morning when the guests began to leave, saying their thanks and good-byes with hugs and kisses on both cheeks, everyone congratulating Louisa and Zahra on a spectacular evening. The last person out the front door was Mehdi who had danced with most of the beautiful young ladies, as well as with Louisa and Zahra. He held their hands and kissed each on both cheeks, "It was a wonderful evening. You two beautiful girls sure know how to throw a party. Thank you both so much."

"And thanks to you too, Mehdi. The caviar and champagne were a real success. Please come over for lunch later today, about three, and we can all have another glass and talk over the evening at length," Louisa said.

"Oh, no, I couldn't possibly. You two will be too tired. It was a long night."

"Do come over! We'll be rested by then, and half the fun of having a party is the aftermath and gossip," Louisa insisted.

Naturally he did have lunch with the Kadjar ladies that day. During the next few months, he was a visible guest at their home frequently. He took Zahra to dinner and was her escort for parties and other events that she attended. People began to talk about the couple and speculate when an engagement might be announced.

One morning, as they were having their tea,

Louisa said, "Zahra, I think it's wonderful that you're seeing so much of Mehdi. I know your father would be happy to see that you two are a couple."

"We are not a couple, Mama. We are just friends. Why, he's never even attempted to kiss me. We have lots of interests in common like horses, agriculture and charity works, so we have lots to talk about. I enjoy being with him, but I really think he's just being my friend."

"You must be attracted to him; he's so handsome and looks so fit and masculine. If I were younger, I know I would be."

"Mama, you are too much." Zahra thought for a moment, sipping her tea. Then she said, "Yes, I'm really attracted to him, but we have no future. You see, when I was with Tom, I gave him my virginity and I know that a man like Mehdi would only marry a virgin; that is the Persian tradition. Not that I ever expect that he would want me to marry him. But it's nice to have him as a friend."

Louisa didn't look as shocked as Zahra expected her to be with the pronouncement of her lost virginity, which surprised her. "My dear girl, do you really think that girls don't make mistakes here too? Of course, they do. There is a French doctor here in Tehran who specializes in revirginization surgery."

"In what?" Zahra raised her voice in disbelief. "Are you telling me that an operation exists to make girls virgins again?"

"Well, yes. Of course, it is kept very quiet, what this doctor can do. But it is a simple operation that replaces the hymen so that on the first night, when the marriage is consummated, the hymen is actually broken as it would be with a virgin bride. The husband is happy and no one knows the difference."

"But that is making a mockery of the marriage! The whole marriage starts off with a lie. I think that's disgusting. I don't believe it, Mama!"

"Well, my dear, it happens all the time, and I think that you'd better consider the surgery for yourself. I have a feeling that Mehdi Bakhtiar is going to ask me for your hand in marriage and I think you could do a lot worse. I know you like him, and he likes you, and that's probably the most important ingredient in a happy marriage. Love and lust are one thing, but comradery is much more lasting than either of them."

"I'm not so sure Mehdi would want to marry me if he thought I was playing a trick on him. And anyway, I'm not so sure he's the marrying type. He is so involved with his farming businesses and that supposedly amazing herd of horses down at his place in Khuzestan," Zahra rationalized.

Louisa ended the conversation with, "Well, if things do develop between you two, it will be easy to make arrangements."

Zahra decided to talk to Mimi and Avid about what her mother had said the next time they had lunch together. It seemed they both knew about the operation, though neither of them had needed it. They both had arranged marriages when they were in their late teens and had never even been on a date alone with a boy.

"I have a friend who I went to school with, who used to sneak out to meet this boy she liked. She would use me as an alibi, and she did lose her virginity. Then her parents arranged a marriage with the son of friends. She was in a panic until another girl she knew told her about Dr. Lamoure and she was able to have the operation without even telling her mother. She stayed over with me the night after she had it and she told me that it was very easy," Mimi told her.

"Zahra, I think you should have it done. Mehdi has been intrigued by you since he first saw you, when you came home that summer while you were still studying in the States. Ahmad told me that he has talked to him about wanting to marry you, but he thinks it may be too soon, what with your father dying and losing your fiancé in the war. He's had a lot of beautiful women over the years but there was never anyone who had so many interests in common with him," Avid said.

"But I'm not in love with him," Zahra protested. "At least I don't think I am. I will admit I'm strongly attracted to him, and we do get on well with our similar interests, but is that enough for marriage? I was really in love with Tom, but now he's gone. Do I have to settle for less?"

"Yes, you probably do. Neither of us were in love with the men we married, but we've learned to love our husbands, haven't we, Avid?" Mimi commented.

"I'm quite happy with Ahmad and I do love him, especially now that we have children. I didn't even know him when we were married. Zahra, life has many surprises for us, and I think you would be lucky to spend the rest of yours with Mehdi," was Avid's advice.

"Well, it's a bit of a moot point, you know. Mehdi has never given me any inclination that he wants to be anything but a good friend. We go places together but he usually spends most of his time talking to the other men when we're at dinner parties. We do go to the clubs quite a bit and he loves to dance as much as I do. But we never talk about personal things or our feelings about each other the way I used to with Tom. It's always about how our crops are doing or something about our horses. We do go out to ride a lot, sometimes to Nowruzabad and sometimes at his place in Vanak, and we have a great time together riding across the vast desert and up in the mountains where the views are spectacular. Still, I have the feeling he thinks of me as just some young girl to have fun with. I don't know, maybe I'm too cool when I'm with him. It's like I'm afraid to get too close to him. I don't know why."

One night a few months later, Mehdi picked her up at the Tehran house, in his chauffeur-driven dark blue Mercedes, to take her to dinner. This was a big change from the usual rides they took in the red Ferrari. "This must be a special occasion tonight," Zahra commented as he held the door for her.

"As a matter of fact, it is," he answered.

"I'm curious; where are we off to in such a formal car? I hope I'm dressed appropriately for the occasion. I thought you only used this car and your driver when you were going to some royal or ambassadorial event."

"This evening is going to be a special event, but not royal or ambassadorial," he chuckled.

When they arrived at Xanadu, she was pleasantly surprised. It was known as the best restaurant in the city and she hadn't been there since before her father became ill. It had always been her mother's and her favorite place to have dinner when they went out to eat. The restaurant had been established by Zoric Zolghadr, the daughter of a Persian general who had served in the Caucuses and brought his family back home at the time of the Bolshevik Revolution. She had been sent to Paris for her education, and when she came back to her family in Tehran, she'd opened her restaurant which quickly became the place to be seen and had the reputation of having the best faire in Tehran.

When they arrived at the curb, Zahra's door was opened by the chauffer. As they entered the candle-lit entrance of the restaurant, they were ushered into the small garden at the back that was like a paradise, with the silver light of the moon streaming through the branches of tall cedar trees and the scent of gardenias from the small bushes around them. They sat at a candle-lit table in the far corner of the garden and Zoric herself brought a bottle of Dom Perignon, which she opened with a pop, and poured into the champagne flutes.

"Mehdi, I am so glad to see you," she smiled knowingly at him and then said to Zahra, "I haven't seen you since your poor father died. I am so sorry. He was a wonderful man. The world is a lesser place without him. Welcome back, my dear."

"Thank you, Zoric," she choked, as a tear

trickled down her left cheek.

Mehdi took a snow-white handkerchief from his breast pocket and softly dabbed at the tear. She smiled sheepishly, took a deep breath, and held it for a moment. Finally, she said, "I'm sorry, I didn't mean to be so emotional. I don't usually cry but remembering my last time here with my *baba* made me feel sad."

"Don't worry, *Zahrajune*, I hope tonight will be a happy memory when it is over." He'd never before used the endearment *june* and it surprised her. He raised his glass to hers and they clinked blurting out, "*Salam a ti*," in unison, then laughing.

They took their time over a superb meal, starting with iced caviar and blinis which was the signature dish of Xanadu. Then they had mussels in a white wine sauce with freshly baked French bread from Zoric's oven. The lamb shanks and *badenjune* with fresh grown green beans were the main dish. Finally, it was time to take a break.

Zoric, who had served them herself, came over to the table once the dishes and cutlery had been cleared. "I have made a *gateau Mille-Feuille* especially for you," she said looking at Zahra. "When Mehdi told me, he was bringing you for dinner tonight, I remembered how you always ordered it when you came to dinner with your parents. It has very special ingredients to-night and I'm sure you will love it," she said as she winked at Mehdi.

"Please bring along some espresso and two snifters of Courvoisier to go along with it, my dear." He winked back at her.

When the *Meille-Feuille* and espresso arrived, Zahra sat and looked at it, wondering how she would be able to eat or drink another mouthful. She reflected that she had loved the squares of flaky puff pastry layers, interspersed with sweet cream and topped with a white glaze striped with dark chocolate, more than any other dessert when she was a child.

Mehdi watched as she tentatively put her fork in and took a small bite. It was delicious, so she took a larger bite. But then she felt something hard in her mouth that had come from inside the pastry. She wasn't sure what to do. It would be rude to spit it out, and yet she couldn't swallow it. As she glanced up at Mehdi, she saw that he was smiling at her.

"Is there something wrong with the pastry?" he chuckled. "It's all right if you spit it out on the plate. Don't be embarrassed."

She carefully spit the hard thing out on the plate and saw that it was a piece of aluminum foil wrapped around something. She asked, "What do you think this is? Something must have fallen into the cream in the kitchen, I guess."

"Why don't you unwrap it?" Mehdi was laughing and obviously enjoying himself. He did have a funny sense of humor, she knew. Was this some kind of joke that he and Zoric had decided to play on her?

She carefully picked at the foil with her freshly manicured nails, the nails that her mother had insisted she have done for some ridiculous reason. She never wore nail polish but didn't want to argue. It was hard to get the foil from around the small object for it was twisted tightly, but when the object was finally freed, she saw with a start that it was a ring. It was a yellow gold beveled setting with a large emerald as the center stone surrounded by a circle of diamonds. She couldn't figure out what to say or do. She just sat there looking shocked.

Mehdi just smiled at her and asked, "Would you consider becoming my wife, Zahra?"

"I don't understand what's happening," she replied in a quiet voice.

"I'm asking you to marry me. That's what's happening. I've been wanting to for a long time, but I thought it was too soon. I finally talked to your mother to get her permission and she seemed pleased with the idea. Maybe she'll be happy to be rid of her headstrong daughter," he smirked. "Well, will you?"

She sat without saying anything. She'd never really thought of marrying now that Tom was gone. She was enjoying her life as it was. She had good friends, work that she enjoyed, and a nice man, even though he was a bit older than she was, to escort her when she wanted. Then there was that virginity thing that she couldn't get out of her head.

She took a deep breath and said, "I don't know what to say, because I thought we were just good friends who enjoyed a lot of the same things and had similar interests. Why, you've never even really kissed me, you've just pecked me on the cheek like a cousin or a brother. I guess I'm just shocked."

"I didn't want to make improper advances because I was afraid, I'd frighten you away. I am sure people, Avid in particular, have suggested to you that I had serious feelings for you. I've talked a lot with Ahmad who is one of my closest friends and is happily married to a younger wife; I'm sure you must have had some inkling."

"To be truthful yes, Avid did tell me that you had talked to Ahmad, but I thought she was just trying to be a match maker. You know how she is. I love her but she doesn't have many interests beyond her family life. Mehdi, there are things about me that you may not like or be able to live with."

"If you're talking about the fact that you are not a virgin, which I'm sure you aren't – no offence, I hope. I don't care. I'm not one either. I wasn't born yesterday, you know. I know things in the States are different than here in Iran. It's not important to me. I love you in a way that I have never felt before and I know that we can have a very happy life together. Passion is something that will come easily with us, I am confident. I want to be with you and take care of you and be married to you. So, will you please let me put this ring on your finger and tell me yes?"

She sat quietly, thinking about whether this was something she would be happy doing. She had her responsibilities at Nowruzabad and would want to continue managing the farm for her mother. But that probably wouldn't be too much of a problem as Mehdi was back and forth from Khuzestan, where his land holdings were, like a bouncing ball. She would have to move into his big new house in Niavaran that he had just recently completed; she hadn't even seen it yet. She knew he spent more time in the south than in Tehran, and she'd never been in that part of the country. Would she like life in the south that was not nearly as civilized as it was in Tehran?

She really did like Mehdi and was very attracted to him, but would that be enough? Could she grow to love this man who was anxiously awaiting an answer to his question? "I just don't know what to say. If I say yes now, will you let me back out if I decide in a few days that it was the wrong decision? I don't want to hurt you, but I am not one hundred percent sure."

"If you say yes now, I will hold you to it till you die!" he teased her. "No, honestly, if you say yes now and you decide it's not what you want, I'll be disappointed and sad because I know the two of us can have a wonderful fulfilling life together. But I will never force you to do anything. That is a promise."

She held her left hand out to him and said, "Yes, I think I will be happy married to you, Mehdi Bakhtiar Khan." As he slipped the antique ring, that had been his mother's, on her finger, he kissed her tenderly and deeply on her soft lips.

Despite her concerns, Zahra did not back out. It was decided that the wedding ceremony would be held the first of the month of Azar because the weather would be turning cold at that time and it was when Mehdi usually went to stay most of the winter in Khuzestan. The ceremony was held in the great hall of Mehdi's new house which had been decorated with flowers, tulle, and ribbons of lavender and mint green to create a springtime atmosphere in the autumn. Lavender is also a color that is said to invoke a feeling of romance and nostalgia, which Zahra wanted to feel on the day of her marriage.

As was the custom when a father was deceased, she was walked through the room, to the *Sofreh-ye Aghd,* by her mother. A veil covered her face, and she sat down on Mehdi's left so that he was on her right-hand side which designated a place of respect. On the beautiful embroidered tablecloth were a pair of silver candelabra with the candles lit to represent light and fire, a Zoroastrian tradition, and a mirror which symbolized eternity. Additionally, there were many items such as gold coins, eggs, nuts, honey, and incense, which were symbols that would contribute to the couple having a good, productive and happy life together. Zahra's friends, Avid and Mimi, along with four of her girl cousins, held the silk scarf over the couple during the ceremony. When the officiate, who was an old of friend of Hassan, asked Mehdi if he would take Zahra to be his wife, he immediately answered in the affirmative. However, Zahra was asked the question three times, as is the tradition, before she said, *"Bali,"* and then her veil was lifted so that her husband could see her face in the mirror. Next Mehdi lifted the dish of honey and dipped his little finger in it and put it in his bride's mouth, and she did the same for him. This symbolized that they would feed each other with sweetness and sustenance through-out their married life. Finally, all the family and close friends attending the small ceremony rushed up, kissing them both on the cheeks and offering their congratulations, "*Mobarak bash!*"

The *Mehmoonee* (Reception) was attended by a much larger crowd than the *Aghd* because friends as well as neighbors all expected an in-vitation to an important society wedding such as this. It would have been considered rude not to invite even casual acquaintances who might have heard about it.

The buffet table was set up with an as-sortment of kabobs, stews like *gormeh sabzi, khoresht-e-badanjun and feshenjun,* as well as different types of rice and especially *shirini polo* the sweet rice that was meant to bring sweetness into the lives of the guests. When it came time to cut the cake the guests took turns "stealing" the long sword that was going to be used as a cake knife. They took turns dancing to the music that was playing and collecting "ransom money" from the happy couple, passing the sword from woman to woman, each one showing off her dancing skills, while the bride and groom con-tinued to bid on the sword. Finally, when the price was right, it was passed to Mehdi who be-gan cutting the cake into small pieces that Zahra handed out to all the guests. Champagne and other alcoholic drinks were served as everyone took to the dance floor and danced into the early hours of the morning.

When Zahra and Mehdi finally went upstairs to the large master bedroom, they each went into their private bath and dressing room to get out of their wedding finery and prepare for bed. Zahra put on the lavender silk nightgown her mother had imported from Paris. Cautiously she entered the bedroom to find Mehdi already lying under the white satin sheets. When she fell into the bed, it was obvious that they were both too exhausted to find out if they would be compatible in the consummation of their marriage. The morning would come soon enough. They had the whole rest of their lives to be together, she thought. It would be just fine. They both slept.

12

Mount the stallion of love and do not fear the path,
Love's stallion knows the way exactly.
With one leap, Love's horse will carry you home.
Rumi

Ali 1979

Ali walked back towards the steps to Zahra's apartment and saw that Golam Reza was sitting on the bottom step; he wanted to say goodbye to his benefactor and good friend who had always been behind him in the decisions he'd had to make over the years,- a lifetime!

Golan Reza saw that Ali was agitated and said, "Khonume is taking her time to leave. It has always been the same, from the first time she came here as the young bride of Mehdi Khan. I met them at the train station, and helped transfer all the baggage, which was considerable, onto the boat to cross the river. We had the ox cart and the horses waiting with Reza on the other bank to take everything to the big house where they were going to live. You didn't know Reza; he was with the stud during the time of Arab Shebani Khan, Mehdi's father. He was Shebani Khan's groom and servant. They grew up together as young boys. I thought he would die, too, when the Khan was killed in an attack by one of the Qashqa'i tribes. In those days, there was much warring between the tribes. He lived on, though he never got over the loss of his best friend. He ended his life's journey shortly before you came here. Anyway, Zahra Khonume fell in love with this place from the moment she stepped foot on this desert land."

"I am afraid we'll not get to the Ahwaz airport in time for Khanum's flight if she doesn't come down in the next few minutes," Ali replied to Golam Reza's dissertation. He knew he would just have to wait and what would be, would be.

Zahra

Zahra had been looking at the picture of herself and Mehdi as they came out of the house the morning after the wedding. They were a handsome couple, on their way to her mother's house where Louisa was giving the "day after" wedding luncheon in their honor. They both looked serious as they stood in the doorway of Mehdi's Neo-Classic house of which he was so proud. They had successfully made love that morning, but she was still wondering if she had done the right thing in marrying this fifteen year older sophisticated khan. He was so kind and charming, and she knew that he was totally infatuated with her. But the question was, would she be able to return his passion and love?

It had been planned that Zahra and Mehdi would leave Tehran for Khuzestan two days after their wedding. They decided to go by train, which left the station in Tehran at seven in the morning and got them to Andimeshke the following morning. The railway had been built by Reza Shah in 1927, when he recognized that a modern transportation system was essential for the future development of his country. Other countries had erected their networks of rail travel by that time. Even though the foreign powers in Iran preferred an east-west line, Reza Shah felt the more important route would be a north-south line that would connect the Persian Gulf in the south with the Caspian Sea to the north passing through Tehran, the capital. A German

consortium commenced the construction, starting in the north and south simultaneously on
the line that needed to climb and fall more than
two thousand meters at each end. Reza introduced a task-tax on sugar and tea to finance his
venture, which was handed over to the Danish-
Swedish group, Kampsax, in 1933. The project
was completed several months ahead of schedule and well below budget.

Zahra and Mehdi travelled in a private
sleeper compartment in first class that was very
comfortable, even though a bit cramped. The
scenery of the bare landscape was breathtaking,
with steep, craggy mountains, towering rock
faces, and deep gorges through which rivers
rushed, visible when the train was not thunder-
ing through the many tunnels *en route*. As they
got closer to Andimeshke, they followed the
river, occasionally seeing small villages where
the train stopped to either take on or drop off
passengers.

Zahra had a thousand questions for her new
husband while the train was moving southward.
She had no idea what to expect in this south-
western province of Khuzestan, that she knew
was populated by many nomadic tribes. Mehdi,
himself was the head of the Bakhtiar tribe, of
which many people were still living the life of
nomads. She knew it was the Iranian province

with the oldest history and that it was often referred to as the "birthplace of the nation." as it was where the history of the Elamites began. Historically, one of the most important regions of the Ancient Near East, Khuzestan was what historians referred to as ancient Elam, whose capital was Susa. She also knew that Masjed-e-Soliman was a city in the province, where oil was first discovered in 1908. But she didn't really have a picture in her mind's eye of what she would find at the end of the train ride.

"*Mehdijunam*," she said, for he was dear to her now, "You haven't told me anything about your house that we will be living in, or the garden or stables. The only thing that you've said to me is that you have the most beautiful and purest herd of Asil Arab horses in Iran. You told me that I would want to leave my own favorite horse in Tehran because he would look like a *yahbu* when put next to your wonderful horses. Don't keep me in suspense. Please tell me where we'll be living."

"Of course, my *junam*, we will live in a house. If you want, we can live in a stable though; I have a beautiful stable, in the countryside of Aghili, towards Dezful that has a lovely apartment above it. That's actually my favorite place to live while I'm here in Khuzestan. But I want us to live in the house my father built, just on the outskirts of Andimeshke. It's a beautiful house that was built by one of the famous architects during the last years of the Qadjar reign."

"Please tell me what it's like; I'm very curious. Is it like my family house in Tehran?"

"My father had fallen in love with a beautiful girl, my mother, who was from a respected and rich family. He was just a Bakhtiari chief and the father of his love said he would not let her marry my father until he created a house that was at least as beautiful as her family's residence. So, my father hired architects, craftsmen, and workers to come down here from Tehran to build the house that would gain the approval of my mother's father. It took five years to build the house of stone blocks and brick that was made to look beautiful with the ornamentation of stucco designs, which is a technique that dates back to pre-Islamic times and is an art mastered by our craftsmen. Like most houses, it is surrounded by a tall mud wall and has a central garden with a large ornamental pool. The rooms all open onto the pillared portico which surrounds the garden with its roses and bronze and marble sculptures. The rest you will have to wait to see, because I could not do the house justice with my description."

"It sounds so romantic. I can't wait to get there."

The train was pulling into the Andimeshke station and she saw that there were several men wearing the Bakhtiari head dresses waiting on the platform. It seemed that they were there to meet Mehdi and his new bride. They greeted Mehdi, kissing both cheeks. She realized they were very close to him, so they weren't just servants. He held each by the shoulders and she could see the affection in their eyes.

"Zarah Khonume, I want you to meet my people," he said.

"This is Golam Reza, who is my right-hand man here." Reza, who seemed a bit older. was the first of the other men she met. They all came respectfully and bowed to her as they were introduced. The baggage car was being unloaded, so she and Mehdi pointed out the bags and many boxes they had brought from Tehran which were put into the back of an old pickup truck that would take them to the river crossing, for the house was across the Karkheh River from the station. The river would be crossed on a primitive boat, and the luggage would be transferred to an ox cart to take it to the house. There were horses too waiting on the far side of the river when they disembarked from the boat.

"You will now have the best ride of your life, my darling," Mehdi told her as he gave her a leg up on a beautiful chestnut Asil mare. "This mare is one of your wedding presents from me. She is called Khatum. I believe, after you follow me now, you'll never want to ride another bloodless horse in your life."

With that, he vaulted up on a handsome back stallion, dug in his heels and signaled her to follow him as he galloped off across the desert. It was a cool morning with a slight breeze as they rode off along the banks of the river towards a destination known only to Mehdi. As they galloped smoothly across the open spaces, the wind whistled through Zahra's long dark hair, that she had not tied up in her usual manner. She had never been on such a comfortable galloping horse; it felt as though the animal was flying without its hooves touching the ground.

Mehdi pulled up and turned to her, laughing, "Well, what do you think, my beauty?"

She was out of breath but was finally able to blurt out, "Fantastic!"

As they galloped across the rolling terrain, past many fertile fields and through a shallow river, she noticed that there were many round mounds of sand in straight lines across the desert. When she caught her breath, she asked him what they were.

"Those are Qanats. They are a three thousand-year-old marvel of engineering in the desert. Beginning in the Iron Age, when surveyors found an elevated source of water, usually at the head of a former river, they would cut long, sloping tunnels from the water source to where it was needed. The holes were air shafts, bored to release dust and provide oxygen to the workers who dug the Qanats by hand. It was a painstaking task, made even more so by the need for great precision. The angle of the tunnel's slope had to be steep enough to allow the water to flow freely without stagnating, but not so steep that the water would flow with enough force to speed erosion and collapse the tunnel. This part of the world was the first place to carry water from underground channels to the surface.

"Now I'm taking you to my favorite place, the stable at Aghili, the one I mentioned on the train. The water there comes from these Qanats. You'll see; it is cool and clear and refreshing after a fast ride."

They then walked and trotted towards what looked like a garden enclosed by a tall mud wall with a scalloped top. When they arrived at the iron gate, Mehdi shouted and the gate slid open, revealing a large stable yard and a garden of several hectares. There were three stable bocks of about ten stalls each in a horseshoe configuration. The middle one had a second story with an onion-domed roof. There was a man and woman with two young children, who obviously worked there, standing by to be introduced to the Khan's new wife. Once they had met, Mehdi handed the horses off to them as they dismounted. He was very friendly to them and gave the children a peck on the cheek as he took Zahra's hand and led her towards the stairway to the small porch of what must be the apartment.

When they reached the door, he scooped her up, opened the door and carried her across the threshold as she laughed. "You don't have an American groom, so I wanted to carry out the American custom of carrying you over the threshold to make you feel better about marrying a Bakhtiari tribesman," he said as he kissed her passionately on her ruby lips. "Now I want to make love to you in my favorite place."

He crossed to the bedroom which had a large bed covered with a brilliant colored Bakhtiari shawl and many colorful pillows. Slowly he laid her on the soft bed and began to unbutton her blouse, caressing her small but firm breasts and kissing the nape of her neck. As she began to sigh, he undressed himself and lay next to her, stripping her of her remaining clothes. Then the lovemaking began.

It was well past noon when they rose from the bed and showered together in the large bathroom. When they had dressed and went into the living room, they found tea, fruit, and sweets waiting on the library table, that they devoured with relish.

"I really love this little place, Zahrajunam. I had it built while I was away at Oxford getting my degree. I knew that when I got back home, I wouldn't want to live in the house with my mother and father. My father had given me this small piece of land when I turned eighteen and it's where I first became so interested in the Asil Arab horses that have become one of my passions. Now I'm passionately in love with you and want to share it with you."

"I love it here, too. It's so cozy and charming. And Mehdi, I think I'm falling in love with you. I wasn't really sure to start with, but I think we're right for each other. You're a tender and compassionate lover and seem to understand me so well. I want to tell you that I do love you."

"That makes me feel so happy, my *junam*. Now I guess it's time we made our way over to our real residence. Everyone will be waiting to meet the new Khonume Bakhtiar. But tell me first how did you like Khatum, the little mare?"

"You made a believer of me. Now I want to learn everything about your Asil horses. I can't wait to get to know them better."

They rode slowly back across the desert towards the house in Andimeshke, stopping now and then to hold hands or kiss as they went.

13

Her lips aflow with sweet sugar,
The sweet sugar that aflows in Khusestan
Nizami

Ali 1979

As he looked up at the door, willing Zahra to open it and come out, he remembered the time she had taken him with her to visit one of the local sheikhs whose land was an hour's ride from Aghili. It was a sunny, cool day in Azar (November) with hardly a cloud in the sky, definitely a beautiful day for a ride across the desert.

"Ali, ride with me to Mohamad Hossain Khan's. He's having a hunt this afternoon and I know you'll be interested to see that he hunts with birds. Well, actually they're falcons," she told him.

"I have heard that some of the Qashqa'i are still using falcons to capture small animals, but they could never get a gazelle or large animals, could they Khonume?"

She explained that there were large eagles that had been used in the past which could indeed take down a gazelle, as they worked as a team. But Hossein Khan hunted small animals, such as desert rats and rabbits, and mostly hunted for the fun and sport. In the time of Cyrus the Great (6th century B.C.), falcon hunting had been a most important sport. Nowadays there were not many who continued with it, so it was a treat to have been invited by the sheikh to attend his hunt.

When they arrived, it seemed all was ready. There were many people milling around the four birds that were tethered, hooded, on their tall perches beside the black wool tent. Ali and Zahra were greeted, and of course, they were then invited to sit down on the carpets laid out and were served tea and fruits as was the custom. The sheik explained to them proudly that these Saker falcons had been bred by his tribe over the centuries and were believed to be some of the fastest birds in Iran. The best one he pointed out was an almost white bird that was nearest the tent; he would handle it himself. His sons would manage the three others which were varying shades of speckled mahogany brown.

When they set off into the desert towards the

foothills on the horses, there was a melee of riders following. The four falconers each had a falcon perched on his wrist as they headed out towards the hunting grounds. After a half an hour, the followers were signaled to stop, as the hoods were taken off the birds and they were set free. They flew high on the thermals, using their excellent eyesight to spot small animals on the ground below. The white bird was the first to fold its wings high in the sky, go into a swoop and soar towards the ground like a rocket. At the last moment, before hitting the desert floor, it opened its wings again and hit a small rabbit killing it instantly. The Khan galloped up to where the kill had taken place, swung off his horse, and stood a short distance from the bird. As he slowly walked nearer, the falcon spread its wings to protect its prey, but his master folded them back against the bird's body, and without hesitating took the small animal in his hands. He cut off its head and proudly fed it to the now contented bird.

The day continued with many more kills. On their ride home, Zahra and Ali could talk of nothing more than the thrill of the sheer heart-stopping beauty of watching the falcons descend at lightning speed. He would never forget that day.

Zahra

Zahra had been studying the photograph of herself riding Shahab, the beautiful dark bay Asil stallion she had taken to riding when she was out on the land alone. She was wearing a colorful Qashqa'i scarf and dark glasses. The horse was an older stallion of around sixteen years, and knew the lay of the land so she always felt perfectly safe riding out alone on him. He was well trained in hunting gazelle and crossing the desert at a gallop. She was looking to the side of his perked ears and white blazed face, in the picture and she remembered that on that day she felt that she had been born to live in the desert. Mehdi had taken the picture as she rode into the stable yard.

It didn't take long for her to settle into the life in Khuzestan. The house seemed to run smoothly without her having to pay much attention to it. Zahra saw that the servants knew their jobs and did them well. Most of the staff had been with Mehdi for years, and some of the older ones had been there in his parents' time. The kitchen staff had routines for the meals they served that were probably as old as the house. But they were all good, so why make any changes?

Mehdi had many friends and acquaintances who came by in streams to visit him and meet his wife. It seemed during the first few weeks, the big beautiful house was always full of people at mealtimes. Though most everyone spoke Farsi, there were some who spoke a Bakhtiari dialect she knew she would have to learn because Mehdi used it himself with some of the older servants and friends who came by. Khuzestan was inhabited by many ethnic groups including Arabs, Lurs and Qashqai people, so there were many dialects, but most people spoke and understood the Persian language.

Their mornings were spent on horseback so Mehdi could show Zahra his lands. Most of it was within the environs of the Andimeshke area which was in the northwest corner of the province where the fertile Khuzestan plain met the Zagros Mountains. The Karkheh River passed by the city, and there are many natural springs in the region as well, which made it suitable as a habitat for various peoples which dated back to five millennia B.C. Khuzestan could be divided into two regions – the rolling hills and mountains of the north, and the plains and marshlands of the south. The whole area was well irrigated by its many rivers and thus it was well-suited to agriculture. Sugar cane had always been grown in the province and some say its name was derived from the sweetness of sugar.

Both Mehdi and Zahra had an enormous interest in agriculture. She, because of her small farm in Nowruzabad and her two years of studying about it at Cornell University, and he because of his vast land holdings of thousands of hectares of Bakhtiari lands that he had inherited from his father. His farms produced sugar cane, wheat, barley and some legumes, all of which he marketed in the local bazaars. There, it was purchased and sent off to Tehran and some foreign countries. His most recent endeavors included palm and citrus, as well as olives, which were grown in the mountainous areas of his land holdings.

He proudly showed all of this to Zahra, who was enthralled with the whole operation. The only problem, as she told him, was that there were so many rivers and streams that had no bridges in the area. When they rode in those areas, they would have to ford the bodies of water with their horses, and many times they were quite deep. At some crossings, there were boats for people to ride in and carry their goods in, but the animals had to cross the water themselves.

One day, as they were crossing a rather deep stream with the water over the horses' bellies, Zahra said, "I think it's dangerous that there are no bridges to cross the rivers, Mehdi."

"It has always been so," was his reply.

"But it doesn't need to be so! Why can't we build ferries that are big enough for horses and cattle? It would be easy, and they could be pulled by pulleys and ropes from one side to the other. There are plenty of men who need work, and they could man the ferries at certain hours. Think about it, *junam*."

Mehdi looked surprised. "You know, that is a brilliant idea. Why didn't I think of that myself? I guess I just needed to marry an American educated girl from Tehran to come up with a great idea. When we get back to the house today, lets draw up some plans, and then we can decide the most important places to start with these ferries. You know, many animals and some people are lost in the waters when they are high and flowing quickly. This will be a great safety measure. I will fund it myself to start with, but I think if we go to the Khuzestan and the central government, we'll be able to get funding for our project." Now he sounded really excited about the plan.

"Is this something you can just do? Won't you need to get some official approval?"

"Zahrajunam, I am the Khan. I can do what I want, and I want to do this for the people of Khuzestan," he replied. "Have I told you how much I love you lately?"

They designed and built their first model to cross the Ab-e Fath River that needed to be negotiated to get from Andimeshke to Dezful which was a much-travelled route. This was the way crops and animals went to market so it was a good place to start. When Mehdi presented his plans to build more ferries to the Minister of Agriculture in Tehran, who was a good friend of his, the financing was guaranteed almost immediately. And so, travel in Khusestan became much easier and agriculture would grow in this area, the most fertile place in the country. An offhand comment from the new wife of Mehdi Khan Bakhtiar would make a big difference to Iran. It was her first important contribution to her country, but it wouldn't be her last. She had no idea at the time that she would become a very important personage in the history of the Pahlavi dynasty.

Zahra's two years at Cornell had taught her a great deal about farming, and the more she rode around with Mehdi on his lands, the more she realized that the methods used in Khusestan were those of the Dark Ages. The land was extremely fertile and the abundance of water in the area would make it conducive to producing abundant crops if it was properly managed. At the time, the farm workers did all the work by hand or with oxen, mules, or donkeys, using primitive utensils to work the ground and plant the seeds. In New York, there were machines that did the plowing and planting in less than half the time, and the harvest with the large combines reaped more of the produce, thus providing a greater financial gain.

One afternoon when they were at Aghili, they had worked some of the young two-year-old horses in the morning, and then had a lazy luncheon made by Nahid, the young wife of the head groom. Later, they headed to their favorite bed to make passionate love in the cool of the domed apartment in the heat of the day.

Suddenly, Zahra had an inspiration. "Mehdijuman, are you awake?" she asked softly.

"I guess I am now," he said groggily.

"I just had this idea while I've been lying here next to you, relishing how lucky we are to have each other, and how we've grown to love each other so much."

"I suppose you want to build more ferries, do you?" he chuckled.

"No, no. I was just thinking how easy it was for you to get the funding for our ferries and how successful they have been. So why can't we bring over farming machinery to mechanize the farming in this part of the world, like it is in the States? We would be able to produce so much more than we can now with these primitive methods. Khuzestan is the breadbasket of Iran just like the plains are of the States. We could buy the equipment from Europe or America and work some sort of sharing program for the farmers in this area. I think it would be a great idea."

"My darling, you amaze me. I agree with you. It's a good idea, but I'm not made of money. I couldn't afford to bring over large numbers of tractors, plows, seeders and combines and such," he said.

"I think we could go to His Majesty himself with the plan. You're good friends with Prince Golam Reza and you know the Shah. You could ask Golam Reza to arrange a meeting with his brother. Mohamad Reza Pahlavi wants his country to be modernized and I'm sure we could persuade him to fund such a project."

"Zahra, Zahra. If you can get all the facts and figures together, I will talk to Golam Reza. I agree that it is a great idea. Why didn't I think of it myself? Now come over here and let me make love to you again."

There were many pictures in the Big House in Andimeshke that Zahra studied so that she could better understand Bakhtiar family and the life in this part of Iran. During the Kadjar dynasty, Khuzestan had been called Arabistan, and functioned as an autonomous emirate with the eastern half governed by the Bakhtiar khans and the western part ruled by the Qashqai Sheikh Khazal. But when Reza Shah came to power, he dissolved these emirates, along with other autonomous regions in Persia, in a bid to centralize the state. There were daguerreotypes on the walls of many of the Bakhtiar ancestors. They were posted in the reception rooms for all to see the tribe had ruled for so many years.

One picture in particular interested Zahra; it was of a group of Bakhtiari tribesmen with their horses, standing around a felled gazelle with huge long horns. "Mehdi Jun, what is this picture about and who are these men?" she asked one evening as they were walking into the dining room to have dinner.

"That's my father, his brothers, and some of his workers after they had hunted down a fine old male gazelle," he answered. "We used to hunt them on horseback often, but not so much anymore. The horses were trained to hunt almost without direction from the rider. It was fantastic fun."

"I have read about it but why don't you do it anymore?"

"Mostly because we are always so busy with the land and the horses. I really don't know."

"I think it would be fun to do some time."

"We will, one of these days."

A few days after this conversation, Zahra was out riding by herself on a spring evening, checking on some workers at one of the field camps. She was cantering along on the older stallion she often rode that needed some exercise, when suddenly the horse bolted. This didn't worry her because she was an excellent rider, and she knew she'd be able to stop Shahab, but she was puzzled by his action. She looked around, thinking that possibly hyenas or dogs were following and had frightened him. She looked behind them but saw nothing. As she turned back, zip, zip, zip, one, two, three gazelles went flashing across her path! The horse wanted to hunt them.

When she got back to the stables, she told Mehdi about the incident, and he said, "Oh yes, Shahab was one of the best hunters of gazelle. I always loved riding him on the hunts."

"Well, I think we need to go on a gazelle hunt very soon. He would like to do it again. Please, won't you arrange it?"

"I'll get a group together for *Jomeh* if you like. We'll make it a party and have a big lunch afterwards. I'll get in touch with a few of the nearby sheikhs. I'm sure they'll all love a day's hunt."

As the group gathered the day of her first hunt, the men all began talking of hunting in the past. They described feats that had been performed by this horse or that man, and who had killed the finest gazelle, which day, how long it had taken, and which horse was the fastest and best hunter. And on and on. She was the only woman in the party, because generally women in the tribal areas took care of their men and families and were seldom participants in sports activities.

Gazelle hunting by the Bakhtiari method needed a great deal of patience, and good judgement about speed and distance. The chances of the gazelle escaping were about seventy-five per cent. The hunters, once they spotted the gazelle, would start riding at a walk in a large circle around them, usually no more than two hunters together, slowly decreasing the circle. The gazelle would become agitated, jog off a distance, stop, change direction, start off again, and eventually start to canter. All the while, the stalkers had to stay calm, keeping the pace to no more than a fast walk. Not until the prey made up its mind as to the direction of escape, and began to go into a smooth run, and then to run flat out, so that nothing could persuade it to change direction, did the hunter unleash his horse to a converging course diagonal to that of the gazelle. That first burst of speed of the gazelle was about ninety kilometers an hour, and thus there was need for proper calculation. The horse then began to gallop full out. At this point the rider would put the reins in his left hand, and they would be totally loose because that hand would be supporting the barrel of the gun. The terrain was usually fairly flat, but there were rocks, rat and fox holes, dry flood beds, and other debris. It was the horse that had to make the decisions while galloping at full speed. The distance it ran depended on the angle and speed of both the gazelle and the horse. The choice of the angle and maneuvers, when nearing the gazelle, was where the expert and amateur separated. The gazelle needed to pass within a convenient shooting distance in front, if the moves were correctly executed. Too slow, the gazelle was gone. Too fast, they passed behind. The good hunter needed to be a good shot and a good acrobat on a horse.

Zahra watched as a spectator to start with, but once three gazelles were bagged, Mehdi rode over to her, and said, "Now it's your turn. Are you ready to try for your first gazelle?"

Of course, the ever-identified "Tomboy" was prepared to take her chances. Zahra had brought the gun her father had given her on her thirteenth birthday so that she could go into the mountains with him to hunt mouflon. She had been a good shot in those days, but she hadn't done a lot of practicing since she'd come back home. She was game, though. And after all, she was mounted on the proven hunting horse, Shahab. The group rode closer to the mountains to find a herd. After about a half an hour, a small group of gazelles were found at the edge of a rolling field. She and Mehdi began to circle the animals slowly, and after several minutes the gazelle began to canter. The next thing they knew, the gazelles were running. Shahab took off after them without Zahra having given him the signal; he was in control! Her reins were completely loose, and she gripped her rifle tightly so as not to drop it. As the horse veered off at the correct angle, she tightened her leg grip so that she wouldn't fall. When she neared the gazelle, she leaned over to the left and with the horse still galloping, she took aim and shot. The gazelle went down and Shahab, knowing his job was done, slowed down and stopped by the carcass.

"*BARAKHALAH KHONUME!*" The whole group of hunters were cheering, Mehdi loudest of all.

"You are amazing, Zahrajun!" he said. "I can't believe that you shot and killed your first gazelle on your very first try. I knew I married you for a reason." He laughed.

Back at the Big House during a delicious luncheon, it was decided by all that this would be the first of many hunts. They would try to go out as a group once a week. And so, the Bakhtiar took up the sport again, with a vengeance.

As time went on, they would go to Tehran every couple of months for Zahra to see her mother and check on Nowruzabad, and for Mehdi to take care of his own businesses and keep in contact with the many influential friends and politicians that were a necessary part of his life. During the summer months of *Tir*, *Mordad* and *Shahrivar,* they would spend most of their time in Tehran and at the Caspian because during those months it was unbearably hot in Khusestan.

Slowly Zahra began to learn about the breeding of Mehdi's precious Asil horses. She had so fallen in love with the breed that she decided not to bring her own special horses to the south. She left them at Nowruzabad, where she would ride when she was there. There were many strains of the Asil horse in the Middle East, but in Khusestan, where there were still many nomadic Arab tribes that bred them the Wadnan Khersan, Koheileh, Obayan Sharak, Saglawi and the Hamdani were the most prevalent, but of course there were many sub-stains from each of these major strains.

The Arab sheikhs, who were the protectors of the Asil, had certain regulations of breeding that were carefully adhered to by the majority of the tribal peoples. They believed that most traits of the horse were carried only through the female line. For instance, a mare of the Koheileh could be bred to a stallion of a different strain, but the foal produced from this mating would be known by the dam's strain. If it were a filly, it could be again bred to a third strain, and so on. However, the decedents would always be known by the name of the first dam's strain. Most tribes would have no more than two or three strains, usually breeding back to the original strain every second or third generation. The only real danger was in-breeding, due to the fact that the sheikh would be displeased if members of his clan took their mares to be bred to another sheikh's stallion. The stallions were kept by the sheikhs for use by his tribesmen.

The horses were mostly bred for *biaban* (meaning for the desert or the wilderness, for fighting, long distances, speed for hunting, etc.) while a few were bred for *khiabansharbatehm* (meaning horses for showing off, festivities, etc.) The *biaban* Asil that was bred by Mehdi needed first of all to have five specifications of character: Courage, Intelligence, Stamina, Spirit, and above all *Nejabat* (a mixture of nobleness, gentleness, and the ethics of an aristocrat). If it lacked these virtues, no matter how pleasing to the eye, it was considered useless.

Once it was determined that the horse had the five qualities, its confirmation was considered. The forehead needed to be wide, the eyes large and alive, the ears well placed and alert, the neck connection slender and refined, the shoulder sloping, the girth deep, and the canon short. It was believed that an accentuated dish face was a deformity; the head needed a straight nose connecting to wide flared nostrils. The flat croup was desirable only in certain strains, but overall, the tail should be carried like a flag. Each tribe or family that owned a strain considered their horses superior to all the others. No matter which group she talked to, they believed that, and even Mehdi thought that his horses were the best. "But Mehdi, everyone I have talked to says their horses are by far the best, even you. As your wife, I believe that our horses are wonderful but how can I really know which are the best?" she asked him one day.

"Zahra Jun, there are good horses in all the tribes. Arabs are neighbors and warriors. They fight often between themselves, and the conqueror takes all the best stock from the other. In this way good horses are taken from one tribe to another, so it is therefore more accurate to say that the strongest tribe gets the best. At present, the Bakhtiar tribe is the strongest," was his answer.

"So, let me ask you a question. How do you know the pedigree of your horses is Asil or as you call it pure?"

"All the sheiks that have Asil Arab horses know the pedigree of their horses back to six generations," he explained.

"But where do you keep the papers on your horses? I have never seen any," Zahra said.

"'Papers? We don't need papers. We have everything in our heads."

She didn't understand how the sheiks could keep all the information of the mating and births of their horses for six generations in their heads without forgetting some things. It was impossible. In America, the Arab horses were registered with World Arab Horse Organization which managed and recorded the pedigrees of all Arab horses and registered every pure foal that was born, if the owners submitted the information. Each approved and registered foal would be given fancy-looking papers with gold seals that the owners would keep as proof of the lineage of their horses.

The World Arab Horse Organization (WAHO) had its headquarters in England and was the worldwide registration for pure Arab horses. Mr. Williams had shown her some of his Arab horses' papers when she was at their farm in Virginia. She had also seen the papers of Thoroughbred horses that he had. She knew that many countries had their Arab horses registered with the WAHO so why, she wondered, did the Iranians not do that too?

"We have tradition here *junam*; we do not need papers to keep our horses pure. Most of the Arab tribes have been nomadic until recent times and some still are. Can you imagine having to carry all those papers around wherever they went?"

"Well, I'm going to sit down with you and your brothers and whoever else will give me their time and record the pedigrees of every Asil horse we have. And then, when I have our horses all recorded, I will start going to the sheiks I know and record their horses too. Then one day there will be a Persian Asil Arab stud book." She decided this would be one of the goals of her life.

"My darling, you may do as you like but this project will take you a lifetime," was his comment, but she didn't mind.

Mehdi, who was kept very busy managing the agricultural part of his own eight thousand hectares, and the many more thousand hectares of government lands he rented, thought it would be a good idea to let Zahra be the one to manage his precious herd of Asil horses. Even though they spent many hours every week together inspecting the crops and talking to the workers, he knew she needed something that was her personal responsibility to keep her happy. She had less and less to do with the Nowruzabad farm now that she spent most of her time in Khuzestan, and she and her mother had hired a manager who was doing very well with that small farm.

So, one afternoon during foaling season, when they were at the Aghili property having an enjoyable nap after the mid-day meal, he decided to broach the subject. They were lying, spent, on the big bed above the stables after they had delivered a strapping big bay Saglawi colt a few hours previously. He began stroking her back tenderly, "I've been wondering, my love, if you would do something for me?"

"You know I'd do almost anything for you, but right now I'm enjoying just lying here with you, and I don't want to do anything else."

"I don't mean right now," he said. "I've been thinking that since you've developed such a passion for my horses, you should be the one to manage them. It would take one thing off my mind. I believe you have a great eye for the horses, and also since you have been working on the pedigrees, you would enjoy being in charge. In essence, it will become our herd not just mine."

"You would let me manage the care and the breeding program too?" she questioned.

"That is what I meant. You would be in complete charge. Of course, sometimes I would want

you to ask me for advice, so I don't feel completely out of it. You know I never like being left out,"
he chuckled.

"I can't believe it. You really want me to take
on the horses? I would love to and I promise I
will always want your advice. Why, you have the
best horses around, and I want to keep them
that way. Yes, thank you *junam*, you make me
so happy. I will make you proud." She rolled
over to kiss him passionately, and they made
love again.

14

With them the seed of Wisdom did I sow,
And with my own hand labour'd it to grow:
And this was all the Harvest that I reap'd—
"I came like Water, and like wind I go."
Omar Khayyam

Ali 1979

Ali walked back to the Land Rover to make sure Zahra's bags were stacked securely so they wouldn't move around as they drove over the bumpy track to the ferry. He opened the rear hatch which was almost full and re stacked the three suitcases that were all quite heavy; at least they weren't on the roof this time he reflected.

He recalled the time they had driven to Tehran to get some of Zahra's things from the house she had grown up in there. So many things were stacked in the old vehicle that they had to put two of her suitcases on the roof. As they drove down the hilly, winding street, one of the bags fell off and they had to stop and run back for it. Unfortunately, it burst open as it fell from the top of Rostam and there were clothes all over the street. Ali stood in the middle of the road, directing cars to pass around them, as Zahra shoved her things back in the bag as quickly as she could. Cars were honking and she laughed as he, embarrassed, directed the traffic.

Zahra

She had to smile when she looked at the picture of Mehdi sitting on the big red Allis Chalmers tractor. He was grinning ear to ear with the many farm workers and neighboring sheiks standing around to see this, the first of many farm implements they had ordered, as well as plows, seeders and combines.

It had been several years after their marriage that she and Mehdi had gone to Tehran for supplies. On the drive, Zahra began to talk again about mechanized farming. Mehdi had imported a brand-new Land Rover that was very comfortable and rode smoothly even over some of the rough roads they encountered on their desert and mountainous route. The many hour drive was a perfect time for her to have his undivided attention. Their crops had been plentiful the past few years, but she still felt with tractors and combines, they would be able to harvest much more wheat and barley, which were the prolific crops that were being grown in Khuzestan at the time.

Zahra had read in the newspaper that came to the Andimeshke house every morning that the Shah was planning to institute a type of land reform. Minister of Agriculture Hassan Arsanjani had announced that many of the large land holdings would be redistributed. At present, most of the Iranian land was owned by wealthy individuals and cultivated by peasants in a cooperative type system, with the main profits going to the land holders. In the tribal areas, the Khans owned large tracts of land around their villages, which the tribal peasant members farmed. The majority of the income went to the Khan and the rest was divided up amongst the tribesmen. Mehdi rented open government lands as well as cultivating his own nine thousand hectares, so this redistribution would probably affect him personally. It was reported that the minister wanted to introduce profit-oriented and mechanized farming, along with giving the peasants, who he believed were capable of running their own affairs, a stake in the product of their own work. She believed that this plan would take some time to implement, but meanwhile her idea of mechanized farming was definitely in the air.

Zahra threw her ideas out to her husband whenever they came up. "I'm thinking, Mehdi, that this time when we're in Tehran, it would be a good time to get together with Prince Golam Reza and tell him about our plan to bring mechanized farming to Khuzestan. We could invite him to dinner at our house and see what he thinks about it. Then maybe he could arrange something with his brother," she started the conversation.

"Zahrajun, you are too much! You mean *your* plan!" he replied. "You have been going on about this for quite some time now. Yes, I think it would be good for Khuzestan but, do you really think that you would be able to persuade His Majesty to fund such an expensive program?"

"I do. Especially after reading that he wants to introduce some type of land reform. I have all my facts and figures and just need the opportunity to present them. I am very persuasive, as you know, and I know that the Shah wants the best for his country. Why if enough wheat is produced, Iran could become an exporter and compete in the world markets. If Khuzestan can prove that mechanized farming works, the whole country could have it."

"Now don't get carried away. We'll start with Khuzestan. I'll try to see Golam Reza tomorrow and broach the subject with him, but don't expect much to happen," he promised.

The following day when she arrived back at the house after having spent the day at Nowruzabad, she was surprised to find Mehdi in the library waiting for her. He was usually home late when they were in Tehran, because he needed to spend time with his brothers, three of whom worked for the National Iranian Oil Company (NIOC) in important positions, and they were all quite the talkers when they got started. She had thought he was going to be with them that afternoon.

"Come here my little magpie," he said taking her in his arms and kissing her. He then went over to the bar where there was a chilled bottle of champagne. He opened it and poured two glasses. "A toast to my brilliant wife!"

"Well, thank you, but what brings this on?" she asked.

"When I had lunch with Golam Reza and mentioned your plan, he was really interested. He thought it was an excellent idea and is going to talk to his brother about it tonight when they have their usual *Chahar Shanbeh* family dinner. He said he'll telephone me in the morning and let me know what the Shah says."

The next morning, when Zahra was spending time with her mother, she could hardly contain herself. Louisa noticing how distracted she seemed, asked her what was the matter. She blurted out the whole story and couldn't seem to stop talking. Her mother had never really recovered from the shock of Hassan's death, so she enjoyed seeing how exuberant her beautiful daughter was feeling.

"Zahra, it makes me so happy to see that you are so enthusiastic about your life and that you're truly happy with Mehdi. You remind me of myself when Hassan, may *Allah* rest his soul, and I were first married. I'm so happy things are turning out well for you after the losses you endured a few years ago."

Three nights later, she was carefully dressing to go to Niavaran Palace to have dinner with the Shah and Shahbanou. She had gone over her facts and figures a hundred times that day so that she had all the projections memorized and wouldn't have to be reading some paper scrunched in her hand. She had never before been to the palace or met the Shah, but she knew Mehdi had many times, because he and the Shah were about the same age and had known each other as boys.

"I'm so nervous, Mehdi. I just hope I don't make a mess of this presentation," she said as they were getting into the chauffeur-driven Mercedes.

"You don't need to be, Zahrajunam. Mohamad Reza is a pretty down-to-earth guy and Golam Reza has already broken the ice for you. If he wasn't really interested in your plan, he wouldn't have bothered to invite us to the palace."

As they drove through the gates into the lush Niavaran parklike garden, she saw the large clean-lined modern building of marble tiles, bronze and glass, lit up on all sides. The car drove up to the obelisk-pillared portico and they walked up the wide, marble steps to the tall solid glass doors which were opened to them by a liveried servant. They were ushered across the black stone floor of the great hall that had an aluminum sliding roof. The roof was open to the clear evening star-studded skies. They entered the alcove that she later learned was the family room, with its French designed furniture and magnificent Kerman carpet that depicted kings back to the time of Achaemenes.

As they entered, the Shah, who had been seated on a sofa with the Shahbanou, rose to greet them. "Mehdi, it's so good to see you. It has been a long time. And this is your wife, Zahra, about whom I have heard so much. I'm so pleased to meet you." He put out his hand, which she took, and then she curtsied as she thought she should to her king. He introduced both her and Mehdi to the Empress Farah.

"Sit, sit, please," he told them as the servant came to see what they wanted to drink. Mohamed Reza did not drink alcohol, just wine occasionally, so they both opted for tea, Iran's national drink.

When Golam Reza arrived (he had been divorced from his first wife a few years before, so he was alone) the subject of mechanized farming for Khuzestan was broached and Zahra was given the floor. Her palms were wet, and at first her voice shook a bit, but as she talked, she gained confidence for she knew her facts.

By the time she had finished, the Shah who had been listening attentively, was smiling broadly. "*Barakalah*, Zahra. That was an excellent presentation and a brilliant idea. I will definitely present this plan to my cabinet and I can guarantee that Khusestan will have all the equipment needed to bring the farming level to modern times. To tell you the truth, I think we need to implement this plan in other parts of the country, too. Mehdi, I'm going to appoint you to head up the project, with Zahra's help of course. As soon as it is ratified, we'll get started." Mohamed Reza Pahlavi was definitely a man of action.

With the help of the Shah and the government of Iran, Mehdi, as the chief of the Bakhtiari tribe, was the benefactor of the project, providing financial aid along with his knowledge and time. Zahra and Mehdi worked tirelessly with the local chiefs, introducing them to the machinery and the more modern and efficient ways of growing their crops and feeding their animals, so that they would have a better income in the ever-changing life in Iran. The crop production in the Province of Khuzestan increased, the project was a great success and continued to be in the "Breadbasket" of Iran.

Over time, life in Khusestan became better than Zahra had ever dreamed it would be. The horses occupied a good part of her time and she was helping Mehdi with the massive amounts of paperwork her farming project had handed him. The fields and planting needed to be watched over and then there was the harvest time and the marketing of vast tons of grain that was being produced. She had become totally, completely, in awe and love with her wonderful, exciting, and handsome husband. Things could not have turned out better for her. She thanked *Allah* and God every day.

One early evening, she had come into the Big House in Andimeshke after a day at the Aghili stable, and she was getting ready to have a shower before dinner. The house boy knocked on her door to tell her that her mother was on the phone for her. She was a bit concerned as Louisa seldom called her; it was usually she who called her mother. Louisa told her that Anne Williams had telephoned to speak to Zahra and she had given her the Andimeshke telephone number. Apparently, Anne had something important to tell her.

Zahra was surprised because she and Anne had not kept up their correspondence over the past years. Anne was happily married and had at least two children and Zahra too, was happy in her life. She couldn't imagine why Anne would be calling her.

The following day as she was about to leave the house the phone rang, and she instinctively knew it was Anne. She picked up the receiver. "*Bali,*"

"Zahra, is that you?" The voice cracked over the long-distance line.

"Yes. Is that you, Anne? Mother told me you were trying to contact me. What's up? How are you?"

"I'm well. It's good to hear your voice. I have something to tell you. Are you sitting down?"

"Do I need to be?" She wondered what Anne had to tell her.

"Tom is alive! He was captured in battle and

we thought he was taken to a Korean prisoner of war camp, and he was declared dead. But it turned out he escaped and was hidden away by a Korean family. They took care of his wounds, and when he recovered, he assimilated into the life of these people. He lived with them in the countryside of North Korea where life was terrible, but after five years, he was finally able to get across the border to the South, and he's being flown home as we speak."

She couldn't speak. She had a new love and was married and living a blessed life in her country. This had nothing to do with her life. She had loved Tom, certainly, but he had no part in her life now. What was she expected to do about this? She was happy he'd survived but their love and life together were finished. Should she feel guilty that she couldn't love him now? What was Anne expecting her to say?

"Oh, Anne, I'm so happy he's alive. Your mother was right to have faith that he would come home. For me, my life has changed. I've grown to love my husband and I'm very involved in life here in Iran. Please tell him I'll remember our times together with great fondness, but I'm now a different person and things can't go back to the way they were."

"I thought that's what you would say. One of the first things he asked when we spoke to him was how and where you were. I, of course told him you were back in Iran and married. He seemed disappointed, but if he has endured all he has, I'm sure he will be fine with things. Do you want me to give him this number so he can call you?" she questioned.

"No! I don't think I could handle it. I mourned his death when you told me he was presumed dead. I'm sorry, but I just can't go back. I wish him the best and I'm sure that, like me, he'll find someone to be with and learn to love, but I just want to keep my good memories. Talking to him would cause me too much anguish. You are my good friend, so please understand."

"I guess I do. I, stupidly, have just been hoping you would want to come back to him."

"Anne, you must understand that I couldn't possibly do that. I know that I told you I was dubious when I agreed to marry Mehdi, but I've grown to love him, and he adores me. I'm happy and have a place in life that is fulfilling to me. We're working on farming improvements that will help our whole country. The Shah himself backed our plan of mechanization which was so exciting. We spend most of the time here in Khusestan, which is the most beautiful place imaginable. No, I wouldn't change my fairytale life for anything. I'm sorry." She then asked about Anne's husband, children and her parents, who were all well, it seemed. Then each wished the other a fond farewell and they hung up.

Because of her commitments to Mehdi and her busy life in Khuzestan, Zahra wasn't able to spend as much time in Tehran and her interest in Nowruzabad had been waning. According to Louisa, the manager was doing a fine job, but profits were small and she felt it was too big a responsibility for her to handle alone. Also, without Hassan's business deals, money was becoming a problem. It seemed that one of the neighboring landholders had offered her a very good price for the property, so she felt it was sensible to take the offer. She would sleep more easily with a little nest egg in the Bank-e Melli, she told Zahra. Zahra was not happy with the idea, but she realized it made sense. She knew her mother was getting older and still felt the loss of her *baba*. She kept herself occupied with her afternoon teas and the card games with her other widowed friends, but she didn't seem her old self. She couldn't be persuaded to visit Andimeshke for some unknown reason, and so she spent her time with a few servants in the big house in Tehran. Zahra missed spending time with her mother, but they did speak on the phone almost every day.

One spring morning after the planting had been finished, Mehdi told Zahra that they were going to take an excursion. He'd heard of a Saglawi mare that he wanted to buy from one of the Arab sheiks of the Hoveishi tribe that was camped nearby on his way to the northern summer grazing pastures. She was excited because she had become greedy about collecting mares of that strain, so they set out on their horses for the ride across the desert. When they arrived at the camp, Sheik Salman first invited them into his tent, where he served them tea, sweets and fruits. They passed the time of day discussing the new farming methods, and the merits of this or that horse, until Mehdi finally broached the subject of the mare of interest.

When the said mare was brought out for them to view, they were disappointed because she did not look the typically Saglawi. She lacked the good looks expected by the strain. She was quite tall and muscular with a lean body and a neck longer than normal for the Saglawi. Her head and eyes were not as well shaped as expected, though she did have a fine sloping shoulder and good depth of girth. Just the same, Majid liked her, but no matter how he tried, the sheik kept politely refusing to sell the mare. He offered him a Jeep, any type of armament he wanted, planting crops for him, and any other ridiculous things he could think of, but still the sheik refused. Finally like the fox with grapes he couldn't reach, who decided they were sour, they consoled each other, deciding that she was not a good representative of the strain, and they left.

Several months later, Zahra was driving back from the fields during harvest time when she saw a rider galloping full speed on the plain. What arrested her attention was that he was not moving in a straight line, but circling, zigzagging and turning back on his own tracks, all at full speed. Puzzled she drove closer and saw that there was a gazelle running in front of the horse, which she recognized as the Saglawi mare ridden by Sheik Salman. She stopped at a distance and watched as eventually, the gazelle exhausted, lay down beneath a bush and Sheik Salman descended and cut its throat.

When she drove up to him, he smiled saying, "Now do you understand why I cannot part with this mare? She is fantastic. I have owned and seen many horses, but only one out of a hundred can do what she can do. For this reason, I have not bred her, though she will shortly be ten. I will wait a few years more."

That evening as she was telling Majid the story about the elusive Saglawi mare, the servant came to tell her that there was a call from Tehran. She excused herself and went to the hall where the phone was located, expecting it to be

Louisa. Instead, the voice of Dr. Riahi came over the line. "I'm so sorry to tell you this," he said. "Your mother was found dead this afternoon. She had been having some arrhythmia with her heart the past month or so. She was resting after lunch, and just didn't wake up."

Mehdi heard her howl and went running into the hall to see what was wrong. He took her in his arms and hung up the phone. When he finally got her calmed down, they went to their room to pack their bags and then got into the Land Rover to make the long drive to Tehran to commit Louisa Kadjar into the hands of *Allah*.

Zahra had barely recovered from the loss of her dear mother when she arrived at the Aghili stable early one morning to check on one of her mares that was due to foal. Golam Reza was waiting for her at the gate and seemed agitated, which made her think that there had been a problem with the mare. "No, Khonume! It's not your mare. She's fine, but it's two other horses. Bahram, the Khan's favorite horse, seems to be having trouble breathing. His breaths are very labored and then the mare you bought from Sheikh Khabir last week is coughing a lot. They're both sick. Please come and look at them. I'm worried."

She went to see the two horses, both of which

seemed to be in distress and depressed. She went to the feed room to fetch her thermometer so that she could take their temperatures, and when she did, she saw that they both had a high fever. She told Golam Reza to get two grooms to take them out to give them a cool bath while she prepared syringes of phenylbutazone to inject into their veins which would help bring down the temperature and stop inflammation. She had no idea what could be wrong with the horses but she didn't want the other horses to be in contact with them so she moved both of them to an out-building at the far end of the stable yard, and told them to have their vacated stalls disinfected with soda lime powder and not to put other horses in them. She thought probably the latest addition to the herd had brought in some sort of infection.

After a busy day checking the fields and visiting with several nomadic groups that were camped nearby, she decided to go back to check on her two sick horses. As she entered the stable block, she heard coughing. She knew the sick horses were not in the main barns, so she followed the sounds and saw that one of their best breeding mares was coughing up a frothy fluid from her nose and mouth. She quickly prepared a syringe to inject the mare, for she could see she had a fever without taking the temperature, for she was sweating profusely. She told the Golam Reza to bathe the horse with cool water and then walked by every stall, looking in to examine each horse. She discovered that several were coughing and had a white discharge coming from their nostrils, and a couple were standing stretched out with their heads hanging between their front legs, obviously having difficulty breathing. What could be wrong with all these horses?

She'd done some equine study while at Cornell, but though she searched her mind, she couldn't pinpoint the symptoms she was seeing. She told Golam Reza to take the temperatures of all the horses and have any that had a fever bathed in cool water. She would ride back to the house in Andimeshke where she had her Equine books to see if she could discover what was afflicting her and Mehdi's beloved horses.

After about an hour of reading, she came across the disease that she thought her horses must have, African horse sickness! According to her book, there were three forms, pulmonary, cardiac and fever. The pulmonary form which she was sure was the strain affecting her horses was the worst. It said that the disease was characterized by high fever, depression, and respiratory symptoms. The horse would have trouble breathing, start coughing a frothy fluid from the mouth and nostrils and show signs of pulmonary edema within four days. The lung congestion would cause respiratory failure and result in death within hours. It said that up to ninety per cent of infected horses die.

As she read on, she learned that it was variant of the Bluetongue virus of sheep which was principally carried and transmitted to horses by the Culicoids species of midges or mosquitoes. The disease was seasonal, usually associated with drought followed by rain, which was just the weather they'd had in Khusestan. Surprisingly enough, it was not directly contagious but could remain in infected horses for many days, enabling it to be transferred via biting insects. The only way to prevent the disease from spreading was to use insecticides to kill the insects and screening. The latter would be impossible, but they did have some insect sprays in the stables, and she knew they would be able to get more sent to them quickly.

She and Mehdi decided to move to their apartment over the stable at Aghili so that they would be near the horses and be able to help keep them as comfortable as possible. They wanted to supervise the administration of the spraying and wiping the horses down to help eradicate the insects There was no known cure for the disease and so they knew they'd have to watch as their precious animals died. Mehdi, who truly loved his horses, decided that he didn't want to see them suffering, so when he could see that one or the other was in real distress, he would take out his pistol and shoot it directly in the head so it would suffer no longer. They both felt so completely helpless, they could hardly speak to each other nor to their faithful grooms and their families.

For two weeks everyone at Aghili was like a zombie, watching horses die and then be dragged way out into the desert where they would be devoured by vultures and wild animals. When there were no more sick horses, only thirteen mares and three stallions were left from their herd of seventy. They slowly realized that, compared with many of the other sheikhs, they were lucky, for many herds had been left with only three or four horses and some had lost all. They were still young enough to rebuild the herd that had been in Mehdi's family for generations, and which his father had left to him as his legacy. Of the sixteen horses they now had in the stable, luckily each one went back the six generations that Zahra had been recording in her now diminished stud book. She would be tearing out pages from the book, but she would also have to visit the many other khans to see which of their horses had survived.

15

Ali 1979

Finally, he heard the door above open and he saw the Khonume step out onto the porch. She was dressed in loose white cotton pants with a colorful striped jacket and a white headscarf covering her now greying hair, which was tied in a knot at the nape of her neck. She had a large shoulder bag made from a piece of Bakhtiari carpet on her arm. She was wearing large sunglasses on her tanned face. She looked spectacular, he thought. She walked slowly down the stairs to where he and Golam Reza were waiting, and he could see that she had been crying when she took off the glasses; her eyes were red rimmed and misty looking.

She walked over to Golam Reza and touched his arm. "You have been a good and faithful friend to me all these years I have been at Aghili. I want you to know how much I appreciate everything you have done for me and all your support. I'll miss you when I am gone, but I will come back, and I pray to Allah that you will still be here then." She hugged him close to her.

Zahra

The picture of her and Mehdi on their horses in the stable yard at Aghili was one she loved, because the future had looked so promising to her on that occasion. Together they were going to rebuild their herd and they were also going amongst the tribes' people to help to make their lives more profitable.

The Shah's White Revolution was intended to be a non-violent regeneration of Iranian society through economic and social reforms, with the ultimate goal being the transformation of the country into a global economical and industrial power. Novel economic concepts such as profit-sharing with workers and massive government-financed heavy industry projects, as well as nationalization of forests and pasture-lands, were introduced. The most important aspect was the land reform programs which saw the landed elites of Iran lose much of their influence and power. Socially, the platform granted women more rights and poured money into education, especially in the rural areas.

The changes did not really affect Zahra and Mehdi, with the exception that Mehdi was expected to sell a small portion of his lands to the government at a fair price. The government then sold it to peasants at thirty percent of the market value, giving them a loan payable over twenty-five years at a low interest rate. For him, it actually turned out that those who bought his land threw it in with his holdings and they sharecropped as they had previously, with the exception that they gained a larger portion of the profits.

There were some problems though, in some of tribal areas not far from them. The Qashqa'i confederacy began in the eighteenth century as an amalgamation of diverse tribal groups including Turks, Lurs, Kurds, Arabs, Persians and Gypsies. They practiced a mixed economy of nomadic pastoralism (sheep and goats, with camels and horses used as transportation), cultivation of grains and weaving. Their long seasonal migrations of over three hundred miles between their winter lowland and summer highland pastures in the Zagros Mountains took them by the large southern city of Shiraz, where they marketed their goods. These tribespeople, who were almost all still living the nomadic life, would not agree to mechanized agriculture when it was offered to them; they did not want to settle. So, slowly land was taken from them and pasturelands were nationalized; tribal land that the Qashqa'i had regulated and controlled became government land and its use was restricted. This caused the tribe to take up arms and have skirmishes with government authorities and other tribes. They felt that the land reforms, which were rumored to be backed by the United States, did not consider the interests of the local people.

Shortly after the African horse sickness ordeal, the Governor of the province dropped in to see Zahra and Mehdi. He wanted to discuss the farming project that Mehdi was heading as well as the devastating loss of horses that had been incurred throughout the area. As he was leaving, he mentioned that he had been asked to tell them that the Minister of Agriculture and Tribal Affairs, Amir Khosrovi, wanted to see them in

Tehran on their next trip there.

The Minister seemed extremely pleased with the way the mechanized dry farming project was progressing and praised Mehdi for all the work he was doing to promote it to the landowners. However, he had a surprise for Zahra. He wanted to appoint her in charge of tribal affairs in their region, which would include Khusestan, Esfahan, Fars and Lorestan. She was shocked when he told her this, for she didn't feel she was knowledgeable enough about the tribal systems in the area as she had not lived there her whole life and how could she truly understand the situation.

"We feel confident that with your husband's guidance you'll be able to deal with any situation you come upon when you're working with the tribes. We're trying to get more tribes to desist from their nomadic migrations and settle down on lands that have been redistributed. As well we have government lands that need to be farmed and the tribes could gain better income from that. We are also planning to make it mandatory for the nomads to obtain grazing permits before they commence their migrations," Amir told her.

She knew that the government had been trying to persuade the nomadic tribes to settle in permanent homes in villages, but she personally believed they should be able to live the nomadic life they had been living for centuries. Their economy was based on livestock, mostly sheep and goats and some cattle, which they would sell as needed when they passed through villages and towns. Seasonal migrant tribes moved in the spring to their more northern countryside and spent part of the spring and summer months there. Then in the autumn, they would return to their southern winter quarters where some had clay or stone houses. Shepherd nomadic tribes migrated from one place to another during the year, lived in tents, followed the pasture and the water and had a single-based economy in livestock-keeping. The men tended the animals and any crops they grew, while the women were the homemakers and wove the colorful woolen tribal carpets. How could she represent the government in tribal affairs when she disagreed with its tribal policies?

"Your Excellency, I do not believe I am qualified for the job. My husband would be the more experienced person to hold the position," she said.

"Khonume Bakhtiar – may I call you Zahra?"

"Of course."

"It has been decided that you will have the post. His Majesty was the one to make the recommendation, so it would be impossible for you to turn it down. You'll be reporting directly to General Hossain Pakravan, the new head of *Savak*," was his reply. "We expect you to mingle among the tribes to see what the overall consensus is about settlement and if it's true that the majority of the tribe's people do not want to desist from their nomadic ways. We want to give you a platform that may persuade them otherwise."

"*Aghaye* Khosrovi, during the time I've lived in the south, I have spent considerable time travelling about among the tribesmen and their families. But I've always been with my husband, and our mission was to encourage agriculture or find new Asil blood for our herd. I have no influence with any of the tribes, so this will be a difficult task for me," she reiterated, for she really did not want this position that was seemingly being forced upon her. The Minister seemed unwilling to change his mind, though, and their conversation finally came to an end.

Upon their return to Khuzestan the following evening, they went directly to the stables at Aghili. They wanted to see how the horses that had survived the plague were doing, and to spend a quiet few days in their favorite home without having people drop in all the time as they did when they were at the Big House in Andimeshk. Zahra, as she had promised, had written down the pedigrees of all their horses for six generations. After dinner, she got her ledger out and she and Mehdi sat side by side studying the lineage of the sixteen horses they had left. Occasionally they would look at the breeding of one or the other of the lost horses with regret that the lines were probably lost forever. Between them, they decided that with only three of their own stallions left, they would have to find surviving stallions and mares of quality, with bloodlines that would be compatible with their own horses, which were owned by other tribes and sheikhs. It would be a long process, but they agreed that they would build their herd to be the best in Iran no matter what it took.

After they reviewed the breeding lineage, Zahra discussed her potential new position with her husband. "I hardly know where to start as far as the tribal affairs are concerned. And I will tell you, Mehdi, I am nervous about reporting to the general. I've never met him, but on the few occasions I've seen him at functions, he appears to be an intimidating man. I guess that's why he was appointed as the head of Savak; it is an intimidating organization," she commented.

"Well *junam*, I think we can work at building up the herd and at the same time, we can discuss with the tribes the idea of a sedentary life that would be easier and more prosperous.

We'll need to travel about, seeking out the few good quality horses and bloodlines that remain in order build up our Bakhtiari herd, and what better chance to talk to the nomadic people?"

But Zahra was skeptical. "You know how hard it will be to persuade any of the sheiks and khans to sell us their horses. Remember the Saglawi mare? And then to try to persuade them to give up a life they've been used to for thousands of years; it's crazy! I can't imagine it working, ever."

"All we can do is try, my love, on both counts," he said, always the eternal optimist. "I think I had better fill you in on a little history of the Bakhtiari so that you'll have a better understanding of us and of this part of Persia." He put his arm around her shoulders, and she snuggled up to him as he began his tale about the tribe of which he was one of the most important khans of the day.

It was in the fourteenth century that the name Bakhtiari first appeared as the name of a *tayafah* (tribe) when it had entered Persia from Syria. The *tayafah* was made up of smaller sub-tribes called *tirahs,* which in essence were families or clans, and each had a *khan*, or leader. It was historically considered a dauntless, uncivilized, and unprincipled group of herdsmen on a ceaseless and ageless quest for pastures for their flocks. They feuded with each other and raided villages and farms, terrorizing the sedentary peasants and other Persian tribes in the area that straddled the Zagros Mountains of Khusestan and Esfahan.

It was difficult to trace the history of the tribe because the Bakhtiar dialect had no written form, but by the eighteenth century, their leaders had emerged as major contenders for power in the country. They participated in the deposition of Muhammad Ali Shah and the restoration of the constitution.

Meanwhile petroleum seepages had been evident for centuries, in what had become Bakhtiari territory. Since time began, gas and liquid oil excretion, called *bitumen,* that oozed through cracks in the rocks, had been used as mortar for brick laying, linings for water channels, caulking for boats, setting jewels, and lighting fires. So it was that the Russians, Germans and British all became interested in investing in Persia. It was, however, the British William D'Arcy who secured the concession for exploitation of natural gas, petroleum and asphalt in the Bakhtiari lands in 1901.

Finally in May of 1908, oil in commercial quantity was found at the drilling site near Masjid-e-Suleiman. This discovery was a milestone and a turning point in the history of Persia and it also brought the British and the Bakhtiaris together out of necessity and mutual goals. The Anglo-Persian Oil Company was formed with fifty-one percent of the shares being bought by the British Government. The company would purchase lands from the tribe and there was a protection agreement under which the Bakhtiar Tribe would protect the installations and the pipelines that were being built to transport the oil. In addition, the Bakhtiari Oil Company was formed from which the tribe would receive three percent of the profits of their part of the parent company. All had been happy with the arrangement.

Then when Reza Shah had himself elected king, he set out to break the power of the tribal leaders who might try to threaten his attempt to centralize the government. The autonomy of Bakhtiaris began to diminish as he, intent on reducing their influence, at first through military power and later through economic and political reorganization, arrested and imprisoned their leaders. He divided the Bakhtiari lands between the provinces of Esfahan and Khuzestan, and finally ordered the khans to sell all their shares in the oil company to the central government. At the same time, the British chose not to support the Bakhtiari and their khans.

The politics of the Second World War forced

Reza Shah to abdicate because of his pro-German leanings. At the time, though some of the old Bakhtiari khans were still living, most did not seek their old positions, as their armies had been depleted and the young men were not trained to be tribal leaders. Instead, they concentrated on restoring their lands that had been confiscated by Reza Shah. By that time, most of the *tayafah* leadership was divided. Given inherent family rivalries, decreasing incomes and uncertainty in relations with both the central government and the other tribes, the great khan families were unwilling to commit their assets to re-arming the Bakhtiari and re-establishing a political role for themselves from a tribal base.

After he explained their regional history, Mehdi kissed her on the cheek and said, "You see my father and his family were able to regain all of their lands in 1941, when Mohamad Reza took over from his father. One reason was that my father had gone to school in Switzerland at the same school, though he was older than the Shah by several years, and he'd taken the shy young Persian boy under his wing to help him get adjusted when he arrived at Le Rosey. The other reason was that, after his divorce from Princess Fawzia of Egypt, he married my cousin Soraya Esfandiari-Bakhtiari, whose father was Persia's ambassador to Germany. When she became Queen, her influence helped us regain the land and we were paid a settlement of millions. And then the Shah appointed my father, Arab Shehbani Khan to the head of the NIOC. That's why we are so well situated now."

"So, you're telling me that your family or clan became the most powerful of the Bakhtiari confederation because of their connections with the Shah?" she asked him.

"I would say yes to that. There are many other *tirahs* (sub-tribes), but lucky for me, my father, descending from his own father and uncles, became a great khan and thus my brothers and I have many advantages over other khans. You see, we also accepted sedentarization while most of the others refused and are still nomadic," he explained.

Zahra and Mehdi began spending at least two days a week visiting the tribespeople in the area to see what horses had survived the plague. They also used these visits to talk to the head men about the advantages of accepting lands that were being given out by the government to any of the nomadic people who would consider settling. When they went to visit the nomads, they would usually have Golam Reza scope out the area to see where the nomads were camping and then ride out on their horses. On days they had to travel a distance, they would take one of the Land Rovers and drive across the slightly rolling brown desert sands, often ending up in the foothills of the Zagros where the Qashqai were most often found. It was sad to see how few of the fine Asil horses were left. They lamented their losses with the khans and sheiks and often offered to buy this mare or that stallion. But seldom were their offers accepted.

In their part of Khuzestan there were many tribes in addition to the Bakhtiari. Close by there were Arab tribes, and of course the Qashqai were prolific. Each tribe or sub-tribe was known for the foundation of certain strains of the Asil, and each time they went to visit a different tribe they heard tales from the past of the horses of the strain the tribe was known for.

One cool, rainy day they went to visit Sheik Hajat who was said to be one of the most authoritative men who knew about the dispersal and fame of the Asil strains in Khuzestan. He had an enormous brazier of red-hot charcoal set out for them, and once they had warmed themselves with tea, and had partaken of sweets and fruit, the conversation turned to the discussion of the different expectations of certain strains of horses.

"From the Hamdani, you will find courage; from the Obayan Sharak, lightness and mobility, causing it not to tire quickly and to be useful for fast maneuvering. From the Koheilans, and there are many strains, stamina and the ability to outrun other strains over long stretches such as when chasing gazelle," the sheik told them. He continued by stating that the Djelf was tough, but he ridiculed its wide-spaced ears.

"And what about my Saglawi?" Zahra asked.

"Oh, they are just for show," Sheik Hajat said. Zahra was incensed that he did not think highly enough of her favorite Asils.

Sheik Farham of the Al Kathir tribe, whom they visited one day, told them a story from the past about his tribe's horses. At one time, there was a tribal war going on between his tribe and the Kaab, who were being supported by the British. Sheik Farham was worried because he knew that the Sheik Khazal of the Kaab had obtained nine cannons with which to attack the Al Kathir tribe. They were apparently approaching from the foothills and at the time, were hiding with their cannons behind a hillock, waiting for an opportune time to attack. The Sheik had sent all of the women and children to an island in the river to hide, and if everyone was killed by the cannons, as he was certain they would be, they were to do away with themselves so they would not be taken by the Kaab.

About that time, his son came riding up shouting, "Father, you have forgotten that we have the Hamdani. They will not be afraid of the cannon fire. How many cannons do they have? No matter! We shall jump into their stockades with our Hamdanis and do away with the men firing on them." So, they mounted and attacked the fortifications of the nine cannons of Sheik Khazal, jumping in with the Hamdanis and beheading the men manning the guns. That tale demonstrated the courage of the Hamdani Asils, the sheik told them.

Another sheikh who was from a family of *Seyyid*s (descendants of the prophets) whose *Tefagh* (tribe) was known for its line of Koheilan Adjuz, told them the story of how their Asils became so revered in the history of the Arab horse. In ancient times the grandson of Sheik Ahmad, the head of the tribe, was in serious trouble. It was said that the only way for him to save himself was to get to Bagdad and get the rulers to intervene for him. As the sun set, and he was in danger of being pursued, he mounted his strongest Koheilan mare and rode toward the distant city. He continued until he reached his destination, stopping only for brief rests and to give his mare a handful of barley and restricted amounts of water. The distance was eighty-eight *farsangs* and each *farsang* was six kilometers. which was a total of five hundred and twenty-eight kilometers. When the sheik's grandson arrived in Bagdad, he was declared innocent and was saved. The mare became known as "Koheilan 88 farsangs" and her descendants had been sought after by many since that time. The day they visited, the Sheikh was obviously in a generous mood. No, he would not sell the yearling filly that descended from the mare, but he would give it as a gift to Mehdi Khan Bakhtiar. This became their first acquisition after the plague.

As they entered the courtyard of Majid's friend, Sayyid Nour, one midmorning, Zahra noticed a grey stallion standing saddled and bridled with the reins tied behind the saddle. She was taken by his lean and tremendously muscled body, strong legs, and the sloping croup of the Koheilan. Shortly after arriving, Zahra had walked back though the courtyard to get something from their Land Rover and noticed that the stallion was no longer there. As they were sitting drinking tea and eating fruits, she heard the clattering of hooves from the courtyard and guessed that the horse had returned. Arab women were so used to unexpected guests, who were not allowed to leave without first being given a meal – lunch or dinner, depending on the time, – that something was always produced in an unimaginably short time. On this day, however, they waited quite a long time. When the food finally arrived, there was a huge platter of grilled gazelle meat which was a real treat and a rarity. Usually, the meal consisted of cooked lamb under a bed of rice with an accompaniment of dates, yogurt or possibly grilled chicken. Sayyid Nour asked their forgiveness for the tardiness of the meal, explaining that he was aware of the Bakhtiari fondness for grilled meats, particularly game, and upon their arrival he had sent his son out with the grey Koheilan to catch a gazelle!

And over the next months and years, they spent their time searching for Asils that would fit into their breeding program. They were seldom able to buy mares because the sheikhs and khans would never sell or trade a mare of good lines. However, they would sometimes give them as gifts, and as time went on Mehdi and Zahra were gifted several additions to their herd. It took many years but the Bakhtiari herd finally reached the number forty.

Zahra began to travel the countryside, working with the tribes alone and searching for horses, because Mehdi was spending more and more time in Tehran. He was selected by the Shah to supervise several joint ventures that had been signed by Iran and the United States. There was an aluminum plant that was being built in Arak by Reynolds Metals Company, a deal to build General Motors cars and several other projects that were being handled by the Iranian

Development and Reorganization Organization (IDRO), and he was expected keep an eye on them. It didn't please her, but she realized that the country was developing and would hopefully become a world power. Who was she to criticize that?

She loved the life in the beautiful country-side of Khuzestan and began to feel that she too was a tribesman. She even began to wear men's pantaloons and a Qashqai cap on her head. As the years passed, she would seldom go to Tehran with Mehdi unless there was a meeting or event that she was expected to attend. She still owned the house in which she had grown up, that had been left to her upon her mother's death, but she had rented it out to expat Americans since then. There were times when there were social obligations and Mehdi wanted her with him so she would grudgingly do as he asked.

But more and more, she was becoming anti-social. Occasionally she would go to the city to report to General Pakravan, and since she had been able to persuade several tribal groups to accept government lands and settle, he was pleased with her work. She still believed that the nomads should be able to live the life of their choice, so she was not overly enthusiastic when discussing the sedentary life with the tribal leaders, and seldom went out of her way to do her work in tribal affairs.

When Mehdi was able to come home for a few days here and there, they would be kept busy planning their farming strategy, the management of which had fallen into her lap now that he was not able to spend as much time as he wanted at home. They'd always find time to ride out in the desert and the foothills, looking over the land and crops as well as visiting with their neighbors and nomadic friends. They needed to show their presence at the house in Andimeshk while he was in Khuzestan, but they always made a point of spending a day or two at their love nest at Aghili. There they could forget all their real-life problems and enjoy each other without interruption.

Zahra had been working on her book of pedigrees since she first began to manage Mehdi's horses those many years before and she had collected information on Asils from many of the sheikhs and khans in the region. So, her stud book was becoming a tomb. The compilation actually consisted of several large ledgers, each labeled for one of the many strains or sub-strains of the Persian Arab horses. She was proud of her work and always excited to show her dear Mehdi what she had accomplished since their last time together. In return, he was always amazed and full of praise for the intricate and tedious work she was doing to record the lineage of the horses that were so dear to him.

"Zahra *junam*, you are an amazing woman. I never dreamed you'd be able to record the pedigrees of all these horses," he said one evening as they were sipping a glass of cognac after dinner on the porch of the apartment at Aghili.

"I'm not nearly finished, you know. There are so many more horses to be recorded, I sometimes wonder if it will ever be done. As sad as it is, the many horses that died have made the job a bit easier. Luckily, however, many of those famous old horses do have a few progenies that will hopefully carry the lines forward."

They had developed a special close relationship over the past few years that allowed each of them their independence, though they relied on each other for undying love, understanding and support. Mehdi and Zahra both felt they were the luckiest people in Iran. When he was away without her, she knew he enjoyed his life of work and social obligations, hob-knobbing with the elite of Tehran's society, but she knew he would never think of cheating on her. She was happy staying in Andimeshke and Aghili, taking care of their land and horses, and being amongst the good people of the tribes.

It was late in 1970 that she received a gold

embossed invitation to attend a meeting of the newly formed *Anjoman Sultanate Asb* (Royal Horse Society). The Shah himself had a love of horses and wanted the Persian breeds to be saved and recognized. The Master of the Horse, Bahman Mansarpour, had been instrumental in starting the society and had named Crown Prince Reza as its patron. The aim of the group was to preserve and improve native Iranian breeds, to establish official stud books for the breeds, and to promote and develop equestrian sports.

At that time the most prolific breeds were Asils, Turkomans, Kurds, Fars and Darashuri. However, the American wife of a Prince of the Kadjars had rediscovered an ancient breed dating back to 3000 BC. It was actually this discovery that had precipitated the idea of this new organization. Louise Firouz had been looking for small ponies upon which to teach riding to her young children and their friends when she discovered a few small horses near the town of Amol in the Caspian area. She was taken by the elusive beauty of these small equines that were only about eleven hands (44 inches) at the withers. She began to do research on the small horses that she'd found on the lush shores of the Caspian Sea.

Her research into their nature and historical

precedent, which started in 1965, proved that they were the forerunner of the Arab, and had been thought to be extinct. Dating back to the time of Darius the Great, these small animals' images were found on ancient coins and the carvings at Persepolis. She had started a breeding program with seven mares and six stallions and was instrumental in persuading the powers that, be that Iran needed a registry for all the horse breeds. This was like a song to Zahra who was already working on her Asil stud book.

For Zahra, it was a reason for her to go to Tehran with Mehdi, who had taken up flying and bought himself a four-seater blue and white RC-3 Seabee that was an amphibious plane. The plane was well suited to Iran and the lifestyle of Mehdi, who could land either on an airfield or on the water such as the Dez Dam which was so close to Andimeshk. The dam had been completed in 1963, becoming the biggest and the highest dam in the country; its primary purpose was to produce hydroelectric power and irrigation. The Seabee reminded her of a fat swallow with its bulging belly, but it did make the trip to Tehran much more palatable for it took many hours off driving. Mehdi had been lucky to find the plane through one of his friends who was in the Air Force. Now he'd be able to get back to his beloved Khuzestan and wife more frequently.

She first rode the plane on her way to a meeting at the *Anjoman*. As she boarded, Zahra said, "Mehdi, I can hardly believe that we're actually going to fly to Tehran. This is so exciting! When you told me, you were learning how to fly, I never thought we would have our own plane." He held her hand to steady her as she stepped onto the plane from the dock. As the little plane gained speed over the clear blue water of the dam, and soared up into the sky, her ears popped.

Once in the air, she gazed down at the beautiful Khuzestan countryside, shades of brown dotted with green oasis and long straight lines of round, sandy mounds denoting the paths of the *ganats* (underground streams). As they ascended, the rugged Zargos Mountains loomed ahead with the wide desert on the north side of them. They flew towards the majestic Alborz range and on toward Tehran where they landed at Doshun Tape, the air force runway that was in the southeast part of the city right next to the Shah's Imperial Stables.

The meeting, held in the office of Bahman Mansarpour in the Imperial Court office complex on Pasteur Avenue, was quite productive. It was decided that there would be a main stud book for all Iranian breeds that would be sub-sectioned to include the Asil (pure Arab), Caspian, Darashouri, Fars, Kurd and Turkoman horses. Zahra was made the director of the Iranian Asil section and of course Louise Firouz would head up the Caspian horses. The plan was that each breed would have its own director, and the equine sports would each have their own autonomous department. The Royal Horse Society was to mandate and control all equine interests in the country. The Society would be a part of the Imperial Court of the Shah, which meant that there would be court ministers and well-connected military personnel that would be inputting their opinions and trying to gain control as those types were wont to do.

One night, when they were getting ready to leave the big Tehran house to go to a dinner party, Zahra said, "I think this organization is a great idea for the horse world of Iran, Mehdi." She added, "I do think, though, that poor Bahman will have his hands full. With me, Louise and the Canadian trainer of His Majesty's horses, Cathy Johnson, who he has made head of show jumping, all three women, and basically not really Iranians, it will drive the old colonels mad. And they in turn will drive Bahman mad. You know what they're like, -so officious! And they all resent the fact that Bahman was given his position of Master of the Horse. You know how he got the position, don't you? His father stepped down in order to let him have the job, so he could gracefully get out of the military, which he didn't particularly like."

"I wouldn't worry about Bahman, Zahra Jun. He's clever, and having been brought up in the court, he understands all the nuances of it. As well, he is one of the Shah's personal assistants so he will have his ear. No, he's a strong man who I'm sure will be able to keep things under control."

After a week full of meetings for them both, during the days, and dinner parties and receptions in the evenings, they were happy to get in their small plane to fly back to the more sedate desert life of the Bakhtiari. They checked on the crops and the goings on about Andimeshk, and of course got in a little gazelle hunting with their tribal friends. They spent several days at Aghili, enjoying their time together and planning the breeding of their slowly growing herd of Asils as well as riding across the desert lands for the sheer joy of it. For Zahra, it was the perfect life, to be with her partner in love, in the land she loved. How lucky she felt.

One morning early, when they were at Aghili, the telephone they had installed, much against Zahra's better judgement, began ringing as they were having their breakfast of fresh orange juice, squeezed from their own fruit, along with date compote, fresh *nun-e-barbari* and tea. At first, they ignored it but as it began to ring incessantly, Mehdi excused himself and went to answer it. He was gone for quite some time, so Zahra was convinced it must be from Tehran, which would probably mean that he would have to go back for some reason. She had plans to work on her stud book and to go about the countryside gleaning information from some of the sheikhs from whom she had not yet been able to get full pedigrees of their horses. She knew how important this would be, especially now with the new registration book being planned for the whole country. She had no intention of going back to the bustling, traffic-filled metropolis where she would be expected to don her uncomfortable city wardrobe and entertain or be wined and dined by Tehran's social set. That life bored her. She would stay put.

"Who was it, so rudely calling this early on a *Jomeh*?"

"It seems there's a problem with the aluminum plant in Arak. As you know, the celebrations to commemorate the beginning of the Pahlavi regime will be underway in *Shahrivar* [August] and there is a need for massive electrical power to light all the decorations across the country for this event. It has been asked that the plant shut down part of its reduction facility in order to supply the extra electricity that's needed. The engineers are saying they can't do that because it will freeze up the metal in the pots which, before they are put back into production will have to be drilled out with jack hammers to free the frozen aluminum, and that is a very expensive proposition. I need to go first to Arak, to try to negotiate with them and then to Tehran to make my report. Why don't you come with me?"

"I don't want to go to Arak. It's in the middle of nowhere in the desert. What would I do when you're having your meeting? No, you go alone, and then you can come back after you finish in Tehran. Anyway, I have things here I want to do."

The following morning, Zahra drove Mehdi to the marina at the dam, where the Seabee was maintained and kept. She walked out on the dock holding his hand, carrying his briefcase for him. He put down his bag and turned and engulfed her in his arms, kissing her passionately, "Are you sure you won't come along with me? You know I'll miss you."

"No *junam,* I'll miss you too, but you'll be back in a few days." She hugged him tight and they kissed again.

She watched from the dock as Mehdi's little plane surged on its belly through the crystal blue waters and gradually took to the air. He circled and waved the wings at her before he headed towards the north and the mountains. She walked back to the Land Rover climbed in, then drove slowly towards the house in Andimeshk. She had accounts and orders she needed to take care of for the farming operations, so she thought she'd need to spend a couple of days in town before she went back to Aghili and her horses.

On *Se Shambeh* (Wednesday) in the evening, she was just finishing her light supper of *baghali polo* (rice with beans) *khoresht-e-badanjun* (eggplant) and *nun,* in the office when the phone rang. It was Mehdi.

"*Azizam* (my darling), how are you?"

"Other than missing you, I'm just fine. I've stayed here in Andimeshk to catch up on some things that needed attention to do with the farming, but I hope to go to Aghili tomorrow and will wait there for you there when you come back."

"That's the problem. His Majesty wants me to go up to Ramsar for the weekend. He has some investment people coming and he wants me to talk to them about a new project. I'll fly down to pick you up in the morning and then we can go on up to spend the weekend at the house up there," he told her.

"Oh no! I don't want to go. You know I don't love the Caspian the way I used to. And I know there will be the usual partying every night. Please *junam,* let me beg off this time," she pleaded.

"I want you with me, but I understand how you feel. I don't really want to go myself, but I have no choice. Here's what I'll do. I'll fly up tomorrow and spend *Jomeh* there. Then I'll fly back home that evening and hopefully avoid any dinner party that night."

"That sounds like a great idea, my love. So just call me. I'll be at Aghili. Let me know what time to pick you up at Dez."

"Will do."

"I love you," she said, and hung up.

She rode Shahab out to Aghili on *Chahar Shanbeh* (Thursday), after she had finally finished with the paperwork that had taken her much longer than expected. The old stallion was kept at the Andimeshk stable, along with a few other semi-retired horses; he was still a joy to ride though he was now in his twenties. As she slowly sauntered along the track, she remembered the time she had shot her first gazelle from his back and thanked *Allah* for a blessed life. She thought she would leave the old horse in the stall to rest when she got there and get on one of her younger mares. Then she could go out to the desert with Ali to find Sheikh Khabir, whom she had heard had acquired a beautiful mare of the Koheilan strain just recently.

As she rode in the gate, she saw that Ali and two other grooms seemed to be looking up at the telephone pole, pointing and arguing. "What's the matter, Ali?" she asked.

"Zahra Khonume, there is no telephone. I tried to call you this morning but there was no sound on the line. We don't know what the matter is."

"Don't worry about it. I'm sure it will be fixed by the time we come back from our ride today. Will you please get Arrus ready for me and one of the youngsters for you? I want you to ride out with me to visit Sheikh Khabir so I can see his new mare."

It turned out that the sheikh was camped at quite a distance from her home and it took a couple of hours to reach him. But when they got there, they were of course served tea and fruits to start before they could see the new mare. When she was brought out for inspection, her light, golden chestnut coat seemed to shine like a new copper *rial*. Her head was straight with the hint of a dish, a large prominent eye, large nostrils and a muzzle as small as a teacup. She had a straight back and flat croup with a proud tail gaily carried. The magnificent animal had a pedigree to match her looks that went back the required six generations. Zahra, who had brought her camera, took many pictures and recorded the lineage as the sheikh told her. Naturally there was then a large meal to be served to the guests, so by the time she and Ali left, it was late afternoon. They would have to ride fast to get home before dusk.

When they rode into the stable yard at Aghili, Zahra asked, "Has Mehdi Khan telephoned yet?"

"Khonume, there is still no telephone, it is broken."

Oh well, she thought, when he landed someone from the marina would surely take him to the house in Andimeshk, and he would come out in the Land Rover. There was no need to worry. She sat down on the porch having poured herself a glass of *sharob* (wine) to wait for Mehdi. As the dark sky began to fill with bright desert stars, she wondered why he had not arrived yet. But then, as the moon came up, she decided that indeed he had been persuaded to stay for dinner and would probably not fly home until the next morning. He'd probably tried to call but with no telephone service, could not get through. She ate a solitary meal served by Golam Reza's wife and reflected on the enjoyable day she had. She couldn't wait to tell Mehdi about the mare. She knew Sheikh Khabir well and felt sure that if they offered him enough for her, he would sell them the beautiful Koheilan.

She awoke early and decided to ride Shahab back to Andimeshke in the cool morning air so that she could be ready to meet Mehdi when he arrived. Surely, he would call the house to let someone know when he would be arriving. On the ride across the rolling sands towards the river, the old stallion was feeling good and jigged and bounced, looking for gazelle. Once they had crossed the shallow river, she let him have his head and he galloped like a youngster. She felt the wind whistling around her ears and through her flowing hair. What a day it was!

As she got closer to Andimeshk. she saw dark clouds forming on the horizon and the wind began to blow, so she moved Shahab on, in order to avoid the rainstorm that was brewing. These sudden storms often blew in at this time of year, and she hoped this one wouldn't delay Mehdi's arrival for she knew he wouldn't fly in stormy weather. As she rode in the gate, she felt the first big drops of rain on her face. She patted her horse's neck affectionately, as she handed him to the boy in the stable yard, and then ran to the house, climbing the wide marble steps two at a time. She stood laughing, dripping wet, in the great hall.

As she entered, Azizeh, who had come to Khuzestan after Louisa's death, walked in to greet her with a grim look on her face and tears in her eyes. "Khonume, you are wet! Please sit down," she sobbed, ushering her to the ornate carved oak bench that had graced the hall since its importation from Europe by Mehdi's father when he'd first built the house for his bride.

"What's wrong, Azizeh? Why are you crying?"

"Khonume, there has been a crash! Mehdi Khan's plane crashed into the mountain in the north. He is dead, Khonume! He is dead!" She held Zahra in her arms as she began to howl, rocking her back and forth.

"No! No! No!" Zahra screamed and began to cry uncontrollably.

16

Death is a wedding feast,
And the secret of that
Is that God is one.
Rumi

Ali 1979

Golam Reza went to the passenger's side of
old Rostam to open the door for Khonume,
but she shook her head, saying that she wanted
to go to the stable before she got into the vehicle.
He and Ali both walked with her, but as she approached the main door, she signaled them to
wait there for her. They saw her enter the cool,
dimly lit building and knew she had gone directly to the stall of her favorite mare Khatum,
whom she had ridden for years across the desert to visit the many friendly sheikhs she knew.
She had often taken one or two other mares
that were ready to breed along with her, but

she never took another person. Then a couple of days later she would return with stories of her ride and hopes that the mares were in foal to this or that famous stallion of the Saglawi or Hamdani strain, which were her favorites. She would also go say farewell to her black stallion Arrus IV, who was the fourth generation of the Bakhtiar's most famous horse, Arrus, who had won many cross desert races in his life and had been one of the best gazelle hunting horses the tribe had ever had, according to the stories.

When she came out of the stable, they saw that she'd been crying. She had put on her dark glasses, but they could see wet patches on her cheeks. Together they walked across the sandy yard to the Land Rover and as Golam Reza held the door open, she got in. She gave him one more hug. Ali started the motor and she drove away from her beloved Aghili.

Zahra

As Zahra walked up to Khatum's stall, the mare nickered and walked to the front, to be patted by her mistress as she nuzzled her shoulder.

She reflected on the many exhilarating rides she had had on this beautiful chestnut mare with her flowing mane, riding beside her dashing husband on one of his favorite stallions during those wonderful years they had been lucky enough to spend together.

Majid's mangled body had been flown to Andimeshk on one of the Shah's military helicopters by his friend Manuchehr Khosrodad, so he could be buried at his family home next to his parents. All his brothers and sisters with their families had miraculously arrived in time for the *Khatm* that was held on the third day after the actual burial. The memory of that day, with so many family members and tribal sheikhs and their families filling the big house was just a blur in her mind. The only thing she wanted to do that day was to mount one of the horses in the stable and gallop across the desert to their favorite home at Aghili. This, of course was not possible, so she did her best to be the stoic grieving widow she was expected to be by all those who had come to give their respects to Mehdi Khan. On the *Hafteh* (seventh day) the family and many close tribal friends visited the grave to once again pray for the departed and read verses from the Quran.

Finally, the following day, she bade farewell to the many members of the Bakhtiar family, who were still staying in the Andimeshk house, and she rode to Aghili. She wanted to be alone to hopefully bring the spirit of Mehdi close to her. When she arrived, Golam Reza and his wife greeted her tearfully with open arms as the stable boys stood solemnly by. She went directly to the stable to see the horses that she and Mehdi had so lovingly cared for. She went up to each horse to stroke its face and neck and whisper, "Mehdi Khan has gone to be with Allah, so it's just you and me now. I'll do my best to care for you as if he were still here."

On the fortieth day she rode back to the Andimeshk house to be with the family and mourners when the black marble stone, identical to that of the ones of Mehdi's parents, was placed over his grave. The ceremony, presided over by the local mullah, was short and final; though it was forty days she knew she would never stop mourning the loss of her best friend, love, and husband.

During the open house that followed the graveside ceremony, she had noted the four remaining Bakhtiar brothers talking together, looking her way. She wondered what the scheming four were up to but didn't dwell on it. There were so many friends and acquaintances she needed to welcome and thank for coming. It was a long day, so she decided to spend the night in the Andimeshk house and go back to her beloved Aghili the following morning.

She was enjoying her breakfast of *nun-e-barbari* with butter and fresh pomegranate jelly and of course, tea, when the brothers entered the small office where she was sitting at Mehdi's desk.

"*Sob beher, Khonume,*" Majid, Mehdi's brother, the second oldest of the five, greeted her.

"*Sob beher, baradaram,*" she wished them good morning as her brothers.

"We have come to talk to you about a delicate matter," Karim, the third brother began. "You see, now that the forty days of mourning has passed, it is time to discuss the disposition of our dear departed brother, Mehdi's, assets. It is the custom of the Bakhtiar that when the Khan dies, his possessions go to his legitimate get, if he has children. Unfortunately, you and Mehdi never had any children and so, as is the custom, all his possessions, financial assets and land go directly to the next eldest brother, who becomes the new Khan. So, you see, Majid will become the Khan of our family and tribe and will take over everything that has belonged to Mehdi, and he will as well take on all his duties as the head of the tribe."

She sat there aghast, not daring to open her mouth to say a word. What did this mean, she thought? Were they telling her to leave? Were they telling her that she had no horses? Were they telling her that she had no money? Would she have to leave her beautiful Khuzestan? Silence rang in the room until Majid spoke.

"Zahra, you made our brother very happy and shared his love of horses, so we decided that as the new Khan, I will give you the *bagh* at Aghili and the twenty or so hectares of land that it encompasses. Of course, I will also give you all of Mehdi's beloved horses, for I know they are like your children. And also, some money to get started with. We hope this will make you happy. We feel badly that there is not more for you, but this is the way of the Bakhtiari, so you understand."

She sat there sipping her tea, unable to speak. She should have known she would be cast out of the family when Mehdi was killed. She was not born into the tribe and had not produced an heir for him. Though they'd wanted children and had never used any form of birth control, it just wasn't to be. They'd never really worried one way or the other about children because their lives were so full, as it was. She should be overwhelmed with gratitude by Majid's offer to give her some land and horses, but somehow, she still had the feeling she was being cast aside.

She'd almost singlehandedly managed the

farming operations over the past few years and she knew she would miss that; she loved checking the crops and spending time with the tribal workers of whom she had become fond. She loved riding across the land, seeing the green lines in the brown dirt turn into the golden heads of barley during the growing season. And then the huge combines, crawling across the fields of gold, spewing out clouds of chaff and collecting the nuggets of grain that brought prosperity to all those involved with the process, made her heart sing. She had always felt comfortable in the lovely Andimeshk house. Even though she loved being at Aghili, she would miss the life of being the wife of the Khan and the social prestige it meant, but why should that matter to her? They were giving her the horses and Aghili; she didn't need anything else.

"I thank you Majid Khan – if I may call you that – for the generosity. Mehdi and I never discussed the fact that either of us would leave this earth. It never crossed our minds as we were both still young enough and in good health. We did not imagine that the hand of *Allah* would take either of us for a long time. I know that he would want me to be able to spend the rest of my days at Aghili taking care of his horses and continuing to rebuild his herd for posterity, so I am grateful to you and your brothers for allowing me to do so."

"*Gorbon-e-shoma*!" The four brothers bowed their heads to Zahra as though she were still the wife of the Khan.

"I hope you will give me a few days to collect my things to move them to Aghili. And, of course I will be taking Azizeh with me; she has been with my family since she was a young girl and will want to be with me."

"No hurry Zahra take all the time you need," said the new Khan. "We will miss Azizeh and her heavenly touch in the kitchen, though. You, of course, will always be welcome to visit this house and stay in your room whenever you wish. We do still consider you a sister, Zahra June," the new Khan replied.

She knew she would never come back to the place where she and Mehdi had lived their formal life of being in charge of the tribe. No, she would be perfectly happy living her life at Aghili and taking care of her beautiful herd for the rest of her life.

She and Azizeh spent the next few days packing the things that were hers, most of which had come from her family home in Tehran. She took some of Mehdi's personal possessions and several of the tribal carpets they had bought when they travelled around the countryside during their years together. The small lorry she hired to transport everything the few kilometers to Aghili was full to the brim and laden down so that the tires bulged from the weight. In the end it took two trips.

Once she was settled in at Aghili, she realized that she couldn't stay the nights in the small apartment she and Mehdi had lived in; his ghost was there every night and she couldn't sleep a wink. This surprised her, for she had thought that being in their special place would comfort her and make her more secure, but it seemed that was not to be.

She decided to take some of the money the Bakhtiar brothers gave to her to build a small house for herself and her two German shepherd dogs. It would make sense for her to have a house that was big enough to entertain in and have a place to put the furnishings that had come from her parents' house in Tehran. The small apartment above the stable would make a suitable guest house for overnight visitors or even paying guests who might come to the area as tourists.

She enjoyed drawing up the plans and supervising the construction of the mud and stone building that would become her new home. The low foundation was made from stone and dried mud in the method of old that would survive for hundreds of years. The walls and domes were made of powdered mud mixed with straw and water that, after drying in the hot summer days, would last for a millennium as had the castles and forts that had been constructed before the Sasanian times which were still standing in many parts of the country. She kept the Old Persian architecture with domed ceilings in all four of the main rooms, while the kitchen and bathroom were appendages jutting out on the side with flat roofs that could be ascended by outside staircases and be used for sleeping under the stars in the warm summer nights.

It took just over three months to complete her house, and once she'd moved in it was time to think about breeding the few mares, she felt had the quality and pedigree needed for commercial sale. As much as the tribespeople did not ever want to sell their horses, she realized that she would need a way to make money to support herself and the herd, so she could be one of the very few people in the country who would sell young Asil horses of good conformation, temperament, and pure bloodlines. She believed that her horses would support her, not the other way around.

The three stallions she and Majid had left in the herd had crossed as many mares as it was possible considering their pedigree and conformation, so now it was it was time to bring in new blood. There were five foals that had been born the previous spring that looked like they would be very saleable when they turned a year old in a few months. They were being groomed and handled every day so when she visited the sheiks and khans, she would try to get interest in them in hopes of creating some income for the year. She would also go to Tehran where Asil horses were becoming popular; many wealthy men were interested in having show horses because they felt it gave them prestige. Show jumping, polo, and racing were important sports in and around the capital and some other big cities, but Arab beauty shows had begun to catch the eye of many people. Her young horses were exceptionally well-conformed and eye catching, so the show market should be a good place to offer them.

Her first step was to research the pedigrees of the stallions she knew were within a reasonable distance of Aghili. Since the sickness had killed so many horses she'd entered in her stud book, it would be difficult to find a stallion with the best pedigree to nick with her beautiful mahogany bay mare of the Koheilan line which was the first of the mares on her list to breed.

After much deliberation she decided on Sheik Amir's well-known stallion, Bahram, if the sheik would permit such a mating. Before she set off for the sheik's camp, which was a full day's ride away, she watched the mare, called Aziz, carefully to make sure she was in the most advantageous time of her heat cycle for breeding. It was a beautiful sunny, yet cool morning as she mounted her favorite riding horse Khatum, and started across the desert, leading Aziz.

Sheik Amir sat in his tent, proudly gazing over the sandy desert, observing his fifty sheep and his now small herd of horses that had been carefully mated for hundreds of years by his tribe. Suddenly he saw a cloud of dust, the indication of riders approaching. As the cloud got closer, he saw that the rider was the widow of Mehdi Khan Bakhtiar who had taken over his herd after his death. She was beautiful, but she was dressed as a man, wearing pants, a loose-fitting jacket and a Qashqai cap with the ear flaps folded up, as it was a spring day. She was alone but riding one horse and leading another. The horse she was riding was a lovely chestnut mare with a flowing mane and a wide white blaze on its face, but the mare she was leading was magnificent; it was a beautiful bright bay with a long graceful stride and an amazing presence.

She pulled up in front of the few small mud buildings and tent that were his winter home and said, *"Salam Alekhom."*

"Welcome" said the Sheik. "You have come a

long distance with your two mares. Come down and I will give you some tea and sustenance." He snapped his fingers at the servant boy who was seated outside a small building in the sand and the boy took her two mares, leading them to the water trough where they drank. Then the boy tethered them in a small enclosure beside the sheik's small stable.

As they sat drinking their tea and eating the sweets that had been brought by the old Sheik's concubine, they talked pleasantly about Zahra's ride from Aghili to this distant place. The Sheik brought his nomadic family there in winter as the weather was warmer and more pleasant than in his summer home near the mountains of Hamadan.

Finally, the Sheik asked Zahra why she had come to see him. He was not surprised when she told him that she had come to ask him to allow her to breed her beautiful mare to the sheik's famous stallion, Bahram. The sheik smiled and said, "I do not breed him to just any mare, you know. You must give me the lineage of your mare, back six generations, of course."

"That I can do. The Bakhtiar tribe also is very careful with our breeding program, as I'm sure you have heard. All of our breeding stock have pedigrees that go back six generations."

"I also need to examine her to see if she is

pleasing enough to my eye for me to permit Bahram to jump her when she is ready."

"I'm certain that she will be ready by the morning, as I have kept a watchful eye on her myself and I am sure you do not have a better conformed mare yourself that moves so well and has such a good disposition," she told him.

"There is one other condition you must fulfill, once I have approved your mare and her pedigree," the sheik said with a sly smile on his face.

"And what is that?" she asked, knowingly.

"If my stallion Bahram breeds your mare, so must you bed me."

Zahra knew of the sheik's reputation as a womanizer and had been prepared for this condition; to her it was not a problem. She knew she could easily give herself without passion, she had little or no money to pay for the services for her mare; her budget was very slim, and she had been dipping into her capital. She looked at the sheik, "So be it! The deal is done. My mare should be ready to breed by tomorrow and I will be yours tonight."

And so, for the first time ever she sold her body to help save and improve her small herd of horses. As it turned out, Sheik Amir was a kind man and was very considerate of her privacy. After a delicious meal of *khoreshts-e-badenjun* (lamb and eggplant stew), rice, and a mixture of many different greens, they sat drinking Turkish coffee and eating sweets served by one the sheik's concubines. When the meal had been cleared away, the concubine showed Zahra into a tent made from goat hair with many carpets on the floor and beautiful Qashqai hangings decorating the walls. She directed her to an area behind a screen where there was a long white cotton robe for her to put on. She was told to let her hair fall loose down her back for it seemed the sheik enjoyed caressing hair before he made love. She was ushered to a pile of pillows that were on the carpets beside a hookah pipe which she realized was ready to be puffed.

As she sat down, the sheik came into the tent in a long white robe with his colorful headdress still secured on his head by ropes. They began by enjoying the hookah, which she thought had a small amount of opium in it, as she began to relax. She had made love with only two men in her life, so she was nervous and not sure what to expect. But the sheikh was tender and very careful in his approach. It took more than the seven minutes she had read about in a book one time, but afterwards, they were both satisfied and she did not feel defiled as she had expected to. The sheikh got up slowly and left her in the tent, where she slept like a kitten until early morning.

When she heard the noises of the camp commencing for the day, she washed herself in the basin behind the screen and dressed in her travelling clothes. Then she went outside to see what was happening. She strode across to where the women were having breakfast of freshly baked *nun-e-barbari* and tea and helped herself. Shortly, the sheikh came to tell her it was time to breed her mare and they went across to the stable area. After examining the mare, it was decided she was ready, so the stallion was brought out and the coupling took place. Once it was finished, she thanked Sheikh Amir, mounted Khatum, and lead Aziz away towards Aghili.

As she rode into the stable yard late in the afternoon, her people were all waiting for her, eager to hear about her trip to visit the sheikh. She proudly told them about the mating of Aziz to the great stallion Bahram, which would, with the help of Allah, produce a beautiful foal in eleven months.

"Khonume, I was expecting that Sheikh Amir would only let you breed to one of his lesser studs; rumor has it that he doesn't usually breed Bahram to mares that have not been specifically selected by him alone. Either he was very impressed by Aziz or you were very persuasive yourself," commented Ali.

"It was a little of both," she answered. "Aziz

presented herself well, but I was a good nego-
tiator." Of course, they would hopefully never
know how she negotiated.

She spent the next few weeks going over
her herd carefully planning which other mares
she would breed this spring. She decided that
she would only mate five mares again this year,
which was the number she and Mehdi had been
breeding while they were building the herd
back up. It was a manageable number considering the size of their property and the number
of grooms they had to help with the work. Now
she had twenty-eight horses in the herd. There
were three stallions that could not be bred to her
young mares because their bloodlines were too
close, but she could duplicate two or three mat-
ings from the previous years, which would leave
only one other young mare that she could breed.
She'd have to find an outcross stallion that she
felt would bring good blood into her band.

Her final decision was to breed the five-year-
old Saglawi mare she called Mojghan, to one
of Sheikh Khabir's younger stallions. She and
Mehdi had been on extremely friendly terms
with him over the years and he'd always bred
superb horses. She knew he'd been building up
his herd carefully after he had lost all but two
of his stallions and four mares. She trusted his
judgement to select the best of his young ones

for her, and she surely would not have to bed him for he was known to be a devoted family man with only one wife and no concubines. A rarity for a tribesman. She knew she'd have to hurry though, because he always migrated to the north with his horses in late spring and the weather was becoming warm. Within the week, she was on her way with Mojghan to the Khabir winter quarters.

She had brought Ali along with her to ride one of the younger horses that would benefit from the two-hour ride across the desert. She rode her favorite Khatum and took turns with Ali leading the rather skittish Mojghan. She began to think that maybe the mare was too young to be bred but she was a beautifully conformed bright chestnut with a flaxen mane, and if she threw her color which was dominant, she would produce a greatly-sought-after horse that would hopefully bring an excellent price. She hated that she kept thinking of the money she hoped her breeding venture would bring her, but she had begun to realize that it was expensive to live the life she led with all this help and horses relying on her to support them. Additionally, she still had the worry of the house her mother had left her in Tehran, that at present was without a tenant. She was surprised how her funds were dwindling.

When Mehdi was with her, she never had to
worry about the money situation. She hadn't realized how much he spent on their lifestyle and
especially their passion for the horses. She'd
thought the money his brothers had given her
was plenty; that was why she had spent so much
on the house she built. But now she knew she
would be in trouble soon if she didn't find a way
to raise more funds. She wondered what Mehdi
was thinking now about her situation. Would he
be cursing his brothers for not giving her more
and keeping her a part of the family? Or would
he expect her to pick herself up and become
more realistic and scale down her way of life.
No, she couldn't do that. The horses were their
children; they were their life. He would want
her to find a way to continue and build up the
Bakhtiar herd to what it was before the sickness.
She would find a way!

Sheikh Khabir greeted her and Ali with his
usual hospitality of tea and sweets while they
passed the pleasantries of the day. When Zahra
told him the reason for her visit, he seemed
quite pleased that she wanted to mate one of her
young Saglawi mares with one of his yet untried
stallions.

"Khonume, I am flattered that you feel my
young horses will meet your high standards.
We're all in the same situation it seems, since

the African horse sickness. We must try to breed horses that will be equal to or better than so many of those that were lost to that dreadful disease. We must infuse new blood into our herds, but we need to have definite proof that we can trace the lines back six generations. You and I and a few others of our kind are being very careful, but I know of some that will try to cheat. We must be sure to keep the standards. I know of your stud book and I want to warn you now that you must be even more diligent than in the past to be sure that our Asil stud book is true."

"You know I will be," Zahra answered. "As you know, I'm on the board of the Royal Horse Society and one of our goals is to have our Persian Asil horses recognized around the world. When we get to the point of applying for recognition, my book will be scrutinized and inspectors from other countries will come to inspect our horses. Our records and horses will need to be close to perfect."

"So now, let's go see the stallions, so you can pick which one you want to be the sire of your bright hussy's foal."

The three young stallions were tethered to sturdy posts on long ropes alongside a grazing area that had a sparse covering of soft green spring grass. One of them was as jet black as Arrus IV, who was at home in his stable, having luckily been spared from the sickness. He'd been Mehdi's favorite having come down the line from the original Arrus that had been his father's famous horse. Black Asil horses were not common because the gene was genetically suppressed by the more dominant Agouti gene that created the black points on bay horses. In some areas, black horses were considered a bad omen but to the Bakhtiari they were a valued treasure. She could not breed Mojghan to the black no matter how beautiful he was for fear that the Agouti gene would produce a foal with black points.

There was a tall gray horse that had a beautiful straight nose with big flaring nostrils and an elegant compact body that she was taken with, but she didn't think it would be the best idea to breed her chestnut to a gray. All Asil horses had black skin except under their white markings and gray horses were born bay, black or chestnut. Then they got progressively lighter as they aged, until their hair coat eventually turned pure white or became "flea-bitten" gray. Their skin remained black throughout their life and there was no such thing as a genetically white Asil.

And then she saw a magnificent chestnut horse with a typical Arab type head, broad through the forehead with an ever so slight dished profile and small pricked ears. He had a compact muscular body with an arched neck, a broad deep chest, rounded quarters and a flat croup with a high tail carriage. Shahin, as he was named, was about 15.2 hands tall and would make the perfect mate for Mojghan.

"Oh!" she gasped. "That chestnut fits my mare's confirmation perfectly, Sheikh Khabir Khan. Will his pedigree also fit with her lines?"

"We'll have to check on them, but I believe it will be a good fit for the Bakhtiar line."

Later in the day, after it had been found that the pedigrees of the two horses would work well, they decided that as long as the mare was ready, the breeding would take place the following morning. The sheikh and his family hosted Zahra and Ali for the night, entertaining them royally with a wonderful meal and dancing to the music of the *sehtar* (Persian instrument similar to a guitar) and flutes around the fire while they drank Khabir-made wine late into the evening .

Ali and two of the Khabir grooms held Mojghan while the sheikh washed her down in readiness for her maiden breeding. Though the stallion was young, he had serviced several mares that season, so he had the experience needed for breeding a mare that had never been covered by a stallion before. He'd been washed down carefully by the two stud grooms before he was led across the yard, prancing and nickering as he knew what enjoyment he was about to have.

Mojghan's hind legs had been hobbled with ropes to prevent her from kicking her soon-to-be mate and she began winking as the young horse, with his erect penis, was brought close to her, showing that she was ready to accept the stallion. She stood still, her front legs firm as he reared up to mount her, but his weight made her hind end sag momentarily as the grooms guided the penis into her accepting vagina. As he entered her, he nuzzled her neck, covering her whole body with his, shuddering and shaking for a minute or two. And then it was over, and he climbed off with his flaccid member still dripping semen.

"I would say that was a good cover, Zahra Khonume. Now we will let her rest for an hour or so and I will take you to see my own young horses before you take your mare home to incubate a hopefully perfect foal that will enhance your herd in the future," said the sheikh.

Zahra was impressed with the quality of the yearling and two-year-old horses that Sheikh Khabir showed her; they were all of good flesh, had shiny coats and had the mark of the true Asil horses. His herd had grown to over forty horses since it had been decimated from the sickness those years before. "We'll be leaving for our migration to the north in a week or so. All my foals of this year have been born and they are almost ready to set forth on the journey. Why do you not take your herd to the cooler parts during the heat of the summer?" he asked her.

"I have never thought to. When Mehdi was alive, we were too busy farming and going back and forth to the capital for his business and our social life, so it wasn't possible then."

"You should think about it now. It is so good for the horses to escape the sweltering summer heat of Khuzestan, and the journey makes them become stronger and more sure footed. The trip is always interesting, all sorts of things happen, and you will meet many others while travelling. We all feel so invigorated while in the cool of the mountains, away from the heat."

"My father's family still has land near Hamadan. I suppose I could get in touch to see if they would be amenable to my bringing my horses there for the summer next year. Yes, it might be a good idea; I will certainly look into it. Thank you for the suggestion."

After having been served tea, sweets and fruit, Ali and Zahra mounted their horses, and leading the now proud Mojghan, they headed for the long ride to Aghili.

17

For most of these long nights I stay awake
And go to bed as dawn begins to break;
I think that eyes that haven't seen their friend
Might get some sleep then...this is a mistake.
Jahan Malek Khatun

Ali 1979

Old Rostam's motor purred loudly along the dusty road like a tiger, as they passed through the gates of Aghili and towards the ferry crossing. Ali couldn't figure out why Mehdi and Zahra had not built a bridge across the Karun River closer to their own place. They had been in charge of supervising the building of the many bridges as well as ferries that had been erected by the government in the fertile Khuzestan area, to facilitate transportation of agricultural goods. He knew there must be a good reason, otherwise these two dedicated people would have had a bridge. The road was bumpy, and he had to drive slowly so as not to jiggle the old Land Rover apart. Why had Zahra Khonume not been given one of the newer vehicles that Mehdi Khan owned? The Bakhtiar brothers had plenty of cars and trucks of their own, as well as those that had belonged to Mehdi and Zahra, so Ali always wondered why she had been satisfied with old Rostam that was always having problems. Of course, he'd become a good mechanic himself and could always seem to keep the old goat running, but it would have been nice to have a newer version.

He glanced to the side to look at Zahra who was sitting rigidly with her hands in her lap twiddling her thumbs, a habit she had commenced since she'd made the decision to leave her beloved life in Persia and go to the land where her mother had been born. This drive would be the worst of his life. He didn't want her to go. He had a feeling of foreboding about this whole crazy idea his boss and mentor had planned. She'd been his inspiration for all these many years he had been in her employ. He had loved her from afar, and yet when she told him he must find himself a bride, he had done as she had bidden; he had married a young Bakhtiari girl from Sheikh Khabir's tribe and now had two lovely children, Ahmad a boy of five and young Zahra who had just turned two.

Zahra

Zara smiled as she looked at the picture she had taken of the mares and their young foals grazing in the large pasture on spring grass. She had waited for almost an hour, watching the mares and the frolicking youngsters until they finally settled, and she could press the shutter button to get the photograph. That photograph, when developed, turned out to be an almost true-life color picture that she cherished,

Life at Aghili had continued to be full for Zahra. She spent the days with her horses and grooms, training, grooming, treating the injuries and sicknesses, for though they are large animals, horses are quite delicate and tend to attract affliction frequently. Foals were born in the springtime, which gave her great joy as she watched them frolic with the mares and each other. She kept the number five as the maximum for several years, but even so her herd began to grow. She was able to sell almost all the yearlings either to the sheikhs in her area or to stud farm owners from Tehran who had heard of her horses through the *Anjoman* (Royal Horse Society). She had continued to be a member of the board of directors, though she seldom attended the meetings.

She often went to visit her many tribal friends nearby who were also trying to grow and improve their small herds that had been so devastated by the sickness. Her stud book was again growing. Most evenings, with a glass of wine by her side and her typewriter clacking, she would pour over generations of Asil horses which she had recorded on sheets of manila paper that would go into her binders. She vowed she would complete her project before she died, and she would get the Persian horses recognized worldwide.

The summer after she had bred Mojghan and Aziz to the Sheikhs' stallions turned out to be a dreadful time in Khuzestan. There was a terrible drought that destroyed the grain crop and there was no fodder for the horses to eat. Zahra was able, through her connections with the *Anjoman*, to have hay and barley delivered to Aghili on the military trucks that Bahman Mansarpour was able to commandeer through his connections with the Shah's Imperial Stables, but it was not cheap to buy. When the few of her neighbors who did not migrate heard of her fortunate link, they asked if she would help them

too, for their horses were suffering and growing extremely thin. Being the woman, she was,
she ordered more truckloads of feed, which she
paid for personally, and which she persuaded
Bahman to send down to her. These she distributed to her friends for their horses. As autumn
arrived so did the rains luckily, but now she had
a huge debt with the feed company in Tehran.

When she received the invitation to attend
the board meeting at the *Anjoman* in the mail
in early *Aban* (October) of 1973, she decided she
really needed to go to Tehran to attend it, and
also settle up some of the debts she had incurred
over the past years. She had still not rented out
her mother's house and it was costing her to
keep it, so she thought she should try to sell it.
Her funds were slowly dwindling, and though
she had faith that her horse sales would bring in
some income she realized it would probably not
be enough for all the expenses she had.

She and Ali drove up to Tehran early one
sunny morning, arriving at her house just before dark. Nahid, the caretaker, and her husband Davoud were waiting at the gate, for she
had called the day before to let them know she
was coming. Even though it was costing her too
much, she had kept the telephone line at the
house because they were very difficult to obtain
and the foreign renters always needed to have a

house with a telephone line; perhaps that would also help in the sale. They sat down in the almost-bare dining room and enjoyed a delicious meal of *gourmet sabsi* (lamb and greens stew) and rice with a crisp golden brown *tadique* (the crust on the bottom of the rice).

The next morning Ali dropped Zahra at the door of the Royal Horse Society office, which was a part of the Imperial Court office complex on Pasteur Avenue in downtown Tehran. "Shall I wait for you, Zahra Khonume?" Ali questioned, for there was no parking allowed along the street where these important offices were situated and there were plenty of police and imperial guards monitoring the traffic.

"No, no, Ali, I'm sure there will be someone at the meeting that will be willing to drive me back to Shemran after we have finished. There are many people I know that will be there. Go home and enjoy a restful day in the garden with Nahid and Davoud. You had a long drive yesterday."

She walked up the barren white plastered stairway to the second floor of the court building where the offices of Bahman Mansarpour were located. She thought it was strange that the entrance to the office of the assistant to the Shah who was also Master of His Majesty's Horse and president of the Royal Horse Society was so plain and unassuming. Most of the other court offices had large carved wooden doorways and carved pillars with large chandeliered entrance halls to welcome their visitors. But she knew that Bahman was a son of the court whose own father was in charge of the personal financial assets of the king, so perhaps he felt more secure with an inauspicious entrance to his domain.

Bahman's pretty young secretary ushered her into the large office where she had met with people from the horse world many times before. At one end of the large office was Bahman's carved mahogany partners' desk, with its oversized black leather chair behind it and the two matching armchairs on either side for visitors. There was a brilliant red and black Turkoman carpet in front of the desk to remind people that Bahman was in fact from one of the major tribes of that area in the north of the country. Already seated at the large shiny conference table at the other end of the room were Bahman and the twelve other members of the board; she was late as usual!

"Good afternoon, Khonume Bakhtiar," greeted Bahman sarcastically, as it was just a few minutes after ten, the time of the meeting's commencement.

"Good morning to all. I'm sorry to be the last one here, but as you know, in the south we're not as punctual as you seem to be in Tehran. I apologize if I am tardy."

The main topic of the meeting was the fact that the society was thinking of sending a group of Iranian bred horses to the Salon du Cheval, an international horse show and exposition in Paris, France. This particular show had been established in 1971 to promote the world's horse breeds, and horsemanship, including horse care and products, as well as sporting highlights including show jumping, dressage, harness, vaulting and the World Arab Horse Championships. While Bahman was on a trip to Paris the previous year, with their Majesties, he saw an advertisement for the event and managed to spend a few days enjoying the atmosphere of what he called *the most wonderful horse show in the world*. On the plane ride home, he'd discussed the possibility with the Shah of sending a delegation from Iran the following year. The Shah seemed to be enthusiastic about the idea.

"Seeing as our Persian horses are not world recognized, do you think we would be allowed to enter and compete in this exposition?" Zahra questioned.

Bahman replied, "His Majesty has spoken to his ambassador to France who is going to look into the details for us. I've talked to Cathy, who you know is the Imperial Stables trainer and has extensive experience in international show jumping. She thinks we could definitely send one or two horses to compete at some level in those events.

"Zahra, you've been working for years on your Persian Asil stud book, so it might be a great opportunity to let the world see some of our pure horses even if we aren't recognized and won't be able to compete, as such. We could send an exhibit of our horses for people to see and hopefully make contact with the World Arab Horse Organization," he added.

The meeting went on for about two hours. In the end it was agreed by all members that the Salon du Cheval would definitely be a goal for the society the following year. As the meeting adjourned, Bahman told Zahra that he wanted her to stay behind as he had a few other matters to discuss with her. He'd be happy to drive her up to Shemran when they were finished. It was on his way to Niavaran where he had a meeting with His Majesty.

She'd known Bahman for many years as he had always been involved with the horse world. He loved to ride and was in the process of developing show jumping into a major sport. The Shah also enjoyed his riding and was a supporter of horse racing and polo. Now, thanks to Bahman's interest, he was also developing and buying a stable of fine show jumping horses.

As they drove up the Vanak Expressway towards her house, Bahman had a question for her, "Zahra, I hate to bring up uncomfortable topics, but I've heard you have a large, long-standing debt with the feed company which I don't understand. I know your herd is growing, but how big has it become?"

"Well, as you know, we had a terrible time in Khuzestan with the drought a couple of summers ago. You kindly arranged for transport of feed to me from the north. When my neighbors, whose horses were beginning to starve, heard this, they asked me for help. I admit I took advantage of you and the society by using your generous offer of transportation for my friends too, but I personally charged all the feed you transported to my own account. I didn't realize how much it was going to cost me. The feed company has been patient, but now I am here in Tehran trying to figure out how I'm going to pay all my debts, not just to the feed company, but others as well."

She hesitated for a moment, and then continued. "You know that Mehdi's brothers gave me the land at Aghili, the horses and some money after he died. Because they were Bakhtiaris and I was not, and had no children with Mehdi, the rest of his estate, which was very large, went to them. I am not good with money, so perhaps

I have spent some foolishly; I built myself a small house and made commitments I probably shouldn't have. I've been trying to work it so the horse sales will help with the expenses, which they do, but somehow there is never quite enough. I'm going to try to sell the house that I grew up in, which should bring in enough money to pay most of my debts, but it seems there is always something else that needs to be paid."

"You may remember that Jamshid Khan, who is Mehdi's youngest brother, and on our board, although he couldn't make it today, is a close friend of mine. He has talked to me about the treatment you received from his brothers, which he feels was very unfair to you. He wants to find a way that he can help you out with your financial problems without incurring the wrath of his brothers. We're having dinner together this evening to talk about what we think we can do to help you and to protect the Asil horses of Iran," he told her.

Zahra was surprised to hear that her brother-in law had spoken to Bahman about the situation because the brothers usually stuck together. But Jamshid had always been friendly to her when he visited Andimeshk, which was seldom because he was President of the NIOC (National Iranian Oil Company) and he didn't get the opportunity to visit Khuzestan often. Of Majid's brothers, he was the one she felt most comfortable with. A couple of times a year, he always came to see the horses and ride out with her when he was able to take the time to visit his family home. She couldn't imagine what he might propose, but she'd find out soon enough, she knew.

On the drive to Shemran with Bahman, they discussed the possibility of sending two or three Asil horses from her herd to the Exposition in Paris. They both doubted they would be accepted as competition horses in the Arab division, because their horses were not recognized by the WAHO, but surely, they'd be able to introduce the Persian Arab horses in the exposition. Zahra was excited that she might be able to go to Paris. She'd always loved the times she visited with her mother and father when she was young. She had not left Iran since she came back from college those many years ago and the thought of travelling abroad was something, she had thought would not happen again. They agreed that she would meet him the following morning at his office to discuss what plans Jamshid had that would help Zahra and her horses.

When she walked into Bahman's office the next day, he had a telephone at each ear. He signaled her to sit in the chair opposite him. She watched him speak into one phone, then say, "Hold on," and address the other mouthpiece, then back to the first phone, and so on. It almost made her dizzy to see these antics, which she had viewed almost every time she came to his domain; she had no idea how he could carry on two conversations at one time, but it obviously worked for him. He was successful in his many positions and was well supported by the Shah and liked by his colleagues.

Finally, he hung up one phone, and after another few minutes of discussion, he put the second headpiece in its cradle. "I'm sorry to keep you waiting, Zahra. I just had a few things I wanted to tie up before we talked. I had a good conversation with Jamshid Khan at dinner last night. He said that he realized his brothers had been unjust in their distribution of Mehdi's estate when it happened, but there was nothing he could do, for the majority had ruled. And as your husband did not leave a will, the traditional Bakhtiar passage of chattels was the law; the eldest brother would become the Khan and he could disperse the estate as he wanted."

"I knew that was the way things were and I have no problem with what they did. They were kind enough to let me have our horses and the Aghili property. It's not their fault I'm not the best at dealing with money. I have no complaints about how things turned out."

"I know you don't but Jamshid feels badly and

worries that you will need more funds as time goes on. You've worked hard on the stud book, which will become a part of the *Anjoman,*for years with no compensation. You've also spent a great deal of your time visiting the Sheikhs and persuading them to help you record their own horses' bloodlines to keep the Asil pure. These are things that benefit our organization and Iran."

"You know I do it because I love the horses and I want to be part of the Persian Asil horses as they become recognized by the World Arab Horse Organization. Research has shown that the first Arab horses came from the deserts of the area in and around Khuzestan. For that reason, our horses should be acknowledged internationally. I really enjoy everything I do with regard to the true Asils."

"Well, Jamshid proposed a plan that will benefit both you and the Royal Horse Society if you will agree to it," he told her.

He explained that her brother-in-law had proposed that the Royal Horse Society would become the protectorate of the Bakhtiar Stud Asil horses, which would mean that all expenses in supporting the horses would be borne by the society. Zahra would be given a handsome salary to manage the stud and continue her work on the Persian Arab Stud Book in hopes that the

Iranian Asils would be recognized.

Zahra was a little concerned by this plan, though. "Does that mean that the *Anjoman* will then own my horses? And how will the society be able to pay for all this? I've seen the budget and it seems to me that there's not a great deal of reserve money after all the other expenses have been covered." she wanted to know.

Bahman explained that the horses would still be owned by Zahra, but they would be considered under the protection of the society. Jamshid had agreed to donate the money to finance the project himself. Zahra was flabbergasted to hear this. Jamshid, the youngest of the Bakhtiar brothers, would be the one to save her from what she knew would eventually have been poverty? Of course, this proposal would have to pass the board which, Bahman told her, was not a problem; he was sure it would be a shoe-in.

It was decided that when she had finished her business in Tehran, she should go back to Khuzestan and continue her life as it was. But she must try to decide which horses of the Persian Asils would make a good representative to send to Paris at the end of the following November.

With a song in her heart and a light skipping step, she descended the stairs of Bahman's office and hopped into the old Land Rover that Ali had parked illegally near the door of the building. "Ali, you won't believe it! We've been saved by the hand of Jamshid Khan Bakhtiar."

She went on to tell him about the proposal that had been made to her, which hopefully would be ratified by the *Anjoman* board at the next meeting. "Now, I need to sell the house here in Tehran so I can pay the many debts I've incurred over the past few years. So many people have been patient with me, but I don't like owing money. Never before in my life have I been in debt and it frightens me, Ali," she told him.

When she got back to the house, she immediately telephoned to the estate agent that she had listed the house with to see if there were any prospective buyers in the works. The agent said a young doctor and his family who had just returned from the United States had been to see the house twice, and he was expecting that they would make an offer in the next few days. She decided that it would be prudent for her to stay in the capital for another week, even though she was itching to get back to Aghili.

She arranged to have lunch with Louise Firouz, who would be in charge of selecting which Caspian horses might be going to the Salon du Cheval. She also invited Cathy Johnson who had a couple of jumpers that would most likely compete in the international show jumping section of the exposition. They discussed the criteria each of them would use to select horses to represent Iran which had never before sent horses abroad. Of course, it wasn't definite that they would be allowed to exhibit the Caspian or the Asil horses, but they felt sure that with the Shah's good connections with France it would most probably happen and they wanted to make sure they were prepared for the exciting event. What fun the three of them would have in Paris together!

When her old friends realized she was in town, Zahra found herself being entertained at numerous dinner parties given in her honor in several of the big new modern houses that had been built in the Niavaran area north of Shemran, which had been the place to live when she was growing up. She was used to the quiet life in her desert home, so these social gatherings, which didn't usually commence before nine-thirty or ten in the evening and continued into the wee small hours, were quite exhausting. But she did have fun reuniting with friends and acquaintances, most of whom she had not seen since Mehdi's untimely death. She was able to spend many hours at Avid and Ahmad's home, playing with their children and reconnecting with close friends with whom she had lost touch over the past few years.

When the news came that the house had been sold, she realized she'd have to stay in Tehran longer in order to clear out the house and make arrangements for the long-time caretakers, Nahid and Davoud. There were closets full of clothes that had been hanging since before her father's death. Her mother had never had the heart to throw his things away and Zahra had not attempted to go through her mother's belongings; now she would have to arrange what to do with everything she did not want to take to Aghili. Her own closet was full of clothes from the past, most of which, with her lifestyle in the desert, she would never again wear. There was still furniture, which had been left for the renters, but most of the antiques she had previously sent to Khuzestan where they were either in her apartment or in the new house, although she had left a few of the bigger pieces in the Big House in Andimeshke.

The sale of the house went smoothly and quickly. It turned out the doctor and his wife wanted Nahid and her husband to stay on to assist them, so that problem was solved. When they heard that Zahra was going to sell most of what was left of the furniture, they agreed to buy it all. Before she knew it, she and Ali were on the road back to Khuzestan and the life she loved so much.

18

However old, incapable,
And heartsick I may be,
The moment I recall your face
My youth's restored to me.
Hafez

Ali 1979

As they rumbled along the desert track towards the ferry, Ali remembered the day a few
months before when Zahra told him she wanted
him and his family to move into her house. "But,
Zahra Khonume you don't want to have my little ones running around under your feet. I don't
understand."

"Ali, I will move back up to my apartment
above the stable and you'll have the house for your
family. The little ones will not be under my feet!"

"I still don't understand."

"I will be going away, and I want you to manage

everything here. Your family will grow, so you'll need more room than the small house you have now. I love the little home Mehdi and I had, and when I return here to visit, I'll stay there."

"But when will you come back, Khonume?"

"I really don't know just now, Ali, but in several months I'll be back. Do not worry yourself."

He couldn't believe that she was really going to leave. All along he had hoped that she would change her mind. Why did she want to leave the home he knew she truly loved? He knew she had lived in America, her mother's country, when she was at school, but why would she want to go back now? The Bakhtiar Stud horses were now famous here in Iran. They'd started breeding more mares each year because the yearlings were commanding high prices, and except for the one or two she decided not to sell from each crop they were all sold to wealthy people in Tehran. Was she becoming senile?

Zahra

It was only a couple of weeks after she arrived back from the trip to Tehran that had made her life so much easier, that she had a call from Bahman Mansarpour. "Zahra, it has all been arranged; The Royal Horse Society of Iran will be sending horses to the Salon du Cheval in Paris in November."

"Oh, that's fantastic."

"The Imperial Stables will be sending two show jumpers that will compete and we'll be sending an exhibition of three Asil horses and two Caspian horses. I want you to select the three horses you think will represent our Persian Arabs the best and I'll come down to see them in a few weeks. In early October, we'll bring them up to the Imperial Stables where all the horses going to Paris will need to spend a few weeks in a quarantine barn to have the required inoculations and blood tests for the trip. His Majesty has given us the use of an Iranian Air Force C130 transport plane to make the trip. I'm very happy that this is going to happen."

"I think it is wonderful, Bahman. I'm very excited about the trip as I am sure Louise and Cathy are. Just let me know when you want to come down to look at the horses. I've almost decided about two of the three horses to take and I'm sure you will approve, but you have the last say."

"I knew you would have already started to make your selection. I'll be down in a week or two. I'll call first." With that the line went dead.

When she had arrived home, she couldn't stop thinking that there might be an opportunity to take three of her horses to the Salon in Paris, so she had spent many hours each day observing and scrutinizing her herd. There were many magnificent specimens, but which ones should she choose? She felt disloyal to all those that she would not be selecting. It was like having to pick one of your children as the favorite. She watched them when they were out on the desert grazing, when they were prancing in through the gate to come into the stable at feeding time, when they stood in their stalls eating. And then she had every horse led out into the yard to stand up in a conformation pose.

It took days, but she finally selected the stallion, Zahhak, who was descended from the line of Arrus, the most famous of the Bakhtiar stallions. She had named the colt Zahhak after the evil mythical Persian King of Zoroastrian times, because he had been so naughty as a foal, constantly taunting the other foals and even attacking his own mother. He was a dark mahogany bay with a refined chiseled head, and a large star and stripe on his slightly dished face. His neck was strong and crested, flowing into a straight back with the high carriage of his black tail that had a white streak in it. With his three "fit for a king" white socks, he was a strikingly beautiful animal that would represent the Persian Arab perfectly.

The mare she selected came from the line that was descended from the breeding of Mojghan and Sheikh Kabir's beautiful stallion, Shahin. The flaxen mane and tail of Mojghan had continued in this line and the young mare she called Farah, after the beautiful empress, with her diagonal white sox, high flaxen tail and almost perfect conformation, would certainly be an eye catcher. It took some time to decide on a third horse. Zahra knew she wanted a youngster, but weanlings often went through growth spurts that weren't always attractive. Yearlings too, had their "ugly duckling" stages, so she decided that a two-year-old would be the best choice. However, she had eight of them and just couldn't decide which one she should ready for the November trip that was now just six months away. She telephoned Bahman, who had still not come to look at the horses and asked him to come down to help her with the decision.

Bahman agreed to come to Aghili the following *Chahar Shanbeh* (Thursday, like Saturday). He told her that he would get Manuchehr Khosrodad to fly him down in one of the military helicopters so they could land right next to the stables in Aghili. She was thrilled that he was coming so quickly, but wasn't so sure that

---

she wanted Manuchehr there, too. He was the Commanding General of the Imperial Iranian Army Aviation, had been a dear friend of Mehdi, and was very close to the Shah. He and Bahman were almost inseparable because of their mutual love of horses and show jumping. However, he was very opinionated and thought he knew more than anyone about most subjects. He did have a good eye for a horse, though he was mostly interested in Turkomans and European Warmbloods, whose conformation was quite different from the Asil horses.

She had all eight of the two year olds groomed and tied up in their stalls when she heard the faint clacking of the chopper approaching. She had told Bahman to make sure they landed far enough out in the desert that they wouldn't frighten the horses. She got into old Rostam and drove through the gates to see where they had landed, so she could pick them up. Just the week before, Manuchehr had established five world records in altitude and time-to-height categories with a Bell 214 helicopter, so she was sure he would be full of himself. When she drove up to where they landed, the rotors were still whirring, and it took several minutes for him to shut the engine down.

But once he and Bahman were on the ground, Manuchehr took over. "Zahra June," he hugged her tightly. "It's so good to see you again. The last time was not so happy an occasion, when I brought Mehdi home to his resting place. You look wonderful. These years have been good to you. You don't look a day older than the last time I was here, which was five, or was it six years ago?"

"It was almost six long years, Manuchehr," she answered. Though he was good friend of Mehdi, she had never been overly fond of the handsome, dapper general who so resembled the Shah himself.

She turned and addressed the Secretary General of the Royal Horse Society. "Bahman, thank you so much for coming down to help me with my choice of a third horse to take to Paris. I am so happy to see you."

Azizeh had set a table under the veranda of her house with fruits and sweets along with thirst quenching *hendovaneh sharob* (watermelon juice) so she ushered them over there to take some refreshment before she brought out the horses, which she would show on the lush green grass lawn in front of the house. It took a lot of water and care to have such a beautiful lawn in the hot dry Khuzestan climate; she hoped the visitors would appreciate it.

"I want to show you the mare and stallion I have selected first, and then I'll have the two-year-olds brought out for your inspection. We can select, jointly, the one that should go to the exposition."

"Why do you want to take a two-year-old? Why don't you send a three or four-year-old?" piped up Manuchehr.

"We decided to send a mature mare and stallion and one young horse so people can see we are looking to the future," said Bahman.

"Well if you want a young one, why don't you send a weanling or a yearling? That's what I'd do," the expert interjected.

Zahra explained the reasons to him and then signaled to Ali to have Zahhak brought out to be shown to her guests. She was delighted that they both thought him a beautiful specimen of the Asil horse and approved her first selection. Next came the four-year-old mare, Farah, who was led out by her groom, prancing and flagging her full flaxen tail. Both men were impressed with the showy mare. "She will surely steal the show in Paris," Bahman said.

Now began the selection of one of the two-year olds. Zahra had told the grooms to bring all eight out on the lawn at the same time, to walk them in a circle so they could be seen as a group. Then she would have the horses that were selected out of that group by all three of them brought out individually so their presence and conformation could be analyzed. She was quite surprised when it turned out that the general, Bahman, and she all agreed that the most impressive two year old was medium height for his age, an almost black colt, whose high-crested neck held a finely chiseled head with a diamond-shaped star. His pedigree went way back to the lines of Arrus. She had named him Arrus VI in honor of the Bakhtiar line.

After eating a lunch of rice and *khoreshts,* they all went into the house where they could nap for an hour or so before Manuchehr and Bahman flew back to Tehran.

On a cool sunny morning in October, she loaded Zahhak, Arrus VI and Farah on an army truck that had arrived the previous day for their long ride to the Imperial Stables in Tehran where they would begin with the shots and quarantine necessary for their export to France. Zahra would not go to the capital for a couple of weeks, for she wasn't needed, as the care at His Majesty's stables was excellent. The Irish resident vet was a good horseman and strictly supervised the horse care and she would call Cathy every few days to see how her horses were fairing.

Louise Firouz had selected an exquisite little bay mare that looked like a miniature Asil and a sturdy chestnut stallion with a wide chest and strong looking hind end to represent the Caspian horse which she had rediscovered in 1965. While she and her husband, Narcy, had been living near Persepolis, the ancient Persian Empire capital, they had viewed the elegant small horses that were carved in bas reliefs on the great staircase of the old palace there. It was believed that the Persian Shah Dariush had demanded tributes of only first-class animals to be carved on the walls of his palace. Unfortunately, the fine little horses he so valued disappeared from history after so much was destroyed in the great Mongol and Islamic conquests. Almost no further mention of them was found after 700 A.D., so most modern scholars believed that they had become extinct, until one day while Louise was in the north of the country in a remote village near the Caspian Sea, she happened to see some small horses that looked like replicas of the carvings. She collected a number of these petite horses, the size of small ponies, and began her breeding program. Research proved that the modern Caspian was in fact, descended from the great pool of quality stock that was bred during the days of the Great Persian Empire.

Cathy Johnson had decided to send one of His Majesties Akhle Tekeh stallions, a line of the Turkman breed that came from the north of the country, to compete in the one meter twenty division of the Show Jumping. This seven-year-old stallion was just sixteen hands high, but had a powerful, stylish jump. Cathy had been successfully competing with him in that division for the past two years. However, Bahman wanted him to be shown by an Iranian, so she would have Davoud Bahrami, the talented young junior rider whose father was the Shah's personal *dgelodar* (groom), ride him in Paris. Davoud would also compete with the lovely grey Arab/Turkoman cross mare, Shirin, in the same division.

When Zahra arrived in Tehran, she stayed with Louise and her husband at their house on Damghan Avenue, in the heart of the city, just a few minutes' drive from the stables. They had all been friends for years, and they had allowed her to store some of her things there when she sold her mother's house. During the two weeks before they were due to leave for Paris, there were a number of cocktail and dinner parties given in honor of the delegation that was being sent to the Salon du Cheval. What with working with the horses during the day and partying at night, she and her colleagues were exhausted before they left for France.

Tehran could be cold and even snowy in mid-to-late November, but the weather was good to them before their departure. The morning they were due to leave dawned sunny and mild, so the horses were walked by imperial grooms the two kilometers to Doshun Tape, the military air base. From there, they would be flown to France in one of the Shah's C130 transport planes. Zahra, Cathy and Louise were waiting on the tarmac as the seven horses, led by the grooms, walked up the winding, tree-lined drive of the base and onto the airfield.

The crates in which the horses would be transported were waiting beside a large metal hanger, though the plane had not yet arrived. They had been told that departure would be at nine o'clock, but it seemed the air force was working on Iranian time. It was almost ten when they heard the drone of the huge fat swallow of a plane, which had fueled at Mehrabad before coming to pick up the entourage destined for Paris. The horses were held at the edge of hanger as the plane landed and taxied over, close to the crates. Once the pilot shut down the engines, the horses were loaded onto the crates, two to a pallet, with Zahhak in a single, as he was the only mature stallion. The forklift drove over to the pallet with the two Caspian horses first, and slowly moved it close to the open back of the plane. Then it was lifted up level with the floor where the grooms, Jamshid and Sefola, were ready to carefully push it on the rollers to the front of the hold of the plane. The small horses, pony size actually, nickered few times, but settled down as the hay net was hung from the plane's ceiling and the pallet was secured.

There was no problem with the pallets holding Farah and Arrus or Roshan and Shirin, but when Zahhak was lifted into the air, he began to scramble in his crate, whinnying and trying to rear up. Young Davoud Bahrami, who was to be the rider of the two show jumpers in the competitions, quickly and quietly climbed onto the pallet and soothed the frightened horse, which calmed down as he was rolled into the plane. With all the equine passengers on board, the personnel climbed the stairs into the front of the plane. When everyone was settled, the big cumbersome aircraft began to roll along the runway, slowly picking up enough speed to leave the ground and climb high into the sky.

The plane landed at Orly Airport at dusk. It was a cool misty evening as the passengers watched the forklifts offload the palates with the horses onto the tarmac. The van that had been hired to transport the horses from the airport to the stabling area in Montsouris Parque where the Salon du Cheval would take place,was standing by to load the seven tired horses and move them to what would be their home for almost two weeks. Davoud, Jamshid and Sefola began to lead the horses from the palates to the large van with its narrow steep ramp, while Louise, Cathy and Zahra tended to those still in their crates. The horses were used to being loaded onto the open army trucks from a bank, when they would step directly onto the floor of the truck from ground that was the same level. To the horses, the ramp would probably seem strange and spooky. The two small Caspians walked up the ramp without a moment's hesitation and were secured in their stalls. Farah and Arrus VI were a little more hesitant, but slowly walked up the ramp step by step. Shirin and Roshan had both been used to shipping to various horse shows in the Imperial Stable's fancy Lamborne lorry with its ramp, that had been purchased the previous year at Cathy's insistence, so for them it was not a problem.

But Zahak was a different matter. He'd always been difficult, but he was well trained, so Zahra felt he wouldn't be a problem. She was wrong. He refused to step a foot on the ramp as Jamshid led him. Instead, he reared up and wheeled, dragging the poor groom with him. When he was finally under control, Jamshid began to put the chain of the shank over his nose.

"No Jamshid!" Zahra shouted moving forward to the fractious stallion, "He'll only fight the chain and it might mark up his face. Let me have him. He'll do as I tell him." When she took him from Jamshid, she led him away from the van and walked him in a circle, talking to him quietly until his eyes, that had almost popped out of his head, became soft and docile. She patted and stroked him until it was evident, he was again calm.

By now the mist had turned into a light rain and everyone was anxious to get on their way to the exhibition grounds, but Zahra would not hurry. She cautiously led the stallion up to the narrow ramp with tall wooden sides that made it look like a tunnel and began to pat him on the side of his neck and speak softly to him. She let him stand, looking at the frightening walk-way into the tall horse box for several minutes, until he finally breathed a deep sigh and blew out a long soft breath. Then she walked him in another big circle and led the now soaking-wet animal up into the truck. He did not hesitate but followed her with confidence and quietly backed into his waiting stall. He stood still as she hooked both sides of his halter to the chains and put up the breast bar.

She too, was now dripping wet and chilly, but she insisted that she ride in the van with the driver and grooms, because she wanted to be with her horses when they reached the stabling area. The embassy had sent a Mercedes limo for her, Cathy, and Louise, as well as a box van to take all the tack trunks and trappings they would use in their display during the expo. But she knew the horses would arrive first and she just didn't feel comfortable leaving them, especially Zahhak, to be offloaded without her supervision.

The drive along the wet, traffic-jammed Paris streets was slow. Happily, the horses were travelling quietly behind her in the van, so she struck up a conversation with the driver. She didn't use French often, so she was a bit rusty, even though she had been almost bilingual earlier in her life. "It isn't a very pleasant evening to be driving around Paris with a load of horses," she began.

"Oh, it is no problem for me, Madame. This is my job. I drive horses all over Europe for my company, so I'm quite happy to be spending a few days in Paris transporting horses to the Exhibition from the airport and train station. I've already driven this route three times today. I will also be driving your horses on the return trip."

"So, it seems there will be many horses in the Salon du Cheval."

"Madame, it is said that this exposition is becoming the world's leading event for horses and equestrians. This is only the third year it has been held, but it has become a sensation already all over the world. I know that you come from Iran, and you must have beautiful Arab horses, but there will also be exhibits and shows for other breeds. And then on the final days, there is wonderful show jumping which I will definitely be there to watch. The best riders in the world will be here. I love the jumping events," he told her.

"Please call me Zahra; that is my name."

"And I am Jean."

"Jean, we've brought five horses that will be on exhibition only. People will be able to see what beautiful horses we have in Iran, but we have also brought two show jumpers for the lower level classes."

"Then I'll be sure to watch them. I think they compete during the last two or three days, but I will find out for sure. I don't really enjoy the showy Arab classes or the dressage, but I love the jumpers. There will be several hundred horses in the whole exhibition and there are many, many booths for equine related items. Your horses will probably be stabled in the second hall where there are exhibits of different breeds of horses that are not competing. I think your jumpers will be in the competition barn, which is close by, but spectators are only allowed in those stables certain hours when the horses are not competing."

As Jean eased the big horse van through the beautiful gates with statues of rearing horses on either side, several officials of the Salon were there to direct him to the off-loading area, which was full of other horse transports. Zahra climbed down from the tall cab and walked up to the man in charge. She gave him the information he needed and the envelope with the horses' papers and credentials that she had in her handbag. She was shown to the stalls and to an area designated for Iran in the huge covered arena that was the exhibition hall. Then the little mustachioed man walked her over to the competition barn where there were three stalls ready, one of which would be a tack room. The vans slowly took their turn to unload the horses and just before it was their turn, the rest of the contingent arrived.

Even though everything went smoothly, it took more than two hours to get the horses settled and all the traps out of the box van. So, it was decided that, due to the late hour, they would all go to a bistro nearby for a late supper and a glass of wine. After a "night check" of the horses, the embassy driver dropped the boys off at their nearby hotel, first showing them the path, they were to take when they walked to the stables in the morning to feed and do morning chores. He made sure they each had their credentials so they would have no problem getting admission to the exhibition grounds. Zahra was worried about three handsome young Iranian boys left alone in Paris. She reiterated the instructions they had already heard, telling them to be careful and not to be late to feed the horses in the morning.

"Leave it, Zahra, they're not babies!" Louise admonished her. "You've lived in the sticks of Khusestan too long. These boys live in Tehran; they can take care of themselves."

The driver drove the three exhausted women to their hotel which, fortunately, was not more than fifteen minutes away. They were all there to work and didn't want to spend hours in a car driving from the hotel to the exhibition every day. The Palaise de San Jean had three deluxe rooms ready for them, arranged by Bahman, who would be arriving a few days later.

They told their chauffeur to pick them up at eight the next morning so they could spend the day working with the boys to set up their display area and to help with the horses that would all need a long hand walk. Then they decided it was time for a nightcap in the quiet little bar they had spotted from the lobby. At the long mahogany bar with its brass foot rail, there were a few people talking quietly, so they sat at a corner table with plush red velvet chairs and each ordered a Cognac.

"I must say," said Cathy, "I'm really surprised at how well things worked out today. I really expected a nightmare. You know how things in Iran can be a mess when it comes to Iranian organization!"

Louise said, "Well, you haven't had the good fortune to travel abroad under the auspices of the Imperial Court before this. I promise you; we will be treated like queens while we're here. It's most important that Iran puts on a good face when it sends representatives out of the country. I know because I've been sent on several trips for the Royal Horse Society and they've all been amazing. I think His Majesty himself makes sure things go well when his people travel. You know how he keeps himself informed, especially with the horse world. You will see, we're going to have a great time here," said Louise.

"And we are going to put on a great show to make Iran and the Shah proud," Zahra replied.

The following morning when Zahra awoke and looked at her watch, she saw that it was five-thirty, her usual time to rise. She bounced out of bed, ready to shower and get dressed so she could have a good breakfast in the hotel dining room before leaving for the exhibition. When she returned to the bedroom from her shower, wrapped in a towel, she glanced at the clock on the bureau. It said four o'clock! She had forgotten that there was a two-and-a-half-hour difference in the time and she hadn't changed her watch the previous night. She decided to read the information pamphlets, instructions and program for the Salon du Cheval de Paris that they had been given as they left the stables the night before. There were reams of instructions for both competitors and exhibitors, with maps and time-tables, rules and regulations, on and on. When she finished reading all the material that she felt was important to her and the Iranian contingent, she picked up the glossy thick official program. The cover was striking with a picture of a chestnut show jumper, jumping a magnificent pure white Arab, standing in front of the Eifel tower. It captivated her. Slowly she turned the pages that had beautiful pictures of horses and information about the event.

At breakfast she pointed out the program, which she had brought with her, to Cathy and Louise. "Did you see this magnificent program?" She held it up.

"Are you kidding?" Cathy said, "I was so tired, I didn't wake up until a half an hour ago. I didn't read any of the stuff they gave us."

Louise hadn't seen the program either, but she picked it up and glanced through it. "Oh, look." She held it up to a centerfold page that was dedicated to Iran's exhibition. There were pictures of Davoud jumping Roshan, head shots of some of the other horses, and a picture of the three of them that had been taken by Bradley Davis, the official court photographer, at one of the board meetings of the Royal Horse Society in Tehran. There was a three-page article about Iran and its horses. As Louise read it, they were all pleased with what had been reported by their friend, James Underwood, the English journalist who worked for the daily paper, the Tehran Journal.

She passed the magazine back to Zahra, who flipped through to the page of officials. "Do you think you will know any of the officials, Louise? You've been abroad so many times and you are American, so maybe you will know someone."

Louise began looking down the list of organizers but knew no one. "Perhaps I'll know some of the judges." They waited as she looked at the list. "No there is only one American judge and one Brit, and I don't know either. Someone called Sir Anthony Parsons from England and a Dr. Thomas Williams from the United States."

"Oh, my God!" Zahra gasped and turned white.

"What's the matter, Zahra? Are you all right?" They both said in unison.

"It can't be possible! It just can't," she whispered almost to herself. She sat with her head in her hands breathing deep, almost painful sounding breaths for several minutes.

"What's wrong, Zahra? Please tell us," Cathy said touching her shoulder.

"I don't believe it could be the same person!"

"For goodness sake, what are you talking about?" Louise questioned.

"You know that I went to school and university in the States. Well, before I came back to Iran when my dad was so sick, I became engaged to this American boy who was my good friend and roommate Anne's brother. Well, actually, he asked me to marry him and gave me a ring just before I was to fly home and he was on his way back to military boot camp. We spent a coupleof blissful days together in New York, at the Plaza. I thought I was very much in love with him. My mother knew, but at first I didn't tell my father because he was dying of cancer and I didn't want to upset him.

"My fiancé ended up in Korea and was captured and presumed dead. I mourned him for a long time, and then, to make matters worse, my father died. After what seemed like ages, I decided that I needed to get back to my life.

That's when Mehdi started courting me and we eventually married. Several years later, Tom's sister, Anne called to tell me her brother had been found alive in Korea. He had escaped from a prison camp. I didn't want to talk to him because I was married and amazingly in love with Mehdi. His name was Tom Williams."

"It's a very common name, Zahra. There must be thousands with the same name. And this judge is a doctor. Was he studying medicine?" asked Cathy.

"No, as I recall, he graduated from Cornell with a Business degree. You're right. It couldn't possibly be him. Although –" she hesitated for a moment. "The family did have horses, both Arabs and Thoroughbred racehorses."

Louise got up. "Well, we better go – I just saw the chauffer peeking in the door. We only have two days to set up our booth and get the horses settled in before the Salon du Cheval opens its doors to the public."

All the personnel from the Salon were extremely helpful to the Iranian group, none of whom had ever been to such a large, multifaceted exhibition. A guide took them around to see the premises, which covered many hectares. Not only were there equine exhibits, but there was also a large hall with hundreds of retail booths. Several restaurants were set up in and around the complex so it wouldn't be necessary to leave the site until they went to the hotel to sleep, after the gates closed at eight p.m. each evening.

The non-competing horses, of which there were many, would be exhibited on the opening day in the Great Hall competition ring. The Iranian horses would be on formal display in the ring from ten a.m. until eleven, following a display of Fiord horses from Iceland. Once they had their day of parading around the ring, they'd be in their stalls next to the Iranian booth, except when they were being exercised or hand-walked in designated areas where people would be able to gather by the fence around the rings to watch and ask questions of the handlers. Sefola and Davoud both spoke quite good English but Jamshid hardly knew a word. Louise had decided she would handle her small horses herself when she as not manning the booth, and Zahra insisted that only she would handle Zahhak. Cathy and Davoud would help out as well, when they weren't riding or training the two jumpers. Luckily, there was a lot of space to ride and exercise them, as well as a large covered schooling arena that had jumps.

The night before opening day, they admired their work on the booth and were all pleased. It looked like the inside of a Qashgha'i tent with Turkoman, Bakhtiari and Kerman carpets hanging on the three walls. They had put a *tang* (a long narrow piece of carpet) at the top around the walls like a border. There were camel bags, and pillows made from carpets on the floor around the small room for seating. There was also a beautiful inlaid table in the center that held many artifacts and pamphlets about the horses. On easels in front of the booth, they had huge pictures of Asil horses standing and rearing, and one picture of Davoud on Roshan clearing an imposing looking jump. There were two small carved wooden benches for seating on either side of the door. As they walked past some of the other exhibits, they felt theirs was the most eye catching. The horses had settled in well, so they were pleased with their first two days in France.

They decided to look in on the Great Hall, where the horses would be exhibited the following day, before leaving the grounds. The glistening off-white sand had been dragged smooth and the kick board around the ring had been covered with a deep, royal-blue fabric. On one side, there was a long row of tables covered in white tablecloths, a place to display the ribbons and trophies. On the other side there was a small pavilion, draped in a soft fluttering blue fabric, with about ten seats and tables, for the army of judges who would be on hand when the official show commenced.

Bahman had arrived in the afternoon and was waiting in the hotel lobby for his three horsewomen as they walked through the large glass revolving door. He opened his arms to each one, kissing both cheeks as was the Iranian custom. "You beautiful ladies look like you need a glass of champagne after your busy day. Let's go into the bar and sit at a table so you can tell me how things have been going here in Paris, and then I will tell you my news."

They all sat down at the same corner table that the girls had been frequenting each evening before they went off to their rooms for a much-needed sleep. The *garcon* nodded to each of them in recognition with a friendly, "*Bon soire, mesdammes.*"

"It seems that you ladies have been frequent-ing this charming bar since you've been here. I'm glad you've been enjoying yourselves." He ordered a bottle of *Moet &Chandon brut.*

They clinked their glasses for the *Salamati* (Cheers) and each took a deep sip of the deli-cious bubbly. Zahra and Louise spent several minutes relating the activities since they had arrived, filling Bahman in on all the details. He listened attentively, occasionally interjecting a question, until they were finished. Then he said, "And now, Cathy, please tell me how my jump-ing horses are doing."

"They're both settling in well. We hand-walked them the first day and today we gave them long slow flat work in the covered ring. Tomorrow I plan to give them both a school over fences with Davoud riding. We don't actually show until the end of next week, so I'm sure they'll be well-prepared for their classes. I haven't had time to look around see what the competition is, but I'll be doing that in the next couple of days. There are quite a few riders here that I know from past competition in the States and here in Europe, so I look forward to reconnecting with them."

It seemed Bahman could barely keep quiet. "So, wait till you hear my news!" he said enthusiastically.

They were all anxious to hear what the news was, but Bahman kept them waiting as he signaled the waiter to order some caviar and blinis. Then as they waited for their order, he brought them up to date with the happenings back in Tehran at the horse show the previous week. When the caviar arrived, they each served themselves a generous amount on a flat white blini with a small squeeze of lemon juice.

Bahman took a bite of the caviar and said, "Mmm, delicious. Not as fresh as we get at home, but it suits the occasion. I had dinner with His Majesty and the Empress a few nights ago and she seemed most interested in our showing of the horses here in Paris. This surprised me, because she really doesn't have much interest in the horse world. As you know, culture, art and the people are her passions. She asked me for the dates and wanted to know what we would be doing here. And then she informed me that she was planning a visit to France and would put a few hours at the Salon du Cheval on her itinerary when she was in Paris next week."

Louise smiled. "How absolutely fantastic. That's going to be great publicity for the horse world at home," she said. "And of course, having the Empress of Iran at the Salon will be amazing for attendance here, I would think. Do you know which day she'll be here?"

"I think she's coming next Friday afternoon if it works out with her schedule."

This news made Cathy concerned. "Oh my God! That's when Davoud shows Roshan in the Meter twenty class. It will make him too nervous if he knows she's there watching."

"Don't be ridiculous. Davoud has been raised at the Imperial Stables; he doesn't get nervous when he sees her there. And remember, his father is the Shah's personal groom when he comes to ride. It won't bother Davoud in the least. She's like family to him."

"Well, it's going to make *me* nervous," Cathy admitted.

When they'd finished their champagne and caviar, they all went to the dining room to enjoy a leisurely dinner before retiring early so they'd be ready for the first day of the big event.

The day of the exhibition went off extremely well. Zahra dressed in Qashgha'i pantaloons and a colorful coat. Wearing her felt hat, she galloped in on the brilliant stallion, Zahhak, with his head and tail held high, to the Persian music of Bijan Mortazavi's *Sharh va Gharb*. Jamshid and Abdula, dressed in colorful tribal outfits, followed, leading Arrus and Fahra with long multicolored braided leads attached to the red tasseled rope halters used on the Persian Arab horses. During their allotted fifteen minutes, Zahra rode Zahhak at a trot, canter and gallop, to demonstrate his excellent fluid movement. Meanwhile, the boys ran this way and that with their charges to show them off advantageously. Finally, they all stood stock still before sedately leaving the ring. The remainder of the day the booth was inundated with spectators, full of questions about Iran and its horses. It was a tired group that left the hall shortly after ten that night. Day one was complete, with just nine more before they'd return to Tehran.

The second and third days were for the Arab horse competitions which Zahra was excited to watch. She arrived at the stables before the others because she wanted to groom her horses and ride Zahhak out in the park early so she could spend the day watching the classes. She was interested to see what the champions of the World Arab Horse Organization looked like and how they compared with her own herd and those of the other Iranian breeders.

The Arab beauty contests were the first events for the WAHO registered horses. She had never before seen classes like this. First the competing horses were all lead into the ring together by their handlers and walked in single file around the ring with their heads held high. The panel of judges (there were at least six), sat in the pavilion on one side of the stadium in an area cordoned off by thick white ropes and colorful potted flowers. They had about ten minutes to observe the entrants as they paraded through. The whole group of horses then left the arena and came back to be judged individually.

Each handler came running in with the horse on a long rope so that it could rear and play, circling the ring and changing direction to show off its style of movement and agility. Finally the judges, who had all moved into the center of the ring, asked the handler to stand the horse up in a conformation pose, while they wrote down the points they felt the horse deserved for movement, head, eyes, ears, neck, back, fore-arm, hind legs, tail and all the rest of the body parts of the animal. Once the horse had depart-ed the arena, the announcer gave out the scores which were then averaged to one final number. When all the horses had performed, the win-ners were announced to a fanfare of music and applause.

There was a whole day's schedule of differ-ent divisions which included a separate class for stallions and mares, in age groups for yearlings, two-year olds, three-year olds, four-year olds and senior horses(five years and up.) Zahra was fascinated and began to try to judge herself, pleased when she picked the same winners as the judges did several times. She also kept her eyes on the judges, who seemed to change for every class. She wanted to see if she could spot Tom, but she didn't see anyone she thought could possibly be him. She was sure she would recognize him if she saw him.

On the second day of the Arab Show, as Zahra took her seat in the exhibitors' section of the arena to watch the competition, Bahman joined her. "I'm sorry I missed the show yester-day. I had some commitments I needed to take care of for Her Majesty's impending visit. Did you enjoy it?"

"Yes," Zahra replied, "it was really interesting

to see how they have the horses trained to display their movement and agility on the end of a long rope. To me, the handler finds himself in a precarious position at times, where it would be easy for the horse to connect with a swift kick, but the training and control didn't seem to let that happen. I plan to speak to some of the handlers while I'm here and hopefully to get some lessons in how they accomplish what they do.

"Today the classes are all mounted, so I think it would be fun to watch the different divisions for another full day. Most of the classes are still divided by age. For instance, there are three, four and five-year-old classes and then the older horses compete in the Senior or Open divisions. The final classes of the day will be the costume class where the horses are ridden around the ring by riders in supposedly Arab costumes. I've been told that it's quite a spectacle. It amazed me during the beauty classes how grooms and other people were running around the outside of the ring waving long sticks with flags on them and hooting and hollering in order to make the horses take notice and snort and shy. It was a bit crazy to me. I'll be interested to see if they do the same thing to the horses while they are being ridden."

As they sat together watching, Zahra kept her eye on the judges to see if perhaps she would spot Tom. Late in the afternoon she thought she saw him when the costume classes commenced. There was a tall man wearing a beige suit with a cowboy tie, carrying a clipboard with a pen stuck over his left ear. She could see that he was sporting shiny brown cowboy boots and his blondish grey hair was slightly receding. Her heart started beating fast and she breathed in sharply. Was it really him?

Bahman touched her arm. "Is everything alright, Zahra? You seem agitated all of a sudden."

"I think I saw someone I knew years ago when I was going to school in the States, though I'm not really sure it's him."

"Where is he? Point him out to me."

"The judge with the clipboard who's walking up to the gray horse with the woman in the purple and gold Shahrazad-like costume."

"You know there is a reception in the members' lounge being given by the WAHO this evening at seven? I was planning to go. Why don't you, as the Persian Arab expert, accompany me? I'm sure the judges will all be there, so you might meet up with this fellow and see if it really is your friend."

When the Arab show ended about five, Zahra went over to the booth to relieve Louise who had spent most of the day answering questions and telling the boys when to take the horses to the display rings for inspection by spectators. Cathy and Davoud had been occupied with schooling the jumpers and meeting up with riders and trainers who would be their competitors in the show jumping. Bahman came by the booth to remind Zahra about the reception later that night. He suggested she take the car and driver to the hotel so she could change out of her Qashqa'i outfit into something more suitable for a Paris function. He would be waiting for her in the lobby at seven.

On the ride to the hotel, Zahra began to worry about what she would wear to this party. She had brought several outfits left over from her social days with Mehdi, but they were probably dated. Once in her room, she took time to luxuriate in a hot bubble bath which she hoped would help her relax. She opened the closet and there was a very chic, soft turquoise Chanel suit that she liked, but thought perhaps it was more for a luncheon engagement. She had brought two long evening dresses, one a Dior and the other a Pierre Cardin, but they were both too formal.

Then she spotted the blue chiffon Persian-designed fabric that her designer friend Bijan had fashioned into a dress with a mid-calf length flowing skirt, a slightly dropped waist, round ruffled neckline and beautiful bell sleeves. She had worn it several times in Tehran to dinner parties and she thought it was quite flattering to her less-than-perfect forty-five-year-old figure. She pulled her long, wavy brown hair back, rolling it into a chignon, put her mother's double strand of Oriental pearls around her neck, fastened pearl earrings on her ears and looked at herself in the mirror. Next came a daub of powder on her face and a little blush on her cheeks. Was she ready? No, she needed a bit of lipstick and mascara on her long lashes.

Knowing the weather would be cool, she'd brought her one remaining mink coat, which she now threw over her shoulders. As she walked out of her room she glanced down at her work-worn hands. On her left hand, she wore Mehdi's beautiful emerald and diamond engagement ring and her gold wedding band. For some reason she couldn't fathom, she had put the diamond ring Tom had given her on her right ring finger when she'd discovered it in her small Kuwaiti chest in her bedroom the day before she had left Aghili. She'd almost forgotten about it until she opened the chest to get her passport. It had been locked away for all these many years. Now as she looked at it sparkling at her, she decided it was an omen. She glanced at her image in the mirror by the door as she left her room; though she knew she wasn't the beauty she'd been years before; she was still a striking-looking woman.

As she entered the lobby from the elevator, she heard a whistle, which upon investigation she realized had come from her boss, who was waiting by the concierge's desk. "Well, don't you look fantastic this evening, Zahra Khonume. Are you all dolled up in hopes of meeting your old 'friend'?"

Zahra smiled at Bahman. "I wanted to look my best when representing my country. I see you're looking quite dapper yourself in your Yves St. Laurent suit and Royal Horse Society tie and handkerchief. Are you planning to meet some *femme fatal*?"

He chuckled as he took her arm to walk through the lobby to the waiting car outside. They were, of course, fashionably late as was the Iranian way, but were cordially greeted by the president of the WAHO and his wife, who were still in the receiving line with another couple whose name and position Zahra had missed. The reception room was packed with people, many of whom Zahra had seen at the show. She worked the crowd, introducing herself, conversing with trainers and owners whom she would like to get to know well enough to discuss their methods and her project of attaining recognition for the Persian Arab horses. Meanwhile she kept her eye out for the man that she thought was Tom, but she wasn't able to find him in the throngs.

Waking next the morning, she felt quite disappointed that she hadn't seen Tom at the reception. She knew she had looked her best, which was how she would like him to see her if they ever met again. She felt a niggling guilt that she hadn't wanted any contact with him once he was found alive and back in the States. Had she been cruel, or was she afraid to talk to him because she was so happy at the time? Or was it that she felt iniquitous because she knew he had such a difficult time, while she was living a wonderful, easy life?

At breakfast, Cathy and Louise both wanted to hear all about the reception. They would each be accompanying Bahman to the reception for show jumpers and foreign breeds within the next few days, so they wanted to know what the attire would be. What did Zahra wear and did she feel appropriately dressed?

Cathy asked, "So tell me did you see your old fiancé that you thought you saw judging yesterday?"

"No, I didn't see him. There was quite a crowd, but I looked hard and I'm sure he wasn't there. I was sure he would be, being a judge and all, but then maybe it isn't Tom at all."

Once at the stables, Zahra checked on her three horses, and then she and Jamshid took

Zahhak and Fahra on a long ride in the park. It was a beautiful cool November day. The sun shone through the almost leafless trees, casting small shadows at which the horses occasionally shied and jumped. The riders laughed at their foolishness.

Zahra said, "These horses have been inside for too long without having any turn out. That's why they're being so silly. By the end of our stay they're going to be bucking us off, Jamshid. Let's go over to the exercise track and let them gallop around a few times. That'll make them happier and a bit tired, let's hope."

After they'd finished letting the horses run and had settled them back in their stalls, Zahra walked slowly towards the exhibition booth to take her turn talking to inquiring spectators. Just before rounding the corner to their aisle, Cathy stopped her. "Zahra, I think your friend is at the booth! He's tall and quite good looking. He came up to me asking if there was a Zahra Bakhtiar with our group. He said he knew you years ago when you were at school in America. I told him you were out riding, so he said he'd wait. He's been hanging around asking questions and looking at the horses in the stalls for over an hour. You and Jamshid must have taken a long ride."

"What? Are you serious? Look at me! I'm

a mess! The horses needed a good run. I can't meet Tom like this, wearing this Qashgha'i outfit. My hair is a mess under my cap. I need to go back to the hotel to change."

"No, you look just fine. You're in your working clothes. They've been good enough for the spectators so far. Why aren't they good enough for an old friend?"

"You don't understand. I was engaged to him. We were lovers. I don't want him to see me like this!"

"Well, you'll just have to get over yourself. Let's go see him."

Zahra straightened up, touched her cap and hair, and walked around the corner to see a tall, older, but still handsome Tom Williams smiling at her. He opened his arms and gave her the best hug she'd had in years.

"Oh, my God! I can't believe it's you, Zahra," he whispered into her ear. "I've missed you so much all these years. You were never out of my thoughts."

She couldn't answer because it made her feel badly; she had thought of him often, but she'd also had such a wonderful life that he wasn't in her forethoughts.

He released her and held her at arm's length, staring into her dark brown eyes, with his sparkling blue eyes reflecting joy. "You look fabulous.

The years have been good to you, my darling."

She was still unable to speak. What could she say? And then her eyes spilled with tears falling down her cheeks and a sob emitted itself from her throat. She collapsed onto one of the wooden benches, putting her head in her hands as she cried. Tom sat down next to her, putting his arm around her shoulders to calm her.

"I'm so sorry!" She was finally able to find her voice. "I don't know what hit me. I'm not usually so emotional. Please forgive me."

At eight thirty that night, the time they had arranged to meet for dinner, Tom was waiting in the hotel lobby as Zahra stepped out of the elevator. As she came towards him, with a big smile on his face, he held out his hand to her. She had taken more time with her appearance than she had the night of the reception. She wore a flowing rose colored chiffon Pierre Cardin dress that she had had for years but this was one of her favorites. It was slightly off the shoulders with a softly pleated bodice and a loose waist. Again, she had her mother's pearls around her neck and her two beautiful engagement rings on her rather large, well-worn hands, over which she had put black kid gloves to stave off the cold of the evening air.

"You look wonderful, Zahra," Tom said as

he gave her a kiss on both cheeks and led her through the front revolving door to the car and driver he had waiting. "I made a reservation for us at Maxim's. I know you've been there many times before, but this is my first visit to Paris, if you can believe it, and I want to dine at the most famous restaurant in the world."

"You're right. The first time I had dinner at Maxim's I was a teenager. You may remember my parents came to Richmond for my graduation. Then after going to see Cornell, we went to Europe for the summer. We spent some time in Paris, and while my father attended to his business, my mother and I toured the fashion houses. We ordered all these beautiful clothes, most of which I never wore. We had dinner at Maxim's, more than once as I recall. Brigitte Bardot was there one evening wearing no shoes. I was so excited to see a real film star even though she wasn't one of my favorites. I would have preferred if I had been Marilyn Monroe."

"I hope you won't mind going there again."

"Oh, no. I love the place and it'll bring back some good memories for me. I haven't thought of those times much lately. Do you know much about the history of the restaurant?"

"No, I only know that it's reputed to serve the best food in the world."

"Maxim's was founded as a bistro in 1893 by

Maxime Guillard who had been a waiter. When he sold it to Eugene Cornuche, it slowly became one of the most fashionable and popular restaurants in Paris because he decorated it in the Art Nouveau style and installed a piano for dancing. He made sure it was always filled with beautiful women. Why, he would even have a beautiful woman sitting by the window, in view of the sidewalk, to entice people to come in. In the 1930's it was sold again, this time to Octave Vaudable, who began by carefully selecting his clients, preferably those who were famous or rich, such as Aristotle Onassis, Maria Callas, the Duke of Windsor and Wallis Simpson. It was the beginning of a new era of prestigious catering under his family name, and it's lasted more than thirty-five years. Now, you and I, neither rich nor famous, will be dining at Maxim's."

The driver stopped at the curb in front of the red awning, opening the Peugeot's rear door for them to alight, and Maxim's doorman opened the heavy wooden, framed, glass door. As Zahra walked in, she caught her breath. It was so beautiful, just as she remembered. The lighted stained glass beveled ceiling with its colored leaves and flowers drew her eyes upwards. The walls were covered in mirrors, art deco flowers, and paintings of beautiful women of many époques framed by tall slender Roman

Corinthian columns, gold embossed at the top. They were ushered by the maître d' to a round corner table with its sparkling white tablecloth, small shaded lamps, and a silver rose bowl, filled with a half dozen red roses. As she sat down on the red velvet covered banquet, she felt as if she was in a different world and time. Tom sat opposite her in the red-cushioned wooden armchair, taking her in with longing eyes.

Neither of them spoke, and for a moment there was an uncomfortable silence. Then they each began to speak at the same moment. They stopped, laughing, as the waiter approached to take their drink orders.

"Shall we have champagne to celebrate our chance encounter?" Tom queried.

"Why, yes, I never turn down champagne. especially when it's a celebration."

After ordering a bottle of Moet Chandon Brut, Tom held his hand out for her to take, which she did willingly. "You may wonder why I said chance encounter," he said. "I'd actually planned to leave Paris to go back to the States today, but when I missed the reception last night I decided it was ridiculous not to stay a few days and see Paris. I was so tired after the two days of judging that when I went back to my hotel room to change for the party, I sat down to rest and fell asleep.

"When I awoke it was well past midnight. I ordered something to eat and drink from room service and began leafing through the Salon's program. That's when. by chance, I saw the article about Iran and your picture. I couldn't believe it! All these years I've put you out of my mind as best I could, But every now and then, I'd let a memory creep in, only to tell myself that you were living the life you should be living and hopefully you were happy. At first, I told myself that I should just go sightseeing today and stay away from the Salon, but then my impulses told me that I needed to find you, and here we are."

They studied the ornately printed menu, deciding on *Caviar de Persia et ses Blinis* to start, for it was the only thing a sophisticated Persian girl would order. Next, they had a *Foie Gras de Canard* followed by *Sole Rotie avec Sauce Vermouth* and *Legumes de Saison.* They talked through dinner, or Zahra talked, while Tom asked questions. He wanted to know all about her life after she had left New York that day more than twenty years before. So, she told him all, or almost all, that had happened, from the time she arrived back in Tehran when her father was so ill. They were able to laugh together about the good parts and she shed a tear or two as she related the deaths of her father and her much-loved husband.

"I suppose I should tell you about the day Anne called to tell me you were alive. I was at the big house in Andimeshke about to leave for the day to attend my duties at the Aghili stud farm when I heard the phone ring. I almost didn't answer, but my mother had called me the night before to tell me that I should expect a call from your sister, so I ran back up the front steps and answered the phone which was in the front hall. For once the reception was quite good. I was glad to hear Anne's voice for we hadn't been communicating much by that time.

"Then she told me to sit down for her news, which was that you were alive and, on your way, back to the States. She wanted to give you my number so you could call me, but I told her not to because I knew I would not be able to handle the situation. I had mourned you and my father together for a couple of years until I told myself I was wasting my life and needed to move forward to accomplish something instead of living like a widow who didn't know how to have fun. That's when Mehdi and I began our courtship. After I hung up and I rode towards Aghili on my faithful Shahab, I let my mind drift back to the times you and I had in our innocent youth and smiled with joy at our young love and dreams. I began to have pangs of guilt at the fact that I was – I guess afraid is the word – to talk to you.

I decided that the decent thing would be to wait a week or so and call you. Of course, that day never happened. I was so busy with the horses and the agricultural innovations we were trying to implement in our tribal area, that I just didn't find the time or have the inclination. Every now and then, I would think of you and vow to make the call, but I'm sorry to say I just didn't do it. I can only apologize now and ask your forgiveness."

Tom said, "Not necessary, but you have it."

They ordered *Plateau de Fromges* and port for the final course. While they were waiting, the piano began to play so they joined other couples on the dance floor. As he led her expertly around the small dance floor, she felt as though she were floating. He held her softly and put his cheek against hers and she was a young girl once more. It just felt so comfortable to be in his arms again.

Back at the table he took her hands and held them. "I'm so happy to see you are wearing our engagement ring, even though it's on the wrong hand. Maybe you'll move it back to where it belongs one day."

"It's strange you know. I hadn't worn it since I became engaged to Mehdi all those years ago, but when I was retrieving my passport from my lockbox before coming on this trip, I saw the box. I don't know why, but I just decided to wear this beautiful diamond. I believe it was an omen or something mystical that made me do it," she said giggling. "So, you've heard enough about me. Now I want to hear about you and your life since we've been apart."

"That will take at least one more bottle of Moet, maybe more. Shall I order it?"

She nodded in assent, "The night is still young, and I know this place stays open until dawn. Why not?"

"So, this story I'm going to tell you is long. The last time we were together was our romantic visit in New York when we became engaged. I had so much joy in my heart as I boarded the plane back to boot camp, but it sure didn't last."

He looked off into space for a moment, then continued. "That dreadful Korean War started when the North Korean People's army suddenly invaded the Democratic People's Republic of Korea to the south. You see, after WWII, Korea was divided in half along the 38th parallel with the Russians occupying the north and the Americans the south. The dictator in the north was communist and the United States was anti-communism, so after the invasion President Truman readied his troops for war against communism itself. Even before we stepped in, nearly ten thousand North and South Koreans had been killed in battle.

"I flew back to Alabama and finished my basic training, which was rigorous and full of harassment by the officers, but I survived it. After a week at North Cliff, I was flown to Seattle where I boarded a Liberty ship with about four thousand other men and spent a dreadful sixteen days crossing five thousand miles of the Pacific Ocean. We landed in Japan with its beautiful Mount Fiji, one of the largest volcanoes in the world, that I could see from the front porch of our building where we were billeted while waiting for our orders.

"I was surprised when my orders came because I was being sent to the Eta Jima Specialist School for thirty days of training as a medic. Eta Jima is a small island off the coast near Hiroshima, where the Japanese Naval academy had been before and during WWII. It was a beautiful, idyllic place where the accommodations were almost luxurious. The great admirals of the Japanese Navy had attended this school early in their careers. This is where I began my interest in medicine, which became my life's work – but that's another story.

"From Eta Jima, we went by rail to the seaport of Sasebo, for shipment to Korea. At the port, we were given all our fighting gear, then boarded a flat-bottom landing craft where we slept in our sleeping bags for the crossing. It was a pretty rough ride, as I remember. As morning broke, we viewed the rough mountainous coastline of the South Korean peninsula. We disembarked at the Port of Pusan, which is one of the largest cities in the south and had become a sanctuary for hundreds of thousands of refugees who fled from the North Korean invasion forces. As we boarded a narrow-gauge train that would take us north to the war zone, we saw that the city was a mass of hungry, dirty and homeless people living in despair. Along the two-hundred-mile route, we saw children congregated along the railroad tracks. Whenever the train stopped, which was often, we gave them C-rations or whatever food we had to spare. The kids were orphans, living day-by-day in cardboard or corrugated tin shelters or in caves nearby. Some of the older ones were taking care of their younger siblings. It was cold and there wasn't a soldier on that train who wasn't concerned for the welfare and future of these children."

"Oh, that sounds so sad and cruel!" Zahra interjected.

"The little train chugged up the mountain terrain and finally stopped at a small town in a valley alongside a dry riverbed. We were told that we would make camp about three quarters of the way up the ridge in a grove of pine trees.

Each man had a folding cot over which we fashioned a sort of tent with canvas shelter halves. It was nice not to be on the cold ground. We of course dug fox holes just in case, but that first night, we didn't have to sleep in them. However, we listened to gun and mortar fire all night long, in the distance, so we didn't get much sleep.

"We'd been there for only a few days when we began to notice South Korean soldiers wandering along the dry stream below us. We didn't think much about it because their troops weren't as well-disciplined as ours. They kept wandering south in twos and threes. Then one morning we awoke to the news that there was no South Korean infantry in front of us to the north, between us and the North Koreans and Chinese. Our reaction was to get the heck out of Dodge, but our commanding officer had a different idea. We were to stay and fight. We had conflicting emotions – the adrenalin rush that told us to fight and the mental, prudent wish to flee. But we didn't have a choice.

"Soon we heard the artillery fire of the North Koreans on the other side of the ridge and then mortars began falling near our encampment. We began to fire our guns in retaliation and the battle had commenced. Ammunition was brought to the village by trucks and carried up the mountainside to our position. Mostly we had small arms, mainly carbines, but we also had some 30-caliber machine guns and a couple of 50-calibers. With the tremendous barrage of sound, sleep became impossible. Each gun lit up the sky when it was fired. The bombardment went on for about four days, with the combined artillery pieces putting up a constant boom-boom-boom that created a rain of steel, fire, and destruction over the ridge. Then just as it began, all went quiet. And we thought that was it."

"Was it?"

"That night we had sentries posted with two hour rotations so that some of the men could get much-needed sleep. I was to do the second shift, so I dropped onto my cot after we had a less than delicious stew and biscuit supper. I awoke with a start to find our encampment was surrounded by North Korean soldiers. In minutes, we were all taken prisoner.

"They strung us together with long ropes and chains and marched us in a line up to the top of the ridge and down the other side to a narrow road that ran alongside another dry riverbed. We walked all night, until dawn, when we were marched down a small rocky path away from the riverbed. We were taken to a collecting point that was a compound of timber-lined caves dug into the side of the hill which were rooved and covered with soil. The small room that we were in had a window in the corner for light – it was barred with small timbers. My first thought was to escape, so I started to twist the bars to see if I could get them loose. With the help of a couple of my platoon buddies, we finally got them loose enough to be able to take them out and replace them at will. We planned to wait until dark to escape.

"Just as we finished our escape route, the guards came in with a huge bowl of rice and some water. As we reached in with our hands, they stopped us. While one guard held us at gunpoint, the other went out and came back with a handful of spoons. We tried to get some sleep, lying on the rough ground that day, for we would need to be alert for our planned escape that night.

"Unfortunately, at dusk that night, they came into the cave, and herded us all at gunpoint, outside and into a truck. We travelled all night over rough roads, which was hard on our hind sides. At first light, we stopped and were ordered to enter a small hut just off the road in a grove of trees.

"We weren't offered any sustenance and sat or lay in the hut all day until the guards came in that night, removed our boots, and again tied us together. Then they ushered us, with their rifles, out of the hut and down a path that led to a stream that did have some water in it. There, we scooped it up with our hands, drinking thirstily, for we had not had any water since the night before.

"Next we had to march across the river and up the mountainside on small rocky paths that were treacherous for our feet. It was extremely cold, and some of the men fell on the path due to pain and frost-bitten feet so they were shot there and then. We started out with about twenty-six of us, and by the time we had trudged down the other side of the ridge there were only fifteen of us left. We continued marching all that morning with only rest stops when the guards seemed to need them. They had canteens with water and ate from pouches, but they offered us prisoners nothing.

"At just about dusk, a North Korean armored truck came up beside us and an officer got down and said something to the soldiers who were guarding us. They then began to shoot us with their rifles. I felt the searing pain through my side and legs. I fell to the ground as my comrades fell in a heap, one on top of the other. Finally, when the gunshots stopped, I thought I heard the soldiers shouting and then climbing into the vehicle, and they just drove off."

Zahra was stunned. "Oh my God Tom, that sounds terrible! So, what happened next?"

"I lay there not moving, freezing cold, for a

long time. Finally, I must have passed out, for the next thing I remember was waking up in the small hut of a North Korean family. I don't know how long it was before I regained consciousness, but when I did, I was very weak and confused. I'd been shot in several places, but the wounds had been cleaned. However, they were still open and quite painful.

"It was hard to communicate with the family for I knew no Korean and they knew no English. The husband and wife were in their forties, but they looked much older. They had a son who was twenty and a beautiful daughter who had dark, almond-shaped eyes, a lovely kind smile and long black hair. She was eighteen. This family took care of me for months as I lay prone on a small cot, they had put me on. They lived way out in the boonies behind the North Korean line, but they were totally able to subsist on this narrow piece of land, an oasis hidden in the woods at the base of barren, rugged, impassable hills. There was a small lake nearby where they would go with a two-wheeled tank that was pulled by their oxen, to get water.

As I improved and was able to start moving around, I began helping out with the duties around the farm. I slowly learned the language so that we could communicate better. They were terrified that soldiers would find them.

They explained to me that I must stay with them unless I wanted to be killed again. They had considered me dead when they found me on the side of the road under a pile of bodies on one of their return trips to the nearest village which was about ten kilometers away. They said as they passed the bodies, which had begun to smell, they heard a sound and so they investigated and found me almost dead. They searched my pockets and found my billfold, that miraculously my captors had not taken, and realized I was American and probably worth saving."

"You were so lucky that those kind people were brave enough to rescue you."

"Oh, I know. They were simple but altruistic peasants. The real heart of the earth. I stayed with them through two more winters. We had no communication with the outside world, but we would sometimes hear gunfire and explosions in the distance. Then there were planes that dropped bombs all around where we were, so we knew the war was still going on. As time went on, I became part of the family and grew very fond of them, especially the daughter Chin-Sun, whose name means 'truth and goodness.' I have to admit, we actually became lovers, with her parent's consent, of course. Finally, the war noises stopped so I figured it was over, but by that time Chin-Sun was pregnant, so I knew I couldn't leave until after the birth of our child. They all accepted the fact I would eventually try to get back home, so they were appreciative that I was staying even though the bombing had stopped."

"You're a wonderful person, Tom. I'm so glad you did that. So, tell me about the baby."

"There's not a lot more to tell. I helped deliver our beautiful baby. The birth was so simple; Chin just squatted down and the next thing I knew there was a baby boy in my hands. She acted as if nothing had happened. Her mother, Eun, and I took care of the umbilical cord and cleaned him up and that was that. To me it was a miracle, and that's when I decided that once I got back to the States, I would go to medical school and go into gynecology and obstetrics. I stayed with the family until our son, Dae-Ho, began to walk at twelve months. It was a tearful good-bye for all but I needed to go home. I knew you and my family would have believed me dead, and I felt I still had a real life to live. Chung-Hee, Chin's father, walked with me to the village and gave me instructions on how to get back across the border into South Korea hopefully without being spotted. I still had my billfold and dog tags, so once in the south I wouldn't have a problem getting back home. It was a long arduous journey, but I finally made it. After some interrogation in South Korea, I flew to D.C. where my family met me. And here I am finally reunited with my one true love."

"But that can't be the end of the story! What happened to Chin and your son and the family?" Zahra sounded concerned.

"They were finally able to escape to South Korea and contacted me when they arrived there. I began sending them support money. When Dae-Ho turned 16, he came to Virginia where he lives with me and goes to the Hill School in Middleburg. He took English at school in Korea and spoke it quite passably when he arrived. He's turning out to be a brilliant student. I'm hoping he'll follow family tradition and go to Cornell in two years when he graduates from Hill." Tom stopped talking and refolded his napkin in silence.

Zahra said, "But you're still not finished. What happened to Chin and her family when your son left for America?"

"They had no desire to leave their country. Chung-He and Eun have a grocery store in a suburb of Seoul and Chin-Sun studied to be a legal secretary and then married a big-time lawyer. I, of course have returned to visit them almost every year. That's one of the reasons this is my first visit to Paris. I don't have a lot of time to travel. With my practice, which is in Warrenton, and my commitments to the WAHO, I'm kept pretty busy."

He told her about going back to Cornell to study medicine and then interning at Presbyterian Hospital in New York. After that, he told her about going into practice with an older doctor who retired a few years later. He'd taken up riding again when he moved back home and became interested in breeding Arab horses. The next thing he knew, he was on committees and judging shows. He was now the President of the American Arab Horse Association.

It was almost three in the morning when they drove back to her hotel. She sat close to Tom in the back seat beside him. He put his arm around her shoulders and held her tight. He would come to the exposition around noon the next day so they could spend more time together. Hopefully she could get away to do some sightseeing with him.

The final days of the Salon flew by like a lightening flash. Davoud and Roshan won the championship in the One Meter Twenty division and riding Shirin he was second in two of the three classes. There was much celebrating at the Iranian exhibit and the group was inundated with curious spectators. Zahra spent as much time as she could with Tom, but she had her responsibilities to her horses and had to man the booth. Tom came in the early morning to ride on Farah out in the park while she rode Zahhak; they had some exhilarating rides which they both enjoyed. They were able to do some touring of Paris and went to dinner together every night. Some evenings they were joined by Cathy, Louise, and Bahman, during which time Tom learned about Zahra's stud book and the Persians' desire to have their Asil horses recognized by the WAHO.

It didn't take Tom many days to persuade Zahra that she should transfer her things to the San Rafael Hotel where he had a suite. He arranged for his driver to take her back and forth to the Salon, but most days he went with her himself, anyway. He had committee meetings to attend and enjoyed being there to watch the classes and wander through the exhibits.

The final evening of the show, there was a Grand Finale with all the exhibition horses and champions being ridden or led around the main arena to a full house of VIPS and spectators. Zahra wore a colorful Qashgha'i skirt, blouse, and headdress as she rode Zahhak, while Jamshid on Farah was dressed as a tribal chief. There was much applause for the whole Iranian contingent, which made Bahman especially proud as the Empress, who had enjoyed her first visit watching Davoud, had decided to come a second time, and was at his side in the Presidential box.

Tom was due to fly out the next afternoon, and Zahra would be busy helping pack up the booth and ready the horses for their flight back to Tehran. So, they decided to have a farewell dinner at Maxims, their final night together. They drank champagne, ate a delicious meal and danced until midnight when the driver came to take them to the hotel.

After making tender love, they lay together talking about what the future might bring for two people that lived at such a geographically undesirable distance from each other. Tom had a life in northern Virginia practicing medicine and running North Cliff, where he lived now that his parents had moved to Middleburg where they had a smaller house with less upkeep. The farm would eventually belong to him and Anne, but she had married a stockbroker who himself owned a large Thoroughbred farm nearby in Upperville where they lived, and she wouldn't want the family farm when their parents were gone. He'd agreed to take over the management of the place, where he ran a well-organized Arab stud farm. His parents and sister and her husband still had horses racing but he had not become involved in the sport due to his preference for the Arab horse.

He didn't envision himself ever living elsewhere; he loved his life of bringing babies into the world and being a part-time farmer. He had a great farm manager in Roy, who'd been working for the Williams for almost fifty years. Roy had been on the farm since he was a teenager, was an excellent horseman, well-versed in agricultural practices and totally dedicated to the family. His main fault was that he was opinionated and stubborn. Tom, who himself worked on the farm with the horses, mucking stalls and making hay in the season on the weekends, had learned to handle Roy with kid gloves. Without him, Tom could not feasibly run the farm, so he always tried to agree with the older man and make his own suggestions seem like they were Roy's ideas.

He knew that a strong woman like Zahra would not easily be able to cooperate with Roy and some of his old-fashioned ideas. She had her own life in a country that Tom had never visited and could not imagine. When he tried to picture it in his mind's eye, the primitiveness of his farm life in Korea came to him, but he knew it wasn't really like that. When she talked about her time in the desert visiting the tribal chiefs, dealing horses with them and searching the horses' pedigrees her eyes lit up like diamonds; she truly loved her way of life and he knew he would never have a part in it. He truly loved her still, after all these years, but both their lives were different now, and he couldn't imagine that either of them would give up what they had; they were both happy with their place in life.

So, he broached the subject cautiously. "Would you consider coming to North Cliff for a visit any time soon, my darling?" he asked. "You know, now that I have finally found you again, I don't want to be without you."

"Tom, I love you with all my heart but there's no way I can come to America. First there's my work with the Asil Stud Book. It needs to be ready soon, now that WAHO has agreed to send inspectors to Iran so that our horses – which have the oldest lines in the world, by the way – can be recognized by them. Then there's the farm that I run, there's my work with the Royal Horse Society, and I don't have the money to travel. And finally, I'm now a true Persian and I love my life and country, so I can't imagine leaving all that. I do love you, but let's face it, it's not the young immature love we had all those years ago, when there was nothing stopping us. This is a mature sensible love and unfortunately, we will have to love from afar. We can keep in touch by phone and write to each other, but it wouldn't work for either of us to relocate to each other's life. I know you have a fulfilling life with your babies and horses, and I have a life that I love in the desert."

"We will just have to play it by ear then. We will keep in touch from afar and as time goes by things will move into place. There is no hurry since we've waited so long to reunite, so I have a feeling between the two of us we will work out a solution," Tom said as he leaned over to kiss her tenderly.

19

For in and out, above, about, below,
'Tis nothing but a Magic Shadow-show
Play'd in a box whose Candle is the Sun
Round which we Phantom Figures come and go.
Omar Khayyam

Ali 1979

The ferry was on their side of the river, so they were in luck. Zahra got out and boarded the aging contraption, chatting amiably with the tenders who she had known for so long. She handed them some *rials* as was her norm. Ali carefully drove onto the ferry, watching as Zahra went to the bow where she would always stand during the crossing. He watched her, thinking about the past few months.

Life at Aghili had not changed when Zahra arrived home with the three horses that had performed so well in France. The breeding program continued well, and the numbers of the herd grew. Each year, the money from the horse sales had increased, and though almost half of it went to the Royal Horse Society, the portion that was paid to Zahra went towards maintenance and was distributed to her workers. Everyone living at Aghili seemed to be happy with their life. It seemed that more and more of the nomadic tribes were settling in the area as was being encouraged by the central government, so there was more intermingling amongst the tribes' people. Life in Khusestan was very pleasant.

About four years after the Paris trip there were rumors of unrest in the county, but it was not evident in or around the Dezful/Andimeshke area of Khuzestan. It was so far from any of the major cities that it seemed to be a different country, and the people, who were mostly of Arab decent, were not interested in politics. Many of the nomads had settled, but there were still many who migrated, and as long as they had grazing lands, they didn't care about much else. Under Shah Mohammad Reza Pahlavi, they hadn't been tormented with like they had when his father was the shah.

Towards the end of the month of Shahriar *(August),* 1978 there were reports that the theatre in Abadan had been burned down with four hundred and thirty people inside, all of whom had expired. At first this massacre was blamed on the Shah, but eventually it was found that the fire had been set by Islamic militants who barricaded the doors preventing the people from fleeing. This dreadful event shocked the whole country. Since then, there had been reports that slowly leaked down to Aghili that there were riots happening in most of the big cities, but it was all so far away that it had no effect on what was happening in their part of the country.

When Ali asked Zahra about the rumors, she told him and the others who lived and worked for her that she had spoken to Bahman Mansarpour who, as well as being the head of the Royal Horse Society, was the right hand man to the Shah himself. He told her, "Yes there is some unrest but it's not important. The average age of the protesters is about seventeen. We don't see any real problem." That was in the month of Aban (October) and it was now the middle of Dey (early January) and she didn't think things had become any worse. There were still protests, but since the day that had been called "Black Friday" it seemed that things had settled down, according to what little news filtered down to them from Tehran.

Zahra

When the plane arrived at Doshun Tappe Air Base from Paris, it was late afternoon. Shadows fell across the runway as the horses were off-loaded and everything went smoothly. Extra grooms had arrived from Farahabad to help lead them back the two miles to the stables and the military truck was ready to have all the trunks and paraphernalia from the exposition loaded up. What surprised everyone was that Bahman and General Khosrodad were there to greet them with three of the Imperial open coaches drawn by the gray horses that were used during the opening of Parliament and other special state occasions.

"We're all going to ride in the coaches to Farahabad," said Bahman. "His Majesty wanted to have a welcoming party for our horses that performed so well in France. He suggested we have a parade, in order for the people to view them and congratulate the whole entourage."

As the coaches drove out of the gates, Zahra saw that there were crowds of people on both sides of the road, waving flags and cheering. Just what the horses needed, she thought, after their long arduous trip, but she had to admit it made her feel proud to know that the event had been well publicized at home. The horses all behaved well on the two mile walk and the most exciting thing of all was that His Majesty and the Empress were waiting in the stable yard, which had been decorated with streamers and lights and signs of congratulations. A large group from the horse community had also been invited to attend the fete.

The Shah opened the event with a toast. "I want to congratulate everyone who was involved with Iran's first ever international showing of horses. I'm very proud that you all made such a good impression, whether it was exhibition or competition. The Empress told me all about the jumping competition which was won by Davoud and Roshan who also placed second with the mare, Shirin. Louise and our Caspian horses were very well received, and Zahra put on a spectacular showing of our Persian Asil horses. As you know, my dream is for Iran to become recognized internationally in every field. Our football team made it to the World Cup Finals this year, and now our horses are in the international eye. I want everyone to toast the horses and the people who made this possible." The Shah held his glass of champagne high as did everyone else. He toasted, "*Mobarak! Salamati*!"

There was a buffet table set up in the royal pavilion with mounds of caviar and many delicious dishes of rice and *khoresh*. After circulating for a half hour or so, the Shah and Empress flew off in their helicopters, but the rest of the crowd stayed eating, drinking and dancing to Iranian music into the late hours. It was a good home coming.

Before she knew it, Zahra and her horses were back at Aghili and life had not changed at all. She now needed to be diligent about getting her stud book ready. She'd been told by the powers that be in the WAHO that she would first have to present a copy of what the Persian Arab Stud book contained, to date. It needed to be in English and every registered horse must have a pedigree that went back six generations. Whenever possible, they also wanted pictures of the stallions.

The beginnings of the Arab horse had been hidden in the ancient desert sands. It was thought that the ancient Persians were the first beings to tame the horse to be beasts of burden, for which *Allah* had put them on the earth. The common history of the Bedouin tribes and the horse went back to 3000 B.C. during which time keeping meticulous records of pedigree commenced. The hardiness of the breed was the result of a harsh desert climate and terrain. Often the horses would be brought into their owners' tents for protection from theft. Early selective breeding for traits included the ability to form a cooperative relationship with humans. This created a horse breed that was good-natured, quick to learn, and willing to please. They also developed a high spirit and alertness needed in a horse used for raiding and war. In Khuzestan, where the majority of the Persian or Asil horses were raised, they were meticulously bred by the families some of whose names they bore.

The stud book Zahra had been painstakingly working on complied with the requirements but there were strains of the Asil that still needed to be added, pictures had to be taken and then she needed to translate it all into English, the international language. She knew this work would consume every moment of her free time. She would need to go to the few families she hadn't yet approached about her project though she was sure they knew about it, for amazingly, news travelled fast in the desert.

She arose early in the mornings so she could attend to all the things that needed to be done, so if she planned to visit any of the breeders, she and Ali would be able to get to their destination by noon. She tried to be back at Aghili by mid to late afternoon so that she could work on the stud book which she did, on into the night. She tried to write to Tom once a week, for his letters came that frequently. They had made a plan that if he were to call her it would be between six and seven in the evening her time, which was mid-morning his time. She was living a happy fulfilling life, for it had a purpose and routine.

It took almost a year for her to complete her work on the studbook so that it filled all the requirements of the WAHO. When it was ready, she contacted Bahman who wanted her to deliver it personally to the *Anjoman* offices. She decided to drive to Tehran on her own. Ali needed to stay at Aghili to supervise the farm because she was doing some renovations to the stables and the paddocks just in case the WAHO accepted her pedigrees and came to Iran to inspect the horses.

She'd made the trip so many times over the years that she knew every rock on the roads, which had been improved greatly thanks to the Shah's development program. But the first hundred or so miles were still over well-packed sand and gravel tracks through the desert. Once she left Aghili, she crossed the Dez River on the old ferry that was still in operation. As she drove the few kilometers towards the river, she took in the arid beauty of the desert with its still blooming purple, red and yellow flowers scattered over the sand and rocks. She reflected on the memory of when she and Mehdi had been in charge of building the bridges in the area. They didn't build one on the route between Aghili and Andimeshke, mostly because they didn't want their place to be too accessible. And they were concerned it would look like they were using funds for their own benefit which would not look good to those in power, so they left the ferry they had constructed years before in operation. They usually rode from the big house to Aghili anyway, and there was a shallow area in the river that was an easy crossing for the horses, so they really didn't need a bridge, though many of their friends and workers felt they'd been foolish. On approaching the ferry dock, she saw that there were two keepers waiting on it with fishing lines in the slowly moving, murky water. Another reason for not building a bridge; what would the families of the ferry minders do if they had no job?

"Zahra, Khonume, we have been waiting for you. Word came to us that you were on your way to Tehran. It's a long drive, so you must hurry if you are to arrive before the sun sets," an old man with a gray beard called to her as she drove onto the dock.

"No worry, Behruz, if Old Rostam doesn't break down, I should be there well before dark," she said as she inched the car forward onto the rickety old ferry. Once it was safely secured, she got out and stood at the bow of the boat, taking in the mountains in the distance on the other side of the river. The morning breeze felt refreshing on her cheeks for those ten minutes before they landed, and she hopped back into the Land Rover. She stopped on the dock and got out to hand both the men who had helped her some *rials*, "Khodafez, I'll be back in a week." She waved goodbye as she drove away towards the north.

Once she reached Khoramabad, which was a two-and-a-half-hour drive over a mixture of broken tarmac and dirt roads, she turned onto the main Tehran highway which was beautiful smooth pavement. She stopped to fill up with *benzine* (gasoline) on the outskirts of the city, and then headed for the industrial city of Arak where the Iranian Aluminum Company (Iralco) reduction plant had been built as a joint venture between Reynolds Aluminum and Iran in the early 1970s. The town was now a bustling complex of many industries, including tool and die plants and Aluminum manufacturing companies. It was a good place to stop to refuel and to grab a quick bite to eat before setting off for Tehran. She calculated that it would take another five hours to get to the home of her friends Louise and Narcy's house on Damghan Avenue where she would stay while in Tehran. She had been driving conservatively, reminiscing as she travelled along, and Old Rostam was behaving well. She would arrive around seven in plenty of time for dinner.

The following morning, she had an appointment with Bahman at eleven. That gave her time to have breakfast with her hosts on the patio overlooking the beautiful rose garden that was Narcy's pride and joy. Over the many years they had lived in the Damghan house, he'd been cultivating many varieties of the rose. Some he had brought from America when he made trips to visit Louise's family, but his favorite was the red rose that was the national flower of Iran. This was a perennial flower said to be a symbol of love and beauty, with its large, full, bright red bloom, thick round thorny stem and bulbous fruit that was called rose hip, and was full of seeds used to produce jellies, jams and juices that were said to have medicinal properties and be full of vitamins.

"Narcy, the roses are absolutely beautiful, and it is the middle of *Mehr* (early October)," Zahra commented.

Narcy loved to talk about his flowers. "Roses usually bloom from *Jordan* (May) through the end of *Shahrivar* (September) here, but due to the fact that our garden is well protected by its walls, I'm usually able to enjoy a few extra weeks of the fragrance and flowers," he told her. "For five thousand years, the rose has been resplendent in our country. Its allure represents the passion of living, and the thorns represent the difficulties one has to endure to reach that state.

"At the time when Europe was still subservient to Roman occupation, the Sasanian Emperor Khosro the Great (531-579 BCE) had poetic couplets about roses and love posted on the palace gates. Surrounded by these splendid flowers, I often remember the lines of the famous Kashani poet Sohrab Seperhi, *'Our job is not to discover the 'secret' of the red rose. Our job is, perhaps, to float in the charm of the roses.'* As you know I have a passion for these magnificent flowers."

Zahra loved hearing his stories, but suddenly realized that she was running late. "Oh, I'm sorry I must run. The time got away from me enjoying your garden. I'm due to meet Bahman at eleven. He usually rides at six with Cathy and then has a leisurely breakfast, arriving at his office on Pasteur by then ,and I want to make sure I'm the first to get to the waiting room because you know what it's like there. He always has many appointments made for the same time and Parvin, his secretary, lets you into his office in order of arrival. I don't want to sit around all morning in that uncomfortable little waiting room." Louise told him.

When she walked into the court offices, Parvin told her that Bahman had not yet arrived but luckily, she was the first of many. So, at eleven fifteen she was ushered into the opulent office of the Shah's assistant and head of the Royal Horse Society who had been her good friend and savior for so many years. In Mehdi's old leather briefcase, she had the results of years of work on the stud book for the Asil Horses of Iran in both English and Farsi. Bahman stood as she entered, embracing her and kissing her on both cheeks.

"It's so good to see you, Zahra. It's been a long time since you were last in Tehran."

"As you know, I've been spending every moment I could on the stud book in hopes that it will be approved and the inspectors will come here to see the horses," she said as she put the briefcase on the mahogany conference table, opening it and revealing the two books she had bound with heavy string. They sat down, side by side to examine her work, leafing through the books as she explained the organization and information she had compiled.

"This is really amazing, Zahra. I congratulate and thank you for doing such a detailed and comprehensive job. I will have the court press print out several copies that we will have bound so we can send it quickly to the WAHO in hopes of having the inspection in the spring at the Aghili Stud Farm. We of course will have to discuss it, but I thought to have the presentation in Khuzestan, where we can call on the tribes' people to come and help us put on an authentic Arab celebration that would be very impressive for the foreign inspectors."

"Bahman, that is brilliant! I was hoping we would have it at Aghili. I know many of the tribal chiefs would be honored to be a part of such an event. I'll start making a plan, with your approval, of course. The spring is the perfect weather for it to take place."

"Once I get the word from the WAHO, I'll let you know and then I'll come down to stay with you for a few days so we can formulate a good plan." He couldn't wait to take the stud book to show His Majesty, who he knew would be thrilled with the prospect of world recognition for the country's horses.

Zahra stayed in Tehran for a few more days, catching up with friends and shopping for supplies that were unavailable in Khuzestan. Then she got into her ancient vehicle and headed back to Aghili.

The first day she was home, she was sipping on a glass of *sharob* (wine) on her porch before her evening meal when she heard the telephone ringing in the house. She walked in the front door and sat at the chair next to the small table as she answered, "*Bali.*"

"My darling, I've called for the past three days and no one answered. I was getting worried. Thank God I'm hearing your voice, finally," Tom said.

"I wrote to you that I'd be going to Tehran for a week or so to take the final copy of the stud book. Didn't you get the letter?"

"I did, but I wasn't sure when you were going. I was so happy that you had finally finished that I guess I didn't realize when you would make the trip. How did things work out?"

"Bahman was thrilled and he's getting the book printed so that it can be sent to WAHO soon. If it's approved and they agree to inspect us, we're planning to have it down here with a true Arab theme. We are hoping for some time in the spring, if all goes well."

"That sounds wonderful. I think I'll put my name in to be one of the inspectors. What do you think?"

"Oh, that would be wonderful. I so want you to come here to see what my life is like and to learn about our Persian ways. You know I miss you terribly and want to be with you. It would be a dream come true to have you here. I'm going to say a special prayer to *Allah*. And you, how have things been for you?"

"All's well at North Cliff. The weather is beautiful, and the colors of the trees are gorgeous this year. We had an early frost that turned them brilliant red, orange and yellow."

"I remember how it was in New York when we were there all those years ago. I always loved the fall because of that."

"I delivered six babies this week and they all arrived in the middle of the night, so I haven't had much sleep. But it makes me happy to bring new little beings into the world. I guess I'll never get tired of the miracle of birth. You have your horses that foal every year so I'm sure you understand the feeling."

"Yes, I do indeed. I am sorry to say I haven't written you all week because of my trip to Tehran, but once we sign off, I'll start a letter. I have so much to tell you."

"I hope it's that you love me."

"You know I do, with a passion!"

"I love you too, with all my heart. Now I must go to the office and see my patients. I love you, Zahra. Bye, bye."

The line went dead so she walked back to the porch with her glass of wine to watch the scarlet setting sun.

It was in late *Azar* (November) that word came from WAHO that the Iranian Asil Stud Book had been conditionally approved and they would be sending a team of four inspectors to

Iran. They were due in late March (*Farvadin*) which would be just a few days after the *Now Ruz* holiday and *Sizdah Bedar*. That gave Zahra and the society just over three months to make their preparations for the big event. It would be difficult because no one worked during the Now Ruz period.

The Persian New Year, occurring on the day of the Vernal Equinox, marked the end of the old year and the beginning of a new one. It celebrates not only the New Year, but also the arrival of spring and the rebirth of nature. The holiday is over three thousand years old and is supposed to be linked to Zoroastrianism. *Sizdah Bedar,* which is the thirteenth day, is considered the final day of the celebration and is a day that everyone spends out of doors having picnics, hoping that a happy time together as a family will cleanse their minds of "evil thoughts."

Bahman flew to the Dezful airport in one of the Shah's six-seater King Air turbo prop planes that were used for short flights of imperial personnel to fly from place to place on missions for the court. Zahra drove the twenty minutes to the airport in the old Land Rover to meet him. She was excited to spend as much time as she could with him on this two-day visit during which they would plan the presentation of the Persian Arab horses to the WAHO. The plane was just landing as she got out of the car, so she waited by the gate of the small airport that was used for the military and government only. She was well known to the guards on duty, so they didn't even ask for her identification papers. She watched as the sleek, beige airplane glided to a stop at the end of the runway and taxied to the gate. Bahman, smartly dressed in a well-tailored tweed jacket and khaki pants, waved to her as he came out and descended the steps to the tarmac. They kissed both cheeks, then passed pleasantries as they waited for his bag, which was brought down the stairs by the copilot.

As they headed off towards Aghili with the windows open letting in the fresh cool November air, they began to discuss the plan for the visit of the inspectors which Zahra had formulated in her mind. She hoped that Bahman would agree with her plan, for after all she was the expert on the Arab customs, and he was only a lowly Turkoman from the steppes in the north. They rumbled along the rough desert road heading for the ferry to Aghili.

"Zahra, what are our auspicious guests going to think of us when they find they have to take a rickety ferry across the river to your place? Why, they will have had two or three days of being entertained in the best hotels and restaurants in Tehran, they will have visited palaces and seen the crown jewels, as well as having been flown down here in a private jet. Then we take them on a rough road and across a primitive ferry instead of a bridge. I just can't imagine what you and Mehdi were thinking when you neglected to build a bridge over the Dez to your farm."

"It was not our money to do so. We were building bridges where they were needed to transport agricultural products to help the farming industry, not for our personal advantage. You may not know, but we actually designed and built this 'rickety ferry' ourselves with Mehdi's own money early on in our work with agricultural in the area. I love this ferry; it was the beginning of our adventures and I don't want it ever replaced in my time. Anyway, I think it will add to the atmosphere of our guests' visit. Let them know they're truly in Arab country," she answered.

"Well, I guess I'll have to get a decent vehicle driven down to Dezful to transport them in. I don't think your Rostam, as you call it, would add to the atmosphere. I don't know why you insist on keeping this old thing."

"This 'thing' as you call it has been a part of Aghili forever. It still runs well and is trusty, so why get rid of it? Anyway, I can't afford a new one."

"The horse sales have been very good the past couple of years, so I don't understand why you can't. What do you do with all that money we pay you?

Zahra sighed, "I have to take care of my people and their families and there's always someone out there who needs help. You know me, I don't like to see my friends in need. The money just goes."

They crossed on the ferry and drove the few miles across the desert to Aghili in silence.

The two days that Bahman stayed were very productive. Zahra showed him the drawings she'd made of the small tent compound she and her tribal friends would put up within the walls of the beautiful *bagh* (farm area) with its fruit trees and flower gardens. The inspectors would stay in the apartment over the stables where she and Mehdi had lived. Except for Tom, who would hopefully be coming and would stay with her. But that subject she didn't broach.

Four of the Sheiks had committed to bring their tents and to decorate them in the old Arab way with colorful *tangs* (long wide woven belts), carpets and wall hangings as decoration. The grassy area in front of her house had been enlarged so there would be room to show several horses at a time. The inspection would last three days, during which time the plan was to give their guests a true desert experience. They would serve authentic Persian Arab food and have entertainment every evening. The horse inspections would be scheduled during the mornings when the weather was the coolest. A big lunch would be served before the free time, when people could nap or whatever. In the late afternoon, the guests would be taken sightseeing to local antiquities and to some nomad camps.

Bahman was so impressed with Zahra's plans that he told her she had a free hand to complete everything that needed to be done. The funds needed would be borne by the Royal Horse Society which itself was funded by the Shah. He would arrange for the transportation of the guests while they were in Iran and for the security but everything else would be in her hands.

20

Don't put your trust in all the tricks
And games that you've created;
It's said there are a thousand ways
For kings to be checkmated.
Hafez

Ali 1979

A li drove onto the dock once they had crossed
the river and Zahra, waving to the ferry op-
erators, walked off and got into Rostam. He
headed along the desert road for Dezful, where
they would stop to fill up with *benzine* and then
take the highway towards Shush.

The news from Tehran had filtered down
to Khuzestan that strikes were occurring, and
people were refusing to work in the big cities.
Marches against the Shah were taking place and
people demanded that he leave the country. In
Khuzestan, it was said that General Ja'farian, the

commander of the military, had troops marching through the streets of Ahwaz supporting the
Shah. Then a few days later, tanks and troops
were reported to be suppressing the people, but
Ali was not sure which side they were on, that of
the Shah or the revolutionaries. He had heard
it said just yesterday that Shapour Bakhtiar had
resigned as prime minister and the whole country was in a state of anarchy.

It was said that the Ayatollah, whom the
Shah had banished from the country in the early
1960's, was planning to come back to Iran to
save the people from the dreadful tyrant that
had been ruling them for so many years. Neither
he nor anyone he knew wanted to be saved by
that nasty old Ayatollah. Few people in their
part of Iran worshiped in the mosques anyway.
What was happening to their world?

And then came the news that the Shah had
left the country and a week or so later Ayatollah
Ruhollah Khomeini arrived in Tehran from
France with the blessing of the United States.
There had been millions of people to welcome
him at Mehrabad Airport. How stupid were
these city people, with the women all covered in
black chadors looking like crows? He wondered
now if the Aghili Stud would still be supported
by the *Anjoman*. Would this new Revolutionary
government take over the Royal Horse Society?

How would all the bills be paid if there was no money coming from Tehran? Zahra had explained to him how to manage the books and pay the bills when she was not there, but he wouldn't be able to pay if the money from the court was not transferred to the bank account. He'd pay most of the outstanding receipts in cash which he would withdraw from the bank, but if the account had no money, he wouldn't be able to pay. There was cash that Zahra kept in the safe in her office, but that wouldn't last long. Now there was more reason for Zahra to stay where she was. She must realize that she was needed and that nothing would be the same without her.

Zahra

The cool winter weather was perfect for travelling by horse across the desert to meet up with the sheikhs who said they would help Zahra put on her production, for that's what it was. She and Ali spent many days riding across the expansive brown terrain into the nearby rugged hills where Sheikh Khabir, Sheikh Houshang

Farshid, and others had their winter camps.

Over the years, the sheikhs had been helpful as she recorded pedigrees of the Asil horses that they bred. Four of them had promised they would bring a tent and decorate it in her *bagh* for the days of the inspection. They all wanted to bring their families with them during the event. Sheikh Farshid told her that he wanted his wife and daughters to cook the luncheon for the foreign guests one day, in order for the visitors to experience a true and special Arab meal. She had planned to have Azizeh and her own people do the meals but Sheikh Khabir had told her he would do the noon day meal, barbequing a gazelle on the final day so Azizeh would only have to cook one luncheon. It had been planned by Bahman that the guests would be taken out to dinner each evening after their sightseeing expeditions, but Zahra insisted that the last evening would be spent at Aghili, with an informal supper and music from some local musicians.

Before she cold blink an eye, it was *Chahar Shanbeh Souri*, the ancient festival that dated back to the early days of Zoroastrianism. This festival, a prelude to *Nowruz,* which marked the arrival of spring, was celebrated the last evening of the old year. Ali and the workers collected twigs and branches from in and outside the Aghili garden and piled them up into small bonfire piles during the day.

Zahra had invited some of Mehdi's family with whom she was still friends, and several of her tribal acquaintances, to come to the *bagh* for the jumping of the fires. This tradition, to jump over the small bonfires singing, '*Sorkhi-ye as to man; Zardi-ye man as to,*' which means, 'Your fire red color is mine; my sickly yellow paleness is yours,' was a purification rite that means you want the fire to take away your paleness, sickness, and problems and in turn give you redness, warmth and energy. It was believed that with the help of fire and light this unlucky last night of the year would bring the arrival of spring and longer days. Traditionally, it was believed that, on this same night, the living were visited by the spirits of their ancestors, so the children wrapped themselves in shrouds and costumes and ran around the fires banging pots and pans with spoons to beat out the spirits and bad luck.

During the evening, the garden was filled with the joyous shouts of children and adults, and all partook of a delicious meal set out on a long buffet table on the large porch of Zahra's charming, domed house. After the meal, the children were given sparklers and they danced in the darkness as the bonfires were jumped when they were lit.

Majid came up to her and touched her arm.

"Zahra Jun, it is always such a pleasure to come here to your *Chahar Shanbeh* Souri celebration. I thank you for myself and the whole Bakhtiar family. I know we don't come every year, but when we do, we always have a good time mingling and getting reacquainted with many of our old friends. The children all love your party, and now as you see, there are many grandbabies to enjoy the fun. I want to ask you from the whole family to come to our *Nowruz* reception tomorrow. It's been many years now and you have not returned to your home in Andimeshke. Your room is still awaiting you; we've kept it ready for you all this time."

"I thank you, Majid. It's been hard for me to return, you must understand. At first, I really felt that I had been cast away by the Bakhtiar family, though I did appreciate your generosity in giving me this home. When I've gone to Andimeshke for supplies and such these past years I would often pass the Big House, but I never felt that I could stop by. I had so many wonderful memories of my time there with Mehdi, and I've felt an emptiness for so many years. I had financial difficulties that I didn't want you to know about because you were generous to me, but things are better now. So, thank you – I look forward to coming to your celebration." They kissed on both cheeks as he said his farewell and then collected his children and grandchildren to leave.

The *Nowruz* holidays lasted thirteen days, during which time most families had an open house every day so their friends and relatives could come to wish a happy New Year to them. But the first day of the year was the day when close family came together. So it was that Zahra did indeed go to Andimeshke to be with the Bakhtiar family for the first time since Mehdi's death. As had been the norm, she rode over on horseback, enjoying the lovely spring weather and shy flowers that were beginning to pop through the sandy soil of the desert. Khatum was feeling fresh, so she pranced along the desert path as they left the *bagh*. But when Zahra asked her to canter on towards the river crossing, she felt as smooth as glass. They had ridden many miles together over the desert during the years since the mare was gifted to her by Mehdi more than twenty years ago and she had filled her rider with joy every step of the way.

When Zahra arrived at the Big House, she rode into the stable yard and handed Khatum to Babak, the old groom who had been with the family almost all his life. "Zahra Khonume, *Mubarak*. It is so good to see you on this first day of the year. It has been too long that your place here has been empty," he greeted her with a wide grin of happiness.

"*Mubarak,* Babak," she answered as she put some coins into his hand as was the custom during the New Year celebration, when guests gave a tip to the workers of the family they were visiting. The employees of the households were always given an *aide* (gift) by the family they worked for and she had given all of her own employees one month's extra salary and a new set of clothing.

It felt strange to be walking across the yard she had crossed thousands of times and up the grand steps of the house where she had lived for so long. She felt nervous, but as she entered everyone smiled and clapped calling, "*Mubarak* Zahra June, *khoshke omadid!*" They were happy she had arrived, and one by one they all held her in a welcoming embrace.

In the large entrance hall was the traditional *Sofreh Haft Sin* (seven "S" table display) that had many more items than seven. She contemplated the symbolic meanings of what she was observing on the round table covered with its damask cloth. The *Sabsi* (wheat sprouts growing in a dish representing nature and exhilaration; *Sib* (apple) for health; *Senjed* (dried fruit) for wisdom; *Serkeh* (vinagre) for disinfection; *Samanu* (sweet wheat paste) for power and bravery; *Sumaq* (sumac) for patience and tolerance; *Seer* (garlic) for stimulation and contentment; *Shamdan (candlesticks)* for light; *Sekkeh* (coins) for wealth. There were also items that did not start with "seen" such as *Ayyaneh* (mirror), another symbol for light, and *Pisces* (goldfish) used to indicate the start of the New Year. It was a beautifully arranged setting that reminded her of the constant renewal or rebirth that could happen when one transcended and balanced the material mind with the immaterial spirit, by letting life flow through oneself in a perpetual allowance, amazement, and appreciation of each moment as it happens.

She had a delightful afternoon, which stretched into evening, as she talked, sang and danced with family members and friends. The delicious traditional dishes of the *Nowruz* table, *Sabsi Polo* (rice with herbs), *Kuku Sabsi* (green omelet with herbs), *Fesenjan* (chicken walnut stew) and many sweets were devoured by the guests, only to be replenished by the maids as each plate was emptied by the hungry crowd.

Majid and his wife came up to her as she contemplated leaving and asked her to spend the night in her old room, to which she acquiesced. They would serve an early breakfast so she could go on her way the following morning.

In the morning, Majid rose from his seat at the head of the table as she entered the dining room. "*Sob Beher*, Zahra June. I hope you slept well."

"Thank you, Majid Khan. It was like the old days, though without my dear Mehdi."

Slowly other members of the family straggled down and sat at the table so that it was soon full.

"Zahra, the Bakhtiar family has a gift for you before you leave. So please come out to the front of the house when you've gathered your things. We'll meet you there," Majid told her as the meal was finished.

When she came down from her room with the few things, she had brought with her, and stepped out on the grand verandah that over-looked the drive and stables, she saw what looked like brand new tractor with a front-end loader. The Bakhtiar brothers were all milling around checking it out.

"Your gift, Zahra," called Majid as he pointed to the beautiful machine. "We heard from the workers that the old tractor at Aghili has been giving you a great deal of trouble and we had this one here that we have had only about two years, so we wanted to gift it to you for *Nowruz*."

Zahra said, "I'm in shock. I can't believe you are all being so kind. This is a much better tractor than mine, which doesn't have a front-end load-er. Even when all the tractors were imported for the agricultural program, Mehdi refused to take one for us at Aghili, so ours must be at least twen-ty-five years old. It's been a good servant, but of late it won't start, no matter who works on it. The mechanic told me it's finished, so this is wonderful surprise. How can I thank you?"

"No need, we're all happy that we can help you some. We know in the past we did nothing about you and your problems, so now we're pleased to be a help to our sister," Karim spoke for his brothers. She went up to each brother and hugged him with tears in her eyes. For the first time since Mehdi's death, she felt she was again a part of the Bakhtiar family, and it was the only real family she had.

Sizdah Bedar was a sunny warm day with a hint of a spring breeze. All the members of the Aghili family rode across the desert to the banks of a small tributary stream of the Dez River to have their picnic. They tethered their horses and spread carpets along the bank on which they put out the decorative tin and copper pots filled with various rice and stews. Ali started a fire where they would grill the kabob of mouflon which had been shot the previous day. There were of course, several dishes of the favored *Kuku Sabsi* that had been made by the women of the families.

Once the food was laid out, they sat around jovially, laughing and talking of things past and what would come in the New Year. The impending horse inspection, which would commence within the week, was number one on the list of topics. Everyone was excited to show off their horses to these international experts, who couldn't possibly have ever seen more beautiful Asil Arabs anywhere else in the world. Those who played instruments had brought them along, and once the repast had been eaten, they began playing traditional music to which the women and children rose and danced. A game of football was organized using branches to designate the goals; instruments were put down and all those not playing stood on the sidelines cheering for their favorite team.

The final event of the day was to throw the *Sabsi* from the *Sofreh Haft Sin,* which every family had in their home, into the swiftly flowing stream. The action of throwing away the *Sabsi* represented removing negativity from one's home. It was believed that the *Sabsi* collected all the negative and ill in the household during the thirteen days it had been growing there. Releasing it into flowing water symbolized new beginnings, as all that was sickness and ill was removed from one's home. In mythology, water represents purity, so this symbolic gesture meant that the evil which was in the *Sabsi* was literally transported away in the purity of flowing water.

The *Shanbeh* (Saturday) following *Sizdah*

Bedar was the day the inspectors were due to arrive. Zahra scurried around checking that everything was ready. The sheikhs had done a magnificent job with their tents. She had expected the usual black felt tents that were very plain outside but well decorated inside. That was not what she got. As she looked across to the far side of the *bagh,* where she would be planting forage for the horses soon, she saw four unusual tents.

Sheikh Khabir had constructed a whole tent with colorful carpets that had most probably been woven by his wives and children. One side was open so she could see inside. The walls were also of beautiful Bakhtiari carpets, as he was of the still nomadic, Bakhtiar tribe. The floor was covered with colorful *ghilims* and around the sides were many seats made of camel bags and small stuffed carpets. There were several tooled copper tables on short trellis legs, and he had two carpet looms set up at which sat young girls dressed in colorful skirts and wearing multicolored scarves to cover their long dark hair.

Her old friend Sheikh Amir had been only too happy to come for the event with his "formal" tent used when he had visiting sheikhs. It had a tall center pole, giving it a dome-like ceiling. It was made from dark brown felt that was trimmed with off-white geometrical designs around its perimeter. Sheikh Hajat's tent was of the traditional black felt with small multi-colored woolen tassels rimming the outer edge at the top. Sheikh Farshid's tent was a loosely woven dark brown fabric that was used in the warmer weather as the air could permeate the upper walls, which made it cooler. He had large tassels of red, orange, yellow, and blue hanging from the tent ropes that were holding up the tent. It was an authentic Arab camp in a comprised setting, but it would certainly impress the westerners, she hoped.

She checked that the apartment above the stables was ready for guests. There were two bedrooms, the master with the ensuite bathroom that she and Mehdi had used, and a smaller twin bedroom. In case Tom elected not to stay with her, she had put another twin bed in the alcove that was the library. Her own house had been scrubbed and tidied within an inch of its life. She and Azizeh had even organized a lot of her clutter that usually covered tables, counters and any surface that would hold it. Her office was immaculate, with the Asil Stud Book open on the large carved walnut desk in front of her chair.

She had talked to Tom by telephone several times during *Nowruz,* so she knew that he was flying from Washington to London where he would spend a few days visiting medical acquaintances. Then he planned to meet up with the three other inspectors who would all fly to Tehran on Iran Air. She had met General Ali Mohammad Khademi, who was a close friend of Bahman, several times in the past. He was president of Iran Air, so she felt certain Tom would have a safe ride.

Zahra felt like a schoolgirl as she waited for the arrival of her guests. She was nervous to meet the three she didn't know, but she was itching to see Tom again. It had been a long four years of letter writing and phone calls since the trip to Paris, when they connected after twenty some years. She had wanted to go to Tehran to be a part of the sightseeing trip that Bahman had organized for the first three days, but there was no way she could leave Aghili; there was too much to do and so much was riding on this inspection.

About noon she had a call from Bahman telling her that they would leave Tehran in the late afternoon, flying to Dezful and arriving about seven. He wanted her to make dinner reservations at the Dezful Inn, which had a quaint Persian restaurant that served excellent food. She was to meet them there.

What would she wear? She'd planned to meet them at the airport in her usual garb of balloon pants, colorful shirt, and Qashgha'i hat, but she couldn't go like that to meet strangers at the restaurant even though she wouldn't have had a hesitation if she were just meeting locals. And now she would have time to take care of her looks for Tom. She spent the afternoon meeting with her staff to make sure they all knew their respective responsibilities for the next three days and brought some of the horses out to the grassy showing area to make sure the grooms knew the walk they would each make while the horses were being inspected.

By the time she got to her room, it was past six and she only had time for a quick shower and to throw on an old navy dinner dress that was the first thing she'd seen in her closet. She put on the ever-useful pearls from her mother and the engagement ring Tom had given her on her right ring finger and was ready. She jumped into old Rostam and quickly drove through the desert towards the ferry, leaving a cloud of dust behind her. When she got to the ferry, she told the tender that she would be returning along with another vehicle in a few hours, so they were to be sure to have people on duty to wait for them.

She arrived at the inn before Bahman and the group. The minutes ticked along slowly until she finally heard voices in the entrance hall, so she headed towards them. Brahman was first to embrace her and peck both cheeks; he then stood back to introduce her to the inspectors. But the next thing she knew she was in Tom's arms and he was kissing her, holding her tight. When he finally let go, he held her at arm's length and said, "It's so good to see you. It seems I've been waiting forever. Now let me introduce you to my friends."

He introduced the Irish, Ruth O'Reagan, first. She was one of the top Arab judges in the world and had travelled inspecting horses many times. Amr Salama was an Egyptian representative of the WAHO who had been mostly in Middle Eastern countries, though this was his first trip to Iran. The third inspector, Oskar Pawel, was from Poland and spoke English with a decided accent when he greeted her. She led them to the table where their first course of *ash reshte* (lentil soup) was waiting at each place. Bahman arranged the seating, with the ladies at each end of the table. He sat next to Ruth and directed Tom to take one of the seats next to Zahra. There was much discussion of the past three days that had shown the foreigners all the best that Tehran and the environs had to offer. They were full of admiration for the Shah who had met with them at Farahabad and arranged for them to tour his beautiful stables and shown them some of his Iranian-bred horses. They were amazed that he had such a good knowledge of the equine.

"His majesty's great love has always been

his horses," Zahra commented. "The Empress often would tell him he spent too much money on them but he, lucky for me, never listened to her. Bahman here was instrumental in persuading him to fund my Asil Stud through the Royal Horse Society, when I was almost out of money."

After the meal was finished, they went out into the cool spring evening to get in the vehicles to drive to Aghili. Bahman, as promised, had a brand-new powder blue Land Rover that, by its color, was obviously from the Imperial garage; it was parked behind rusty dusty Rostam.

"Tom, if you think you can trust that contraption Zahra is driving, why don't you go with her and we'll all follow in my car," Bahman laughingly addressed him.

Tom nodded and got in the passenger's side of the old vehicle. "Is this your only mode of transportation, my love?"

"This and my horses are all I need. My brothers-in-law did gift me a lovely tractor for *Nowruz,* which I suppose I could call transport, though."

"How do you keep this thing running? It must be as old as the hills."

"Yes, it is old, very old, but Ali is a good mechanic and is able to keep it running. They don't make them this well nowadays," she answered.

Shortly afterwards, they left the pavement in

Dezful and drove along the desert path towards the ferry. She could tell Tom was a little concerned about their direction so she said, "This road leads to the ferry that will take us across the river to Aghili."

"You mean the road doesn't go all the way to your farm?" he asked.

"No, when the bridges were being built down here, Mehdi and I didn't want a bridge that would make it easy for people to come visit us. Anyway, we did most of our travelling around on horseback, so we didn't need a bridge," she answered as they drove onto the dock and the waiting ferry. She got out and went back to Bahman's car to explain that the ferry would come back for them in about ten minutes and she would wait for them on the other side. All went smoothly, and soon they were driving into the gates of Aghili. The Bedouin tents were lit up and each had a fire burning in front, so the atmosphere, with the lights lighting the arches of her stable blocks and house, was truly Persian. To her it was a most beautiful sight.

She had Ali and her stable boys in attendance to carry bags to the rooms and ushered her guests to her front porch where Azizeh and Golam Reza had fruits and sweets set out on the large wooden table, along with a tall pitcher of wine. They sat on thick Persian cushions chatting and listening to the soft music of a sitar (three stringed instrument) and nez (wooden flute) played by two of the young boys who worked for her, for an hour or so. It seemed that all the guests were enchanted with this Persian evening and they all seemed to enjoy the ride on the ferry, as she had told Bahman they would.

After the others had retired, Zahra and Tom sat quietly on the porch, observing the almost full moon and brilliant stars in the sky as they drank the red wine that was made by the Bakhtiar family. Finally, Zahra rose and took his hand saying, "Shall we?" as she led him to her room.

As couples grow older their lovemaking becomes less urgent and theirs that night was slow and tender, with both of them coming to a climax together as the moon slid behind the horizon. As they awoke when the roosters began to crow, Tom tenderly stroked her cheek.

"Zahra, my love, it feels so good to be here next to you. To me it has been an age since we left Paris."

"It has been more than an age," she whispered as her eyelids fluttered and she slowly opened her still deep brown eyes.

"Zahra June," he said using the Persian endearment, "will you marry me? I know it will be complicated, but I know we can work it out"

"That it will be but between us I'm sure we can figure it out. Yes love, I will marry you, somehow sometime."

He took their engagement ring which was still on her right hand and removed it replacing it on her left hand. They were now engaged again.

The three days of the inspections flew by. Each morning, the four inspectors, sitting under a colorful Qashgha'i canopy, watched horses walk, then trot a triangle, before they stood for them to study the conformation, all the while studying the pedigrees that had been placed on the table in front of them. The horses were shown in age divisions and the Aghili horses were interspersed among the horses from the many sheikhs who had wanted to be included in this inspection to have their horses known throughout the world. A dazzling luncheon was served at noon each day at the front of Zahra's house when the breeders and inspectors could get to know each other. Zahra and Bahman were kept busy translating, which they enjoyed as they were able to get an insight into what the inspectors were thinking about their Asils. Tom had told Zahra he could not discuss his judging with her, which she understood; he needed to be impartial to do his job properly.

After an hours nap they took a trip in the blue

Land Rover to see the sights of Khuzestan. They visited the Mohammad Reza Pahlavi Dam which at two hundred meters high, was considered to be the biggest dam in the Middle East, with a lake that covers six thousand hectares. The Dezful Jame Mosque in the central city square that dates back to the third and fourth centuries AD and the five levelled ziggurat, Chogha Zanbil that dates back three thousand years and was built by an Elamite king to honor his god Inshushinak were seen in one afternoon. They also visited Susa, one of the oldest cities in the world that began as a small village in the Neolithic Age around 7000 B.C., was rebuilt, and became the favorite residence of the Persian king Darius the Great (522-486). Then they went to Masjed-e-Soloman where oil was first discovered in Iran by the Englishman William Knox D'Arcy. He had been given a 60-year oil concession in 1901 by Mosafar al-Din Shah and finally struck oil in contract with Ali-Qoli Khan Bakhtiar, Mehdi's grandfather in 1908. Oil was still being produced at the well, after almost seventy years.

The first two evenings, they stopped at local restaurants on their way home to sample some of the traditional Persian foods like *chelo kabab* (lamb kabob with rice)and *ab goosht* (a thick potato soup). Later they sat on the porch at Zahra's house drinking wine and listening to traditional folk music played by the musicians from the sheikhs' families. The final evening, Azizeh, with the help of the wives of the sheikhs, produced a truly Arab meal of wild game and several types of rice for the whole group including the sheikhs' families and all the workers. As the desert of sweets such as *baklava, basbousa* and *Zainab* fingers, all of which were sweet with honey syrup or powdered sugar, were served, the music started, and people began to dance to the rhythmic tunes of the desert.

When the party finally ended late in the night, Zahra and Tom sat on a Persian cushion against the back wall of the porch to talk. The only time they had been alone together the past few days was when they were in her room at night, and there hadn't been a lot of discussion then as more carnal things had been on their minds. Now he was leaving the following morning and who knew when they'd be together again.

"I know you can't tell me the results of the inspection, but when will I know what has been decided by you inspectors?" she asked as she snuggled up to him.

"We'll discuss and make our decision on our flight back to London, but I will tell you that I'm almost certain it will be favorable. The horses we've seen are as beautiful as any in the world and I know I'm not the only one of us to have been so impressed. But I want to talk about 'us,' not the horses. When will we be able to be together again?"

"I don't know. It's difficult for me to travel out of the country. I'm so involved here with the horses and my commitment to the *Anjoman* is not going away."

"But I love you and want you to marry me. I know you love me, but do you love me enough to leave this place?"

"I do love you, but I also love this place and my life here. It will be a hard decision to make; maybe one I can't make."

Tom sighed. "I don't think I could make my life here. I've loved seeing how you live and meeting your people and I think this is an amazing place, but I too have my life. In Virginia I have a farm to run, and I have my practice which I love and from which I earn a living I think you could adapt to the life there. We could bring some of your horses over and you could breed them like you do here. North Cliff has lots of room for horses now that Anne has her own farm for the racehorses. I have several Arabs but would love to get into the breeding and sales business with your Persian Asil horses. The market for Arabs is growing in the States right now. I'm sure I could keep you as busy there as you are here. And with time, you will gain the prestige and prominence you have now."

"The prestige is not important to me. I do what I do because I love the horses and I love my life here in the desert. Virginia is beautiful, but I don't know if I could live in a place that wasn't free and open like it is here. If I want to ride to Andimeshke for supplies, I can go to the stable, saddle my mare and ride across the open land without seeing anyone until I get to the town. Can you imagine what people would say about your crazy wife if she rode her horse to Warrenton? I'd probably be killed by a car anyway for there's so much traffic."

"That you probably would," he answered with a sadness in his voice. "Promise me one thing. That you'll think on it. We have time. We've waited all these years and it hasn't killed us."

"I really want to marry you, Tom, but it will be a difficult path we have to take, for both of us."

"I have a plan. Why don't we try to meet someplace every few months while we're deciding what to do with this situation? Have you ever been to Venice?" She shook her head. "Well, let's meet in Venice in September. I've never been there either, but I've read about it and am dying to go there. With its romantic atmosphere, art and music, I think we could have a wonderful week or two together. I'll make all the arrangements and send you a ticket."

And so it was decided.

21

Ah, Love! Could thou and I with Fate conspire
To grasp this story Scheme of Things entire,
Would we not shatter it to bits and then
Re-mold it nearer to Heart's Desire!
Omar Khayyam

Ali 1979

After filling up with *benzene,* they headed towards Ahwaz on the almost brandnew highway that had been finished just a few months before. The ride was smooth, and he pushed Rostam to the maximum because they were behind schedule. Zahra kept mentioning things that he should do once she was gone, and then would say everything was written down in the logbook she'd given him. There was a list on the wall in her office, too. He also had her telephone number in Virginia, and she said he should call if he had any questions or problems.

She was sure everything would be fine, and she was planning to return in a few months anyway.

He'd heard Zahra talking on the phone and understood that Bahman Mansarpour had left the country with the Shah. He was Zahra's savior and he knew that she was upset that he had left. She told Ali that he had said that the Shah was leaving for a holiday, but once they heard that Khomeini had formed his government under the Islamic Revolutionary Party (IRP) they knew he wouldn't be back any time soon. Amazingly, the regular money transfer had arrived the previous week so Zahra felt sure that the new government would continue to support the previous government's projects.

There were rumors that Khomeini had set up *komitehs* (Islamic committees) around the country that were allied with the IRP (Iranian Revolutionary Party) and aligned with the Militant Clergy. Their main task was to keep order and security, but they were arresting people and executing them after trying them in front of an evil judge called Sadeq Khalkhali. Things were definitely not good in Tehran, but Ali didn't think much else was happening in Khuzestan just yet. However, he was not really sure whether there were still tanks in the streets of Ahwaz or not.

As far as he was concerned, he had loved the

Shah and thought this was an unnecessary revolution. His Majesty had done so much for the country. His actions were why the farming and highways were much improved. And the beautiful Mohammad Reza Shah dam that he had built on the Karun River near Dezful irrigated the farmland all around and produced electricity for all. And most important to Ali was what he had done for the Aghili Stud. He had been a wonderful shah and had done so much for his people. Ali couldn't believe what was happening.

Zahra

Official notification of the acceptance of the Persian Asil Arab horses by the WAHO arrived at the Royal Horse Society office just two weeks after the inspections. Bahman called her to give her the news. He would send a plane to Dezful for her to come to Tehran because the Shah was going to make a presentation to her during the announcements at the dinner, he had each year for the national sports governing body. It was lucky that the acceptance came so quickly, and it could be a part the current year's celebrations.

The Iranian football team had made it to the World Cup finals again and the Iranian Show Jumping Team had won the overall title, under Cathy's guidance, at the International Show that had been held at the Aryamehr Stadium the previous *Azar* (November) when teams from France, Italy, Germany and England came to Iran. Now with the acceptance of the Persian Arabs to the world, it would be quite an international acclaim for Iranian sports.

Zahra was sure the Shah would be ecstatic. The dinner was held at the Saadabad Palace, the complex of which was originally built by the Qadjars, Zahra's ancestors, in the 19th century. Reza Shah had built the White Palace between 1932 and 1937 and used it as a summer residence, as did his son, Mohammad Reza. The main hall was decorated with flags and pictures of football players, show jumpers and many of Zahra's beloved Asils. Presentations were made to the members of the football team first. Then the riders of the show jumping team and Cathy were honored. Then His Majesty motioned for Zahra to come up to the head table.

"Finally, I want to present Zahra Kadjar Bakhtiar, who has worked for many years to get our own Persian horses recognized by the World Organization. Her husband Mehdi was one of my best friends before he so tragically died in a plane crash. Zahra has been working on pedigrees and an Iranian stud book for years, and just a few weeks ago international inspectors came to Khuzestan to see our horses and gave them recognition in the World Arab Stud Book. I had no doubt that they would accept our horses, for the Arab horse originated in Persia more than five thousand years ago. I will now present Iran's Gold Medal of Honor to Zahra in thanks for all she has done for our country."

Zahra bowed her head as he placed the shiny gold medallion with its ribbon of red, white and green over her head. He then held her shoulders and kissed her on both cheeks, "Thank you Zahra, not just for this accomplishment, but for so many others in the past," he whispered in her ear.

She was almost in tears, thinking of the time she and Mehdi had spent together working on agriculture and tribal relations. "I thank Your Majesty for this great honor you have placed around my neck. Everything I have ever done to deserve this was out of love for you, my country, and my horses. I Hope *Allah* will give me time to continue serving you."

When she got back home to Aghili her work with the stud book continued as it would for years to come, for there were always new foals being born that needed to be entered in it. She was looking forward to seeing Tom again. Before she knew it, September had arrived and she was boarding a plane for Italy.

The trip to Venice had been magical. Tom met her at the airport and they were taken into the city situated on a group of one hundred and eighteen islands separated by canals and linked by over four hundred bridges in the shallow Venetian Lagoon that lies between the mouth of the Po and Piave rivers. The Republic of Venice (697-1797) was a major financial and maritime power and center of commerce and art from the 13th century until the 17th century. It was considered the first real international financial center, which made it a wealthy city throughout history. The buildings of Gothic, Renaissance and Baroque architecture seemed to be in essential harmony even though they were from such different periods. Zahra and Tom saw the buildings crowded together along the Grand Canal. Tom had booked a suite at the St. Regis Venice that was just a block from the Piazza San Marco and the old town center.

They spent ten blissful days together riding in gondolas and visiting the sights and art museums of the old city. In the 16th century, Venetian painting was developed through influences of the Paduan School and Antonello da Messina, who introduced the oil painting technique of the Van Eyck brothers. Titian, Tintoretto and

Veronese were some of the early masters who painted in the city and the grand landscape canvases of Canaletto and Tiepolo brought revival to Venetian art in the 18th century. Zahra and Tom spent hours at the galleries as they both had a true appreciating of art itself. They attended concerts a few evenings, listening to the moving classical music of such composers as Vivaldi and Monteverdi, but mostly they spent time alone in their suite, taking in the views of the Grand Canal, making love, and trying to find a way to spend the rest of their lives together.

When they parted at the airport, they had made a plan to visit Ireland together in February; meanwhile they would write and call each other as often as they could.

It seemed like no time before they were together again. They met at Dublin Airport where Tom had arranged to rent a car to drive the two hours to Adare where they would stay at the Dunraven Arms, a charming and casual, but proper quaint inn. The inn was owned by Lord Dunraven who lived across the road in the ancient stone castle that had been in the family for two centuries. To get there, they had to drive in heavy rain for some time. When they pulled up in front of the long low gambrel-roofed inn, they jumped out of the car, heads down, and ran into the lobby. A ruddy-cheeked Irish boy, dripping wet, brought their bags into the reception area and on up to their room as instructed by the attractive red-headed woman at the front desk. She was the manager of the Dunraven, Miss Maurine O'Sullivan, who escorted them to their room to make sure they would be comfortable.

The room was at the end of a long, carpeted hallway that groaned and creaked as they walked along. The large and cozy room had two wide windows overlooking the main street. The big double bed with its many pillows and comforters would definitely be well used! After lovemaking and a luxurious hot bath in the long claw-foot tub, they went downstairs where they had champagne in front of the huge fireplace in the lounge. After a meal of smoked salmon, grouse, fresh vegetables and a custard tart for dessert, they retired back to their room till the following morning when they would be going fox hunting.

The cheery Irishman, Benny Supple, who had arranged for the hunt and had procured their horses, picked them up at nine to drive them the one and a half hours to the meet. Zahra was a little nervous because she hadn't been fox hunting since college more than twenty years before. Tom still hunted regularly during the season with the Warrenton Hunt. It was an overcast but not cold morning with little wind, the perfect conditions for scent, as the hounds were cast in a covert by a big old stone manor house. Hounds spoke almost immediately, and they were off galloping across the lush green Irish countryside, navigating banks and ditches and flying over gates.

They had a wonderful two weeks, fox hunting for five days, driving around the countryside sightseeing and enjoying being together again. She loved fox hunting and told him she would take it up regularly if she moved to Virginia. Tom was concerned with the news he'd been hearing about the political situation in Iran. Zahra tried to explain that she was sure the press was relating false news, as usual. Why , Bahman had told her there wasn't really a problem. There had been some demonstrations in Tehran and the larger cities, but the average age of the dissidents was seventeen and the Shah and his government had everything under control. There was no evidence of the problem in Khuzestan.

"I'm just concerned for your safety, Zahra. I don't want anything to happen to you. I know that you own your farm yourself, but you have some convoluted agreement with the Royal Horse Society that I don't understand. If something happens to the Shah, what will happen to you?"

"Nothing is going to happen to him. Don't believe what you read in the papers," was her answer.

They wouldn't be able to see each other again until September, because Zahra needed to be home during foaling time which would not be over until the end of May, and Tom had two medical conventions during the summer. They agreed to meet in Athens and then take a cruise in the Aegean for a week.

Life at Aghili continued as usual that spring, with more than fifteen foals being born, all beautiful and healthy thanks to *Allah*. The new tractor made preparing and planting the fields much easier and quicker. She couldn't imagine how they had survived without a front-end loader all those years. Lifting and moving things became no problem, where before they had had to use rope, chains and lots of manpower. The training, buying, and selling of young horses kept Zahra so busy she hardly had time to write Tom, but they did have at least one phone call a week.

The news from Tehran was not good. Bahman told her that the Shah was not doing well. He had not been told what was wrong with him, but he knew that French doctors came frequently to see him. The Empress said she had no idea what the problem was either, but that he'd been losing weight and he tired very easily. There had been mass demonstrations by Khomeini supporters in Tehran and martial law had been imposed in response to them. Bahman still felt they were of no consequence, so she headed off for her trip to Greece with Tom, though she was worried about what was happening in her country. Maybe Tom would be able to tell her what the international world was saying about it.

For the first few days, they enjoyed themselves as usual, making love with abandon, seeing the sights around Athens, eating, drinking retzina and dancing into the night in the Tavernas. When they boarded the sailboat they had fun fishing, swimming and diving in the clear waters. In the evenings, they began to talk more seriously about how they could marry and spend the rest of their lives together. Tom was worried about what he was hearing about Iran. He knew that President Jimmy Carter had spent a luxurious sixteen hours over New Year's Eve in Tehran in the company of the Shah and his ministers, but the scuttle bug in the States was that because Carter was such a human rights advocate, he had cooled on any relationship between the two countries. It was said that he thought the exiled cleric Khomeini had been treated badly and might be a better man for the job.

Tom didn't want his one and only true love to be trapped in Iran if things got bad. He didn't want to lose her again. He begged her to leave Greece with him when their vacation was over and go to America with him. Of course, there was no way she could do that. She couldn't just not return to her responsibilities and the people she loved. And the horses – she couldn't just leave them there without making plans for their care.

As they discussed their plans, Zahra finally said, "Here's what I'll do if you'll let me. I'll go home and make plans for the farm and horses; Ali is capable of running the place if he's able to be in touch with me. I'll plan all the breeding for the spring and leave detailed instructions for everything. When I feel comfortable that things will run smoothly without me, I'll fly to Washington and we can be married quietly, shortly after I arrive. But you must promise me that I can go back to Iran whenever I want to or when I'm needed. Probably every six months or so. Why, you can come with me and we'll make it like a holiday."

He had tears in his eyes when she finished, "You mean you'll really come to live in Virginia and marry me?"

"As long as I can go back home when I need or want to, yes. I love you and I want to spend what is left of my life with you." He held her tight, and closing his eyes, prayed that he was not dreaming.

"I don't want to pressure you but, how long do you think it will take before you can come?"

"I'm not sure. A few months. I'll have to get someone to take over my position at the

Anjoman and make sure all foals are recorded, which will mean a lot of time spent with the sheikhs. Many of them don't read or write, but all their children do, thanks to the Shah's great education programs, so they'll have to be taught how to keep the records of their herds. There will be so much to do, many things I haven't even contemplated yet. So yes, it will take several months. But once I'm finished, we'll be able to start our real life together."

They parted at the Athens International Airport, hoping their plan would come to fruition sooner rather than later.

When Zahra arrived at Mehrabad Airport in Tehran, she took a taxi to Damghan Avenue. She was going to stay with Louise and Narcy for a few days so she could meet with Bahman and organize things at the *Anjoman* for her departure. She talked with Louise, who was happy for her, but not really enthusiastic about taking over her job as the head of the Asil division. Zahra thought it would be a perfect fit, but Narcy was against it. He told her that with all the trouble that was going on in the city, they were spending most of their time at their farm in the Turkoman Steppes in the north. He didn't want to have to come into the city for meetings or be at Bahman's beck and call.

"Narcy, I spend my time in Khuzestan and

only come to meeting every couple of months. After all, Louise is heading the Caspian division. It won't be any more difficult to take over the Asils too," she told him.

"Bahman may not even approve it," interjected Louise. "He may not let you resign,"

It took several days of meetings and long discussions for Bahman to come to the decision that he would have to think about it for a while. There was no hurry, for she had to go home to formulate her plans there and he needed time to digest things and pick a replacement for her. He thought it would be too much to have Louise take her position. He would find someone soon, he promised her. She was not satisfied as she made her plans to fly to Dezful. It was so Iranian to put things off, but what could she do?

Meanwhile shocking news came from Iraq. Ayatollah Khomeini's house in Najaf had been embargoed, his political activities had been banned, and he'd been told to leave the county. Iran had been making noise and, as her ally, Iraq had acted. Khomeini headed for Kuwait and Syria but both refused him entry. Finally, with the help of the United States, France had accepted him, as long as he wouldn't create political problems there.

Zahra couldn't wait to get home, where hopefully the news wouldn't reach her. She knew she was being an ostrich with its head in the sand, but she just did not want to hear any more bad news. Her life was going to be wonderful with Tom, and she had confidence that Ali could manage without her being physically with him. The telephone technology had improved so much over the years that she would be only a phone call away. But she realized her work was cut out for her, to persuade him and give him the courage that she knew he sometimes lacked. It took her several days of settling in before she mustered up enough fortitude to tell him of her plans. When she did, he told her he would do anything for her, but he could never take her place.

"You won't be taking my place, Ali. I'll still be the one who makes the final decisions. You'll be my manager, and you'll be able to talk to me on the telephone any time you need to."

"But Khonume, you will not be here. You've always been here to take care of your horses and your people. You won't be here is the problem, and how will I know what to do? When I have encountered problems or decisions, I'm not sure of, I can always come to you to ask you what I should do. If you're not here, I won't be able to do that."

"Ali, you've worked for me for many years, so you know what needs to be done. You know the horses and the land. You have planned the planting and harvest for years, you've helped me with the breeding program and you've always foaled out the mares. The only difference will be that you will be in charge, and now everyone will answer to you. You've always done that when I was away. I'll just be away for longer periods of time, and I'll be available by telephone any time you want. Are you not happy for me, that I'll now have a husband to love me again?"

"I am happy for you, and I know *Agha* Tom is a good man, but why can he not come here? Why do you have to leave us?"

As the days passed, they mounted their horses to ride across the desert to talk to the neighboring sheiks. They explained that Ali, the son of Sheik Karim Salih, who was one of the most eminent breeders of the Asil horse, would be managing the Aghili Stud while the Khonume was in America. All seemed to accept the fact without a doubt, as they had known Ali all these years he'd been riding by the side of Zahra Khonume.

One cool cloudy morning, they rode to Andimeshke in order to meet with the Bakhtiar brothers, who would be the least likely to accept the fact that she was leaving the beautiful *bagh* they had deeded to her after Mehdi's death. After leaving their horses in the stables, they walked across the yard to the Big House. Both Karim and Mehdi Khan, now chief of the tribe, were there to greet them as they entered.

Majid welcomed her as he ushered them into

his office. She sat in one of the chairs before his desk while Ali sat nearby. "When we saw riders entering the gates, we thought it was you, Zahra June. It is lovely to see you here. As usual, *jah-e-shoma khali shodid* (your place has been empty), but I hear by the grapevine that you have been travelling abroad recently. As you know news travels with the wind in these parts. I pray you have been well," he said.

"I have been very well, Majid Khan, and my travels have been most enjoyable. I have visited Venice in Italy, and Ireland where I went hunting for fox. And I also traveled to Greece."

"But why would you hunt fox? That animal is not edible!"

"It's a sport where riders follow hunting dogs, called hounds, that chase the fox. It's wonderful fun riding across the lush green fields, jumping over gates, banks and ditches. The fox is vermin and kills the farmers' chickens and lambs, so they are happy when one is killed by the hounds."

"So they are dogs like our salukis?" asked Karim.

"Yes, similar, but salukis are sight hunters and these foxhounds hunt by scent."

They chatted on for several more minutes enjoying hot tea and fruits that were brought in by the young kitchen girl. Finally, with trepidation, she broached the subject of her decision to marry and move to America, but she was pleasantly surprised when they both wished her happiness and said not a word about Aghili having once belonged to the Bakhtiar clan.

Finally, the Khan turned to Ali. "Ali, you may come to us any time you need to. We'll be only too happy to help or advise you in every way if you need it," the Khan addressed him sincerely. Zahra sighed in relief. It was a comfort to know that Ali would have the support of the prominent Bakhtiar tribe.

The conversation turned to the happenings in the country. The brothers, who were never as close to the Shah as Mehdi, wanted to know what Zahra had heard recently. She explained that she didn't read the newspapers and did not have a television like they did, so they probably knew more than she. She told them what Bahman Mansarpour had said about the Shah having everything under control, but they poo-pooed that and began telling her what they had read and heard on the television. The Shah had started arresting some of the prominent members of his own regime. There had been peaceful marches around the country demanding the removal of the Shah and the return of Khomeini, who had been broadcasting and sending tapes to Iran and around the world from France.

Their friend, Amir Abbas Hoveyda, had been dismissed as prime minister and their distant cousin, Shahpour Bakhtiar, who had often been in opposition to the Shah, had been appointed prime minister by him and ratified by parliament. From afar, in Paris, Khomeini had formed his Revolutionary council to manage the revolution that he expected to come to fruition soon. The news was not good.

"You Zahra June, are making the right decision to leave now while the getting is good. Once things have settled down, you will be able to come and go as you please. We wish you good luck from all of your Bakhtiar family," Majid told her, as she and Ali walked out the door to get their horses from the stable.

A few weeks later, she was sitting in her office when Tom called her as she was having a glass of wine before her dinner. "My daring, have you heard that your Shah has left his country?" were his first words.

"What are you saying, Tom?"

"I knew you wouldn't know, sitting out there in the desert in the middle of nowhere. You need to leave now, as soon as you can. That dreadful Ayatollah will be coming to Iran and the revolution will happen. Promise me you'll leave now. I'm afraid something will happen to you. You were so close to the Shah; you'll probably be in great danger."

"I will call Bahman to see if it's true; I just don't believe it."

"Zahra, I saw it with my own eyes on the television. The Shah and his wife and a whole entourage boarded a plane today and left. Believe me! You must arrange for a ticket now, please I beg you."

"It's late now, so I can't do it today. I'll get in touch with Bahman to see if it's true. Then I'll get a ticket in a few days. It's not easy to get plane tickets here like it is in the States. I'll have to go to the Iran Air office in Dezful to buy it. But I promise I will do it within the week. I love you and miss you. I'll call you tomorrow to let you know what is really happening."

It couldn't be true! The press was putting false pictures on television. She decided to call Bahman at his home, for he would surely know the truth. When she dialed the number, it rang many times before it was picked up by the houseman, Javad.

She spoke loudly into the phone because she knew Javad was hard of hearing. "Javad, this is Khonume Bakhtiar. I'd like to speak to Agha Mansarpour."

"*Nemitunid Khonume, Agha raft ba Shahanshah, emruz.*" There it was. Bahman had left with His Majesty. She knew he was only going on a holiday, because he had not been well and the situation in the country must have been a drain on him. Well, she would go to Dezful to buy a plane ticket to Washington in a day or two. There was really no hurry.

Tom called her daily, pressing her to make her plans and get a ticket. The Ayatollah had returned to the country on February 1st with a crowd of five to ten million in a frenzy greeting him at Mehrabad Airport. When asked how he felt after having been away so long he said, "*Hichi*(Nothing)!"

A couple of days after Khomeini's arrival in Iran, Zahra went to Dezful to buy a ticket and found that she would have to wait almost two weeks for a seat. Now that revolution had happened, Iran Air was booked up, with foreigners and Iranians alike wanting to flee the unstable country. Tom seemed to be in a panic every time they talked, telling her to keep up with what was going on in her country. As she had no television, she sent one of her boys to Dezful every morning to get the newspaper for her, which she would read in the evening so she could talk intelligently to Tom when he called, which he did almost every night.

Two nights before she was due to leave her beloved country and Aghili, she looked at the front of the morning's paper and saw a picture of four men lying dead and half naked. The headline read "Generals Dead." They had been executed! As she scrutinized the picture, she saw that one was her friend Manuchehr Khosrodad. He'd been the first head of Iran's Special Forces and at the time of his arrest, he was a Major General of the Imperial Iranian Army Aviation. He had been a loved and respected commander. He was not an affluent man and had never abused his position to collect wealth as did some of the other generals. During the revolution and before the fall of the Shah, he'd always reiterated his position that the military should not be involved in politics. He had been reported as saying, "We are soldiers and have nothing to do with politics. I am obedient to whoever governs the country." But this attitude didn't help him when he was tried by Judge Khalkhali, head of the Islamic Revolutionary tribunal, who charged him and the other generals with treason and corruption. Tears flowed down her cheeks as she thought of his beautiful nine-year-old daughter, Shirin, who he had loved so dearly. Now she knew, finally, that she must leave.

When Tom called her that night, she was almost hysterical, "Oh my God, Tom they killed Manuchehr! I don't believe it. He was a good man and he loved his country. He was no traitor! Now I know you're right. The sooner I leave, the better. But I worry about what will happen in this country under this evil man. I pray to *Allah* they don't come for me before I get on the plane. Just two more days and I'll be on my way. I love you and can't wait to be with you."

"My darling, I will be at the airport waiting for you when you give me your flight plan. I can't wait either."

In the early morning the next day, she rose with the roosters as was her norm. Going directly to the stables, she went to her small office to doublecheck the schedules she had written for Ali to make certain that everything was correct and was clear in the logbook she had prepared for him. She also went over the less-detailed notice she'd put on the bulletin board for all the grooms. She stood in the stable aisle listening to the soft munching noises of the horses as they ground the grain and dried grass that was their morning meal with their large teeth. Because horses move their jaws sideways to grind the grain and fodder, their teeth gradually erode due to the grit and abrasive matter found in the nutriment. Therefore, their teeth continue to grow as they age. She had always loved listening to the quiet sounds her horses made while in their stalls, and she knew she would miss it terribly.

She saddled Khatum, mounted and walked her through the gates to the desert beyond, where she would have one last ride over the land she loved. The sun rose slowly over the rugged hills to the east as she began to canter across the loose sand towards the river crossing and Andimeshke. She enjoyed the warm breezy day, and the thoughts that soon the desert would be experiencing springtime once more. Khatum galloped with gay abandon to the top of the small hill that overlooked the Big House and the small town that had been her home with Mehdi. Would she ever see it again? She halted her mare for one last look. Then with a swift pirouette, she galloped off back towards Aghili.

When she talked with Tom that night, she explained to him that she had a sad heart to be leaving her home, her horses, her people, her country, her life.

"My darling Zahra, I love you; I will be everything I can to you. I will give you my love and my life. I will do anything to make you happy. Have a safe trip, and remember I'll be holding my breath until you're in my arms again."

"I love you too, Tom! I'll try to keep positive thoughts about our future together and fond memories of my life past. I'll see you soon," she told him as she put the receiver in its cradle.

Now she was in her dear old faithful Rostam flying along the shiny black pavement towards the airport, towards Tom and her new life. ,

22

The night you leave this world, go, climb
like Jesus through the skies-
Your lamp, a hundred times, will light
The sun as you arise.
Hafez

Ali 1979

As they approached the outskirts of Ahwaz,
Ali saw that there were tanks along the sides
of the road. They didn't seem to be manned, but
there were many army jeeps and trucks driving
in both directions, filled with disheveled-look-
ing men. In the past, when he'd seen any army
personnel, they were always neatly uniformed.
These men were dressed in scruffy clothes wearing scarves on their heads and around their
necks and were wielding guns this way and that,
shouting words he couldn't understand.

"What do you think is going on, Ali?" Zahra

asked nervously as they drove towards what looked like a roadblock.

"I don't know, Khonume, but it looks like we're going to have to stop here, so I'll ask. Why don't you put your scarf over your head? I've heard that the revolutionaries think women should cover their crowning glory."

Zahra covered her hair and straightened her large sunglasses as Ali slowed down to a stop beside a makeshift booth at the roadside. There were two men with clipboards who asked for identification papers, looked at them cursorily and waved them on before Ali could ask a question. A mile or so further on, another checkpoint loomed that had army vehicles parked to the side and five or six armed, unshaven, rough-looking young men holding rifles, standing across the road to stop them.

"Get out of your vehicle!" shouted a long-haired unkempt young boy, pointing his rifle at Ali. "Keep your hands up!"

As Ali stepped out of Rostam, another boy went to the passenger side with his gun and motioned for Zahra to get out and move over to the side of the road where the others were lounging, leaning on their firearms.

"Are you Zahra Kadjar Bakhtiar?" a gray-haired, also unshaven, man who was obviously the one in charge, shouted at her.

"Yes I am."

"You are accused of causing tribal unrest, which is considered treason and corruption on earth, and is punishable by death! You are under arrest!" he screamed.

"This is ridiculous. I will not be arrested! Ali, get in the car. We're leaving," she commanded.

Ali did as she told him, as the men stood by, shocked, wondering what their leader would do. Zahra started walking around to the passenger side of the old Land Rover, intending to get in. The gray-haired man shouted, "Khonume, you may not leave. You are under arrest!"

"I *am* leaving," she said, as she reached for the door handle. There was a loud report from a rifle as she started to get in, and her body fell back onto the pavement. One of the young men who had been trigger-happy had fired his gun at her.

"*CHE KAR MIKONID?* (What are you doing?)" shouted the gray-haired leader, pointing his own rifle at the ragged-looking boy who had fired the shot. "We were ordered not to shoot our rifles at anyone. Are you crazy?"

He screamed at the others, directing them to bring a vehicle to the side of the downed woman.

Ali was in shock! At first he couldn't move, but then he jumped out of Rostam and ran over to Zahra's crumpled body. "My God, what have you done? You've killed her!" He kneeled over her and saw the pool of blood beneath her.

"Not to worry," said the leader, "we'll transport her to the hospital. It's just a short way."

Ali watched silently as the leader pressed a white bandana to Zahra's side, which soon became red. He helped lift her limp body into the back of the jeep and then jumped into Rostam and followed to the hospital hardly able to see the road as the tears blurred his vision.

Tom: February 15, 1979

It had been a crazy day for Tom. He knew that Zahra's plane would arrive at Washington National Airport at seven in the evening, so he'd planned to finish his office hours early, go home to shower and pack a few things in his bag. He knew she would be exhausted from her flight, so he'd reserved a suite at the Mayfair for the night. They would have dinner in the hotel dining room which was noted for its excellent gourmet fair. The next day they could sleep in, as he had closed the office for two days. Then they could drive out to North Cliff at their leisure.

He had made his hospital rounds early, see-ing one of his patients who had had a lump re-moved from her right breast, then checking on several others who were hospitalized for various gynecological problems. The waiting room of his office was quite crowded he saw when he peeked his head in once he had arrived to commence his office hours. By four o'clock he saw his last patient but as he was about to depart, his nurse stopped him to let him know that Sara Church, the daughter of one of his close friends had just been admitted to the maternity ward and was in labor, so he would need to stop by the hos-pital. As it was to be Sara's first child and at the age of forty, he knew it could be a difficult birth. There was no way he could hand this sweet girl off to one of his associates for she was his god-daughter and he held her in a special place in his heart. When he got to the hospital, she had already become dilated so the baby would arrive soon. By the time her bouncing baby boy was in his hands it was past six o'clock and though he was anxious to be at the airport to meet Zahra he took his time with Sara, once again enjoying the wonder of bringing a new life into the word, a phenomenon that would never become banal to him.

Once in the Mercedes he knew he would have to put the pedal to the metal if he was going to make it on time, but then he thought, why speed? Zahra would have to get used to the hours of a doctor and the fact that he often had emergencies that kept him late. Even if he wasn't at the gate, she would know that he would not leave her stranded, so he drove within the speed limits arriving just after eight. When he went to the baggage claim area for her flight and did not see her, he went to the information booth to have her paged which produced no results. He then went to the Iran Air desk to make certain the flight had arrived. There was a long line, so he presumed others were having trouble as well. When he finally spoke to the attractive dark-haired girl who had a lilting accent, he learned that the flight had indeed landed on time.

"I was to meet someone and can't seem to find her. Can you tell me if she was on the flight roster?"

"If you give me her name I will check to see what I can find out," she replied.

"Her name is Zahra Bakhtiar. Maybe she travels as Zahra Kadjar Bakhtiar."

"I have heard of her. She is famous in our country, I think she was involved with our Asil horses. She lives in Khusustan I think. I'll check for her name."

She went through a door behind the desk and disappeared for a few minutes.

"I am sorry sir, but she was not on the flight. She did have a reservation, but she did not get on the plane. You know things in my country are not good right now so perhaps she just missed the plane. Hopefully you will be able to contact her to find out what was the problem."

With a sad heart he walked to the car and drove slowly back to North Cliff. He just knew something terrible had happened, but he couldn't imagine what, of the hundreds of things that could go wrong, it had been.

He walked in the front door of his house and went directly to the telephone to call her number. It rang and rang. For three days he called every hour of the day and night with no response. Finally, on the fourth day a woman's voice answered, "*Bali*." He tried to explain that he wanted to speak to Zahra, but he spoke no Farsi and she did not understand what he wanted. He kept saying Zahra's name but the answer he got was, "Naher", which he knew meant no. He would just have to wait for her to contact him, which he was sure she would. He was heartbroken.

EPILOGUE

During those first days of the Revolution communication with Iran was almost impossible. Tom knew that his father had acquaintances in Washington who he thought could use their influence to help him find Zahra. They were contacted and promised to try to find out what was happening, but it was extremely difficult. Communication with the embassy, which was on lockdown, and unable to get much information at all from Mehdi Bazargan's government was proved hopeless. Khomeini had appointed Bazargan Prime Minister of his coalition government when he arrived in the country so there had been two governments for some days, Bakhtiar who was the Shah's appointee refused to merge with the Khomeini government, and after losing control fled to France.

The only presence the US had in Iran was military, led by general Dutch Huyser who was sent by President Jimmy Carter to try to stabilize Iran during the early stages of the revolution. Messages were sent through the military to try to find what had happened to Zahra, but weeks went by with no information. It would take months for Tom to learn what had happened.

FARSI LANGUAGE GLOSSARY

This is a list of *Farsi* words used in this novel. *Farsi* is the language used in Iran. It comes from the word *Parsa* which is the ancient word for Persia. Farsi is spoken today in Iran, Iraq, Afghanistan, Tajikistan and Uzbekistan by about 110 million people. Also called Persian it has its roots going back to 3000 BCE.

A

ab	water
ab hendenaveh	watermelon juice
aghd	wedding ceremony
anjoman	society
Anjoman Sultaniti Asb	Royal Horse Society
arroz	rice
ashgal	trash
Azizam	My darling

B

ba khoda che kar mikonam?>	for God's sake what should I do?
badenjune	eggplant
bagali polo	rice with beans
bagh	garden or small farm
bali	yes
biaban	desert horses for speed and hunting
bitumen	oil oozing from earth

C

cameron	truck
Chahar Shanbeh Soori	Evening before New Year
chai	tea

D

divoneh	crazy
djelodard	groom for horses
dolmeh	rice wrapped in grape leaves

F

fesenjun	walnut and pomegran-ate stew

G

Gorbon-e-shoma	You are welcome

gorme sabseh	stew of greens and meat
H	
haft Sin	seven S's
hafte	seventh day
I	
ibex	mountain goat with long horns
J	
june	dear
junam	my dear
K	
khan	leader or chief
khaneh tekani	thorough house cleaning
khatm	third day after burial of a dead person
kheli muchekeram	many thanks
khiaban	for show and festivities
Khonume	Mrs., Miss, added to name for respect
khoresh	stew
khoshke omadid	welcome
kabab	grilled meat
kuku sabsi	omelet with greens

M

mast	yogurt
mehmoonee	reception
mobarak	congratulations
mobarak bashe	may you be congratulated
mordeh shoor	washing of dead body
muchekeram	thank you
muflon	urial sheep
mullah	clergyman or teacher of Islam

N

nejabat	nobleness, greatness with ethics
nakher	no
Now Ruz	New Year
Nowruz-e-mobarak	Happy New Year
nun	bread
nun-e-barbari	stone baked bread oblong in shape
nun-e-lavash	unleavened bread

R

rial	currency of Iran
ruz beher	good morning

S

sabs	green

sabsi	greens in food
salam a ti	hello to you
salam alekhom	hello
seyyed	one related to Mohammad
shab beher	good night
sharob	wine
sheikh	tribal leader
sitar	guitar like three stringed instrument
sob beher	good morning
sofreh-e-aghd	marriage cloth
sofreh haft sin	New Year tablecloth

T
taarof	Persian custom: never accept something before declining many times
tadiq	crusty bottom of rice
tang	girth or long narrow woven strip
tefagn	tribe
tira	tribe
tyafah	tribe

Y
yabu	ugly donkey like horse, an insult

Days of the Week

Shanbeh	Saturday, like Western Monday first day of week
Yek Shanbeh	Sunday, like Tuesday
Do Shanbeh	Monday, like Wednesday
Se Shanbeh	Tuesday, like Thursday
Chahr Shanbeh	Wednesday, like Friday
Panj Shanbeh	Thursday, like Saturday
Jomeh	Friday, day of worship, like Sunday

Months of the Year

Farvardin	21 of March
Ordibesht	22 of April
Jordad	22 of May
Tir	22 of June
Mordad	23 of July
Shahrivar	23 of August
Mehr	23 of September
Aban	23 of October
Azar	22 of November
Dey	22 of December
Bahman	21 of January
Esfand	20 of February

LIST OF CHARACTERS

Zahra: Main character
Hassan Kadjar: Her father
Louisa Kadjar: Her mother
Anne Williams: School roommate
Tom Williams: Anne's brother
Joan Williams: Anne's mother
Mimi Zanganeh: Persian friend
Ahmad Zanganeh: Mimi's husband
Avid Motamed: Persian Friend
Mehdi Bakhtiar: Chief of Bakhtiar
                        tribe, became Zahra's
                        husband
Majid Bakhtiar: Mehdi's brother
Jamshid Bakhtiar: Mehdi's younger
                        brother
Bahman Mansarpour: Master of the Horse
                        for Shah and President
                        of Royal Horse Society

Louise Firouz:	Discovered the extinct Caspian horse
Cathy Johnson:	Trainer of Imperial Stables
Dr. Riahi:	Kadjar family doctor
Golam Reza Pahlavi	Brother of Shah
Shah:	King of Iran
Empress Farah:	Wife of Shah, Shahbanu
Ali:	Zahra's groom, companion, stable hand
Golam Reza:	Old groom
Azizeh:	Family servant and cook
Sheikh Karim Sali:	Ali's father
Sheikh Hajat:	Authority on Asil Horses
Sheikh Kabir:	Owner of great horses
Davout Bahrami:	Groom and rider at Imperial Stables

CPSIA information can be obtained
at www.ICGtesting.com
Printed in the USA
FSHW011153200320

9 781977 218728